The Gifted School

Bruce Holsinger is a novelist based in Charlottesville, Virginia, where he teaches at the University of Virginia. He is the recipient of a Guggenheim Fellowship. *The Gifted School* is his third novel.

By Bruce Holsinger:

A Burnable Book
The Invention of Fire

The Gifted School

Bruce Holsinger

REVIEW

The excerpt from the article "Inside the 5th Grader's Brain" by Hank Pellisier
was published on GreatSchools.org and reprinted by permission of the author.

First published in Great Britain in 2019 by
HEADLINE REVIEW
An imprint of HEADLINE PUBLISHING GROUP

1

Cataloguing in Publication Data is available from the British Library

ISBN 978 1 4722 7 2010 (Hardback)
ISBN 978 1 4722 7 1501 (Trade Paperback)

Printed and bound in Great Britain by Clays Ltd, Elcograf S.p.A.

Headline's policy is to use papers that are natural, renewable and
recyclable products and made from wood grown in sustainable forests.
The logging and manufacturing processes are expected to conform
to the environmental regulations of the country of origin.

HEADLINE PUBLISHING GROUP
An Hachette UK Company
Carmelite House
50 Victoria Embankment
London EC4Y 0DZ

www.headline.co.uk
www.hachette.co.uk

For my father, Harry:
teacher, builder, badass

There is something so tantalizing about having a gifted child that some parents will go to almost any lengths to prove they have one.

—Sheila Moore and Roon Frost, *The Little Boy Book*

QUESTION 15

A girl of eleven sits hunched over a test booklet, the cold room hushed around her. In her left hand she holds a pencil and beneath her forearm is a bubble sheet speckled with gray dots. A constellation of what she knows and doesn't, can't and can. Her elbows rest on either side of the open test. Framing her work, giving it bounds.

She starts to fill in the next circle but at the first soft scratch of the pencil her hand freezes in place. She frowns at the booklet. Because the answer can't be *C*—

Or can it?

She glances up at the wall clock, hears its soft pulsing.

Two minutes left.

Another dart of pain shoots through her tummy. She erases the mark and reads the question again.

15. There are four boxes below and five figures to the right. The pictures in the upper two boxes fit together in a particular way. In the second row there is an empty box. Which of the five figures to the right goes with the pictures in the lower-left box in the same way the pictures in the upper boxes go together?

She stares at the lower-left box. The colored shapes swarm on the page. A square, a circle, a trapezoid, a cone, a rhombus.

Blue, red, green, yellow, purple.

She twists a length of hair around a knuckle and tugs until a small patch of pain forms on her scalp. She imagines one of those coin-operated claws from an arcade reaching down into her skull to pull the correct answer from the jumble-jellied mess in her brain.

Her lower lip slips into her mouth. Taste of salt. Her teeth compress the soft ribbon of flesh. Hard. Harder, until it hurts.

But the answer won't come.

Next to her at the table sits a boy taking the same test. His hair is black but his skin is even paler than hers. He keeps rubbing sweat off his pencil hand by swiping his palm against his pants just above his right knee, where the khaki fabric has darkened. It's very annoying and it's very *distracting*.

Another glance at the clock. One minute.

There is a bad quivering part of her that wants to look down at the boy's bubble sheet but so far she hasn't seen their proctor blink once.

Ms. Stark is her name. She warned them about cheating before the test. About keeping your eyes on your own work.

So the girl decides not to look down at the boy's bubble sheet. Instead she looks past Ms. Stark's enormous owlish glasses to the far end of the cafeteria, closed off from the foyer by a wall of mirrored windows. Several panes have been covered in posters, one of them detached at an upper corner and hanging askew. Even without the posters you aren't supposed to be able to see through the glass. Mostly you can't.

What you can see is the faint, swaying silhouettes of parents. They're trying to stay quiet but she can hear their mumbling, their hissing, their breathing. They look like ghosts.

One of them is her mother.

As her gaze wanders across the glass she notices the rectangles and squares of the window panes and especially the shape formed by the folded top of the loose poster and the steel frame above. A square, a rectangle, a trapezoid—

The answer is D.

It comes to her like the bang of a gun, so suddenly she almost says it aloud. She looks down at Question 15 and sees the pattern in the lower-left box. How it goes with the pattern shown in *D* the same way the patterns in the two upper boxes go together.

Her shoulders relax and her nose tingles with the sweet smell of her own sweat. She starts to fill in the bubble but the moist yellow wood slips through her fingers, rolling across the desk and off the edge. A moment later she hears the whack and clatter as the pencil bounces on the floor.

She leans over to retrieve it, grasping the rubber edge of the table with her right hand. The move requires her to push up slightly from her chair and take an awkward half step as she bends forward. She pincers the eraser between two fingertips and drags it back toward her. The whole maneuver takes no more than a few clock ticks, but by the time her head rises above the level of the table Ms. Stark is walking forward and clapping her hands.

The bell rings.

"Pencils down, booklets closed," Ms. Stark calls out over the rattly clanging. Through the big glasses her eyes scan the room like a lighthouse beacon sweeps the shore.

The girl looks down at her bubble sheet. She glances at Ms. Stark. At her bubble sheet again. Her hand glides over the surface of the table until the tip of her pencil has nearly reached the four empty circles for Question 15.

"Emma Zellar, put your pencil down *this instant*."

The girl's hand freezes with the tip of the pencil poised less than a centimeter above answer *D*. The ringing stops. She stares at the empty bubble, willing the cone of lead to lower and fill.

"*Now*."

Voices in the lobby, growing louder. Someone out there laughs.

The parents know. The test is over.

The girl follows the strange movement of her knuckles as she tilts the pencil down and sets it neatly on the booklet. The unfilled circle gapes at her until Ms. Stark comes by and sweeps the bubble sheet away.

PART I

SCHOOLING

*Gifted children are used to
doing very little work to get
the results they desire.*

—VICKI CARUANA,
Educating Your Gifted Child

Crystal Academy / Head of School

The combined Colorado school districts of Wesley, Kendall, Madison, and Beulah Counties, along with the City of Crystal, are seeking a highly motivated and experienced educator, administrator, and advocate to serve as founding director of Crystal Academy, a new public magnet school for exceptional learners. Position to begin February 2018 in advance of initial admissions process. Duties and responsibilities to include the following:

- Deep understanding of and passionate advocacy for the special circumstances and needs of accelerated and exceptional learners

- Administrative oversight of a complex and challenging educational environment with statewide and national visibility

- Supervision of a large body of teachers and administrative staff at two locations (Lower School grades 6–8, Upper School grades 9–12)

- Service to a large student population along Colorado's Front Range, characterized by wide racial, ethnic, religious, geographical, and economic diversity

- Commitment to helping us forge a visionary, equitable, and inclusive admissions process that accounts for difference, diversity, and overall excellence

To apply, visit www.crystalcolorado.gov/humanresources/apply now and search for position #41252. All applications posted by December 1, 2017, will be considered. The City of Crystal is an Equal Opportunity Employer and does not discriminate on the basis of race, color, national origin or ancestry, gender, age, religious convictions or affiliations, disability, sexual orientation, or genetic profile. The City of Crystal maintains compliance with the Americans with Disabilities Act.

ONE

ROSE

It was on the second Thursday in November that Rose got her earliest inkling of the gifted school. Months later she would swipe back through the calendar and finger that day as the beginning of it all. The hours that planted the seed, traced the faint shape of things to come. The school was still no more than a whisper in the air when she saw her friends late that afternoon, a mere ripple of unease as she settled into bed that night with her husband. But it was already a presence among them. A lurking virus, its symptoms yet to show.

She spent that Thursday in the neuro ward, where her most severe case, a girl of fourteen, lingered at the tail end of an induced coma. Brain trauma with swelling, another helmetless cyclist felled on a city street. Her face was uninjured and serene, with good and improving color. Strong pulse, normal blood pressure, lungs ready to take over; on the edge of consciousness, though yet to return. Rose ran through the rest of the teen's vitals, searching for something she might have missed.

The parents hadn't left the room for hours. The mother lay sleeping on the pullout, and the father sat slumped by the bedside. The crescents of skin beneath his eyes had darkened over the last three days, bruised with his fatigue.

"When will she wake up, do you think?" he asked, only half-aloud. His hands stroked his knees, as if petting twin cats.

"Hard to say." Rose touched his shoulder. "But we've weaned her from the pentobarbital and she's breathing on her own. The rest is up to Lilly."

At the sound of his daughter's name he looked up wanly. Rose answered more questions while bending to wipe a line of drool off Lilly's cheek. The moisture had scooped out an indentation on the pillow, a soft cup of foam, and the girl's parted lips vented a sour smell.

When the father closed his eyes, Rose slipped out and strode down a row of rooms to check on an epilepsy case. Though reluctant to leave her patients behind, she would, in less than an hour, be rotating off her autumn cycle as inpatient attending in pediatric neurology, a hospital duty she performed for three two-week stretches each year. Her department chair had tried to limit Rose to shorter stints, deeming her time in the lab more valuable, but Rose loved this part of her job and refused to surrender more of it. On-call weeks were her only chance to heal in the moment, to put a brain scan to a face. There was a part of her that thrived on the machines and the murmured consults, the cleaning agents and the collodion, even the rotten-egg stink of a GI bleed down in the ER.

The admit was an eight-year-old boy with an undiagnosed seizure disorder, doing fine now, though his latest episode had been alarming. Rose left detailed notes in the electronic file, demonstrating a few shortcuts in the new software system to a medical student on neurology rotation. She was back at the nursing station filling in a chart when a text from Gareth shook her phone.

How about Shobu?

??? she replied.

For tonight. Rez at 7:15.

Rose stared down at the screen, longing for a bath, a cuddle with her daughter, a movie—anything but date night. Canceling again, though, would only make things worse. She texted **Sounds good** but had to remind him of her earlier, more agreeable plans: a round of drinks with friends, to celebrate a birthday. Then she would be home by six-thirty for some time with Emma Q before the sitter came.

Did Q practice? Rose texted.

Yes.

Do her math worksheets?

Yes yes. Love u. ☺

Rose set down her phone, even the lazy *u* a mild irritant these days. She didn't like casually texting about love, not anymore, and her nerves were too dulled for an emoji.

Minutes before end of shift a nurse's voice summoned Rose back to Lilly's room, and there she found the parents weeping and their daughter, glassy-eyed but with a weak smile, returned to a world she had almost left forever.

A skin-slapping wind whipped down from the Continental Divide and scared up puffs of dust from the bricks. The brittle November air lifted Rose's spirits as she speed-walked up the Emerald Mall toward Rock-Salt. Pleasingly dark, not too loud, the bar served craft cocktails featuring spherical ice cubes with flower blossoms suspended inside; lavender martinis, hibiscus gimlets, daisy petals melting into gin. The place had become the favored haunt in recent months for the quartet of old friends. Inside, the youngest of the four, Azra, was already perched straight-backed at a high table, busy on her phone.

The two had an unspoken pact and always arrived fifteen minutes before the others. As Rose neared the table Azra looked up through the loose strands of her hair and leaned in for a hug. A climber's strength in her taut frame, a lilac scent wafting up from the collar of her sweater, a cozy oversize knit.

Azra ran a high-end consignment store off the Emerald Mall once owned by her mother and always showed up wearing enviable finds. She was a Crystal native, one of the few Rose had encountered in this valley of new arrivals.

"I can't stay long," Rose complained as she sat. "Date night tonight."

"Oh dear."

"I mean, once a week? Gareth wants to follow the counselor's script to the letter. For me it's just—"

"Pressure?"

Rose picked up a fork, fingered the tines. "I understand why it's important, to show Emma Q we're making an effort. But lately the one-on-one is excruciating."

"Though it's only been, what, four months since you started therapy? Give it time."

"At least he's trying," Rose allowed, thinking: *But am I?* She wondered sometimes, because Gareth had done nothing wrong, really, aside from doing nothing at all.

"I had the same issues with Beck, believe me," Azra said. Rose watched her friend's pretty lips work an olive. Azra had split with Beck after discovering his hook-ups with Sonja, their beloved Austrian au pair. Despite the tempestuous aftermath, the former couple had become oddly close since the divorce, their postmarital intimacy a continuing mystery to most of their friends. Rose almost envied the companionable rapport the two had established in the wake of their split, longed for that easy intimacy with Gareth, though she'd hardly trade her husband's plodding consistency for Beck's erratic bluster. Google *total schlub jacked up on Viagra and Bernie rage*, Azra liked to say, and you'll see my ex-husband's head shot.

"Look, Rose," she said, spitting out the olive pit. "Don't be hard on yourself for trying to save your marriage."

Another thing Azra liked to say.

Samantha breezed in promptly at five, chin up, scanning the place for her minions; she flitted her eyes between the two women's faces and down to their half-finished drinks, an eyebrow raised. She circled to give them each a brush of her lips, glossed in a soft pink, then pulled an empty stool from an adjoining table and squeezed it between theirs, forcing them to shift aside.

"What did I miss?"

They filled her in. Samantha rolled her eyes upward to the exposed ceiling beams. "I hope the Emmas worked on their History Day project," she said to Rose. "Kev dropped the ball on Wednesday."

"We'll see," Rose said. One of Samantha's tricks was to swerve any mention of Rose's marital despair into lighthearted criticism of their husbands' mutual shortcomings. Her own spouse, Kev, came in for occasional barbs, though always couched in terms of his hopelessness in the domestic sphere, which was Sam's domain anyway as the only stay-at-home mom in their group.

"What's the subject?" Azra asked.

Rose said, "Horses. What else?"

"You're so lucky you have boys." Samantha glanced at Azra with a friendly smirk.

Azra stared back, inscrutable. "Blessed by a thousand gods," she said.

Samantha was going on about shopping for a new car when Rose heard a distinctive cough that caused them all to swivel their heads and see Lauren, looking forlornly at two empty stools spaced wide, her friends clustered at the other half of the table. Quickly Azra jumped down to give her a hug and wish her a happy birthday. Samantha slid the extra stool to the next table as Rose shifted left, making them symmetrical.

Lauren: easy to please, but you had to know how. She was a social worker for Youth and Family Services, possessed of a fierce social conscience that showed itself in ways both inspiring and, at times, prickly and harsh— chiding Azra for driving a minivan, Samantha for wastefully drinking through plastic straws so she wouldn't smear her lipstick. For her birthday Lauren never wanted a fuss made, nor a large gathering with the families. They'd tried this once, a surprise party two years after Julian died. Total disaster; Lauren had been miserable the whole evening. Since then they'd kept things small. Just the four of them, for cocktails.

After drink orders and a birthday toast, Samantha brought up Thanksgiving. They'd all been invited to the Zellar house, and Sam wanted to nail down contributions.

"We'll have over thirty this year. Kill me now," Sam said, with an ostentatious sigh. A Thanksgiving busy-brag, quantity of guests as a measure of her family's worth. They indulged their queen bee with talk of cranberries and yams until Lauren's phone lit up.

"It's Xander," she said, as if the president were texting in. Rose watched her turn aside on her stool and tap out a message to her son; like a pecking crow, sharp nose to the screen, head reared back to read his replies. Lauren had an interesting, wedge-shaped face that Rose had always thought austerely beautiful, and like most Crystallites she was fit, though she favored outfits that accentuated her straight-hipped frame. Most often khakis, worn with tucked-in button-down shirts and a cell phone pouch strapped to her belt.

When Lauren looked up, her frown lines softened. "He still doesn't like being left alone."

"That's sweet," Azra said.

"Last week he—"

"Oh god, Emma Z *loves* an empty house," Samantha said loudly, flagging the waitress. "She says it's the only time she can do her reading without her parents getting in the way."

Lauren's mouth tightened. Rose, sensing the tension, spread her arms over the backs of the adjacent chairs and looked across at Azra.

"So, this Glen guy," she said. Azra's potential new beau, chair of anesthesiology at the Medical Center. Rose knew him slightly, though it was Samantha who'd played yenta last month. Their third date had been Wednesday night. "We want the full debrief."

"So did Glen," Azra replied. "Didn't happen."

A familiar joke but they laughed, relieved, because Azra centered them in a way the others never could, weaving accounts of her world they all thrived on, largely because it wasn't theirs. Azra had dated half the single men in the Four Counties, it sometimes seemed, her joint custody of the twins leaving her more than enough child-free time for all the films, concerts, art exhibits, and restaurant openings on the Front Range. The stories she chose to tell, though, usually concerned her mishaps, her uncomfortable fix-ups; they were sculpted to make the others laugh—never to wonder what so much freedom might feel like.

Rose wondered anyway. All the time.

Lauren, on the other hand, had neither suffered nor enjoyed a date since her husband's death eight years ago. Her hardened abstinence was almost a moral stance, all her attention on her brainy son. When Azra related her salty stories, Lauren would listen with her head cocked to the side and eyes blinking in wonder, as if enthralled by an acrobat or a virtuoso cellist: dazzled by a talent she would never possess, nor quite understand.

Samantha reached into her fancy handbag and pulled out Lauren's birthday card. For gifts they always went in for something together, this year a day package from the Aspen Room, a spa three blocks down the Emerald Mall. Salt rub, massage, facial, the whole package probably costing twice their combined contributions. Samantha would have made up the difference.

Once Lauren had had a chance to gush over the present, Azra leaned forward and asked, "So have you made a decision yet, for next year?"

Lauren's face brightened. Another gift: the chance to talk about Xander, her favorite subject.

"Still waffling. I wish Odyssey went through eighth grade, because it's been great for him. But Xander really wants to be with the twins at St. Bridget's."

"They'd be thrilled," Azra said generously, though Rose suspected that Aidan and Charlie Unsworth-Chaudhury would be ambivalent at best about the prospect of Xander Frye attending their school next fall. Xander currently went to Odyssey, a private elementary for high-IQ kids that ran only through sixth grade. Lauren had been deliberating for months—frequently, loudly—over whether to keep him there one last year, put him in the Crystal publics where Rose and Samantha's Emmas went, or enroll him at St. Bridget's, a fancy parochial in Kendall County that Azra and

Beck's twins attended. (Not my idea, Azra would frequently protest, hands in the air, always quick to identify herself as a proud product of the Crystal public schools—but hey, it's Beck's money.)

"The most important thing is that he continue to be challenged," Lauren went on, and they all listened raptly, for her birthday. "It can be hard for him when he feels condescended to. And he has so many social handicaps."

"Not many academic ones, though," Samantha observed.

"Well, no. But if he's going to switch the next year anyway, I'd rather bite the bullet now. I'm starting to resent the drive, the price tag. But I have to say, what you don't find at Odyssey is the slower learners holding kids like Xander back."

Rose wedged her tongue between her teeth.

"So a lot to think about," said Azra, nonjudgmental as always. "But I'm sure you'll do what's best for him." She turned to Samantha. "What about Emma Z?"

"We looked at Odyssey for next year, and it isn't a good fit. Z's just so *social*. We've thought about St. Bridget's too. Same problem. Plus with Kev on City Council it wouldn't look good, having our daughter in a private."

"So she'll go to Red Rocks," Rose said, and it wasn't a question: the Emmas had been inseparable since their earliest months. Samantha had said nothing to her about taking her daughter out of the Crystal publics.

"Most likely."

The snag of doubt in Sam's words hooked Rose by the ear and spun her head around.

"Kev's been looking into other options."

"Like what?"

"Oh, this and that." Waving a hand. "There's this artsy charter school outside Denver. A few closer places. We'll see."

Rose was about to ask more when the server approached.

Closer places? Denver? She never found a good time to return to the subject before they finished their drinks. When the check arrived, Samantha whipped out a Visa and shoved the card and the bill back at the server. Rose started to object.

"You got it last time," Sam said breezily.

Not true, almost never true, but that was Samantha. Rose watched as her friend tipped and signed and studiously avoided her gaze. There was something brittle in Samantha Zellar lately, a pointed aversion to certain matters. When she had insider knowledge, Sam was usually an impulsive spiller, unable to resist sharing what she possessed that others didn't—and right then she knew something, Rose suspected. But she was waffling, playing it close.

Outside, the air had a burning, gassy smell. Two jugglers twirled on the pedestrian mall, their batons wrapped at the ends with flaming rags. An assistant stood by, armed with a can of lighter fluid and an extinguisher. A portable fire pit sparked and flamed between the performers and shrouded their tricks in smoke as the four old friends paused to watch them for a while, to gather the warmth.

ROSE

She edged to the curb along Opal Lane, the dusk-darkened yard warmed by the glow from their craftsman bungalow. Twelve years ago the house had felt both charming and enormous, with three bedrooms, one and a half baths, a half-finished basement. It was a stretch to afford it on one salary, a harsh sentence for a Stanford-trained neurologist saddled with student loans. But if you wanted to live in town and buy west of Thirty-fifth Street—anywhere close to the mountains—you were looking at Palo Alto prices, the agents always said.

Rose set her bag down by the door and shrugged off her jacket, smelling garlic and spice, a doughy waft of home-cranked pasta. Whatever his faults (and they were many), Gareth cooked like a reality show chef, favoring the starchy, carb-laden end of the ingredient spectrum over the brain-boosting vegetables and lean proteins Rose would have preferred for herself and their daughter. But when she was as hungry as she was now, it seemed his food must be the only reason she stayed with him. Sure as hell wasn't the sex.

"Hey, hon," Gareth called cheerily from the kitchen. "I opened a nice Shiraz."

Rose tilted back her head and stood there in the dark, staring up. *A nice Shiraz*, she mouthed, and pressed the gapped teeth of her house key into the meaty flesh below her thumb. Hearing her daughter's barky giggle, she

THE GIFTED SCHOOL | 19

walked down the narrow hall, through the living room, and into the kitchen, where her husband was stationed in front of the stove. A torn gray T-shirt spotted with tomato sauce arced over his softening midsection. Three days of stubble for date night.

The Emmas sat together in front of a laptop, swinging their legs beneath the counter. Emma Q hunted and pecked at the keys.

"Hey, sweetie. Hey, Z." Rose planted a kiss on the crown of her daughter's head. Girl sweat, flowery shampoo. Emma Zellar, Kev and Samantha's girl, got a gentle pat on the back. "History Day?"

Q nodded, intent on her work.

"We made the banner." Z pointed at the laptop.

"To go across the top," Q explained. "Now we're doing captions." Rose squinted at the screen.

THE HORSE IN THE AMERICAN WEST
BY EMMA ZELLAR AND EMMA HOLLAND-QUINN

The two lines were rendered in a rustic font, like a Dodge City saloon sign. The Emmas had been planning the joint project for weeks, the subject perfect for two horse-obsessed fifth-grade girls. Q was swept up in the romance of it, compiling lists of horse-themed novels she'd read, famous Western myths of heroic equestrians. Last weekend, at Rose's urging, Gareth had taken her to Denver for supplies, and they'd come home with old postcards featuring rodeo riders bucking on broncos, Native chieftains mounted on warhorses. In a burst of inspiration Rose had even helped them figure out a way to get clips from vintage Westerns looping on an old iPod, which she'd rigged to a poster board with plastic zip ties.

The result was impressive, though from what Rose could see, Q had done most of the grunt work so far while Z ordered her around, taking over whenever her patience with Q's deliberate pace ebbed—as now, when Z nudged her friend aside and commandeered the keyboard, every inch her mother's daughter. She was a speedy touch-typist, her father's hooded eyes intent on the screen as she banged away, laptop glowing on a heart-shaped face nearly identical to Samantha's, with that same creamy skin and perfect nose.

Emma Q had a more rounded look, like Gareth. Rose kept waiting for their daughter to shed the last of her baby fat, though she had accepted that Q's burly build might become a permanent feature. Her skin was almost translucent, veiny and blue in a certain quality of light. Rose had suffered that skin when she was young. Teachers had regarded her as sickly, a child to be treated with softness and care. She had learned early to take advantage of their regard though still worried sometimes that her daughter had internalized this projected frailty, this deference foisted on her by well-meaning elders.

The Emmas started discussing the captions, every detail a delicate negotiation.

Rose shook her head.

"What?" Gareth said.

"Just those two." She nodded at the girls.

"I know." He sipped his wine. "They've been working hard."

"So have you." Rose wanted to claw the words back, though she knew their therapist would endorse them.

There's a scaffold of kindness holding up every marriage. You two need to rebuild yours.

Gareth blinked twice, visibly surprised by Rose's gentle manner. "Okay, girls, pasta's ready," he said. "Tessa should be here any minute."

He slid two plates across the counter, laden with spaghetti and a Bolognese sauce, fragrant lengths of garlic bread as bookends. Z shut the laptop and pushed it aside, and the Emmas dug in.

The bell rang while Rose was changing in the bedroom. Her husband's heavy step sounded in the hall, then the front door moaned open.

"Hi, Gareth."

"Hey, Tessa."

Rose listened to their small talk, aware of the little shiver of disquiet running down her arms as Lauren's daughter entered their home for the first time in months. She swiped on a raspberry lip stain and walked out to the kitchen. The Emmas had moved their work to the table and now knelt on chairs, bent over a trifold, cutting and gluing. Tessa sat at the counter with her bared ankles crossed, her sketchbook already open. She flashed Rose a tentative smile.

"When did you decide to go back to black?" Rose walked over and smoothed a palm over Tessa's hair, straw-like to the touch.

"Just yesterday." Tessa turned her chin, modeling. "You like?"

"I do, I really do." A lot better than hot pink, Rose thought, catching a chemical scent.

Rose sat with her and chatted, and felt something like a shock to realize what a dazzler Lauren's daughter had become over those first months of her junior year. The newly black hair, cut to bob at the nape of her neck, framed a pale face with an angular chin and smooth cheeks. Tessa was blinking a lot, maybe a contact was loose or dry, though the effect was oddly magical: a pair of butterflies quivering in tandem. Her eyes were a sea blue, perfectly matched by the polka dots covering the silk scarf tied loosely around her neck. Azra had commented just last week on Tessa's unusual flair, how well she wedded her looks with an eclectic style peculiarly her own.

So good to see any kind of beauty budding in this girl again. For years Tessa had been a favorite sitter for the younger kids, an older version of the Emmas. Sweet and open, wicked smart, a bit of a babbler but a joy to have around, the source of her mother's often insufferable pride, for good reason. Lauren had compensated for Julian's death by throwing herself into her daughter's development and education. Advanced math, Chinese, martial arts, flute lessons with the principal player in the Colorado Symphony: by eighth grade Tessa had become a living, breathing benchmark, a proof of concept for the overinvested parenting they all practiced with varying degrees of obliviousness and guilt.

Then, the summer before high school, something snapped.

Rose had never quite extracted the full story from Lauren. A creative sequence of lies. A tenth-grade boy with a bad reputation. A progression of risk that culminated one night when Emma Z, only eight at the time, was left alone for hours. Kev and Samantha had arrived home after midnight to find their daughter weeping under the covers, afraid to leave her bed for fear of the monsters that a wildly drunk Tessa had warned her would slice up her feet if they touched the floor.

Tessa herself didn't make it home until the next morning, smudged half circles beneath her eyes and a CVS bag dangling from her fingertips. Lauren confronted her at the door, but Tessa just snarled at her and disappeared into the bathroom. When she emerged an hour later, her flowing charcoal hair was gone, in its place a chopped salad dyed a cheap inky blue.

As Tessa progressed through her early teens there had been more episodes: drinking, pills, cutting, a shoplifting bust at the mall. Lauren's attempted interventions only made things worse, until finally she was forced to give her daughter a choice: a restrictive boarding school in Missouri for troubled girls or an intensive ninety-day inpatient rehab program in Denver. Tessa chose rehab, and in the six months since returning she'd really started to pull herself together. Shed the nose rings, looked grown-ups in the eye now.

Then, a few weeks ago, Lauren had finally talked Rose into trying her daughter out as a sitter again. Tessa needed a job, she'd pleaded, and the Zellars wouldn't budge, not until the teen had proved herself with the others.

Everyone was rooting for her, or so Azra claimed. Rose wasn't so sure. Samantha in particular seemed to take a guilty pleasure in watching for latent signs of Tessa's next catastrophe.

Rose saw her as a girl teetering on a knife's edge, grasping for a hand.

The doorbell chimed again. Gareth checked his phone and said, "That'll be Kev." He wiped his hands on a towel, looking displeased. Rose got up to answer.

At the front door Kevin Zellar greeted her with a hearty "Hey, Doc!" and that amiable grin he switched on for business types and donors. His windbreaker rustled when he embraced her, and his breath smelled of mint, a taint of bourbon beneath the wintergreen. Kev wore his hair in a sandy sweep, combed but not fastidiously so. Rose followed his athletic stride down the hall into the kitchen.

"Looking great, you two," Kev said, taking in the trifold. He bent to give Emma Z a kiss and reached over to mess Q's hair. "When's it due?"

"Monday," said Z. "We have to finish this weekend."

"Looks ready to go."

"Glass of wine?" Rose asked him, mostly to annoy Gareth. "It's a nice Shiraz."

"Why the hell not," Kev said expansively, shrugging off his wind-breaker.

Behind him Gareth folded his arms. Her husband wanted to leave, get date night revved up, but after a curt nod from Rose he poured some Shiraz into a jelly jar and handed it over. Kev took a drawn-out sip.

"Long day?" Rose asked him, enjoying the moment.

"Oh, you know, Doc, the usual. Disgruntled millionaires, twentysomething tech barons. Plus the mayor's got a stick up his ass this week." Kev fake-grimaced and looked sheepishly at the Emmas. "Sorry, girls."

"Oh, believe me, Q hears worse than that in this house," Rose said, for Gareth again.

Tessa looked up from her sketchbook and laughed. Kev raised his jar and laughed with her, a low broker's chuckle that played well in the political and financial circles in which the Zellars traveled. Kev served on the Crystal City Council while managing a high-dollar equity fund and sitting on a dozen nonprofit boards. A bit of a flirt but rarely boorish or crude, though his attentiveness toward Rose could make Gareth squirm at times. The two men had so little in common, in bearing, looks, ambition.

Rose hated herself for thinking in this cold way about her dutiful husband. But she also loathed dishonesty, as she'd said to their therapist many times—all the false assurances that spouses whisper to themselves to keep the marital boat placid in the water.

"You all set, sweet pea?" Kev asked his daughter.

"Can I stay a little longer, Daddy?" Z wheedled. "Just so we can finish the captions? Please?"

Kev looked at Rose. She shrugged. Kev tilted his jar at Gareth for another pour.

"Fine with us, we're getting sushi," Gareth said, ignoring him. "Tessa, you mind?"

"Nope." Tessa pushed herself off the stool. Her blouse tightened against her chest.

Rose narrowed her eyes. "Tessa," she said pleasantly, "would you make sure Q's lights are out by nine? You'll probably have to take her Kindle away."

"No problem," said Tessa. "I'll just be in here, you guys." She sauntered into the living room with her sketchbook.

Gareth went back to the bedroom for a clean shirt and a fleece. When they left the house, Tessa was sitting by the gas fire and Kev at the kitchen table, helping himself to another pour of wine, watching the Emmas at their work.

THREE

EMMA Z

By fifth grade, the child's brain has created a unique 'self' due to its one-of-a-kind neural pathways. The upgraded analytical ability also enables fifth graders' noggins to become keenly—"

"What's a noggin?" asked Emma Z, lying on her side on Q's bed.

"Oh, sorry." Emma Q slapped her hair with the open magazine. "It's this. Your head."

"Then why don't they just *say* that?"

"I don't know. Sorry," Q said again.

Z rolled onto her other side and looked out the bedroom window. The Holland-Quinns' house wasn't very nice, like Z's, and it wasn't very big. All you could see from this window was the side of a much bigger house going up next door, replacing the tiny one that got knocked down last summer.

All little houses in Crystal are destined for a scrape-off, Emma Z's father always joked.

"Do you want me to keep going?" Q asked.

"Fine," Z sighed.

Q took a loud breath and read on. "*The upgraded analytic ability also enables fifth graders' noggins to become keenly, painfully aware of how they fit, or don't fit, into certain social groups. Partnered with dramatic imagination, your child may feel lonely and unaccepted, a social failure with fragile self-esteem.*" She paused. "Oh. My god."

"What?"

"That's a dangling modifier."

Z said nothing.

Q explained: "Because 'partnered' doesn't go with 'your child,' it goes with 'analytic ability.' So it shouldn't be—never mind. Sorry."

Emma Q was always sorry. Sorry for sounding too smart, sounding too stupid, eating too fast, reading too much, even though Z never cared how Q ate or read or what she sounded like when she talked.

"Is there a more interesting part?"

"I'm getting to it." Q flipped a page. "Ooh, this is good. My mom underlined it. *Your fifth grader is probably sliding into adolescence now, especially if she's a girl. Don't delay! Inform her or him about all the physical changes of puberty: breast development, pimples, bras, pubic and underarm hair, menstruation, larger testicles—*"

"That's dis*gus*ting!" Z screeched and turned around, clutching a pillow. She threw it at Emma Q's face, and the magazine fell from Q's hands and fluttered to the floor.

They rolled around for a while, clutching their stomachs and giggling, because *breast development*! and *pubic hair*! and *menstruation*! and especially *testicles*! which was probably the most revolting word Z had ever heard.

When they calmed down, Z said, "Why does Rose even *give* you stuff like that?"

Q shrugged. "She leaves magazines on the back of the toilet. She says she wants me to know what's going on in my brain and my body. She says most parents think their kids are stupider than they really are, and so they try to hide things from them."

"Well, I'm reading *Island of the Blue Dolphins* right now."

"I read that in second grade."

"Me too." Technically Z hadn't started it yet, but it was sitting by her bed, along with ten other books her mom wanted her to read. Z hated reading but pretended to love it, because it was just easier that way.

"Do you think it's true, though?" Emma Q asked.

"What?"

"That stuff about kids who don't belong. Who start to feel bad in fifth grade because they don't—fit?"

"Of course it's true," said Emma Z, sitting up on the bed, because *this* was something that was actually *interesting*. "There are lots of kids in our class who don't fit with the rest of us. I mean, just think about Katie Johnston."

"She's so, *so* fat," said Emma Q in a whisper, even though they were alone.

Emma Z smiled, looking at Q's chubby arms. "And what about Caleb Bingham?"

"He's just—you know."

Z thought of Caleb Bingham's leg braces, the way he walked. "It's really sad," she said.

"I know."

In the sympathetic silence that followed Z picked up her phone and texted her dad.

Can we go now?

D own in the kitchen Emma Z's father sat at the counter with Tessa, explaining something about money. Z fished a third cookie from a box in the cupboard and ignored Q's frown. Q's mom didn't let her have second desserts.

"Is that a good idea, though, do you think?" Tessa asked him, pushing some black hair behind her ear. Z looked at herself in the window above the sink and tried pushing her hair away like that. Tessa was prettier than she used to be, but the gesture looked better with long yellow hair, like Z's.

"Well, let me ask you," said Kev. "What are these cheapskates paying you to sit Emma Q? Ten, twelve an hour?"

"Fifteen," said Tessa.

His eyebrows went up. "Impressive. So let's say you're on for two hours. You combine that thirty with your next six or seven sitting gigs and buy yourself a two-hundred-dollar CD at two-point-seven percent with a sixty-month term. You with me?"

"Uh-huh," Tessa said. She flashed a cautious glance at the Emmas and tightened her lips.

Emma Z smiled. *Uh-oh.* There was an old joke in the families about her father's money talk, which Tessa's mom had once called *Kevsplanation.* Lauren did an amazing imitation of him that was always in Z's head whenever Daddy started blabbing about investments and interest-bearing checking accounts.

"End of those five years you'll end up with an extra, what, thirty bucks," he went on. "Doesn't sound like much. But you multiply that by ten, twenty, and so on, and soon you're talking an investment of a couple thou, with a return in the low hundreds. Again, not big numbers, but you've got to think long term, Tessa. And that's just a rinky-dink CD. Better idea? Open a brokerage account, maybe a custodial Roth IRA, because then you'd capitalize on—"

A loud giggle burst from Z's throat. Tessa turned away with her hand on her mouth.

Kev leaned back with his arms folded. "Oh, I see. So my life's work is just a big joke to you girls, is that it?" He reached over and pulled Z to his lap. Z giggled wildly until her father spun her around and set her on the floor feetfirst.

"Sorry, Kev," said Tessa.

"Offense taken." Kev smiled. "Point I'm making is, the earlier you start the better. Doesn't matter how."

"I understand."

"And hey." His face got serious. "It's good to see you, Tessa. Out and about."

"Thanks, Kev." Tessa tossed her hair again, but she sounded serious too.

"Good enough." He knocked on the counter three times as he stood and looked down at Z. "You ready, sweet pea?"

From the yard, as they walked to the car, Emma Z looked back through the front window of the little house and saw Tessa sit down with Emma Q on the sofa. Tessa began typing on her phone and Q was reading on her Kindle. They weren't even talking. Honestly, they both looked kind of lonely.

It must be so sad for Q, Emma Z thought, not to have a father like hers. Even sadder for Tessa, not to have a father at all.

FOUR

ROSE

At Shobu they left their shoes in the vestibule and took a corner table low to the ground. Cushions rather than chairs, a space designed for intimacy. *Ugh.* When they were settled, Gareth split apart his chopsticks and toyed with the broken ends, waiting for Rose to crack their ever-present ice.

"The girls' project looks good," she said, treading the familiar. "Thank you for working with them on it."

"Well, I've learned as much as they have," he said. "Did you know there were more than two million mustangs in the Western states at one point?"

"Mm."

"And that it was Christopher Columbus who introduced horses to the New World?"

"Really."

"Though apparently there's a big debate over whether the Spanish mustang should be called an indigenous or invasive species, a native breed or a genetic interloper. Something about whether the same strain evolved in the New World, then crossed the Bering Sea before going extinct over here."

This made her ears perk up. "So there's a scientific angle."

"I—guess so," he said.

"I didn't see that on the trifold, though."

"Emma Z thought there was already too much going on."

"Could they maybe incorporate that into one of the panels?" she suggested. "Biohistory is big these days."

"It's already over the top, don't you think?"

"What do you mean?"

He shrugged. "I don't know, all the bells and whistles. Whatever happened to good old book reports?"

One of Gareth's most annoying tics, these habitual bursts of Luddite nostalgia that made him sound like Rose's father. *Whatever happened to good old rotary phones? Good old typewriters? Good old manual transmissions?*

She placed her stoneware cup of miso soup against her lips. "History Day is competitive," she said between sips, "just like everything else. But Flora Wilson-Bianchi went all the way to nationals last year with a project on the Anasazi, and I don't see why the Emmas can't at least get to states with this horse thing."

Gareth cocked an eyebrow.

"What?" she said.

"States? They're eleven, Rose."

"Mm." She took a longer swallow, enjoying the heat.

Gareth could be so pious about these things, regarding his status as a full-time dad as a license to dismiss Rose's concerns about Q's development and education, to question her parenting suggestions while making her feel guilty for raising them at all. Their differences in approach—the philosopher versus the helicopter, as Gareth had once infuriatingly termed it—were what had finally driven them into therapy over the summer.

Because Rose could handle Gareth's passive attitude toward their marriage, toward Rose's need for intimacy and passion; she had her friends and her work for those. But when it came to their daughter, she worried that his sense of failure and, well, stuckness would rub off on Q, that his laissez-faire parenting style was already having an effect on their daughter's body and mind, whether in Q's overconsumption of the muffins and cookies he baked as after-school snacks or in his unthinking indulgence of her whims—as when he passively allowed her to slog through the Harry Potters for the third time rather than train her voracious reading habits on something new and challenging. Living in a pressure cooker like Crystal could be hard on kids, no doubt; but as Rose's own education and career had taught her, it was possible to control most outcomes if you just worked steadily and planned ahead. She was still holding out hope that therapy might get Gareth to see the benefits of a more directed approach.

"How were things at the hospital today?" he asked.

A return to neutral ground, following the script. Very nice.

Rose said, "Some tough cases."

"Back to the lab next week?"

"This weekend, if that's okay," she said. "The pre-application paperwork is due to the administration in a few weeks."

"The NIH neuro scheme?"

She nodded and smiled, glad he'd remembered. For the past few weeks, and with the support of her chair and the dean of the medical school, Rose had been preparing her lab for a major grant application to the National Institutes of Health: five million dollars to fund a new center for the study of neurodegenerative disease. If she won it, the grant would fund the next decade of her career, take her through two promotions, support grad students and postdocs, procure new machines and laboratory equipment—in short, make Rose the belle of the neurology ball. Putting together the grant would require countless late nights and serial weekends in the months ahead, all worth it in the end, she had to hope.

Still, it was bittersweet, to have Gareth fill her in on the afternoon, share observations about their daughter she herself had been too swamped to enjoy. He made her laugh a few times as sushi came and went, remnants of a writerly wit that had once reduced her to a jittery mess.

Oh yes, every detail of Gareth Quinn. The particular way he crossed his legs when he scribbled or typed. The curls clustered around his ears. How he revised his sentences while speaking, as if an editor's pen were lodged in his frontal lobe; and what a lobe it was, or so the brain-obsessed Rose had once thought.

When they first met, he had just placed his short story collection, and soon after following her from Ann Arbor out to Stanford, he sold his first novel, though part of her must have worried even then that his ambition would be outstripped by circumstance. Because a six-figure advance sure sounds like a lot when your ebullient fiancé first yawps about it over an extravagant wine at Chez Panisse, until you begin to understand some months later that it's a low-six-figure advance, that 15 percent of it will go to the agent and 20 more to taxes, that the money will be arriving in six installments spread out over several years—and that three of these installments will be conditional on the submission of a "highly anticipated" second novel, which your fiancé-turned-husband will never complete.

That this was the case had become clear to Rose only after their move to Crystal. Something changed in their marriage then, in Gareth. An alteration imperceptible at first, but as Rose's career took off, her husband's sputtered to a stop, and with it went much of his charm and all of his ambition. Always a dispassionate intellectualizer, Gareth became ever more withdrawn, never wanting to fight or confront or yell, cultivating instead a studied indifference about virtually everything: whether to buy a new car, try a new restaurant, have a child . . .

Which had always been the plan—Rose's plan. But in the face of Gareth's ambivalence she saw a bleak future with this impassive man. Two months north of thirty-five, she considered leaving him, started having avid fantasies about buying a condo off the Emerald Mall, finding a partner with drive and strong opinions, striking out on her own.

Then, Emma.

She could pinpoint the precise moment of conception: one of the few times they'd had sex in that whole rocky period. Rose had just learned that she'd won a first major grant for her pediatric neurology lab at Darlton. After celebrating over champagne with colleagues, she had tottered home to a five-course celebratory meal prepared by her husband, who had also bought her flowers and chocolates, and so the diaphragm-free lovemaking was at her initiative.

Three weeks later, a missed period for the first time in her life.

And now, twelve years later, this—what?

Entropy. Malaise. Slow, continuing decline. Gareth taught a fiction workshop at the community college every other semester. He kept their household running, made it easy for Rose to spend all the hours she did at the lab. But when he wasn't teaching, Gareth tended to isolate himself, preferring time with the Emmas to ventures out into the adult world, whether for hospital functions or family gatherings. Beck Unsworth, Azra's ex, was the one person in Crystal Gareth saw every now and then for a beer or a film, though Beck called infrequently now, busy with the twins' hectic soccer schedules, plus a young wife and a new baby, the fruits of a sloppy affair. At least Gareth had never cheated, she often mused—though maybe she would respect him more if he had. At least it would show a sense of purpose. A dedication. Zeal.

She looked askance at her husband now, backlit by the sushi bar's soft glow. For the last few minutes Rose had been picking at a sizeable ball of wasabi. Mindlessly she brought the chopsticks to her lips and swallowed it whole, as if it were nothing more than a piece of bread. Gareth stared at her, eyes shot wide, waiting for her to scream or grab for her water glass. Instead, with her tongue and gums igniting, Rose calmly reached her chopsticks into the rice bowl, lifted out a moderate hunk, and popped it in her mouth, heat tears building at the edges of her eyes.

Later she stood in the bathroom doorway brushing her teeth, wishing their bedroom were large enough for a king. Another foot or two at night would do wonders for what was left of their marriage. Settling under the covers with her back to Gareth, she read a medical journal and waited for the touch of his hand at the top of her spine. When it came she tried not to flinch.

"Not tonight, Gareth. I'm sorry, it's—"

"It's the wasabi," he said. She laughed despite herself, turning to look up at him.

"Next time."

"Okay." He nodded, without visible resentment. Which somehow pissed her off.

Then a thought occurred to her. She rolled onto her back and propped herself up on her elbows. "Hey, has Emma Z said anything about school next year?"

"What do you mean?"

"Samantha told me they're looking at other options for sixth grade. Apparently Kev's been poking around. Maybe a charter?"

"Kev didn't say anything."

"Weird."

"That would suck for Q, though, if Z went somewhere else."

"Yeah."

"Should we ask her? Emma, I mean?"

"No, it's probably nothing. I don't want to worry her." Rose turned back on her side and read until the letters tangled and blurred on the page. Her last sleepy impression was of her husband's fingers slipping her journal from her hands, switching off her light.

A Touch of Tessa:
One Girl's Survival Guide to Junior Year
A Video Blog

Episode #28: ALONE AT LAST!!!
. . . 6 views . . .

TESSA [*seated in dim light*]: Hello, no one. It's me again, with a big shout-out to my millions of adoring fans, aka my squad from inpatient. Hey, Deke. Hey, Tiny. Hey, Jessica. 'Sup, Maurice? [*long sigh*] There's something so creepy about an empty house, you know? I mean, not literally empty—the little brat's asleep upstairs and all—but it's quiet. I kind of need that sometimes. So, you guys, this is only my second time babysitting since I got back. It's ridiculous that Q even needs a sitter, I mean, my mom left me alone with Xander when I was like ten so give me a break. Plus she's such a little blob, just sits around reading and does whatever Rose tells her to do because she wants her to be such a "big achiever." So cringey.

[*Camera wobbles as Tessa shifts on sofa; reclining now.*]

Anyway, so the big news, just in case you bitches are actually watching this. I got a job. A real job, not this bullshit. [*Looks around.*] It's at a secondhand called BloomAgain. They sell fancy used stuff on consignment. The owner is Azra, this sweet friend of my mom's, and she's giving me three shifts a week because, quote, Tessa, I've always liked your style, unquote, but I mean, come on, it's a pity job, obvs. But it pays pretty well, and you get a commission on all the stuff you sell, and besides you guys know clothes are my jam. And don't worry, I'm not burning my paycheck on blow or pills or whatever like last time. Though . . . [*looks left*] a girl does have needs.

[Reverse to view of kitchen. Open wine bottle and jelly jar on counter. Tessa's hand pours red wine.]

So, babysitting. Honestly? When you have to change diapers and feed them and all, it sucks. But once they're older and kind of doing their own thing you get paid to basically do whatever. The fuck. You want.

[Raises glass to mouth. Two sips. Pours rest of wine down drain.]

Not exactly an environment conducive to sobriety, am I right? But I'm doing my best, you guys. I mean, come on, two sips?

[Long sigh; phone propped against kitchen wall now, arms on counter, close-up with chin on wrists.]

I'm so glad we have this vlog, cuz I really miss our squad, you know? Like I swear I'd even go back to forty-day group at Sweet Meadow just to see you guys again, and I'm not even kidding. And the way they look at me now? I could have smacked that little worried frown off Rose's face when I walked in tonight. Bitch tried to hide it but she's so transparent, worried that I'll snoop around and steal shit like I used to do, dig through their pathetic little lives. Everybody thinks I'm like Lizzie Borden or some killer nanny from the news, like they'll come home and find their little kids butchered in their beds, or I'll bang their disgusting husbands. They're all so smug, think they know everything because they're grown-ups, but they don't. They fucking don't. *[Bites lip, tears up.]* It's just that it's hard sometimes to figure out why I should bother. What am I even doing this for? What do I even want out of life? It's like group. Oh my god, do you guys remember Dr. Doocy—Dr. Douchecanoe? *[Moves closer to camera; in a low, mannish voice:]* "What's your five-year plan? What's your endgame, people?" *[Backs away.]* That's the question, you know? What's my endgame?

FIVE

BECK

The twins girded themselves for war, equipment yanked from back-packs, affixed to legs and feet. Long striped socks, cleats, shin guards. Charlie Velcroed the captain's band around his upper arm.

Beck took the ramp down to a four-lane and headed west. "You guys need a PowerBar, some Gatorade?" he asked. "A 7-Eleven's coming up. Last chance."

"Nah, we're good," Charlie said loudly, hip-hop flaming from his earbuds.

"Aidan?"

"I'm fine," said Aidan, more quietly.

The great mass of Pike's Peak loomed to the southwest. The dashboard clock read 10:54. A two-hour drive from Crystal for a noon game at the Pike's Peak Soccer Complex.

Travel soccer, elite level. A lot of mileage, a lot of Panera. But Beck loved the drive down here with the guys. They made it at least twice in the fall and once in the spring to play the three major clubs in the area. Today the twins had a league game against Southern Colorado United, a decent team that always gave Crystal Soccer Club a good run.

Beck angled his Audi Q7 off the four-lane and joined a shiny millipede of SUVs and minivans stretched along the entrance drive. He pulled to the curb.

"Kick some butt out there, guys."

"Will do." Charlie tumbled out without a look back.

Aidan stayed in his seat. Beck turned around. "You good, bud?" Aidan gazed out the window as his brother joined a group of their teammates. "What is it?"

"Him," Aidan said.

"Char-Char?"

"Yeah."

"What about him?"

"I don't think he's starting today, Dad."

"Oh, please," said Beck with a loose laugh. "Charlie's team captain."

"He's playing sloppy. Coach keeps pulling him aside. I told you that last week."

"Look, man. Both my guys have started every game since, like, U9. No way he's not starting Charlie."

"Okay." Aidan pressed the door latch.

"Have a great game."

Aidan gave a smirk as he climbed out. "I will."

Beck watched his son approach the throng. It jarred him, to think there might be something to Aidan's concern. True, Charlie had given off signals lately, hints of frustration, subpar play that Beck had been chalking up to bad luck. At last week's game in Littleton—a loss—he'd misjudged a few passes and shanked a shot from point-blank range. Quite a shock, because Charlie had been such a clutch player for so long, team captain since the recreational league, then a top scorer all three years of travel.

The alpha twin: first from the womb, howling like a wolf.

Just before kickoff Beck walked over and joined the other team parents settling in for the game. A good group, mild-mannered on the sideline. With one delightful exception.

"Hey, big guy." Wade Meltzer clapped Beck between the shoulder blades. Wade was the big one, though, six-four and pushing 275, a Louisiana transplant who'd played offensive line for Auburn until blowing out a knee his sophomore year. Now he sublimated his football dreams into the soccer career of his son Bucky, a hulking center back who stalked opposing strikers with an unmatched brutality. (Most yellow cards in the league two years running, Wade was fond of boasting.)

Beck enjoyed standing next to Wade Meltzer at games because he acted as an outrage translator, seconding everything Beck muttered about bad calls and poor coaching but booming it out in a bayou baritone that allowed Beck to elude the judgment of the less intense parents. Wade reduced the teenage referees to tears with his drawling rants. Opposing parents regarded him as a loose pit bull on the sidelines.

Beck also liked Wade because the guy clashed so violently with all the Patagonia parents huddled by the pitch, cheering on their spawn in socially appropriate ways. Crystal's precious child-rearing culture could get insufferable, and there was nothing grander than witnessing the appalled looks Wade could provoke. But he never crossed the line, and besides, the guy was untouchable, a high-powered criminal defense attorney in Denver with a reputation for dogged ferocity in the courtroom. Beck was just glad their sons played on the same team. For now.

They speculated on the comparative strength of the squads, the odds of a win. Wade was concerned about an upcoming tournament in Cheyenne. "We'll need everybody at full strength next weekend," he said. "You seen the brackets yet? Second game Saturday's against the Cosmos."

"That team from Fort Collins?"

"We whupped 'em three-to-one in the semis of the Adidas tournament last year. But now they got that new midfielder, Baashir. Speedy Muslim boy, killed us in the league game in September?"

Beck recalled a wiry left-footer playing the same position as Aidan. Also a dad screaming in Arabic at the side judge. "I think they're Coptics," he said. "From Egypt."

"Whatever the hell they are, we need to clamp down on D. I told Bucky the back line boys need to get their shit together. They say that Baashir kid's the best player in the state in this age group."

"Really."

"Well anyhow he's going to ROMO next year, so we won't have to worry about him then, at least."

Beck frowned. "Is that right."

"That's what I hear."

Beck gulped back a bad taste in his throat. *ROMO.* The twins had been talking for months about the Rocky Mountain Fútbol Academy, the premier youth soccer club in Colorado. A whole league up from CSOC, with games as far away as Arizona and Kansas, plus two tournaments a year on the West Coast. But if this Baashir kid had already received a commitment for midfield, that meant Aidan might be out of the running before tryouts even began.

"Ah, well." Beck tugged at his beard and looked out across the pitch.

Wade Meltzer struck up a conversation with Amy Susskin, the team manager, standing to his right in head-to-toe Lululemon. She was about a third his size, cute but Crystal-prissy and bossy as hell. Amy would always find something passive-aggressive to say about Charlie, who started at striker over her son Will. She laughed, a high-pitched cackle, at some observation of Wade's. Beck ignored them both, his temp set at low brood, waiting for the game to begin.

SIX

BECK

Charlie didn't start.

Aidan was right.

He didn't start.

He still got to be co-captain, greeting the opposing team captains for the coin toss. But when the starting eleven took the pitch, Charlie wasn't among them. Will Susskin came on at striker instead, with Aidan at attacking midfield.

Amy Susskin leaned back and looked down the row of parents. Beck saw her smug smile out of the corner of his eye but ignored it. Over on the CSOC bench Charlie sat forward with his elbows on his knees, staring at the turf.

Beck looked away from his son and sized up the opposition. Some kids on United were brutish teenagers already. Whiskers, hairy legs, hardening jawlines. The CSOC U12s were a small team, but they dominated from the start. Good one-touch stuff, quick and fleet, maintaining possession. True, the bigger kids could outpace half the CSOC defenders, and there was one early play that reached the United striker in a dangerous spot. But Bucky Meltzer slide-tackled him and grounded the ball upfield to Aidan in the middle. Aidan shook a United defender and ran a sweet play with Will, who toed it in. No big celebration after the early goal, just cool hand slaps as the teams reset.

It was funny but with Charlie on the bench the squad looked different, spreading the field, passing with more swiftness and efficiency. Usually Charlie's commands would drown out everything as he made runs and controlled the ball up top. But now the team had a certain flow as Aidan played with his back to the opposing goal, directing traffic, calling out passes ahead of time. He looked solid, assured, confident.

No, more than that. Beck's son looked like a goddamn *artist*, painting the pitch with his zags and his weaves, a full palette of colors in those nimble feet. Or an orchestra conductor, managing the violins, keeping the cellos on beat. When had Aidan gotten so good?

Then he went down. A hard foul by a United defender in the box.

"Hey, now!" Wade Meltzer yelled across the pitch, ready to raise his version of hell, but the whistle blew for a penalty kick, placating him. It should have been Aidan's PK, but he let Will take it instead. Will drilled the ball into the lower right, putting CSOC up 2–

0.

The mood of the game changed. The United side grew frustrated, boys shouting at one another, calling for fouls that weren't there. Wade was loving it, clapping his hands, riling the opposing parents.

When the whistle blew for halftime, CSOC was up 3–0. Aidan had a goal, an assist, and an earned penalty kick. As the happy cluster of Crystal parents milled around, Amy Susskin came up to Beck. "Well. That was something to watch."

"It was," said Beck, wary but pleased.

She put out a manicured hand and patted his bicep. "That was really generous of Aidan, to give Will that penalty kick. He's playing beautifully."

"Thanks." Beck decided he liked the attention. Amy was divorced, he remembered. "Will looks awesome too."

"That's all on Aidan," she said. "They're combining so well. Let's just hope they can keep it up."

"Oh, I suspect they will," Wade said, shaking his large head. "Helluva half."

After the game Beck folded his chair and walked to the parking lot, his thoughts a roiling mix of pride and concern. Charlie had come on fifteen minutes into the second half, subbing for Will Susskin. Amy's son had a hat trick, but all of his goals were assisted or enabled by Aidan, who'd scored two more goals on his own. Charlie had played fine, had even tapped in the team's final goal, though by then the game was basically over.

Beck closed the hatch and stood with his left heel propped up against a faded FEEL THE BERN sticker on the Audi's bumper, watching the team pack up on the far side of the field. A call came in from Azra.

"How was the game?" his ex-wife asked.

"Wipeout," he said casually, not wanting to get into it. "They both played well."

"Good. So listen, Beck. I got a letter from the school yesterday. Aidan was identified for VisionQuest."

"What's that?"

"It's the gifted-and-talented program at St. Bridget's. I mean, it's kind of lame; it just meets for one period every six days. The weird thing is, he tested in last spring, but the school somehow misrecorded his scores, or confused them with Charlie's. The guidance counselor caught it last week during some review of test results they're doing for this new cooperative gifted program with the public schools. But he's in if we want the spot."

"What about Charlie?"

"Here's the bad part." Her voice went soft. "Apparently Aidan outscored Charlie by fifteen points."

"That's batshit."

"I know."

"Then Aidan shouldn't do VisionQuest," Beck said. "We'll just say no."

A pause. "Maybe we should leave it up to him?"

"Joint custody, remember? It's a liberal democracy. One person, one vote."

"Why would you be opposed to this? Is it the exclusivity?"

"Well, yeah."

"Beck, you have a trust fund. You went to Bennington, for god's sake. You come from one of the most elite—"

"Apples and oranges."

"What?"

"Look, I remember the gifted program from elementary school. They called them the Futura kids." He turned to face Pike's Peak. It was all coming back; something about the word *gifted*. "Probably twenty or twenty-five kids out of the entire school population were in the program. There was this whole separate room off the cafeteria, these big windows. At eleven-fifteen the announcement would come over the PA. *Futura kids, report to the Glass Room.* You wouldn't see them again until recess, when they'd mingle with the rabble. Futura kids got to skip out of the boring classes, miss gym. In fifth grade they went to New York for an entire week."

"But not poor Beck."

"What can I say? I never tested in. But I can still give you a list of every kid in that goddamn room."

She laughed.

"What?" Beck said, smiling.

"The things I can still learn about you after all these years. You never told me that story."

"It's one of my great shames, to be locked forever outside the Glass Room."

"Well, this isn't about you, okay? It's about Aidan, and I think he might really like it. Besides, it only meets three times a month or something. It's not like it matters all that much."

"Hmm," Beck said, noncommittal. He looked out over the pitch, noted a new slump in Charlie's shoulders as he trudged along the end line alone, kicking up spits of turf.

During their marriage Azra and Beck had always been on the same page about the twins. No stressing about milestones, no overinvestment in grades and achievements. Azra was a laid-back mom with a Colorado mellow that set her miles apart from her high-strung friends Samantha and

Rose, with their Insta-worthy daughters and their horseback riding on Sunday, violin on Monday, ballet on Tuesday. Then there was Lauren, the worst of them, smugly obsessed with the brilliance of her daughter, and later, when that went south, with the genius of her son. Azra and Beck's only big parenting disagreements had come since the divorce, and they'd all been about sports. Azra hadn't wanted the boys to switch to travel soccer just before third grade. They were too young for that level of competition, she'd argued. Plus, all that time in the car?

Now Beck felt vindicated for pushing it. Find your child's passion, all the parenting propaganda said, and man, had they ever. Soccer was the first activity that had galvanized the twins, brought out their fire. With three-plus years of elite play under their belts his guys had emerged as stars, with a real feel for the game.

Which is why this thing with Charlie was gnawing at him right now.

"Earth to Beck," Azra chirped.

"I'm here."

"They're fraternal twins, but they're different people, Beck. You know?" She sniffed and he thought of her aquiline nose, the smooth contours of her face. "If Aidan has some gifts that Charlie doesn't, then he needs to explore them independently. And vice versa."

"Isn't every kid at St. Bridget's gifted? The school costs fifty grand a year."

"Hey, it's your money, Beck."

It certainly fucking is. A lot of it too, and the tuition was killing him. Just last week Beck had made some discreet inquiries about pulling them out at midyear, figuring he could save twenty thou or so, because he kind of needed the cash right about now. No dice.

"Why don't you talk to Aidan about it tonight," he said. "I should have them at your place by five, five-thirty."

"Thanks, Beck."

"You got it, babe."

"Don't call me that."

"Sorry, I forget."

"No you don't."

He grinned fondly against the phone as his ex-wife disconnected.

I forget. He did forget, more and more these days. No, Beck, it's not early dementia, his doc assured him. Just work stress, twin boys, a new baby killing your sleep, a financial crunch. The world piling on.

Typical early midlife stuff, the doctor had said. Nothing fatal.

SEVEN

BECK

South of Castle Rock, Beck watched in the mirror as Aidan's eyes fluttered and closed and Charlie stared out at the lonely butte coming up on the right. The boys rode in postgame silence, no earbuds. The interstate rumbled below.

"So what was that all about?" Beck asked. His first words to Charlie since leaving the soccer complex.

"What?" Charlie jutted out his chin.

"The—you know. Not starting."

"I don't even care."

Beck licked his lips. A few moments passed. "Coach say anything to you about playing time? Because it was a big change."

Charlie sighed loudly. "Coach wanted to try something different, is all. He said I take over on the pitch, and it makes our game flat."

"Oh."

"He says the team 'defers to me too much.'" Air-quoting now. "He says I need to 'see the field' better. 'Like your brother.'"

Beck winced. "He said that?"

"I don't give a fuck."

"Hey!" Beck said, but Charlie ignored him.

Beck let it go, figuring his son had good reason to use that kind of language right now. Besides, he'd read somewhere that cussing was a sign of intelligence in the young. Soon Charlie joined his brother in slumber.

New Urbanism. That's what they called the architectural style dominating the conjoined cul-de-sacs in North Crystal. Identical houses spaced closely and painted in pastel hues, little picket fences out front: an atrocity to his designer's eye. But Sonja had loved the place, figuring it'd be perfect for all the kids she planned to have, so Beck had squeezed a down payment out the ass of his dwindling trust fund, and here they were.

Beck pulled the Audi into the driveway and reached into the door compartment for his wallet. His fingers grazed against a piece of paper, and that's when he remembered.

"*Goddamnit*," he hissed, startling the twins. Even after an eighty-mile nap in the car they woke up like hibernating cubs, slow, grouchy, starving. "Sorry, guys, just— Go on inside, okay? Tell Sonja I'll be a sec."

Wordlessly they slid their doors open, grabbed their soccer bags from the trunk, and staggered along the front walk.

Beck whacked his skull back against the headrest three times.

Garbage disposal.

The current one was broken. A bunch of old food was collected in the works, stinking up the kitchen. Beck had promised Sonja that he'd replace it himself rather than call a plumber. He'd found a YouTube video laying out the whole procedure from start to finish, and figured he'd save a few hundred bucks while steeped in the soul-nurturing virtues of DIY. He'd been putting the repair off for weeks, but Sonja had made him swear on his bones that he'd take care of it that weekend. The plan had been to grab a new disposal at Home Depot during warm-ups that morning—but the whole business with Charlie had made him forget.

It's just a garbage disposal, he told himself. No catastrophe here. But these days it was the little things that niggled. Charlie's playing time, a few extra pounds, a forgotten errand. That new and worsening wrinkle in his financial plan.

Worms, chewing through his brain.

He lingered in the car, palms moist against the wheel.

In the master bedroom Sonja was nursing Roy. Her yellow mess of hair cupped the baby like an oyster shell, and she had a look of gorgeous bliss on her round face, that charge of oxytocin through her veins. Beck sat on the edge of the bed and dropped a hand on his second wife's knee.

"Did you get it?" she asked.

"You know, babe, I was having some second thoughts."

"Second thoughts, Beck?" Her pouty frown. "About a garbage disposal?"

"I'm in Home Depot this morning down in the Springs, looking over the units. Then this guy walks past wheeling one of those big compost bins on a utility cart. And I got to thinking. What if we composted, you know? Set one up in the side yard, have a bucket in the kitchen?"

She stared at him. He swallowed.

"What?"

"You did not go to Home Depot, Beck."

"Of course I did."

"You are lying," Sonja said, eyes closed as she leaned back against the headboard. "I tracked you on Find My iPhone, and you were at the soccer fields the whole time. You are a liar. I will take Roy and raise him on my own back in Salzburg. It will be easy to find a new husband there. A man who is not afraid to change diapers. A man who knows how to fix a drain."

"Come on, babe, don't do me like that." Beck reached for her soft arms, but she threw up her chin and turned away, shielding Roy from him.

Sonja was so much more a wounded bird than Azra, who'd liked to fight dirty, and always won. Lately, though, Sonja had started to adopt his ex-wife's tactics, going after his basic competencies as a father and a man. It all felt a little too familiar. It panicked him.

Because there were certain things Azra had just never gotten about Beck. The importance of his work at the design firm, his need for spare time at home to flesh out his business plan, to manage the complexities of the family finances. Even back then, when things were less rocky in the dollars-and-debt department, working through it all had required a lot of time on the phone and the internet, nine hours of sleep a night, head space free of clutter.

After the divorce Beck had struggled mightily to understand where things went wrong, and he'd never quite come to grips with what was missing from his first marriage. Maybe he'd needed a softer touch, a more compliant type, without Azra's probing intricacies and all her critiques of his sleep schedule, his laissez-faire parenting style, the habits he maintained to stay young and sharp.

So when he settled down with Sonja, he thought he'd won some kind of spousal lottery, a twentysomething life raft floating him away from the churning shoals of his marriage. Suddenly he had a hot young au pair who was great with the twins, a willing partner in mind-blowing carnality, already intimately familiar with the lifestyle Beck preferred to maintain. Unlike Azra she'd never given him crap about spending from his trust fund when he wanted a new mountain bike, a new guitar to shred, a new kayak.

In fact she looked up to him, Beck could tell. It felt awesome.

So when it was just the two of them, before Roy came along, Beck's days had been blissful. Work at home in the morning, maybe score a nooner with Sonja, then bike down to the office for a few client consultations. Even when Sonja got pregnant, he'd figured his latest spawn would bob gently into the flow of the good life.

Then the baby dropped. And sure, those early weeks were a chaotic blur and he'd helped out some. A *lot*, actually.

But then, to Beck's increasingly unpleasant surprise, his new wife had started demanding things.

Maybe *Beck* could buy the groceries and do the cooking this week.

Maybe *Beck* could make the lunches and drive the twins to school.

Maybe *Beck* could unload the dishwasher and keep the bathrooms clean.

But, hon, you're not working right now, he'd wheedle. I take them to most of their soccer practices and all their games. Plus, I've got three trade shows coming up—

You booked three trade shows right after our due date?

Okay, not the smoothest move. But now they had Tessa coming three afternoons a week. She charged fifteen bucks an hour.

Look at us. We have a nanny for the nanny.

(Beck had never expressed this sentiment out loud. But damn, it seemed like a shitload of childcare, a lot of spare time for a young stay-at-home mom.)

He grabbed his wife's feet and started to rub. He had his own tactics for smoothing things. Eventually she turned back around and presented him with Roy's warm, kicking little body, like some kind of primitive tribal gift to the chieftain.

"Take him," she said. "Just hold him for a while."

Roy clung to his father as Sonja pushed off the bed and left the room. Beck nuzzled the boy's cute head. Peach fuzz feathered his lips as his nose gathered scent: breast-warmed scalp, the milk-sweet tang of Sonja.

This is what it's all about, Beck thought as he inhaled again; man and cub, this animal bond. He swayed on the bed, humming wordless nothings to his third and tiniest son.

EIGHT

XANDER

Mr. Aker would never hurt him again. He'd try to. He'd use his batteries and his pins. He'd use his forks and his skewers. But the guy was a woodpusher and he knew it and he knew Xander knew it.

There was only one thing Mr. Aker could do right now to hurt him. One thing: La Bourdonnais–McDonnell 1834.

He could go

BxP
PxB
B-B4
K-B2
RxPch
R-B7ch
R-N7
PxN

and then Xander would maybe go

P-QN4
BxN

N–Q5

NxPch

NxR(Q7)

K–B3

K–N3

N(Q7)xB

RxP

but he wouldn't see it. Even Xander had barely seen it a minute ago. If Mr. Aker had known he had that one infinitesimal chance—

Nope. Instead Mr. Aker moved queen's bishop to d4.

Predictably.

Xander scribbled a few observations in his notebook, then made his final move. He held out his hand for Mr. Aker to shake.

"Fat chance," said Mr. Aker. "I've still got both rooks and half my pawns. You think you've got me—"

"Look again, Mr. Aker. Look at my knights."

Mr. Aker tilted his head to the side, staring at Xander's knights. Then he shook Xander's hand, conceding the game. "What am I now, sixty and one?"

"Sixty-three and one, actually," Xander said. "Would you like to play again?"

"I'll pass."

Xander packed his cut-glass chess pieces neatly into their appropriate slots, remembering the one time Mr. Aker had ever beaten him, two years ago.

He thought about that game a lot, even now, the unpredictable set of moves his teacher had made after Xander castled. It was an odd flash of brilliance from such a mediocre player. Totally against Mr. Aker's usual tendencies toward self-preservation and conservative defenses.

But then again Mr. Aker wasn't a rook or a knight. He was a human, and humans weren't always consistent and predictable like chess pieces. When Xander looked at the figures on a board, he knew exactly what they were capable of. Sometimes he even felt as if he knew what his pieces were thinking while they were arrayed across the board. As if he were inside their little dead heads and gaming out his plans into a near future bursting with possibilities only Xander could see.

Gonna sit here for two more moves, then capture that pawn, the knight plotted.

I'm pinning the queen right now, speculated the rook. *Does she even know her bishop can't move or she's freaking TOAST?*

Three, eight, twelve, sixteen pieces working together toward a common ass-kick, and Xander was all of them at once, thinking their networked thoughts, plotting against their common enemy. It wasn't like that with people. Who knew what *they* were thinking?

His mother, for instance. Whenever Tessa left the house these days, his mother started closing cabinets too hard and scrubbing the counter as if poison lurked in the granite.

Tessa was just as bad. Not as bad as she used to be, like when she was thirteen, when she'd stop eating or make those little slits in her skin or swipe pills from their mom's friends' medicine cabinets and put them under her tongue and show them to Xander across the table. Now she was hardly ever around, and when she was around, she locked herself in her room, making her actually quite informative vlogs all the time. (Xander's favorite so far was Episode #23: "Virginity Is Overrated.")

Sometimes Xander wished his mom and his sister would play chess with him more often, and not just for the company. When he played them at chess, it was the only time he knew what they were thinking, what they would do. Same with his friends and the parents of his friends. Once Xander had played someone two or three times, he knew the range of moves they would make; he knew what they could see on the board and what they couldn't. Their limitations. Their personalities, even.

Like Charlie and Aidan Unsworth-Chaudhury. They were twins and played a lot alike. But Xander knew the subtle differences between their games. Aidan wasn't great but he was a lot better than Charlie, who was better than their dad, Beck, who was not nearly as good as their mom, Azra, but only a little worse than their stepmom, Sonja.

In chess everyone had a pattern, a tendency. Average human players were invariably predictable. They had grooves in their brains, like furrows in a plowed field out in Beulah County. And the trick to being a great chess player, the masters said, was to be *un*predictable. To get *out* of your groove.

"Get *out* of your groove. Get *out* of your groove."

"What's that, Xander?" asked Mr. Aker.

Xander looked up, wide-eyed, realizing he'd been speaking aloud again. It happened, when he was in a groove like this. Other kids had filtered in from recess, and some of them were staring at him, smirking. Predictably.

"Nothing." Xander slipped his chess set into his bag.

Once they were all back in their seats, Mr. Aker started talking about how serious planning for the science fair would start right after Thanksgiving recess and everyone needed a preliminary idea in two weeks. Xander had already decided he was going to do something about chess. "The Science of Chess," maybe.

Mr. Aker wanted him to work on spider genes. Why are spider populations exploding all over the world? Is it in their DNA? Spider genes were fine, but they weren't as wicked as chess.

For Thanksgiving they were going over to Emma Z's, and that meant he might get to hang out with the twins, if they were there. A house full of people, nobody slamming doors and screaming at one another, and as much mashed potatoes as Xander could eat.

Yes.

Thanksgiving.

Lots of pie. Lots of chess.

You could learn a lot about people from chess.

More than anyone would ever suspect.

NINE

ROSE

The Zellar house was a stately Queen Anne that dominated Birch Street from a corner lot. White cornices and moldings, siding in a daring persimmon hue, two towers, a widow's walk: the sort of home that inspired long sidewalk pauses of admiration from alumni and parents strolling through Old Crystal, thirty-two square blocks of dwellings built for Darlton University faculty but now occupied by software engineers, surgeons from the Medical Center, bedroom commuters to Denver law firms.

Adding to the house's luster was its minor place in the town's history. A mayor back in the early twentieth century had commissioned the home from a Denver builder on the occasion of his daughter's marriage. Samantha, after learning this backstory from the title documents, had applied to put the house on the state register of historic places, a status announced on a bronze plaque now displayed by the front door:

TWENTY BIRCH

A COLORADO HISTORICAL SOCIETY

REGISTERED HOME

A typo, Kev and Samantha had complained when the plaque arrived: it should say Twenty Birch *Street*.

But the Zellars had kept the sign, turning the missing word into a domestic trademark. Now, whenever a gathering was held at the Zellar home, it took place at Twenty Birch. Never *my house* or *our place*, always *Twenty Birch*.

We're having a small fund-raiser at Twenty Birch for Senator Wicke, hope you can make it!

But your living room is so tiny, Rose. Why don't we have Emma Q's birthday party at Twenty Birch?

Are you all coming to Thanksgiving this year, at Twenty Birch? We're having the whole Zellar clan.

By the time Rose and her family arrived, a huge roast turkey was already sprawled on a platter, pies sat in neat ranks on the counter, and chamber music floated softly from hidden speakers. Four men were sampling home brew by the crackling fireplace; at Rose's prodding Gareth drifted over reluctantly to join them. The coziness of the whole thing made Rose wish they'd left their laptops and their own grim living room a few hours earlier, avoiding another of their whispered spats.

The holiday crowd gathered at Twenty Birch had grown since last year. In addition to Kev's parents, his two younger brothers and his sister had flown in with their spouses and broods, a passel of cousins Rose had met several times but could never keep straight. The Zellar crew would leave the next morning for Steamboat Springs, where Kev's parents, Edgar and Suze, had rented a house for a long weekend of skiing and snowboarding.

Azra spied Rose through the throng and signaled her into the kitchen, where she stood with Samantha and Lauren sipping rosé.

"Saved this just for us," Samantha said, pouring a fourth glass. They toasted the holiday, the one quick moment the four of them would steal together, though Rose would remember it as the highlight of the day. Samantha never failed to go out of her way to make her friends feel special, at social events, at the rare fund-raiser Rose attended, even among her own extended family. Always a tasty wedge of cheese for them to sample, a bottle of something she'd set aside. They huddled over their wine until Samantha turned away to check on the gravy.

When Kev called them to the table with some dings on a wineglass, Rose wandered down the hall, looking for Gareth. She passed the powder room, the guest suite, Kev's study. Finally she reached the library, a high-ceilinged room lined with built-in bookcases. Gareth and Xander sat cross-legged on the window seat, playing chess.

Rose stopped in the doorway and felt it, that familiar tug of disappointment in her husband for not mingling with other adults, though she supposed it was nice to see someone paying attention to Xander. As they moved their pieces around the board, the boy scribbled busily in his notebook. According to Lauren, her son kept scrupulous records of every game he'd ever played, whether at national tournaments or at birthday parties, transcribing every move into algebraic notation.

She waited them out, knowing it wouldn't take long.

"I think you got me," Gareth said a few moments later. "I'm oh for four."

"That's correct," Xander replied. They shook hands, then Xander turned his head and saw Rose.

"Hello," he said, giving her a disconcerting stare.

She cleared her throat. "Dinner," she told them. Gareth rose from the window seat and followed her while Xander lingered behind, completing his notes.

The adults filtered into the dining room around the long chestnut table, seven to a side with one at each end. Rose found her name tag, written out in careful calligraphy by Emma Z, next to Kev's sister, Blakey, and directly across from Tessa, who had graduated to the adult table that year. Sixteen guests were gathered in the dining room, many more at the kids' tables set up in the parlor.

Kev stood at the foot of the table, a Denver Broncos apron dangling loosely from his neck. He welcomed everyone with a raised glass and a few off-color jokes before turning things over to his father, a retired physician from Richmond, Virginia, for a formal blessing.

Edgar Zellar cleared his jowled throat for silence.

"Heavenly Father, we thank you for your bounty, for the nourishing gifts laid before us and the hands that have prepared them in Your name and in the name of Your Son, our Savior Jesus Christ. We thank You as well for the loving presence of friends and for the health and well-being of our families, in my case"—he paused for effect, looking over at the kids' tables—"thirteen perfect grandchildren, enough to insure the perpetuation of the Zellar line, especially if my eldest can manage one more."

Some lighthearted chuckles. Rose shared a pained look with Azra, three seats down on the opposite side. Her covered gaze shifted down to Samantha, that placid face taking her father-in-law's ribbing without a flinch. Kev's parents loved to tout the abundance of grandkids produced by their children. An even baker's dozen, Edgar would quip; when can we expect our fourteenth? No surprise that Sam, wife of the eldest, had always been self-conscious about her only child, a rare chink in the Zellar armor and a subject that Kev's parents and siblings alike would often raise in a gently chiding tone that would have made Rose's head explode if anyone had questioned her most intimate choices in this way. Perhaps she was fortunate to have no living in-laws to please. Rose's own folks were lower-middle-class Midwesterners with her elder brother still living in their basement, hardly in a position to judge.

Samantha also came from humbler roots. A sister in Florida she rarely saw; her parents, like Gareth's, both deceased. Understandable that she would cleave so unquestioningly to a family steeped in its own mythology, though when the Zellars gathered at Twenty Birch, the force of their collective self-regard could often be overwhelming.

Rose studied her silver napkin ring as the patriarch finished his prayer.

The school came up a few minutes after the blessing. Edgar was reaching around to refill wineglasses when he asked, "So, Rose, will y'all be putting in for this academy?"

"What's that, Edgar?"

"It's the new—Samantha, hon." He raised his voice. "What's that special school you were talking about with my eldest grandson? The gifted school."

The word *gifted* slashed like a guillotine through other topics. Around the table the talk ceased.

"It's called Crystal Academy, Dad," Samantha said into the silence.

"A private?" Azra asked, apparently as clueless as Rose.

"No, actually." Lauren leaned over the table, her short neck turtling out. "It's a public magnet school for the exceptionally gifted."

"They're hailing it as the Stuyvesant of the Rockies," Kev said grandly.

"A high school?" Rose's question.

"Grades six through eight in the lower school, and the upper school goes nine through twelve."

"Oh," said Rose. *Exceptionally gifted.* Words to make the bones sing. This must be the mysterious "other option" Samantha had been hedging about at RockSalt last week. "What, a city school, just for Crystal kids?"

"Oh no," said Kev. "It's a joint venture between the City of Crystal and the Four Counties."

"All five school districts?" Gareth asked. "But that's a huge pool of eligible students."

"No kidding," said Samantha. "Over a hundred thousand kids for just a thousand spots."

"The one percent," Blakey observed snidely. Everyone laughed, but she was right: one in a hundred. Kev's acerbic sister was enjoying the conversation, Rose could tell, watching the reactions among her sister-in-law's friends as they parsed the news about the school.

"How does admissions work?" Azra asked.

"They're doing it as a test-in." Lauren: happily in the know. "A first round of CogPros in the districts starting in March, then more individualized assessments in a second round."

"CogPros?" someone asked.

"Cognitive Proficiency test," Lauren said knowingly. "It's a standard IQ measure."

Over her wineglass Rose looked a question at Gareth, and he shrugged it right back. Neither of them had heard a word about this school.

"Where are they building it?" Gareth asked.

"The upper school will be out in Kendall County," Kev answered. "But the lower school is going in the old Maple Hill Elementary site."

"About six blocks from here." Samantha nodded vaguely west, in the direction of her back deck.

"It's a done deal," said Kev. "The contractor's an old buddy of mine, and they finalized the building permits last week. The refurbish kicks off in January. They'll be up and running by July, hiring staff this spring for a fall opening. These guys are moving fast."

How do you know all this? The question never left Rose's lips, because the Zellars always knew, and besides, Kev had served on the City Council for the last three years. Any major building project in town, let alone one as visible as a new magnet school, would already be on his radar.

"So, Rose, will you apply for Emma Q?" Edgar asked, still pressing for an answer.

"Who knows." Rose was already seeing years of small classes, innovative pedagogy, Barnard admissions staff cooing in approval. "We might check it out."

"And what about you, Tessa? Think you'll apply?"

The questions came from Blakey. Kev's sister was leaning over her plate, looking at Lauren's daughter in a not entirely friendly way.

Tessa, chewing, held up a finger. "I'm not really the gifted type," she mumbled after she swallowed.

"Well, you're obviously a bright young lady," Edgar said. His gaze wandered down to the top of her dress, a low-cut green velvet or velour, one of her own creations. "And everyone has gifts of some sort or another."

Tessa screwed up her face. "I like to draw, I guess."

"Do you now," he said. "And what is it you like to draw, sweetie? Landscapes, that kind of thing?"

"Mostly fashion. Like clothes, outfits." She pushed a strand of hair behind her ear. "Shoes sometimes."

"Tessa has an incredible sense of style," Azra put in from down the

table. "Tessa, tell them what you told me the other day. At BloomAgain."
She looked around at everyone. "Tessa's been working for me at the store."

Tessa shifted in her chair, and a flush crept up her neck. The table had
remained silent, everyone curious about the exchange. Rose stole a look at
Samantha, who had already started in on the rapid sequence of blinks she
performed when impatient. (Wouldn't do to have the Zellar Thanksgiving
banter hijacked by an outsider, let alone a troubled young woman like
Tessa Frye.)

"You said you think of dressing as an art form," Azra coaxed. "Like
sculpture or painting, right? But instead of stone or canvas you're working
with people."

Tessa's napkin was pressed to her lips. She removed it and started weaving it through her fingers. "Well"—

she looked at Edgar—"it's kind of hard
to explain. Sometimes I can see the shapes of faces and I understand, like,
exactly what kind of outfit would work with those cheeks, or that haircut.
Or what colors people should be wearing to complement their eyes, or the
shade of their skin. I also think about fabrics a lot, like texture and density
and the way things hang. Sometimes I think about what a pair of pants
would sound like when the legs touch, depending on the fabric, the reso-
nance of that. I remember my dad had this barn coat he always wore when
I was little. It was made out of this thick cotton-wool blend that—"

"And who's that lucky fellow—your daddy?" Edgar surveyed the crowded
table, assuming that one of the non-Zellar men there that day was Tessa's
father.

"He's dead," Tessa said.

"Goodness." Edgar looked stricken. "I'm sorry, dear."

"That's okay," Tessa went on, more brightly now, opening up. "Anyway
it was a cotton-wool blend that I've never seen in anything else since. When
I scratched his pocket with my fingernail, it made this beautiful ringing
sound, and I keep thinking if I got some of that cloth and made something
with it, I could hear that same sound again. It's stupid, but."

With her eyes still on Kev's father, she forked a piece of turkey and
chewed it slowly.

"You do sound like a gifted young lady." Edgar reached across Blakey's plate to pat Tessa's free hand. "Quite an imagination. Maybe you *should* apply for that school."

"That's so nice," said Tessa, blushing faintly over her food. "I could show you my sketches after we eat, if you want."

Then—

"Hey Tessa?" Lauren barked sharply down the table. "Let's just see if we can get you through junior year, okay? We'll consider that a victory."

Tessa's eyes flashed then dimmed. She looked down at her plate. The table went still, the only sound in Rose's ears the clink of silver on china. From her angle Lauren's face was obscured, but Azra and Gareth looked appalled, Samantha's lips were pale and taut, and even the children had picked up on the sudden hush. Emma Zellar's eyes roved from Tessa to Edgar to Lauren and back, missing nothing; and there was Q beside her, neck bent over her food, gobbling through a gravy-soaked pile of mashed potatoes.

"Well happy Thanksgiving," someone deadpanned into the silence. One of Kev's brothers, Rose thought. Blakey made a low cruel laugh, and immediately Rose could see how this exchange would be parsed up in Steamboat, the big family cackling over that unfiltered friend of Samantha's who'd been such a bitch to her daughter.

Rose got a patch of heat in her throat, feeling for Tessa—but oddly for Lauren too, the way she had tainted the meal. Only a few at that table knew what their family had endured over the years, the source of these occasional darts.

"Hey, guys, let's get these cranberries moving around." Samantha lifted a cut-glass bowl and the feast resumed. A rough patch Zellar-smoothed.

A Touch of Tessa:
One Girl's Survival Guide to Junior Year
A Video Blog

Episode #34: HAPPY FUCKING THANKSGIVING

. . . 7 views . . .

[*Tessa, in moonlight from window, huddled in bed and sniffling.*]

TESSA: Hello, no one. Well, I hope you guys had a better Thanksgiving with your fams than I did. So today I marched the trail of tears over to the Zellars' house. My first time in "Twenty Birch" since— wait, I mean, who the hell even names their house? But anyways it was my first time in their big fancy Maple Hill crib since the fateful night of Tessa's great fuck-up, when I left their daughter alone. I said a million times I didn't want to go, because I knew I'd get all these condescending questions about my hair, my "unique fashion sense," my "five-year plan." Where would *you* like to go to college, Tessa? Theo's at Princeton, you know. Tessa, where do *you* see yourself in ten years? Plus, my mom always ends up feeling like shit when she's around their big happy family, and I told her we should stay home this year and make our own dinner, you know? Or just do Thanksgiving with Beck and Sonja and the twins, which would have been so nice, because Xander loves those guys and Beck is such a goofball. But Lauren made us go to the Zellars', and it was so—just—

[*Cries; stops recording.*]

TESSA [*wiping nose*]: Okay, I'm back. Anyways I used to love that house, especially after my dad died, when I was over there all the time. They always had the best snacks, bowls of fruit on the counter, fresh bread and muffins. You could just take like an organic grass-fed Fudgsicle out of the freezer whenever you wanted. But going over there today was like—I mean, Samantha? She used to buy me dresses, take me out to lunch. She even took me for my first pedicure. She liked to brush my hair when she was brushing Z's. Ten strokes for Emma, ten strokes for Tessa. Ten strokes for Emma, ten strokes for Tessa. And I remember how she smiled at me in the mirror. Samantha was so beautiful, not a little unibrow troll like my mom, which is probably how I'll turn out. I wanted to look just like her. So I mean the Zellars basically adopted me, like Azra did, and even uptight Rose, but now . . .

[*Sniffs; long silence.*]

The dad's still really nice, I guess. Kev. He has a sister who OD'd and almost died when she was like twenty, even though the Zellars never talk about that and I only know because Azra told me one time when I was hanging out at the store. Yeah, they like to sweep all their shit under the rug over at Twenty Birch so their Latinx housekeeper can vacuum it up three days a week. Now the same sister's some corporate lawyer in New York. She was there today. High-key bitch, totally clueless about other people the same way my mom is. Oh, and my mom? Holy shit. In rare form today, even for her, and I'm like—god it's like she hates *me* because my dad died. How fucked is that? [*Long sigh.*] Sorry, I know I've told you guys all this stuff like a million times. But the whole thing made me think about how different everything used to be. How nice it all was. And that maybe I could find some way to . . . I don't know. Just sort of start over. [*Long silence, blinking into phone.*] Any ideas?

CH'AYÑA

I t's time," Ch'ayña said, rising from her chair.

Atik wristed sleep from his eyes and finished his juice and put his glass in the sink. "Mamay," he called down the hall.

"Coming, coming," Silea answered.

Ch'ayña's daughter appeared in the doorway, wiping her hands on her dress, and the two women rushed to throw their lunch into plastic bags. Ch'ayña noticed Atik's blue fleece draped across the back of the sofa and tossed it to him.

"What's the hurry?" Atik asked. "Aren't they all gone to the mountains, like you said?"

Ch'ayña and her daughter exchanged looks.

"If they left it like last year, it's a big job," Silea said briskly. "Like cleaning a mountain, and then we have the smaller house to do after that." Her busy hands paused as she looked at him. "It's nice, though, Atikcha, that you're coming."

"Your first time," Ch'ayña said proudly, and Atik gave them a sleepy smile. He was a good boy, polite but full of tricks. He'd offered to come along last night, to shorten their day. Silea had refused the gesture at first, because she didn't want him thinking this was the kind of job for him. But there's no shame in cleaning houses, Ch'ayña had pushed back; no shame in hard work. Besides, Atik had insisted. What am I supposed to do on a no-school day, he'd asked, alone out here, where there's nothing to do but TV and origami?

Ch'ayña rubbed a hand across her grandson's hair, tangled and thick and in need of a comb, still smelling of his bed. On the top step she turned to lock the trailer door.

Just after seven, sunrise on the Beulah flats, a single swath of brown. The air smelled of cow shit in the late November cold, and in the distance a tractor roared to life. A bluish haze of exhaust rose from the startled engine.

Ch'ayña opened the cap of the pickup, and Atik slid the half-dried mops into the bed between the bins of cleaners and rags. He hopped in the cab first, taking the middle of the bench between Ch'ayña and Silea. By the time the truck bumped out of the gravel lot between the neighbors' trailers Silea was already nodding off against the passenger door.

"We're going first to the Zellars', then to Ms. Holland's," Ch'ayña said, in Quechua.

"Okay," Atik said.

"Okay," Ch'ayña echoed, gently mocking. She turned left. Always west, toward Crystal and the distant mountains. A few miles on, after they had left the little town of Dry River behind, she said, "Some things to remember." Silence. "You awake?"

He wasn't. She reached over to poke him in the side and he startled.

"Listen," said Ch'ayña.

"I am listening," he said, in his Quechua this time.

"Hollands want the dishwasher emptied but the Zellars don't care."

"Okay."

"When you're doing the showers, pour the 409 all-purpose into the empty green clean bottle under the sink. It does better on the mildew, and Ms. Holland never knows the difference. But Zellar, she'll notice. She's got a better nose, so be careful."

"I will."

"Also Zellar likes the wineglasses polished."

"With a cloth?"

"Paper towels. Hollands drink wine from jars. We don't polish those."

"Why jars?"

"Who knows."

Silea turned over in her sleep, her head flopping down onto Atik's shoulder.

"Ms. Holland will try to speak Spanish if she sees you," Ch'ayña said. "Her Spanish is even worse than mine. But be nice when she does it and speak slowly so she can understand. Also the Zellar father is a pig. But the girl's very clean, keeps her room tidy and makes her own bed and does her own laundry."

"What does she look like?"

"I've only seen pictures. Pretty. But something in her face looks a little—*nasty.*"

The last word was in English. Atik made a sleepy laugh.

The truck stop came up on the right, before the interstate. Ch'ayña pulled past the pumps and handed Atik a dollar bill and three quarters. "Get a coffee," she told him.

He shook his head. "I'll be fine, Awicha."

"You need a coffee. So does your mamay."

Silea made a sleepy moan. Atik shrugged and closed his eyes, seeming content to remain in the truck. She'd get it herself, then.

The door groaned open and Ch'ayña dismounted to the asphalt, a long drop. She got some looks. She always did here, not from the clerks anymore but often from the distance boys ambling in from their rigs.

The store was quiet for a Friday, only a few customers milling slowly beneath the fluorescent pallor. Ch'ayña poured a large coffee into a Styrofoam cup. There was no milk or cream; the three decanters were missing. At the counter a clerk she didn't recognize—a big, white, maggoty thing—rang up her purchase. Ch'ayña owled the girl, because the new clerks shorted you on change sometimes.

"*Lichi?*" Ch'ayña said, on purpose. The new girl wrinkled her nose. "Milk?" Ch'ayña said.

The girl rolled her eyes. "It's Thanksgiving, lady. We're short-staffed." She pointed back to the coffee counter and made a pulling gesture with her hand. Ch'ayña walked over to the coffee again, opened the cupboard beneath the line of decanters, and found some creamers.

Over in the corner of the parking lot the usual gang lingered by the dumpsters, hoping for a work pickup. Good luck on a holiday Friday, Ch'ayña thought. Guatemalans mostly, guys she recognized from Mountain View, their sprawling neighborhood. One of them was perched on top of a dumpster, binoculars to his eyes, looking out for an ICE van rolling down off the interstate ramp.

She saw Tiago, Silea's man who came around. He waved at her and Ch'ayña raised the foam cup a sullen inch before looking away.

She didn't like the fellow. He tried too hard, in all kinds of ways, always bringing wildflowers or candies or packs of beer, staying around to watch American shows with Silea into the night with his feet up, acting like their home was his.

These days his attentions were turning more and more to Atik. Earlier in the fall Tiago had arrived with a baseball, glove, and bat for the boy, then, a few weeks later, a soccer ball. He'd even tried to give Atik an old computer that a cousin of his was selling. *He needs to be connected*, Tiago had claimed. *Linked to a bigger world.*

But Ch'ayña wouldn't have it. *You're not his tayta*, she'd snapped at him—in Quechua but he got the idea. So he had taken the computer back to his cousin, and that was the end of that.

When Ch'ayña climbed back into the truck, Silea was awake with the window down, making eyes at the man from across the lot.

"Here." Ch'ayña shoved the coffee over at her daughter, because Atik's hands were busy. "Share this with him."

Silea took the coffee and reluctantly raised the window. In the distance Tiago turned away.

As they drove out past the pumps, Ch'ayña saw that her grandson had already folded two of his flowers and fruits using the papers in the glove compartment. A yellow rose, its petals lined with machine print. A delicate white pear with a stem fashioned from a stir stick.

Years ago Atik had started with a lily: the one paper trick Ch'ayña had ever taught him, the only one she knew. Now he could fold cars, trucks, flowers, fruits, animals of every kind, and he'd learned them all on his own. Give him a packet of colored paper and he'd make a garden, an orchard, a zoo, a train. A few months ago he'd even folded his jatunmama. Ch'ayña had recognized the paper figure instantly as herself, with a striped dress crafted of ten color strips each no wider than a nail clipping. She pinched his ear for that but still had the figure by her bed, watching her while she slept. The trailer was full of Atik's creations, whole forests of his clever origamis, creeping along the tops of the stove and the refrigerator, lining every shelf, arranged carefully by Silea on half the eating table.

Atik nudged the pear and the rose against the windshield, next to a pair of green tomatoes he'd created last week from Wrigley wrappers.

Ten minutes later the truck hitched over the train tracks and they were in Crystal. Here, the pavement smoothed out. Bigger, lusher trees gathered over the avenue. An electric bus painted deep purple angled quietly away from a charging station, the end of the city line.

"The bus drivers here aren't like Huánuco drivers," Ch'ayña observed. "Never wait for the regulars, they just go."

"We'll be there soon," Silea said, alert now from the coffee.

"Remember, Atik," Ch'ayña continued. "Pledge spray will stain and ruin the suedes and leathers, so when you're doing the floor by the couches, keep the can pointed down."

"I'll remember," he said.

"Also another thing. Zellars want the piano keys whitened today. They've had a lot of guests and a lot of sticky fingers in the house. So here's what you do: you rub the ivory with Colgate, then you buff using a cloth dampened with whole-fat milk. The Colgate will smear on the black keys, and she'll notice if it does."

"So always polish the black keys last," Silea said. "Both sides and the top."

"Also the parts in front," Ch'ayña added. "They're easy to miss when you're cleaning, because they're so small, like your little toes."

"Stop," Atik said. He hated baby talk, more and more since his twelfth birthday.

Ch'ayña patted his knee. "Just be a good worker, Atik Yupanqui. If we go at it hard, we can finish early and maybe your mamay won't make us eat her chicken tonight."

"We'll see," Silea muttered. She drained the last of the coffee and bent her smooth neck back in a yawn.

On Birch Street they pulled to the curb and hauled the mops and bins up the front walk. Halfway to the house Atik stumbled on a paving stone.

"Careful," Ch'ayña warned him. He grunted something, and as he hefted a mop Ch'ayña looked back at the truck and saw the flashes of color through the windshield. Her grandson's rose and his pear and his two green tomatoes stood guard on the dashboard, tiny miracles against the glass.

PART II

THE FIRST CUT

All this can lead to an apparently paradoxical situation when parents who are proud of their gifted child and who even admire him are forced by their own repression to reject, suppress, or even destroy what is best, because truest, in that child.

—ALICE MILLER,
The Drama of the Gifted Child

City of Crystal
SCHOOL DISTRICT
achievement, excellence, equality

TO: City of Crystal School District Families

FROM: Dr. Joe Jelinek, Superintendent

SUBJECT: Cognitive Proficiency (CogPro) testing

March 15, 2018

Dear Crystal Families,

As most of you are aware, we will soon be administering the Cognitive Proficiency (CogPro) test to all children grades five through eleven who wish to be assessed for admission to Crystal Academy for the 2018–19 academic year. The test will be administered simultaneously to students in the school districts of the Four Counties.

The CogPro is a nationally certified standardized test aimed at assessing multiple measures of student aptitude, including verbal, nonverbal, spatial, and quantitative reasoning. The test is multiple choice and will be given to students at two designated times at their current school locations: the first on Saturday, March 24, between 9:00 and 11:00 a.m.; the second, for those who cannot attend the Saturday testing session, on Wednesday, March 28, between 7:00 and 9:00 p.m. Students who currently attend private or parochial schools and wish to be considered for Crystal Academy's first intake are asked to sign up for the Saturday session.

Along with my counterparts in the Four Counties, and in response to many questions and concerns from parents in our districts, I want to emphasize two aspects of this process. First, the CogPro testing is purely voluntary. Your child is not required to take the test or apply for admission to Crystal Academy. Second, a child's score on the CogPro test is but one factor among many that will be used to determine the eligibility of applicants for the first intake. Further details on the next steps in the admissions review will be provided once the CogPro testing has been completed. We ask for your patience as we work through this challenging and exciting process.

Thank you for your understanding, and best wishes for a wonderful spring on our beautiful Front Range.

Joe Jelinek, DEd

ELEVEN

ROSE

The four of them were, Azra had once joked, like mail carriers. Rain, sleet, or snow, the friends met early on Friday mornings for a four-miler, and had for ten years. A ritual carved into the flinty stone of their lives, something dependable, shared since they'd first started trimming up again after the births of their children. Occasionally one of them might be out with an injury or away on a work trip, so they would run in threes or in pairs. But whatever the combination, Friday run was sacred, an unspoken pact.

That day it was just the two of them, Rose and Lauren. A dry March cold had lowered on the foothills, sharpening the air with resin of pine. Lauren always brought a quiet seriousness to these early mornings in the Colorado chill, when mountain birds could seem to be cheeping just for them and deer would linger on the path ahead before bounding off into the scrub. Desert lizards skittered across the trail, avoiding shoes.

At the top of the valley they took a few minutes to stretch and look out over the northern reaches of Crystal, where Route 62 snaked along the Front Range down from Lynn. Pinprick headlights punctured the rising dawn. Lauren bent over to tighten a shoelace, then straightened, hands on her hips.

"Where is Emma Q testing?" she asked, breathing heavily.

"The CogPro?"

"Right."

"Public school kids test at their regular elementaries," Rose said. "So she'll take it at Donnelly."

"Same with Xander. The Odyssey kids test at the nearest public."

They stood there for a moment in their chilling sweat, panting, facing off. A twitch in Lauren's features, more she wanted to say, but before Rose could ask, her friend turned and started heading down the slope. Rose followed. Her thighs quivered on the descent.

The final quarter mile downhill brought them to Fourth Street. Usually they headed south from here, but today Lauren angled across the intersection, making for Maple Hill. Rose thought nothing of it until they had progressed two blocks east.

They slowed and stopped in front of the old Maple Hill Elementary building. The three-story Georgian façade rose above a row of overgrown chokecherry trees. A temporary wire fence ran along the foot of the school's main staircase, and two dumpsters at curbside brimmed with ravaged chunks of drywall and broken lumber. A sign at the foot of the steps heralded the building's new purpose:

FUTURE HOME OF CRYSTAL ACADEMY
THE LOWER SCHOOL

A MAGNET SCHOOL FOR EXCEPTIONAL LEARNERS,
JOINTLY OPERATED BY THE SCHOOL DISTRICTS OF
WESLEY, KENDALL, MADISON, AND BEULAH COUNTIES
AND THE CITY OF CRYSTAL.

FOUNDING HEAD OF SCHOOL:
DR. ELIZABETH "BITSY" LEIGHTON

OPENING AUGUST 2018

FOR ADMISSIONS INFORMATION AND ALL OTHER
INQUIRIES PLEASE CONTACT
THE CITY OF CRYSTAL SCHOOL DISTRICT

Another mounted display showed glossy mock-ups of the classrooms and labs. Modular tables, shiny computers and whiteboards, well-lit rooms teeming with plants and books.

The gifted school had arrived.

A shining promise on a hill, not yet open for business but all the more alluring for that. The subject of admissions came up every time Rose was with her friends now, fleetingly and always with a little edge, accompanied by uninterested shrugs, easy smirks. *Hey, it's one in a hundred*, someone would say. *Might as well be one in a million. What chance does my kid have?*

She heard the topic being batted around by colleagues at the med school and the hospital, neurosurgeons and anesthesiologists and pediatric oncologists, everyone with a brainy kid of eligible age treading this edge of want—because in Crystal, whose kid wasn't gifted?

The school was like a rare wine, or a piece of some exotic fish. Give us one taste and the world will change. My child deserves nothing less than this.

So far it had been all speculation, idle conjecture, abstract and hypothetical. But now, with the approach of the first round of testing, admissions loomed large, assuming sudden weight and substance. The Emmas would take the CogPro on Saturday.

The first cut.

S o here we are," Rose said, sounding stupid to herself as she gazed at the sign and, behind it, the façade of the lower school midrenovation. When Lauren didn't respond, Rose smoothed a hand over her friend's back.

"Lauren, what is it?"

A side of Lauren's mouth lifted. "Just Xander."

"Oh, come on. You know he'll get in. Of all our kids he's the one."

"That's the thing. He doesn't even want to test."

"But why? This place would be perfect for him." *And for Emma Q*, Rose didn't say.

"That's what I thought. But Xander says he doesn't want to go to school with a bunch of freaky nerds."

Rose stifled a laugh. *Pot, meet kettle.* "Where'd he get that?"

"Where do you think?"

Rose considered it. "The twins?"

"Charlie," Lauren said shortly. "Xander stayed over at Azra's last weekend while I was in Minneapolis. Apparently he was gabbing about the academy at dinner and how great it sounded when Charlie jumped in and started ripping the place. You know, why would you want to surround yourself with a bunch of dorkheads? Like you, was the implication. So Xander comes home dead set against it."

"I'm sure he'll come around."

Lauren's head jerked left. "You know how he looks up to those boys, though. The jock hero worship, they're so cool. He said if I make him go he'll deliberately flunk out, or do something to get suspended. It's infuriating."

"Maybe he's just pulling your leg?" Rose suggested. "He has a weird sense of humor sometimes."

She remembered (because how could she not?) what everyone now called the Smoothie Incident. It had started when Lauren came home one summer afternoon with a high-end blender that could supposedly liquefy tree roots. Xander was taken with the machine, using it constantly to make soups, desserts, homemade ice cream for anyone who dropped by. At a Fourth of July gathering he made a pitcher of green smoothies and handed out Dixie cups of the concoction to those gathered in their backyard. Fruity and sweet but with a bitter tang, maybe kale or Swiss chard. After everyone had a taste, Xander stood on the stairs to the deck and called out, "Friends, Romans, Crystalmen, lend me your ears!"

Heads turning, mild curiosity. The Emmas had been standing on the far side of a citronella candle that lit their young faces. Rose saw Z purse her lips, whisper something in Q's ear. *Poor Xander,* Rose thought. So smart, so painfully weird.

"What's the verdict, people?" he shouted.

"It's delicious, sweetie," Azra called over to him, matching his enthusiasm in her affable way. "What's your secret ingredient?"

They waited for it. He told them in three word bursts.

"It's a *PLAINS!* . . . *LEOPARD!* . . . *FROG!*"

Moans, groans, lots of spitting and gagging. But then Xander did a Spiderman leap to the lawn and started a run through the crowd, his arms airplaned as he shouted *Justkiddingjustkiddingjustkidding* in one long stream.

The whole thing had been very strange; very Xander.

"So maybe he's joking," Rose repeated now.

"That's what I'd like to think," Lauren replied. "As long as I can get his little butt in a chair on Saturday it should be okay."

"What about Tessa? When do rising seniors test?"

Lauren scoffed. "Are you serious?"

"You don't think she'd have a shot?"

"Rose, please. Tessa got a 1310 on the PSAT."

As if this were the equivalent of driving drunk, or a bust for shoplifting.

"That's a good score, Lauren." Rose was gentle, trying not to chide, the memory of that awful moment at Thanksgiving still fresh months later. "Most parents would be thrilled with a 1310."

"Well, even so, that doesn't translate into the kind of CogPro score she'd need to get into Crystal Academy. They're saying senior year will be the most competitive of all. They're only holding sixty spots for the first graduating class."

Ah, Rose thought, *so you've already checked it out.*

"And she's being so difficult lately. I mean, I'm glad she's working, I'm really grateful to you and Azra for giving her a chance, but she has this new hostility that scares me sometimes."

"Remember," Rose said, "it's a truth universally acknowledged that teenage girls despise their mothers."

"You think?"

"It's a phase I'm not looking forward to with Emma, believe me. But Lauren, you've guided her through the hardest period in her life. Look at her now."

"Really."

"She was always so talented," Rose said. "I'm sure all of that is still there."

Lauren went into a knee bend. "Well, the only special talent I've seen from Tessa lately is being pretty. It's the one thing she inherited from her dad."

While Lauren squatted the observation sat there, like an unpleasant smell.

"You ready?" Lauren asked, rising to her five-foot height. Rose followed in her draft, those ugly words ringing in her ears.

When they arrived at Lauren's town house, Tessa was just coming out of the downstairs shower wrapped in a skimpy towel. She saw Lauren first and shot her mother a scowl before noticing Rose.

"Oh, hey, Rose," she said, the nasty look arcing up into a beautiful smile. She gave her a little wave before dodging into her room and closing the door.

Lauren turned to Rose. "That's my good morning," she said flatly.

In the dining room the rough farm table was a cluttered mess. A vase of dried flowers and an embroidered runner had been pushed to one end. Two cardboard trifolds were laid out flat and open, the surfaces mostly empty but with shapes drawn for insets of various sizes. An assortment of charts, graphs, and photographs were splayed across an open folder.

Rose stopped. "What's all this?"

"Xander's science fair project," Lauren said. "A molecular study of spider poison, or something. He can't decide between that and chess."

"You're helping him with it?"

"You're kidding, right? He won't let me within twenty feet of him when he has a project like this."

Rose felt it happen, instantly. The part of her that wanted to reassure Lauren about the well-being of her children receded and cooled. She saw the tip of one graph, a rainbow code strand Xander had modeled after the kind found in a lab report. The quantity of diagrams and illustrations in the folder threw her into a mild despair.

Gareth was useless when it came to this sort of thing, but he was the only parent Emma Q would ever allow to help with science and math, despite what Rose did for a living. *You keep taking over, Mom,* she'd moan, and it was true, she did, but there was so much Rose could have been teaching Emma if she'd only let her. *We could design a controlled experiment on memory and cognition across three generations, sweetie! How about a cellular atlas of your own brain?* Instead Q had concocted some sad horticultural scheme involving avocado pits, currently festering in a corner of her room.

Because Q's greatest gifts were, like her father's, verbal. "You read too much, young lady," the one teacher Q had ever disliked told her, which had made her want to read even more. Over the last six years she had consumed whole libraries, going hours into the night with a Kindle propped between her knobby knees, fingertipping her way through a dozen books a week that would show up on Amazon receipts in whirlwind lists of unfamiliar titles that left Rose too overwhelmed to monitor with any regularity. She did worry that the books Q chose were childish, unambitious, repetitive; how much intellectual growth could there be in obsessively rereading the Narnia chronicles ten times each?

Gareth, as always, saw things differently. *Let her lose herself in another world,* he chided Rose, *rather than getting tangled up in yours.*

Maybe he was right. Azra would frequently lament that the twins never picked up a book. In the age of the iPhone, who cared what your child was reading, as long as she was reading? As for those Amazon bills: *Worth every penny,* her husband insisted, quietly proud of their word-loving child.

Rose stopped off for gas and tapped her foot, glancing at her watch while the tank filled. Silea came on alternate Fridays, and Rose liked everyone to be out of the way by nine so the cleaner could work through an empty house. Good for the spirit, to have a mildew-free shower at the end of a long day in the lab; Gareth's haphazard straightenings were a poor substitute for Silea's thorough cleanings.

On the way home she tried to untangle her thoughts. Lauren's distress, Tessa's scowl, Xander's science project. Always comforting to know that other families struggled with their darker moments, and Lauren's crew had endured more than their fair share—genius could be a curse as much as a blessing. Crystal Academy or not, Rose wouldn't trade Emma Q's verbal flair for Xander's unsettling brilliance to save her soul.

Because unlike the others, Rose had never believed that Xander was joking about that pitcher of green smoothies. Her scientist's ear had discerned the biological specificity in his gleeful, creepy announcement. The secret ingredient was a frog, Xander had crowed, and not just any frog but a Plains leopard frog. A world of thought and research packed into that detail. The taxonomic precision of it had stayed with her for years.

Every so often Rose still woke from a bad dream with the bitter taste of Plains leopard frog coating her tongue.

TWELVE

EMMA Z

On Friday she came home from school and ate two of her mother's zucchini muffins and did a math worksheet and practiced violin. Then she went upstairs and noticed three things that were different from usual.

The first thing was in her bathroom. She peed and then stood at the sink. Reaching for the faucet, she saw a small amount of water on the white surface, pooled around the cold handle. She looked down by the drain and saw a dribble of her own toothpasty spit from that morning, and when she looked in the mirror, she could tell that it hadn't been wiped down. Weird.

The second thing she noticed was her favorite yellow sweater, the soft cashmere one her father had bought her in Zurich last time he was there. Emma Z remembered folding it up that morning and setting it on her pillow. But somehow it had ended up under her bed. She squatted down and stared at it for a few seconds, then pulled it out, refolded it, and put it on her sweater shelf. *Also* weird.

Then she noticed the third thing, the biggest thing of all. Emma rarely picked out a book to read, even though her parents bought her books all the time from Crystal Books and Barnes & Noble, as birthday presents or Christmas presents or just random things they thought she would like. They always left them on her bed, and when she came into her room, she would put them on the shelf with the rest of her books. She didn't particularly care where they went or in what order.

But today the books were actually *organized* on the bookcase. The top shelf and half of the second shelf had all her books that belonged in series. All her Percy Jacksons, her Harry Potters, her Boxcar Childrens, her Amelia Bedelias, her Chronicles of Narnias. She looked more closely and saw that all of these series had been sorted, alphabetized by the last name of the author: Coleman, Lewis, Parish, Riordan, Rowling, Warner, Wilder, and so on. The books that didn't belong to series were organized in the same way, from A all the way to Z.

Really weird.

In the kitchen she helped herself to another zucchini muffin and watched while her mom ordered an olive leather jacket off her iPad. After watching her click on the Complete Purchase button, Z asked, "Do we have a new maid, Mommy?"

"What's that?" her mom said, browsing through some blouses now. Z liked the frilly ones but her mom never wore that kind.

"Nothing," said Z, looking around the kitchen and living room. Everything else looked like it normally did on Mondays, Wednesdays, and Fridays, and besides, the stuff in her room wasn't that important, so she decided not to say anything. Silea was really poor and lived in a trailer way out by Wild Horse Stables. Which reminded her.

"Who's driving us to the barn tomorrow?" she asked.

Her mother clicked something and bought the blouse. "Lessons are canceled, actually. Tomorrow you have a test."

"A test?"

"Yes, silly. It's the CogPro, like the ones you've been doing with Cynthia."

"Oh," said Z. Cynthia was her test tutor. She'd been to their house probably twenty million times since Christmas. "The one with the shapes and stuff?"

"That's right," said her mother. "So I'll make your favorite salmon tonight, and we'll have that kimchi broccoli you like. Sound good?"

"Uh-huh." Emma Z finished her muffin. "I like tests."

Her mother reached over to boop her chin.

That night in her room Emma Z found a fourth thing, standing by her
lamp. A paper giraffe the size of a clothespin. She picked it up and examined it closely, trying to figure out how it was made. There must have
been a hundred separate folds in the yellow paper. Daddy had once showed
her how to make a paper balloon that you could actually blow up, but even
he could never make something like this.

She put her thumbs in the giraffe's gapped neck and pulled the pieces
apart, spreading them out. She split the animal's back, unfurled its legs, and
once it was all unfolded, she tried to fold it back together again but couldn't,
not even close. By the time she was done trying, all that was left of the paper animal was a square of torn and wrinkled paper. Emma Z flattened it
with her palm and left it there, curling beneath the light.

THIRTEEN

XANDER

Xander sat in the cafeteria three tables from the front and two off center, filling in bubbles. The CogPro questions were stupid. Like, third-grade stupid.

They never gave tests like this at Odyssey, which was one of the reasons his mother had moved him there in fourth grade.

Leaf-> Maple : Needle-> _____
a. ant   b. cat   c. cone   d. forest   e. spruce

The boy ran _____ down the sidewalk.
a. speedy   b. tastily   c. swiftly   d. fast   e. efficient

They tried to trick you with answers that seemed correct, or could seem correct if you weren't paying attention, like *cone* which could be part of a pine tree like *needle*, or *tastily* which was an adverb like *swiftly*.

The math questions were even dumber. Sure, they'd put two equations in the same problem. But who wouldn't know that

$$x - 7 = 4y / y = 63 \div 9$$

solved for 35? Or that

$$432 \div y = 27 / \sqrt{y} + x = 91$$

solved for 16 and 87? Xander could take one glance at a quantitative test page and know the answer to every question at the same time. It was hardly worth deigning to fill in the dicky little circles with your asshole No. 2 pencil.

He pressed his tongue against the roof of his mouth and looked up from the testing booklet.

Tick tick tick.

With his lips parted he clicked his tongue. Really soft (*ooh, sorry:* softly), so only the nearby kids could hear, and also so it was hard to tell who was doing it. A few turned their heads to look around, trying to figure out where the annoying noise was coming from.

Tick tick tick.

Emma Holland-Quinn's head went up two rows in front of him and one table to the right. She looked to one side, to the other. Xander smiled.

Tick tick tick.

Out of the top edges of his eyes he could see her turn around again. Staring at him. He looked right at her. She stuck out her tongue.

"Eyes on tests," the teacher called out.

Q turned away.

Once, in second grade, before his mother switched him to Odyssey and before the twins went to St. Bridget's, Xander got in huge trouble for taking a pair of scissors from the teacher's desk and lopping off a thick wodge of Emma Q's hair while the class was watching a movie. It was a dare, from Aidan. Q's mom took her to a fancy hairdresser to fix it, but she had really short hair for a long time after that.

He stared at the back of Q's head and remembered what those scissors felt like, slicing through that thick hair. Like cutting up a stack of paper, or making snowflakes at Christmas.

Not as easy as it looked. Not as easy as the next five questions on this asinine test.

He filled in another bubble and sighed.

FOURTEEN

ROSE

C hill out. It's just the first round."

Samantha, a silky whisper to her left.

"Hi, you," Rose said. She relaxed her folded arms, and her skin prickled when she dropped them to her sides.

"Lunch after?" Samantha asked.

"Sure. Finnegan's?"

"Emma Z has the dentist at two, but we should be done by then."

"On a Saturday?"

"If they want my business."

"Poor thing. Q hates the drill."

Samantha waved a hand, dismissive. "It's just a six-month cleaning. And Z couldn't get a cavity if she ate ten cupcakes a day. Those Zellar teeth."

Rose sighed against the glass, remembering Emma Q's last appointment. Two fillings, swollen gums, puffy jowls.

Not Emma Z. Rose located Samantha's daughter in the cafeteria, three tables down from Q. All the other children were slouched over their booklets and bubble sheets, frowning, scribbling away. Not Z. She sat perfectly straight in her chair, face serene, almost bored: ostentatiously so, as if she knew the parents were out there and wanted them to see how well she was performing.

That was Z, always. Early to the finish line, error- and cavity-free.

———

The stop time crept near. More parents arrived, dozens herding tensely into the north vestibule, all put-on levity and forced humor. Rose looked at her watch, and when she looked up again, Samantha's daughter was gone. She frowned. A moment later Emma Z's head popped up above the table, a dropped pencil in her hand.

A bell rang, followed by the muffled voice of the proctor.

Xander was first out, weaving around the other kids and throwing himself like a kindergartner at Lauren, just walking in for pickup. Samantha, texting nonstop, had whipped up a group lunch. Azra would meet them all at Finnegan's with the twins, she said. As the kids pushed their way out of the cafeteria, Rose searched her daughter's eyes for some sign of how the test had gone, but Q was already chatting with her best friend.

The post-testing crowd flowed from the dim vestibule out into the Colorado sun. The stone faces of the Redirons sparkled gold, radiant with the leavings of an early spring snow. On the way to their car Emma Q took her mother's hand, a childlike gesture that surprised Rose. Skin cold to the touch, hand gloved with sweat.

At Finnegan's Wake they shoved tables together at the edge of a cavernous room lined with bookshelves. Students, academics, and earbudded professionals tapped away, buzzed on lattes, happily cloistered in the Saturday crowd. Xander walked over to the chess table and the Emmas settled on a nearby sofa. Azra hadn't yet appeared and wasn't returning texts.

"So," said Lauren when they were seated. "Do you think the Emmas tested well?"

"I guess we'll know next week," Sam answered curtly.

"What do you think the cutoff will be?" Lauren asked with her usual bluntness. Everyone knew Xander's score would be astronomical.

"Maybe one-twenty-five." Samantha scanned her menu.

"Really?" Rose blurted out. "I thought they'd said anything one-fifteen and above would make the first cut." One-twenty was Q's highest score on the CogPro. Hard to imagine she would top that under pressure, despite all the practice tests Rose had found for her.

"That's for the outer counties," Samantha said. "They don't test as well in the boondocks."

"They're weighting it by district?"

"Apparently so." Samantha lowered her voice. "Each school district in the magnet area will have its own cutoff for the first phase. For the City of Crystal and Kendall County it should be five or ten points higher than for Western and Madison counties. And for Beulah County—I mean, who *knows* how those kids will score."

Beulah, the poorer county stretching east over the Colorado plains, five hundred square miles of sprawling trailer parks, small town pawn-and-gun shops, and an agricultural base that furnished carloads of workers, local organic produce, grass-fed beef, and other necessities to service Crystal's moneyed population.

"Is there a specific percentage of Beulah kids they're committed to taking?" Rose wondered how the schools would navigate this delicate ecology of privilege.

"Hasn't been decided yet," Samantha responded. "Everything's up for grabs. Kev thinks they'll intentionally keep it a mystery."

"There's a good reason for that, though," Lauren said, her tone sharp.

Here it comes, Rose thought: subjects like this were kindling between those two. The wealthy matron versus the social worker, both fighting blind.

"You have in-built testing biases, racial and economic disparities in educational attainment," Lauren continued. "We see it all the time at Youth and Family Services, plus social and psychological issues like nutrition and health care. Even nonverbal IQ scores are affected by environmental circumstances."

"And brain chemistry," Rose added, mostly to keep the conversation going. Better than quailing over Q's potential CogPro score.

Samantha's brows, freshly waxed, rose a half inch. "I guess I trust the teachers to know what they're doing."

"And I trust the research to account for difference and diversity," Lauren countered. "Sounds like the school boards want to avoid advantage hoarding and address the excellence gap, and I'm all for it."

"*Advantage* hoarding? Are you serious?" Sam's kombucha bottle thudded down on the table. "So how are they supposed to do that, Lauren? I mean, in a way that's objective and doesn't *dis*advantage kids who *happen*"—here she lowered her voice again—"to be wealthy and white."

"I'm not the expert," said Lauren. "But there are ways of taking account of each student as a unique individual."

Samantha sniffed. "Easy for you to say."

"How so?"

"Oh, come on. Your unique individual's in no matter what."

"We don't know that."

"Sure we do."

As if summoned by Samantha's jaundiced reply, Xander came over from the chess table and stood next to his mother. His thick lenses cast a shadow on his face and transmitted that familiar diagnostic vibe. Azra and Samantha had mentioned it too, more and more in recent months: as if the kid had memorized a psych manual and already had you pegged with a disorder you'd never heard of but fit you like a second skin.

"Are you guys talking about Crystal Academy?"

"Not right now, sweetie." A rare panic on Lauren's face.

His distorted eyes shifted back and forth, landing on Rose. "You don't think Emma Q will get in, do you?"

He asked the question loudly, prompting an awkward silence from their corner of the coffee shop. Rose glanced at Q on the big sofa, mouth hanging open, nose buried in a borrowed book, sweetly oblivious.

"Xander, you're such a *butt*," Emma Z called out. Rose looked fondly at Z's face, the screwed-up frown on that familiar mouth. She could kiss her right now.

Xander turned and flipped her off, double-handed. Lauren gently pulled her son to her side and nuzzled his neck, no hint of a correction. Mama Bear, protecting her cub.

———

They had just asked for the bill when Azra strode in, harried. "Sorry, you guys. I can't reach Beck, and it's making me crazy."

Lauren craned her neck. "Where are the twins?"

"His weekend." Azra flopped down in a chair. "They should have been waiting outside at Donnelly, but I went to pick them up and they weren't there. They missed the CogPro."

Rose blinked. *You put Beck in charge of their testing?*

"Wait, the twins are taking the CogPro?" Samantha asked.

Azra frowned. "Why wouldn't they?"

"I don't know," Samantha said quickly, trying to cover.

"We just assumed," said Lauren.

We? Rose shook her head, wanting no part of this, but Azra was already rising from her seat.

Lauren blanched. "Hey, I just meant—"

"I know what you meant," Azra said. A tightening around her eyes. "I have to pee."

As Azra strode off toward the bathrooms Rose marveled at her composure. It was a boon to their group, a gift Samantha and Lauren had never valued as Rose had, though even she sometimes wondered where Azra got her serenity, and the kindness in her that allowed her to forgive: Beck for his manifold failures as father and spouse, Samantha for her smug, judgmental side, Lauren for the superiority complex that elevated Xander in her eyes miles and mountains over Azra's sporty boys.

And Rose—for what?

There must be something. There had to be, over all these years.

It began, as they began, in the water.

The swim class had beckoned for weeks from posters at the gym: a multicultural assemblage of grinning moms and a few dads and a swarm of floating babies shot from above and frozen in aquamarine, a small masterpiece of graphic design. $H_2OhBABY!$ the posters called it.

A poor pun, hokey; but to Rose the class had a certain appeal, promising company in misery, a venture out of the house, a first taste of postnatal fitness. You should go, Gareth urged her. He had stopped working out regularly, neglecting his fitness along with his writing; but he was always trying to get her to take advantage of their joint membership.

H$_2$OhBABY! did have a few rules. Your child had to weigh at least twelve pounds, with decent head control, and had to wear a swim diaper; parents were required to provide their own flotation devices. At three months Emma weighed in just shy of fourteen pounds. Prior to the first session Rose picked up a packet of lime green swim diapers and tested one out in the bathtub.

What she overlooked was the flotation device. Her eyes must have skipped that part of the fine print; or perhaps she imagined herself as a flotation device, the notion of letting go of Emma's tiny body in a pool even for a moment unthinkable.

She was already running late when she arrived at the Rec Center. A minor crisis at the med school, a grad student turned down for summer funding. Rose made some calls, fixed things, though the effort slowed her down, and she found herself suited up and out at the edge of the pool six minutes after the hour, with Emma clutched to her chest, sting of chlorine in the air.

The instructor, leading the class in opening stretches, greeted her with a disapproving frown. Rose gazed out over the water at the pitying looks from the other moms and au pairs, because despite the gender-neutral ads they were all moms and au pairs, and despite the posters they were all white, like Rose, except maybe one, and they all stood in the pool with their babies tucked into a rainbow of floats and inner tubes, scooping water over the gently bobbing heads.

It's just a swim class, Rose told herself as a burning gathered in her chest. A harried morning at home, then the crisis with the student that made her miss her lab and wonder why she had arranged for so much time off. She started asking herself why they moved to Crystal in the first place when she could have taken a position at Northwestern, in a real city where she could have had real friends. Then, as she began to turn away to slink back to the locker room, a soft alto rang up from the water.

"Hey, I've got an extra," said the voice: low, rich, almost husky. Rose looked down and through the blur of her rising tears saw a sweep of straw-blond hair pulled back from a face that was open, friendly, heart-shaped—the face, it seemed in that instant, of an angel.

"Are you sure?" Rose said.

"Absolutely." The woman pushed herself out of the pool and plucked her baby from an inner tube. In twenty seconds she was back from the locker room with one hand pinning her dripping child to her hip, the other clutching a matching inner tube already half inflated, the nozzle fixed between her teeth and lips.

"Oh, let me do that," said Rose, adjusting Emma on her side.

"Goth ith," the other woman lisped around the nozzle. A few last breaths and the plastic tightened up. "Here." She handed Rose the tube before deftly twisting herself and her baby back into the pool. "You don't mind the duck head?"

"Not at all." Emma was already entranced by it, eyes fixed on the orange bill, the flapping rubber wings. Rose went over the side and situated herself with her daughter, who started kicking gleefully once in the pool. Soon Rose too was hop-jogging in place and feeling part of the class, the water a balm to her spirits and skin.

"Someone always forgets," the woman said.

"You've taken this class before?" Rose asked.

"Only taught it five times."

"You work here?" Which would explain the muscled legs and sculpted arms. The women tilted left, right, left.

"Not since my seventh month. I do personal training, some nutritionist stuff. I'll probably come back at some point." In midtilt she turned and examined Rose's face. Water had beaded finely on her flawless, almost shimmering skin. "I'm Samantha Zellar," she said. "Sam."

"Rose."

"And who's this?"

"Her name is Emma."

Samantha crinkled her eyes in a way Rose liked. "That's funny."

"What?"

"She's Emma too," Samantha Zellar said, and chucked her daughter's chin.

The next week Rose arrived poolside on time, her own flotation device in hand. She looked for Samantha and Emma in the front row but didn't see them. The same lonely sadness welled up just below her neck.

"Rose! Back here!"

At the far corner of the pool Samantha stood, gesturing for her. Rose scurried around the lifeguard, then lowered herself into the water between Samantha and a woman trying to manage wriggling twins who didn't seem particularly happy to be there. Neither did their mother, the only woman in the pool who wasn't white. A pink swimming cap tightened the roots of her hair against the light brown skin of her forehead as she struggled with her twins, now screaming. The mother barked "God, I *can't* with these guys" across the pool, drawing scowls, a prim frown from the instructor. Samantha sidestepped until she had her Emma positioned next to the closer twin. He stopped his screaming long enough to stare at the wide-eyed girl floating in on a pink doughnut. The mom glanced at Samantha, grateful, but by this time the other twin had become distracted by the thrashing of a bigger baby next to him, a white boy with a sizeable head that he enjoyed slamming back and forth against the sides of his inner tube. A giggling fit quickly spread from one twin to the other, and the four mothers laughed in relief.

"Ladies, please," the instructor snapped through her throat mic. "Your classmates are trying to hear the instructions. Can we calm it down back th—"

Screeeeeee!

Feedback whined from the sound system, a shattering volume that caromed around the high-ceilinged pool deck. The women clapped hands to their heads, and the babies in Rose's corner froze, their eyes large with shock, then every child in the pool started screaming at the assault on their delicate ears. Twenty-odd howling infants, panicked and angry mothers and au pairs, but the four women in the far corner shared their first laugh, giddy, like middle schoolers escaping punishment.

For the remaining weeks of the class the four of them clustered with their babies in the back of the pool, where Samantha fed them Rec Center gossip, where they could cast superior looks at all the moms taking H₂OhBABY! maybe a *liiiiiittle* too seriously. Lauren Frye and Azra Chaudhury, it turned out, were casual acquaintances recently brought together by their husbands, Julian and Beck, both avid rock climbers. After the last session they all gathered in the lobby of the gym. Rose wondered anxiously what, if anything, came next.

"Lunch?" Samantha suggested.

They went next door for tacos at Guisados. Strollers and diaper bags colonizing the crowded patio, back-patting baby swaps so they all could eat. There was another lunch the following week, and then Samantha invited them over to her beautiful house on Maple Hill for coffee and cake. Lauren's daughter, Tessa, came along, charming the other mothers and delighting the babies with her sweet attentiveness. Next came a child-free happy hour; another; a first tentative gathering with the husbands a few months in; and by the time the H₂OhBabies turned one, the families had settled into habits that would endure for years.

A sustaining friendship that rooted them in the sandy loam of this unremittingly gorgeous place: Crystal Valley, majestic bowl of earth, stone, sky, the Redirons like gods looking down, orange spikes of suspended sandstone, behind them the jagged ranks of fourteeners marching along the Divide. On a clear day—and nearly every day was clear: *Crystal clear,* inhabitants liked to say—Rose could still inhale the Colorado evergreens and imagine herself nowhere else on earth but here, in this valley, because sometimes it was like a cult.

In Crystal, everyone said or thought, we are happy, we are fit, we are woke, and even our streets are named for gems.

———

Julian had fallen ill when Xander was three, Tessa seven. Osteosarcoma, briefly in remission before it awakened to ravage his bones. Lauren, left alone, had let the others caretake for a while, half-adopt her children, and before long all six kids had the free run of four families. The death had knotted them, Rose saw looking back, establishing new ties of dependence and need among four women with little in common aside from children the same age.

Smaller calamities would follow: Azra's divorce from Beck, leaving the twins to float between homes; Lauren's own bout with cancer, caught early, fended off; and, for Rose, the slow decline of her marriage, which would have been unendurable without the women she had found in the water more than ten years ago.

The changes had only strengthened their friendship, Rose thought as Azra wended her way back through the tables and the chairs, wearing her usual placid expression. These crises and catastrophes had braided the four of them together, like vines around a trunk. Easy to believe those bonds hid no malice in their grip; easy to believe they could hold forever.

A Touch of Tessa:
one GiRL's SURVIVaL GuiDe t⊙ JuniⓄR yeaR
A Video Blog

~~~~~~

Episode #129: Pandora's Box—or Pandora's Bust?
. . . 11 views . . .

[*Tessa in Gareth's basement office, dangling a small key.*]

TESSA: Okay, something slightly different tonight, you guys. A treat for all of you. This evening we're going to have our own episode of *Egypt's Lost Tombs* from, like, the History Channel. But instead of a pharaoh's million-year-old crypt we're going to open the bottom drawer of this filing cabinet behind me. It's locked but I found the key out in the garage. Okay okay, that doesn't sound too exciting. But seriously, who knows what we'll find? I mean I can't even believe this is happening here, live, right now. So the question of the day is: Pandora's Box—or Pandora's Bust? Are you ready? Ten . . . nine . . . eight . . . seven . . . six . . . five . . . four . . . three . . . two . . . one . . .

[*Reverse to filing cabinet. Hand inserts key, turns, pulls out drawer.*]

And here we go! Okay, looks like we've got a long row of about thirty files, and they all have little labels on them. First one: MORTGAGE: 2340 OPAL LANE. Let's pull this out . . . pretty boring. Just a bunch of documents.

[*Shoves papers back in file. Shuffles through next ten file folders, pulling papers out and returning them as she speaks:*]

Next file: CAR LOAN. Um, yawn? Next: HOMEOWNER'S INSURANCE. Next: AUTO INSURANCE. Riveting. Next: BOOK CONTRACT. Ooh, what did Gareth get for that shitty novel? Let's see let's see . . . okay, not as much as my mom said but not bad. Next: EMMA Q: TU-ITION SAVINGS. This might be interesting. Let's see . . . wow, look at that number. Just over twenty thousand dollars! Impressive, should pay for about a month by the time she goes to college, but it's prob-ably more than my mom's saved for me and Q's only eleven. Okay, next is LIFE INSURANCE. And then PASSPORTS. Ooh, fun. Let's just pull these out . . . bad pictures, and Rose's is the only one that's not expired. Back you go. Now what's next?

[*Fingers walking through files, holding some papers up briefly before stuffing them back.*]

These ones aren't even labeled, just a dozen empty—oh, wait, here's some stuff. Let's see . . . awww, look at that, some of Q's drawings from when she was tiny. I think I remember this one, you guys. So cute. And next folder, what's this? Baby pictures, then looks like more drawings, yah yah, a whole other folder of fingerpaintings, shit like that, some old pictures of Q and Z—

[*Hand freezes with fingers parting a file folder.*]

TESSA: No. Way. Okay, straight up? This may be even better than a mummy.

[*Pulls out a short stack of photographs: brief flashes of skin, pictures held mostly out of camera range.*]

TESSA: Umm, content warning: disgusting. Because—Oh. My. *God.* [*Squeals.*] I just can't even. No, I can't show them to you. Okay, so [*clears throat loudly*] what I'm looking at here, you guys, is a bunch of actual porno of Gareth and Rose from when they were, like, maybe in college. God they are *so young*, but you can totally tell it's them. And they're actually *doing* it in these pictures too, like he's actually inside—God, no *wonder* he keeps this thing locked, you know? Anyway, hold on a minute.

[*Stuffs photos back into folder, shuts and locks drawer. Reverse to Tessa.*]

TESSA: I guess some people aren't as boring as they look, am I right? Bye, you guys.

FIFTEEN

BECK

The twins should have been down by now.

We're ready we're ready.

High Anxiety, only their second black diamond. Not the hardest slope on the mountain but definitely a challenge.

We're ready we're ready.

They're not, Sonja had mouthed, but Beck had given them the okay anyway.

They'd started with Risky Business, the easiest black diamond at Breckenridge. Charlie in the lead, Aidan next, Beck's wife scooping along behind. Sonja skied like she was born on a mogul while Beck always brought up the rear, but he would have anyway: he loved to corral his herd down the mountain, watch their agile ease in the snow.

Once they'd finished Risky Business, he let the boys do High Anxiety by themselves. Why not? But that was forty-five minutes ago.

He looked at his watch again. *Forty-seven.* Beck imagined their lanky bodies hurled through thin air, those loose joints and young green bones.

"Come on," he called back to Sonja, pushing off toward the bottom of the lower bowl. "They'll be down in a minute. One more run, then we'll go back to the lodge."

She stayed put, planted on her skis. "Roy has been alone with Tessa since two." Her eyes flickered up toward the mountain.

He saw the worry in them. "Why don't you get a head start back to the condo, babe, so you can feed him. I'll wait here for the boys."

"You will be right behind me?"

"Ten minutes. Fifteen max."

She pouted, then skied away. Beck scraped himself over to the edge of the out-run. A few minutes passed, the blood vessels in his neck throbbing away the seconds. He dug in a pocket for his phone and turned it on. A dozen texts from Azra popped up. Before he could read them, the phone rang in his hand.

The hospital? Ski patrol?

No: Azra.

"Hey babe," he said, working to maintain the calm in his voice.

"Goddamnit, Beck!" Azra ranted into the phone, not like her at all. "I've been calling you all day. You were supposed to drop them off here this morning. What the *hell*?"

"It's my weekend."

"They had the CogPro, idiot. I texted you about it, I emailed you." Her voice caught. "Where are you?"

"Breckenridge. We came up last night."

"You're kidding me."

"You said there were two testing sessions. The other one's next week."

"That's a makeup test, in case you had unavoidable conflicts with today. Fresh powder doesn't count. *Fuck*, Beck."

He scanned the top of the bowl and saw movement at the tree line, flashes of color—and there they were, Charlie in the lead, Aidan's red hat swishing against the snow behind him. The sight of his spawn broke the lump in his chest. The boys flew down the last length of the slope, enjoying the hell out of the black.

"This pisses me off, Beck. It's important."

"Got it," he said, looking away from his guys, listening now. "So, what, you want me to take them to the makeup test?"

"You'll have to. I'll be in Denver for a show. Glen and I have had these tickets for weeks."

Glen and I.

"Email me the details, then. It won't happen again."

"Of course it will." She disconnected before he could reply.

Beck stared at his phone as the twins glided down the out-run, then started sliding off for the condo. He shook himself out of a stupor.

"Wait, you guys don't want to hit it one more time?" he called after his sons.

"We're cold." Aidan clapped his hands, poles clattering.

"And pretty hungry," Charlie added.

"Come on, we can do this. It's the last day of the season—nay, my sons, the last *hour*. How many weekends do we get free of soccer?" Beck pushed himself backward, toward the lift. After that unpleasant exchange with his ex he needed more headspace before returning to the condo. Sure, Sonja would be miffed that they stayed out, but a final run on a gorgeous black diamond with his sons? Worth a little fight. Plus she had Tessa there to help. *At fifteen an hour.* "Think how good that fire'll feel after one more run."

"I don't want to." Aidan shivered and bent his knees. "I'm really cold, Dad. Let's go to the lodge."

Charlie looked over at his brother and mouthed something.

"Am not."

"Are too, douchecanoe," Charlie said.

"Guys, stop it."

Charlie looked at his dad. "Let's do this thing."

"Excellent," said Beck, loving Charlie's spirit. "You coming, Aidan?"

Aidan drew a sleeve across the wet end of his nose and scowled at his brother. "Sure, fine."

It happened halfway down To Your Left, a steep off-piste mogul run with lots of narrow slots and blind rollovers. They'd reached the midpoint in the slope, the edgy part. Beck watched his sons zip into a wooded finger on the left side. He took a more central line, staying behind them to their right. "Slow down, guys!" he called ahead. "Big fall line coming up."

Charlie adjusted his speed before shooting into the steepest part of the black diamond, a mogul-free narrow between two rows of trees. Aidan didn't slow down. He took the fall line at full throttle and screamed in delight at the prospect of passing his brother.

Beck lost sight of them. He bent forward, counting seconds.

"Hey!" he heard Aidan shout. "*HEY!*"

Charlie barreled out first, taking a line in front of Beck and swinging between moguls. When Aidan shot out of the funnel, he was off balance, tottering.

Beck watched it happen, his world slowing down.

First Aidan hit a big mogul at top speed. His arms flew apart. His poles circled in midair. His legs went akimbo and his body tilted, falling.

By the time Beck had come around to the left, Aidan was tumbling, taking snow full in the face. His body windmilled at high speed, skis clattering through the powder down toward a wooded outcropping. His loose body slid and rolled, then plowed into a drift.

Charlie, oblivious, had already disappeared around a bend thirty yards down.

Aidan lay still, half-buried in the snow.

"*He's okay he's okay he's okay,*" Beck panic-whispered as he skidded to a stop three feet from his unmoving son.

"He all right?" a man shouted from the far side of the funnel.

"I don't know."

"I'll call for patrol."

Beck popped off his skis, dropped to all fours, and started brushing the snow from his son's goggles.

"Owwww," Aidan moaned.

Beck's heart lifted.

Not dead.

"You okay, buddy?"

"My leg," Aidan whimpered, trying to sit up. "Charlie broke my leg."

"Wait, Aidan, just wait." Beck helped his son straighten his back.

Not paralyzed.

"Does it hurt or—"

"My ankle. My right ankle. *Owwww.*"

Beck clawed at the buckle and slipped off the rigid boot. With the socked leg cradled on his lap he palpated the soft flesh of Aidan's upper foot and ankle, searching for the injury. Aidan flinched and moaned, and the first image that came to Beck's mind was the sight of his son trawling the soccer pitch. A stepover, an elegant flick of the ball, then a strike, arcing into the net.

These gifted, beautiful feet.

Aidan's lips tightened with new pain, and Beck blinked the ugly thought away. *There are more important things than soccer!* his insides screamed.

Your son's life, for example. Your son's spine.

Your son's brain: a ragged tree stump jutted up not two feet from where Aidan's skull had pressed a neat bowl into the snow.

O ver there!" someone shouted.

Beck looked up. A red-jacketed patrolman was shooting the left finger. He skidded to a halt and lifted his goggles. College kid, mop of brown hair and a hipster beard, rescue sled harnessed to his back. He knelt down next to Aidan and asked his name while checking out his ankle. Beck watched his son's face.

"My brother clipped me," Aidan said. "He clipped my skis."

"But he was in front of you," Beck pointed out.

The patrolman waved him off. "Okay, buddy, now, slowly, can you wriggle it around for me?"

Aidan rotated his foot in a slow semicircle.

"Now the other way," the patrolman said.

The ankle was already puffing up. No bones jutting out, but the skin looked discolored and streaked. As the patrolman helped him to his feet, Aidan put a foot down gingerly, then pulled up with a wince. The guy helped Aidan hop-crawl to the rescue sled and flop down. Beck grabbed his son's boot, sock, skis, and poles as the patrolman fashioned a plastic-and-Velcro splint around Aidan's foot and ankle.

"So is it broken?" Beck asked.

The guy shrugged over his work. "Definitely get him an X-ray. Ice it, keep him off his feet for a while. Probably just a sprain, but you never know." The patrolman glanced over at the spot between the trees where Aidan had landed. "Lucky kid. Maybe go back to the blues for a while?"

Beck's jaw stiffened into a defensive clench. "I don't need a lecture," he said, then regretted it. "Sorry, man."

"No worries," the guy said, and Beck could tell he meant it. Not a care in the world, a trim young dude probably already thinking about ski patrol happy hour.

The condo was a first-floor ski-up at the edge of a center slope. Beck had purchased the place outright with some principal, back in his flusher days. The patrolman hauled Aidan all the way to the door. Charlie slapped the guy a high five before he skied off.

"Come on, buddy." Beck motioned for Aidan to come inside, but instead he spun away and flopped back against the entryway wall, weight on his good foot. Glaring at his brother.

"Charlie made me wipe out."

"Did not," Charlie said.

"He snowplowed in front of me and slowed down and—"

"That's a lie."

Beck showed Charlie a palm. "Aidan, come on, Charlie wouldn't—"

"He would too, and besides I didn't want to *go* again." His face crumpled. "ROMO tryouts are coming up, didn't you *know* that, didn't you *remember*?" Wailing now, fists pounding the wall.

Beck did remember, and it had been eating at him since the wipeout. "Inside," he snapped at Charlie.

Charlie scowled and wheeled for the door. When it closed, Beck reached for Aidan's shoulders, but his son shrugged him away. "Look, sweetie. Your—"

"I'm not a girl."

"Aidan, listen. Your ankle will be okay, and I'm sure ROMO has late tryouts. We can get a doctor's note."

"That won't work."

"We don't know that."

"Yes, we do, and now everything is *ruined* and it's Charlie's fault."

Aidan stomped his splinted foot, forgetting his injury in his fury. His shriek echoed among the condos. Beck reached for him, and this time his miserable son collapsed into him, slender body shaking beneath the bulk of his ski jacket.

"Dad," Aidan said after a minute.

"Yeah, Aid?"

Aidan leaned back and got a serious look on his face.

"I'm not lying, Dad. Charlie did it. On purpose."

"But—"

Aidan reached out and clamped Beck's mouth shut with his palm, a moist patch of warmth on his frosted beard. Through gritted teeth and with a strange look in his eyes, Aidan said, "He's jealous, Dad. He *wanted* to hurt me."

After Beck had arranged a bag of ice around Aidan's ankle, he went back to the fridge for a beer. He popped the top. A tense silence had settled in the condo since they came inside, no one brave enough to break it. Finally some idiotic part of Beck's brain made him say, "Sorry, babe. The boys really wanted a last run."

"That's not true," Aidan said from his spot by the fire.

"Aidan," Beck said.

"It *was* your idea, Dad," Charlie added helpfully, finding a mischievous joy in his brother's misery. He scare-quoted with two fingers and a cheese knife. "'How many weekends do we get free of soccer?' 'Think how awesome that fire's gonna feel after one more run, boys.'"

"Enough, Charlie," Beck warned.

Sonja spun away abruptly and stomped up the stairs, leaving him with Tessa and the kids. Charlie abandoned his slicing task and flopped down in front of the TV, as far away from his brother as possible.

Beck drained his beer. The guys should have known better than to mess around on a black diamond. Those slopes were steep, fast, perilous. Every year you heard about a broken neck or a snapped spine, some paralyzed teenager. That patrolman had been right. Aidan was lucky as hell.

He wheezed out a sigh.

"Another?" Tessa asked, surprising him. Her eyes dropped down to his empty. He held up the bottle, wondering how he'd managed to finish his first so quickly.

"That'd be awesome, yeah."

She fished a beer out of the fridge and tossed it to him. Then she was back in for another. She opened it and took a long gulp before he could say anything.

Beck tried to remember what Julian and Lauren's daughter had looked like at five but couldn't summon it. Crazy how she'd grown. He gave her a cool-dad smile, watching her guzzle. No skin off his back if Tessa wanted to have a few after a day with his baby.

"Your mom would kill me if she thought we let you drink up here," he said.

"I won't tell if you don't."

"Just one, though."

Tessa rolled her eyes. "Okay." She sauntered into the living room and threw herself into one of the big chairs between the twins. With a fuzzy slipper propped on a knee she was gone, lost in her phone.

SIXTEEN

BECK

When they came out and hot-tubbed late like this, Sonja would usually float to him and stay there, clingy and wet, but tonight she lingered on the opposite bench above the hum of an unseen motor, heated water churning white. The chlorine stung his eyes. After a while she leaned over to moisten her face, then pushed up from the bench and stretched to her full length in the middle of the Jacuzzi. Beck's wife was a broad-shouldered woman, and her torso could have served as the centerpiece of some exotic Roman fountain, steam swirling up to sheathe her nude form in clinging wisps.

"Still mad at me?" he said.

"You take all this for granted, Beck," she said. "Including me."

"I don't. You know I don't."

"It feels sometimes to me that you do." She stretched her arms and planted her hands on the sides of the tub. "You think I just have your baby and make pasta and give sex and do it all again next day."

"*Nein*, Sonja, *nein nein nein*." Her perfect English slipped when she was drunk or stoned or, as now, angry.

"I am your wife. I am not your au pair. I am second mother also to Aidan and Charlie and responsible for them too. I do their laundry like you do and I cook for them like you do and I clean up after them like you do."

"Hey, now, no need for the passive-aggressive stuff."

Her head tilted left. "You have to respect my opinions about things I know. Like black diamonds."

Beck nodded, contrite. "That was stupid. I should have listened."

"They were not ready. Aidan could be dead right now. You understand? Your son. *Dead*."

With a low clank the jets died, the timer cycled off. She stared at him across the fogged and calming water. "You are a baby, Beck," she said into the new silence. "Like our Roy. A big baby."

She climbed out and wrapped herself in one of the Egyptian cotton towels stocked by the laundry service. "I am going to shower," she said from behind him. "Will you come to the bed?"

He dropped his head back to look up at her. "Gimme ten minutes."

She held up a hand. "Five."

Sonja went inside and left the sliding door open six inches. Beck gazed up at the tapestry of stars, in dazzling focus on this cold April night at nine thousand feet. The condo shared the Jacuzzi with the unit backing theirs, but no one had taken the place that weekend, leaving the deck nearly silent.

He kept his head there against the smooth curve of the tub. Found Orion's Belt and the twinned lines of Gemini, with the Monoceros horn just beneath. His father had taught him the constellations, over a summer of buggy campouts in the Delaware Water Gap when he was about the boys' age. How many times had Beck taken his guys camping, like ever? Four, five? He closed his eyes, thinking of humid nights in the soft give of a sleeping bag, glow of dying coals. Bear bags dangling from limbs.

W*hoosh.*

The jets went on, startling him out of a doze as Tessa stepped onto the deck. Her towel fell to her feet, and she stood there topless, pale skin luminous in the turquoise glow. She set a water glass and her phone on a bench, then took a step toward the Jacuzzi. Beck gaped.

"Oh god, I'm so sorry." She cowered to cover her chest. Beck turned away, gulping dryly. "I didn't think anyone was out here."

"Hey, it's cool." Beck tried for nonchalant. "Just tell me when you're in."

"Okay, in," she said moments later. He turned back and saw her head popped up above the frothing water. "How's Aidan's ankle?" she asked.

"We'll see. Scared him, though."

"I bet."

"Did Roy treat you well today?"

"He was sweet. He likes whipped cream." She giggled. "Don't tell Sonja."

"I won't."

Silence for a minute or so, and Beck started to get a little uncomfortable with this almost-nude sixteen-year-old sitting across from him. He was about to get out when Tessa reached behind the lip of the tub for a plastic sandwich bag. Inside, the faint white line of a joint, the dark shell of a Zippo.

"Smoke?" she asked.

He considered it. Sonja was waiting. "Maybe a puff or two."

Tessa wriggled a foot closer to him on the bench. The lighter clicked and flared. Her breath hitched. Flame and shadow danced across her young features as she dragged. When she handed him the joint he took a long pull, letting the smoke baste his lungs.

"Another thing not to tell your mom," he rasped on the exhale, handing her the joint.

Tessa sneered. "She wouldn't give a fuck."

"Seriously?"

"All she cares about is Xander, his chess. Plus that lame school he's testing for."

Beck allowed himself a self-righteous sniff. "Azra's all ragged at me because I let the guys skip out on the test today. But there's no way I'm letting them go to that place. I hate all that gifted bullshit."

"You're an awesome dad."

Beck sat up a few inches.

"Because my mom's obsessed with it, whether Xander gets in."

"Your brother's a genius, like your old man. She's actually worried?"

"You. Would. *Not*. Believe. It's all she talks about. Meanwhile I'm just the druggy slut."

"Well, that sucks." Not a surprise, though, knowing Lauren. What had Julian seen in that woman? Beck had never forgotten what a drag Lauren was during those ugly months around his divorce, by far the worst of Azra's uptight friends, taking the opportunity whenever she saw Beck to make fun of his relaxed lifestyle, drop not-so-subtle hints about the wanting intellects of sporty kids like the twins. *They lose half an IQ point with every header*, Lauren once said right in front of him. Azra just ignored it but Beck had stomped out of the room, defensive and furious.

He waved off another hit but watched Tessa as her sucking pulls burned through the rolling paper. Something about the angle of her nose, the shape of that mouth—

"You look like him," he said, "your dad." The memory percolated up through the early high.

Tessa was in mid-drag. The end of the joint stopped glowing and she choked out a cloud. "Really?" she said between coughs. "Because everybody says I look more like *her*. Which, like, fucking kill me now."

"Maybe in the cheekbones. But you got his whole—I don't know." Beck hesitated. "He saved my fucking life one time. Julian."

"Really? That's *crazy*."

"It was two, three years before you came around and—shit, you know I haven't told this story in ten years. I almost told it for your dad's eulogy, but Lauren wouldn't have wanted that."

"Will you tell me?"

The question made him glow. "What the hell."

It had been an idiotic free up Salt Pinnacle, he told her. No ropes, no clips, no helmets. Midway up Beck got in trouble. In trying to get out of it, he slipped down the rock face and ended up hanging on by his hands, his feet scrambling for purchase. Julian was ten feet above him and maybe eight feet to his right. Seeing Beck struggling below, he scooted over to a crevasse and reached out a hand to give him an option. But the closest he could reach was at least two feet from Beck's hand. To save his own life, Beck would have to swing and grab and more than likely take Julian down with him.

"You have to understand," he said, stoned gaze on Tessa's floating chin.

"We were a hundred and fifty feet up, and it was *waaaay* less than fifty-fifty that your dad could stay on that pinnacle with my weight. Stay where I am and I'm dead for sure. But if I go for it and grab him, I'll probably kill us both. I know it. He knows it, I can see it on his face. But he keeps shouting at me, 'Take it, Beck! Goddamnit, Beck, you take this fucking hand,' and so I'm thinking, Do I kill my friend? Do I kill my fucking friend? And I do it. I grab his hand and he swings me to his crevasse and I hug rock until I get my foot in a crack. Then *he* slips a couple feet because of how much it strains him to get me, but I catch him and smash his skinny ass against the pinnacle, and we both just hold on and laugh and laugh and *God*."

He looked at her through the blur of his tears. Tessa was watching him, transfixed by this dangerous gleam out from the void of her father's life.

"Did you keep going?" she said.

"Fuck no. We descended, climbed in your dad's truck, went back to Crystal, and got more shitfaced than either of us had since college. Maybe ever."

"I don't believe it." She dried her hands on a towel and reached for her phone.

"Every word's true, swear to God." He crossed his heart under the water. It felt good, sharing this.

"Thank you for that, Beck," she said, in a low and solemn voice. Looking at her phone, she offered him the joint again.

Ten minutes later he went inside, and when the door slid shut, the weed hit him like a velvet brick. He stopped with his mouth agape and his hand on the back of a sofa. His stomach knotted and churned as he rethought that whole encounter with Tessa and why she'd come out when she did, two minutes after Sonja went inside. It had been gnawing at him since she slipped into the water—or had it?

No, he was pretty sure he was right.

Tessa had been watching them out on the deck. She'd heard every word of their exchange. Lurking, listening, waiting for his wife to leave.

He took a deep breath. *Chill, you paranoid freak.*

He moved through the darkened kitchen, still spinning with his high, when he bumped into someone standing by the island. He sprang back and his towel dropped to the floor.

"Gross," said a voice.

"*Christ*, Charlie." When the towel was around his waist again, Beck leaned against the counter. "Just hot-tubbing." His voice tight. "What's up? You need some cocoa?"

Charlie didn't answer. He glanced out through the kitchen window just as Tessa, still bare-chested, hopped out of the Jacuzzi for a sip of water, skin lit faintly blue by the underwater bulb. Beck sidestepped to block Charlie's view.

His son held up a new jar of Nutella. "I can't open this."

Beck twisted the lid and lifted off the foil covering. *Damn* it looked good. He dipped in and took a big scoop and licked it off his finger. "You want some toast, maybe an apple for this?"

Charlie looked out the window again. "Never mind. I'm actually not hungry," he said softly, walking out of the kitchen back toward his room.

"Charlie, wait." Beck stumbled forward with the towel loosening again. He clutched it tight and smeared it with Nutella. Charlie kept going down the hall. "Charlie, *dammit*."

Charlie stopped beneath the light fixture. "What," he said, without turning around.

"Look at me."

Slowly Charlie rotated the upper half of his body toward Beck, a cold look in his young eyes. Beck swallowed dry air. It killed him but he had to ask. "Did you do that on purpose up there? Slow Aidan down like that, so he'd crash?"

His son's face changed. For a moment Beck saw the flash of guilt, and he waited for the familiar hitch in Charlie's voice. Beck was ready to go to him, hold him, tell him it was all okay as long as he apologized and told the truth.

But no hitch. Instead Charlie's lips made a nasty, hateful curl, almost animal. Beck blinked and the door to the twins' bedroom closed on the empty hall.

A Touch of Tessa:
One GiRL's SURVIVal GUiDe t® JUni®R yeaR
A Video Blog

Episode #138: BRECK WITH BECK

. . . 15 views . . .

[*Beck in a frothing Jacuzzi, taking a long hit from a joint. Holds in, coughs out smoke, leans forward and hands joint off to Tessa.*]

TESSA: So, Beck.

BECK [*stoned*]: Yo.

TESSA: Tell me another story.

BECK: What kind of story?

TESSA: Not about my dad this time. Do you have one about my mom?

BECK: Seriously? That bit— Sorry.

TESSA: It's all good.

BECK: A story about Lauren. Oh shit, I've got one.

TESSA: Awesome.

BECK: Okay. So this was three, four years ago. Kev had this old college friend coming to town, and Samantha thought Azra would like him. You know how she is, the yenta bullshit, always trying to hook my ex up with some D. So this guy, they arrange for him to come out with Kev and Sam to "meet some friends," right?

TESSA: Right.

BECK: Samantha gets this couple they know plus Azra to meet the three of them at the Sky Bar, that restaurant up on Sapphire. Now, I just *happen* to be out with my lovely wife that night at the same restaurant. Sonja and me, we're halfway through our first bottle of Barolo when your mom shows up.

TESSA: Wait wait *what?*

BECK: Apparently Azra let it slip that there was this triple date going on, and Lauren's not invited because she'd be like a ninth wheel—

TESSA: Seventh.

BECK: Seventh wheel. But she comes anyway, right, she's just walking in five minutes after they all sit down. And she just fucking *stands* there, arms folded, staring at them, and they're staring at her. The whole place goes quiet. Really awkward and about to get awkwarder until finally Azra—of course it's Azra—jumps up and pulls a chair from another table and starts to push it around to where Lauren's standing. But—

TESSA: She doesn't sit.

BECK: Your mom just picks up this bottle of wine in the middle of the table, kind of in front of Samantha, she picks it up and slams it down on the table, and a huge amount of it shoots out and sloshes over all the plates, the appetizers. Then she just turns around and huffs out of the place.

TESSA: God.

BECK: Yeah, but you know what, though? I wanted to go hug your mom right then. Because I get lonely sometimes too, and sometimes I wish I had more guys to just hang with, like back in the day when I climbed with your dad. And believe me, I get it, flying off the handle like that. Because some people are well friended and some aren't. I mean, obviously.

TESSA: What do you mean?

BECK: Well just look at Lauren. Who's she got? Who are *her* friends? Azra, Rose, and Samantha. And that's it, man. That's all she wrote, at least as far as I've ever seen, I mean Azra's told me, you know? She says the quad is all Lauren's got, aside from you and Xander.

TESSA [*long silence*]: Wow.

BECK: What?

TESSA: I need more. You want more? [*Reaching out with another joint.*]

BECK: Nah, I should get upstairs to the old ball and chain. The admiral. The buster of balls. The castratrix-in-chief.

TESSA: You are so stoned right now.

BECK: Yeah. Yeah, I guess I fucking am. Anyway, your turn to look away, young lady.

[*Reaches back for towel, then muscles out of the Jacuzzi, everything fully exposed for a long moment before he wraps towel around waist.*]

BECK [*sucking in gut*]: Okay, done.

TESSA: Great stories, Beck. Thanks.

BECK: Just don't tell your mom.

TESSA: That's the third thing.

BECK: 'Night, Tessa.

SEVENTEEN

ROSE

On Tuesdays she would swing by BloomAgain on her way home from the lab to pick up Azra. Sometimes they sat in front of Azra's house for an hour, parked at the curb, processing their lives. This time together was safe, close, precious.

Today Azra was venting about the twins: Charlie struggling in school and soccer, Aidan thriving in both, the brothers diverging in ways she could never have foreseen. They're different kids, Azra wanted Beck to see, with different needs, different talents and strengths.

"That's something I need to remember about the Emmas," Rose offered. "They've been together since daycare. I'm just worried what things will be like, say if Z gets in and Q doesn't."

"Or the reverse."

"Are you kidding?"

"Hey, stranger things have happened," Azra said. "And with Kev's connections?"

Rose frowned. "That's not how this school works, or at least I hope not. Mainly I just don't want our daughters to drift apart. They're like two peas in a pod."

Azra got a look.

"What? Too cliché?"

Azra shook her head. Something in her eyes, or the late-afternoon light playing tricks on her face.

"What?" Rose asked.

Azra dug in her purse for her keys. "I should go. Glen will be by soon."

"Well, thanks for letting me vomit. You're so lucky you don't have to worry about all this."

"What's that supposed to mean?" Azra made no move to get out. A hardness gripped her features, and the temperature in the car seemed to drop ten degrees.

Rose said cautiously, "You know, with the school."

"Go on."

"I just mean– the boys have their soccer, they're such amazing athletes—"

"Have their soccer?" she snapped. "Rose, are you listening to yourself?"

"I thought they didn't test. They weren't there on Saturday."

"Beck took them skiing. I *told* you guys that. So they're taking the Cog-Pro tomorrow night, in the makeup session."

"Oh."

Azra's lips formed a tight line. "So predictable."

"What?"

"You blab all day about Q and Z, the intricate dynamics between you and Samantha and your girls, how brilliant Xander is, a budding scientist like you. But my boys are nowhere on your radar."

"I'm sorry, Azra, I just didn't think—"

"It didn't occur to you, is what you mean. That they would test."

Azra was right. It hadn't.

"The academy hasn't seemed like a priority to you," Rose pleaded. "I think of you guys as contemptuous of it, that's all." She was stumbling, feeling horrible, wondering at this sudden anger.

"You and Samantha sometimes, it's just—" Biting off the words. "Swear to God, if there's one thing that makes me absolutely *insane*, it's the smug parents of well-behaved girls."

This time Rose kept her mouth shut.

"It's been this way since they were tiny," Azra went on. "The boys run around like hooligans, getting into everything, kicking soccer balls through the windows, total fuckstorm. Meanwhile the Emmas are sitting at the table having tea and reading Jane Austen. Do they even burp?"

"That's not fair."

"Not fair? Did you say *not fair*? I'll tell you what's not fair. Potty training, that's what."

"Are you serious?"

"My guys didn't train until they were four and a half, Rose. *Four and a half* and I'm still changing their shitty diapers, one after the other. That's my main memory from those months while me and Beck were first having trouble, the hell of that. And meanwhile your daughter—who trained right after her second birthday, mind you, just like her BFF Emma Z—heads off to the toilet, comes back smelling like a lilac bush, and you're all 'Good job, Emma Q!' in your perky girl-mom voice, right in front of me."

"God, Azra."

"And it's no better now. 'Hey, Rose, what are you up to today?' 'Oh, I'm going with Samantha to Clarita Ranch. We're taking our daughters to ride these cute ponies!' 'Oh, hi, Azra, I'd love to meet for a drink. But you know what? The Emmas have ballet.' Our *daughters* our *daughters* the *Emmas* the *Emmas*."

She bared her teeth and pushed back against the headrest. "It's just hard, when your two best friends have this part of their lives you're shut off from completely. Sweet, studious little girls beloved by their teachers. I don't have that and never will."

Your two best friends. Until that moment Rose had never seen herself this way, on a par in Azra's eyes with Samantha—though not with Lauren, and it was surely no accident that hers was the next name out of Azra's mouth.

"It's one of the things I really appreciate about Lauren. I'm not saying Xander's out there rooting in the mud with my little pigs, but I mean, for all her quirks she's not into the showy girl shit with Tessa."

Rose closed her eyes, wanting to speak up in her own defense. For one thing Tessa had been, until recently, a total train wreck; there was nothing to be showy *about*. But she reached over to press a hand on Azra's fists, clenched together in her lap. "I don't know what to say except I'm so sorry we make you feel this way. I really am."

"It's just different, having boys."

"Azra, I hear what you're saying and I'll think about this, I promise."

"*God* you've had a lot of therapy, Rose."

Rose gasped. Azra raised a hand to her mouth. She burst out laughing and Rose did too, and for a minute they lost it completely. When they recovered their composure, Azra smiled sadly out the windshield. She wiped her right eye with a knuckle.

"I feel better," she said.

"Well I don't," said Rose.

"Good." Azra's face brightened. "You know what Beck used to do?"

"What?"

"He only ever confessed it to me, because it's so unlike him. Bet Sonja doesn't even know."

"Tell me."

"So when the boys were little," she said, rage dissolved, "when Beck was out with one of them at PlaySpace, or one of the climbing structures on the Emerald Mall—"

"Okay."

"Let's say he was sitting and some rando parent sat down next to him and started asking questions. You know, *How old is your son? How long has he been walking?* Where they want to talk about *their* kids so they start by asking about *yours* kind of thing."

"They want to compare."

"Right. So you know what Beck would do, if it was some mom or dad he didn't know? He'd subtract a few months from the boys' ages. Tell other parents they were only nine months when they were a year. Eighteen months when they'd just turned two."

"Why would he do that?"

"It made the boys look like they were more developed. That they had more language, more motor skills. Like they were walking way younger than when they actually did."

"But why?"

Azra's eyes gleamed. "He wanted to see that flicker of worry in the parents' eyes. It would thrill him, to make a self-satisfied mom just a *teensy* bit jealous that some nasty boy was hitting the milestones earlier than her princess."

"Oh my god."

"When he confessed it in counseling, I weirdly loved him for it. I have a little bit of it too, that protective ferocity about my boys."

"We all have that, I think. With our kids."

"But it's different for me, and for Beck too. The fact that you guys don't see the twins the way you see the Emmas, or Xander, see them as smart and respectful and academic and capable of anything—"

Rose started to object.

"Don't," Azra warned, a finger raised.

"Okay," she responded meekly.

Azra's face held an expression that Rose couldn't read. A certain firmness there; resolve. "You know what, Rose? About this test, this school?"

"Uh-huh?"

"I hope Emma Q gets in. Emma Z too. You know I love those girls, and I know the whole thing is important to you and Samantha, to your families. But I don't want to hear about Crystal Academy from you anymore, not for a while. I'm sorry but I don't. It's just not a good subject for us, okay?"

Rose gave her friend a tight smile, the newness of it not choking her up until Azra was out of the car, up the stairs, unlocking her front door. Because with Azra, with the way they talked, there had never been rules, never been limits. Never a taboo, until now.

Late that night, with Gareth and Q asleep, Rose sat out on the living room couch, still shredded from the encounter but distracting herself by prepping an upcoming lecture and slides for grand rounds at the Medical Center.

Seizures, slurred words, loss of motor control, eventual paralysis, and inevitable death: whenever she described her work on neurodegenerative disorders in preadolescent brains, Rose felt as if she were narrating the prologue to a horror novel. The question was how to pitch the subject for first- and second-years, how to spur their interest in this obscure corner of pediatric neurology. The family of diseases she studied in her lab was rare enough that Rose had met only twelve patients with infantile diagnosis since she had started working on the terminal disorder seven years ago. These years of research had convinced her that her team had revealed a new pathway to treatment, that the particular enzymatic mechanism she had isolated held the key to a much wider range of neurodegenerative disorders. Finding that key would require money and time, too much of both, and the field of neurology was fiercely competitive. But give her five years and five million dollars and she would tame this monster tearing through the brains of the young.

Two MRI images glowed from her screen. Close-up cross sections of an atrophic parietal lobe, the decay highlighted in the red PowerPoint circles and arrows she had just added to the slide. Below the image, her cold description of its pathology.

She looked away and into the darkened kitchen. *The brains of the young.* As the stove clock ticked to 2:12 a.m., her thoughts churned over the fraught exchange with Azra, Beck's gaslighting of other parents, Azra's frustrations with her sweet boys and her annoying friends. Rose's work had taught her never to take Emma Q's health for granted, though maybe it was too easy for all of them to lapse into a glib complacency, with these constant parental worries about achievements and test scores, the invidious but inescapable comparisons.

She took one final glance at her screen before shutting her laptop and stealing into Emma Q's room for the day's last look at her little girl, a soft kiss on that forehead. Survivor's guilt, now incarnate in her daughter. Every night Rose came home from her mouse brains and her next-gen sequencer to whisper an agnostic's fierce blessing down through the skull and into the thriving brain of her only child.

EIGHTEEN

XANDER

The problem," said Mr. Aker, scraping his fingers across a dandruffy scalp, "is that what you're doing here isn't really science."

"It's probability, Mr. Aker. Mathematics."

"Yes but only *you* can see the payoff. Do you understand?"

"Not precisely."

Until recently Xander had been working on the biomolecular composition of the secretions and excretions of *Dysdera crocata*, the woodlouse spider, figuring out the cellular information, breaking down the genetics, doing some dissection. Mr. Aker had even made contacts at the university to see if Xander could do some venom testing with mice.

Then, two weeks ago, Xander had grown bored of the biomolecular composition of the secretions and excretions of *Dysdera crocata*. So he'd switched topics. Since then he had been much happier with his project. Now it was all about probability and chess, the equations that explained why certain things happened in the game in particular ways, about how to calculate multiple combinations of pieces and moves.

Xander looked at the formulas and figures on his printout. It was pretty easy to research all this stuff, a lot harder to confirm its validity to his satisfaction. But he had done it, and now these proofs and calculations were even more skull-blowing to Xander than before.

Like Hardy's estimate for the number of possible chess games: ten to the tenth to the fiftieth. Or Shannon's equation for the number of possible positions:

$$P(40) \approx \frac{64!}{(32!)\,(8!)^2\,(2!)^6} \approx 10^{10}$$

Of course, that was only if you factored in every possible game with every possible permutation of openings and defenses and moves and outcomes. But even after just four moves the number of possible positions—according to Flye St. Marie back in 1903—was 71,852. Xander couldn't quite believe that number when he'd first read it, but he'd done the proof himself, and it was true.

"Okay, so let me put it this way." Mr. Aker folded his arms. "I'm a pretty good chess player, right? I can hold my own against you better than anyone else at Odyssey. Agreed?"

"Affirmative. You actually beat me one time."

Mr. Aker flashed a quick smile. "But the folks who will be judging the science fair won't be even as good as I am. So all these tables and charts, the Shirking Hand or whatever—"

"The Shrikhande graph," said Xander.

"It's above the head of basically anyone who would ever judge the competition. You see?"

Xander said nothing.

"Whereas the stuff you were working on a few weeks ago—the genetics, the collagen—*that* was interesting. It's the kind of project that could easily win districts, go on to states, maybe even nationals. So could we go back to *Dysdera crocata*, see if you can get some more questions generated?"

"Why do you *like* the spider project so much?"

"Because it's simple, Xander. You can understand its significance right away. The project is beautiful, complex, smart as heck—but mostly because it's simple."

"I understand."

"Great." Mr. Aker got up and went to talk to one of Xander's classmates, a girl working on water pollution in the Crystal streams. *How exciting.*

Xander stared at the back of Mr. Aker's head, not angry, just bummed out. Mr. Aker was nice, and getting all mad about things, like Tessa did, was an idiotic waste of time.

He looked back at his charts and graphs, four pages of calculations. In one motion he gathered them together and crumpled them up into a ball and tossed it toward the wastebasket in front of Mr. Aker's desk.

Swish. *Eat that, LeBron.*

No big deal. He'd memorized it all anyway. But still.

He spent the rest of science class staring out the window, his chin resting on the back of a hand, trying not to care. Because if there was one thing Xander hated, it was simplicity.

NINETEEN

CH'AYÑA

Ch'ayña waited until she heard Tiago leave before she came out of the bedroom and down the hall to where her daughter sat on the small sofa. She settled next to her and took Silea's good hand in her lap. The other was buried in a white plaster cast up to her shoulder, swirled with Atik's designs in magic marker and pen.

"Where is Atik?" Ch'ayña asked.

"He's out running with Kyler."

The gringo kid three rows down, the only one in the park. Nice boy, though not the brightest bulb; not like Atik.

"I'll call him in," Ch'ayña said.

"Give him a few more minutes. He's been working hard."

"He has," Ch'ayña agreed.

They needed him to. Silea had broken her elbow eleven days ago after slipping on an icy walk in front of the Rite Aid. A serious break, and now Silea had her arm locked out in front of her in a cast-and-brace contraption that made her look like a robot. She couldn't mop, vacuum, shake out a rug, load and unload the truck, or drive.

Since his mother's fall Atik had filled in some at the houses, offering again, as he had last time, without being asked. So far he'd missed three days of school. Soon there would be questions from the teachers.

Ch'ayña said, "For supper I'll do potatoes and those peppers with the beef."

Silea nodded toward the counter. "Tiago brought dinner already."

Ch'ayña looked over. A chicken sat in steaming plastic, roasted at the store. There was also a loaf of bread and a pale sphere of lettuce by the cutting board. "Fine," she said with a huff.

Silea patted her mother's wrist. "Be kind to him. He likes to help."

Those first weeks Tiago had come around, every time he showed up, Ch'ayña would pour him a glass of water from the sink. Back in Huánuco, to offer a guest a glass of cold water was an insult: *For you, I can't even be bothered to boil water for tea.* But Tiago took the glasses of cold water as signs of approval, even fondness. He'd started smiling at Ch'ayña, trying to talk Spanish with her, maybe thinking of her already as his new *suyra*. She stopped with the water after that.

Footsteps on gravel, familiar stomps, door swinging open. Atik came in, breathless, looked at them on the couch, and glanced at the stove clock. "I have to be there at seven," he huffed. "Can we go now?"

"Go where?" Ch'ayña asked.

"To school."

"To school at night? That's what the *wawa* wants?"

"He has a test," said Silea.

"He has chores," Ch'ayña countered. "There are dishes, there's trash."

Yes, he was helping out at the houses, but when it came to chores around their own place, Atik had a habit of squirming out of them, and too often his mother let him.

Silea shrugged. "I can do the washing up. Or I can take him myself."

"No driving," said Ch'ayña, wagging a finger. "Not with that arm."

"You'll take him, then?"

Ch'ayña shrugged an assent and looked over at Atik. "Get something for yourself, at least. Some of that chicken. A good hunk of bread."

Atik went to the counter and opened up the chicken container.

"Rip off a leg," said Ch'ayña. "Take the other leg too. Both legs."

Atik worked the drumsticks from Tiago's bird, tore off some bread, used a knife to cut himself a wedge of lettuce. He put it all in a plastic square from the drainer.

"Wash your hands," Ch'ayña ordered him. "And get some paper towel." He obeyed. "Now get in the truck." She kissed Silea on her forehead and followed Atik out.

"Is Kyler going to the test?" she asked her grandson. The gravel crunched beneath them in the dark.

Atik sniffed but didn't respond.

"Does he have a ride to the school? We could drive him."

"He's not going."

"Why not?"

"It's not his strength, Awicha."

They reached the truck. She boosted herself up onto the bench and started the engine, letting it cough a few times before releasing the brake and edging down the row.

"Is it a numbers test?"

In the truck, when it was just the two of them, they spoke only Quechua. Silea didn't like it, wanting him to sharpen his English, but that was her problem.

"It's an everything test," he said.

"Eh?"

"Math. Shapes. Words. Everything."

The truck rumbled out onto the highway. "Well, you'll get an A for certain," she said. In Peru they had number grades, but in the schools up here it was all letters. "My *wawa* always gets an A."

"The test isn't for a grade."

"No?"

"It's for a school." Atik bent over the supper in his lap and took a bite of chicken. "A new school in Crystal," he said around his food. "The teachers are talking about it all the time. If you beat the test, you might get in."

She was convinced she'd misheard him. "Thirty-five miles, just for school?"

"Tiago said there'll be a bus."

"What does Tiago know?"

"He looked it up."

"What about Kyler?"

He laughed shortly and a tiny piece of bread flew from his mouth. "He could never get in."

Ch'ayña looked back at the road, and while Atik ate she told him a story. There'd been a boy she fancied back in Huánuco, before she'd met Atik's *jatunpapa*. The boy's father was a zinc miner, but the boy wanted to be in tourism. He even went to school for it in Lima. So glamorous, he was like a man you'd see on television. But when he came back to the village, he had changed. He acted like a mine boss, haughty and cruel. He would hardly glance at Ch'ayña anymore, and when he did, he looked down at her as if from the peak of Gagamachay.

"You have a good school now, Atikcha," she told him, "and your teachers like you. Listen. You don't want to be like this man, this false, newborn Limeño."

Atik crunched his lettuce like a little rabbit. "It's not that kind of school. It's not for tourism, or like that."

"What kind of school is it, then? What sort of kids will go there?"

He crunched some more, thinking about it. Finally he swallowed and answered: "Crystal kids," he said, in English.

TWENTY

BECK

COGPRO TEST REGISTRATION. The printed sign hung from a cafeteria table in the lobby of Donnelly Elementary School. Three signs in a smaller font indicated where to stand, depending on the first letter of your child's last name: A–H, I–P, or Q–Z. The line was only four deep at Q–Z, so Beck figured he'd reach the front inside of two minutes. Meanwhile Aidan hobbled over to a display case filled with trophies, plaques, and other memorabilia archiving the history of Donnelly. Charlie followed him.

Beck glanced at the guys and did a double take. The twins were staring up at a framed newspaper spread high on the lobby wall, a *Crystal Register* from last spring featuring a banner headline:

THE EMMAS EMCEE!

Below it appeared a huge color photo of Emma Holland-Quinn and Emma Zellar, leaning in with their ponytailed heads touching. They looked for all the world like conjoined twins, microphones clutched to their mouths, running the end-of-the-year talent show. He remembered Azra saying something about that night, how she'd taken the boys because they had wanted to see their friends onstage. When she'd dropped them off afterward, she had been crying and he hadn't understood why. Next morning, *boom!* The Emmas on the front page of the city paper.

Cute girls. Beck had known them since they were babies, maybe six, seven months. He hadn't seen them since Thanksgiving and they already looked older than they did in the newspaper shot from just a few months before.

Time. *Shit.*

"Sir, your child's name?"

A haggard teacher sat planted behind a box of file folders. "Names, actually," he said. "Charlie and Aidan Unsworth-Chaudhury."

"That's quite a mouthful."

He stared at her.

"And their grades?"

"Solid-B students, like their dad."

She looked unamused.

"Fifth grade. They go to St. Bridget's," he added unnecessarily.

A mom standing in the next line whipped her head around and gave him a lofty glare. Beck smirked, ignored her. To some parents around here, sending your kids to private school made you worse than a child molester. The teacher slid a short stack of forms across the table. Three for each kid, standard boilerplate about disclosure, confidentiality, reporting of test results. None of which Beck bothered to read as he scribbled his signature and filled in his email address.

"So when do we find out if they're in?" Beck handed her the forms.

She clipped the papers together and tucked them back inside their folders. "Oh, this is just the first cut," she said.

"Seriously?"

"This is the CogPro. The Cognitive Proficiency test, for the initial round."

"This isn't the actual admissions test?"

"It's a process, sir." She leaned to the side and looked at the growing line behind him. "Once the results come in, there will be portfolio review, perhaps interviews. Now if you wouldn't mind stepping aside—"

"*Interviews?* But Crystal Academy's a public school. You can't have an interview to get into a public school."

"It will all be covered in the orientation sessions."

"Well, it's bullshit," he huffed.

She looked up at him as if he'd just pulled out a gun. Charlie had a huge grin on his face and Aidan was slumped on his crutches, wide-eyed and embarrassed. Beck scanned the small crowd of tight-ass Crystal faces.

He whirled toward the trophy cases. "Come on, guys, we're out of here."

"Excellent." Charlie looked like he'd just dodged a prison sentence. "Can we get ice cream instead?"

"Hell yes."

"Dad," said Aidan.

Beck ignored him. He waist-bumped the panic bar and pushed out to the circular drive in front of the school.

"Dad!"

Beck rehearsed what he was going to say to Azra. He pulled out his phone. Remembered she was at a concert or something in Denver. Texted her *911* anyway.

"*DAD!*"

Beck stopped. Aidan stood on the curb with his arms dangling down along his crutches, scowly and pissed.

"What is it?"

Aidan shifted onto his good foot. "I'm taking the test."

"Are you serious?"

"Try-hard," Charlie muttered.

For once Aidan ignored his brother. "Mom said I could."

Beck stared at his sons, marveling at their differences. Charlie wore every emotion on his face, never hesitant to blare out his thoughts. Aidan had this wordless reserve, a waiting distance on the world, as if he'd made a conscious decision not to talk about his inner life.

"She promised, Dad."

Beck looked down at his phone, thinking it through. If Charlie didn't take the CogPro, he couldn't fail it. If he didn't fail it, he wouldn't lose face if Aidan somehow scored high enough to get in.

"Well, if she promised," he said reluctantly. The thought of going back in there, though.

"Do I have to take it?" said Charlie.

"We'll go get ice cream while your brother's testing."

"Do I get ice cream?" Aidan asked.

"Not if you take the test," Charlie said, and gave his brother a satanic smile.

"That's not fair." Aidan was now close to tears.

"He's kidding." Beck ruffled Aidan's hair. "Now let's go back inside."

You nine-one-one'd me," Azra said ten minutes later. Beck walked angry circles in the parking lot, phone in hand. "What is going on?"

"We're at Donnelly. For the test."

"I'm at a show, Beck. What is the emergency?"

"You said it was one test. You did *not* tell me everything that was involved in this."

"Yes, I did. Two times."

"They're not going to that entitled school, Azra. I will chain myself to the panic bars to keep them from walking in. I will lie down in front of the fucking *bus* if I have to. I will go Tiananmen."

"Right."

"This is about privilege. You can't see that?"

"Listen to yourself, Beck. Our sons go to St. Bridget's on your trust fund, and you're squawking to me about privilege?"

"That's totally different," he sputtered. *And what trust fund?*

Azra said, "Let's get you off that high horse, cowboy. Let me know once you've dismounted."

He spun and kicked a lamppost, hurting his toe. She'd said the same thing to him at therapy one time and he'd screamed at her, but then they'd both started laughing and couldn't stop until the end of the hour. Their best session ever. Since then Azra had pulled out that comeback whenever she needed to quash one of his frequent rants about bourgeois values, rampant capitalism, and white privilege. ("But never your own, Beck," she liked to point out. "Have you noticed that?")

"Okay, boots are on the ground," Beck said, chastened.

"Good." Azra's voice changed when she was calming him like this. Sounded more like his mom's. "Now look. The CogPro is just the first test, okay? Chances are they won't score high enough to make the first cut, and even if they do, we have choices. They could get an admission offer, and we could still decide to send them back to St. Bridget's next year. It's just one test they're taking."

He used his free hand to trace diminishing circumferences around the mound of his gut, like tree rings. "Not *they*, technically."

A few seconds ticked by. "What did you just say?"

Charlie was in the courtyard, kicking a soccer ball off the school wall. "So Aidan wanted to take the test. Charlie refused."

"Wait, he's not in there?"

"No."

"But Beck, *Jesus*. This is the makeup session! If he doesn't test tonight, he has no chance."

"Okay, high horse aside, Aidan's the one who got tapped for that VisionQuest thing," he pointed out. "Plus there's no way in hell Charlie would ever go to Crystal Academy. Nine to four every day with a bunch of dweebs?"

She exhaled loudly. "You're probably right."

"*Thank* you," he said. Azra rarely conceded a parenting point to him, but when she did, it felt like a bong hit.

"I need to go. And Beck, never *ever* nine-one-one me again unless one of the boys is in the hospital. Do you understand?"

"Yes."

"I'm serious. It's not okay."

"I get it. I'm—"

—*sorry*, he'd been about to say, but then she was gone, phone probably dropped in her big bag, already breezing back to whatever Tinder-swiping motherfucker she was dating right now.

Five years since the divorce and still he hated disappointing her. He stood by the lamppost looking off into the dark and felt a yearning for something he couldn't name.

Beck kept an old photograph in his basement, hidden beneath the keyboard of his docking station. Nothing porny, just an old shot of him and Azra at Burning Man the summer before their engagement. Azra wrapped in a lavender sarong and Beck at his muscled best, barefoot rock climber in some old jean shorts low-riding on hip bones that were actually visible back then. They'd eaten mushrooms half an hour before the shot was taken, and this DJ wearing a papier-mâché donkey's head was playing an electronic dance mix inspired by *A Midsummer Night's Dream.*

But mostly Azra. The smooth slide of that bare arm over his shoulders. The sun dancing through her hair in that desert heat.

In college Beck had taken a course on medieval dream visions, and the professor had taught them this old idea of the Wheel of Fortune. Not the game show but a symbol for changing circumstances and fickle luck. Everyone was stuck on this slowly turning wheel that could bring you up or take you down. Even kings and emperors sitting on top of the world would be brought low once the wheel started its inexorable rotation. King Lear, Julius Caesar, Richard Nixon, didn't matter. Sometimes Beck looked at himself in that Burning Man shot and thought, That was it, man. Look what you had. You were perched like a fucking eagle on top of that wheel and you didn't even know it, did you? And he'd never made it back to the top, not even close. Despite his sons, despite Sonja, despite the way his whole spoiled existence had gifted him with so much to be thankful for. And now here he was, watching someone else go through the motions of his pathetic, shrunken life. Stuck near the bottom of the wheel and dangling there, waiting for a final drop into the trough.

He wriggled his toes. When he turned around, Charlie had his soccer ball tucked under an arm, the other hand planted on his waist, staring blankly at his dad.

Beck rubbed his palms together. "Ice cream?"

"Awesome." Charlie broke into his youngest smile. That grin: maybe that's what he needed. Beck opened the car door and held it for his son.

TWENTY-ONE

ROSE

Wild Horse Stables occupied a patch of flat grassland at the far northern edge of Beulah County with an expansive view of the Rockies low to the west and, to the south, a not-so-great vista onto Mountain View, a sprawling trailer park one had to pass before turning off the rural highway. The whole area was a world away from Crystal. Rusted remains of trucks and tractors sulked in front yards, pawn shops and McDonalds the sole businesses in a string of two-stoplight towns with names like Sandy Bend and Dry River.

That morning, though, the forty-minute drive to the county's upper reaches was a luxurious pleasure for Rose, riding high in a Buick Enclave, the highway smooth and muted beneath the brushed leather seats and fluid suspension. It was a loaner car—their battered VW wagon was in the shop, the transmission acting up again—and one thing she noticed immediately was the quiet. Their regular car was thin-skinned, reacting to every bump. A passenger sitting in back had to raise her voice to be heard by the driver. Not so in the new Buick: like headphones on wheels, the outside world muffled, shut away. Only as the big SUV glided gently over a set of train tracks did Rose's temporal lobes process what this difference between the two vehicles allowed.

In this car she could hear the Emmas.

———

Since before they acquired language the girls had carried on a running stream of commentary whenever they got in a car together. Babies in backward safety seats goo-gooing and touching hands. Toddlers playing tug-of-war with stuffed animals. Little girls making worlds with dolls and toy horses. Car Talk, Kev Zellar had once called their chatter; the label stuck. The Emmas shared so many interests and activities that they were in someone's back seat at least three times a week, and Car Talk had become a sweet fixture in their intertwined lives.

Recently, though, the girls' chatter had begun a slow decrescendo: more often private now, whispered and secretive rather than voluble and open. When they lowered their voices, Rose often couldn't make out a single word.

A natural part of growing up, Samantha had avowed. They're eleven now, genuine tweens, heading for middle school. Of course they have secrets. Of course they don't want their parents listening in while they talk about their annoying teachers, or the gross boys they're finding new ways to despise.

But Rose missed it, the sweet babbling of those little girls. So now, sitting in the front of an unexpectedly quiet vehicle, she listened eagerly.

Two words stood out right away: *Crystal Academy.*

Emma Z brought it up, asking Emma Q, straight out: "So what was your best practice score? On the CogPro?"

Rose felt a spasm in her lower spine.

"One-twenty-five?" Q said, with a soft question mark, perhaps a twinge of conscience about the lie. Q's highest score on any practice test had never exceeded one-twenty. She'd added a full five points.

Z pushed harder. "Your average or your best?"

Q hesitated. "Um, my average."

In the rearview mirror Rose saw Z wriggle, a tiny tense uncoiling. "That's *really* good, Q," she said, her intonation so much like her mother's when Sam was in Lady Bountiful mode. "My average is one-thirty. But once I got a one-thirty-five."

Rose felt her body go heavy in the seat.

It got worse. Soon the Emmas began rating the admissions chances of their classmates and friends. Z called one boy a "drooler," and then Q opined, world-weary, that someone named Connor would get in because of his father's big prize in astrophysics. Rose heard a vicious analysis of Caitlin Comstock, a hilarious girl who'd come to their birthday parties for years, always bearing a thoughtful gift.

"Caitlyn can't even finish a book," Q observed, her pitch too high.

"I know!" Z's laugh, belly-deep. "She's had *Order of the Phoenix* in her backpack for, like, six months!"

"That's just sad." Q pretended to be pained.

"I know, right? She pulls it out and just, like, *thunk*s it on her desk and opens it so everyone will think she's reading a big thick book."

"What about Stephie Turner?" Q asked.

"She can't even *talk* like she's smart."

Q laughed. "You're right. But Xander's good at that."

"Good at *what*?" Z snapped.

Rose looked in the rearview. Emma Z's pretty face had contorted at the mention of Xander's name.

"Sorry, I just mean, he . . . he's good at *talking* like he's smart," Q stumbled. "Xander can read anything, right? But it seems like he doesn't *understand* a lot of what he reads. Because of how he *is*. He just doesn't *get* it. He doesn't get—*context*."

Q had lingered a beat over the last word, like a taste of milky chocolate on her tongue. *Context*: a recent acquisition, and she was clearly thrilled to be deploying it to such good effect.

Then Z's wicked laugh again, approbation for her friend. "*Yaaaaasssss!*" she said, tickled by Q's insight. "Yes, that's *totally* it. It's like—it's like he's actually *not* as smart as everybody thinks. Because what he doesn't get means that the stuff he *does* actually know, like all that chess stuff, is just . . ." She paused before her punchline. "It's just *wasted*."

And these girls were only eleven.

––––––––

For Rose the last five minutes of the drive passed in a trancelike state of despair, her ears gathering more of their hateful chatter as they went along. They had moved on from the subject of the academy and were now cycling through the other girls in their riding class, sorting the decent riders from the poor, the skillful from the "pathetic"—

another lovely new word.

There had been some small behavioral issues with Emma Q over the last year, all of them at school. A call from the principal about passing notes. A half-dozen girls rebelling against the gym teacher for making them run laps in the drizzle. Minor stuff.

This was different. The Emmas had suddenly metamorphosed into mean girls. Little bullies, preadolescent vipers ruthlessly judging those deemed inferior. More than that: Emma Q sounded like a different person when she was talking to Z. Withering, ungenerous, casually cruel. Like someone else's child.

By the time they arrived at the barn, Rose's skin was sheathed in a cold, almost feverish sweat. She wasn't paying attention to her speed in the unfamiliar SUV, and as she drove through the gate into the parking lot, she almost hit a signpost. The Buick skidded before coming to a stop, the wheels kicking up a haze of dust that lingered when the doors slid open and the girls tumbled out, Z on the passenger side, Q on hers.

Rose climbed down from the high driver's seat. Q was already slipping on her riding boots. Rose stood over her.

"We'll talk about this later," she told her daughter.

For a moment Emma looked scared, or ashamed. But then she shrugged, buckled her riding helmet, and ran off to join her friend. The Emmas skipped together to the barn.

Rose unloaded her bike and within two minutes was helmeted, sunscreened, and clipped in, pushing up County Road 346, bearing due north. She could get a good thirty miles in before the lesson ended at noon.

The strain of her pumping thighs and tightened abs soon worked like a Xanax, calming her thoughts.

Perspective. It wasn't as if the Emmas had been outright bullying other girls at school, or their parents would have heard about it. Nothing they'd said in the car indicated they had acted on their appalling dissection of their classmates.

But kids could be so cruel. This Rose knew from her own childhood as the geeky poor girl who'd always raised her hand first. Oversize glasses, hand-me-down clothes, the wrong brand of shoes, slant-toothed and too broke for braces, and despite all that Rose would never have stood out if she hadn't participated so avidly in class, strived so hard for the approval and attention of her teachers.

Smarts, she had seen early on, might be the only way out, success in school the one thing that might lift her away from an environment that had depressed her even then, though she understood the real weight of it only once she got to college. A full ride to Lehigh on a merit scholarship; after that, Michigan for her PhD, then the postdoc at Stanford, and finally a multimillion-dollar neurology lab here at Darlton. Pole vaults, all the way up.

Character-building, though growing up like that had also taught Rose how much she didn't want to raise her own child the same way. No, they didn't buy Q the latest fashions in jeans and shoes. No, they wouldn't be springing for a new SUV any time soon. But they'd been comfortable enough on her salary to give Emma Q what she needed, and much of what she wanted. Problem was, what she wanted was starting to match everything her wealthy best friend got: riding lessons, maybe someday her own horse, boutique summer camps. But Gareth's adjunct pay was low and unreliable, and faculty salaries didn't keep up with inflation even in the medical school.

Besides, they had always agreed that they wanted Q to grow up without a sense of entitlement, that unearned air of privilege you saw in all too many kids in a town like Crystal. To succeed on her merits, not her social status. Rely on hard work, not "good genes," like the Zellars', or a trust fund, like Beck's. Because success in life didn't just happen. Things didn't always work out, no matter where or how you were raised. The thought of Emma Q sliding back into that world filled Rose with a shivering fear. Slow death by lower-middle-class angst.

So it was no mystery why she wanted Emma Q to have a shot at Crystal Academy. A public magnet school that measured student worth not in money or social status but in pure ability and smarts? If Rose had had something like that growing up, it would have saved her years of misery. She would never have taken its existence for granted, let alone its admissions requirements.

She ascended a low hill, then let herself coast down the other side to the western bank of the Silver Lake Reservoir, two hundred acres zithered by breeze and flashes of sun. She circled the oval, pushing herself—up to twenty miles an hour, twenty-five—pumping and pumping until the endorphins jump-started the better half of her thoughts.

With her bike stowed Rose strolled over to the main paddock to watch the last part of the session. Five riders, all girls, had their horses in single file moving in a serpentine line around the arena, playing a game of red light, green light. Janelle Lyman, their beloved instructor, got them all lined up in a single rank at one end and did another version of the stop-and-go game, calling out when she saw a resistant side step, a rein too quickly pulled. After five minutes of this the riders broke up to work on their maneuvers. Emma Z was closest to Rose's end. Samantha's daughter attempted a figure eight around one of the gates, but her horse was resisting.

Just then Emma Q glided by, ignoring her mother's presence. She reached the far corner and executed a smooth turn along the rail.

A voice said, "Yours?"

Down the fence stood a man wearing mirrored aviator glasses on a sharp and narrow nose, his muscled arms straining at the sleeves of a navy polo shirt. Rose had seen him out here once or twice but hadn't met him yet. Some girl's dad.

"Yes. Emma," she said, nodding toward her daughter. "And which one is yours?"

"Caitlyn, in the purple jacket." Rose saw his daughter struggling around one of the far gates. "So how long has Emma been riding?"

"Oh, I don't know, I think this is maybe her tenth or eleventh lesson?"

His head cocked back. "You're kidding."

"Maybe the twelfth?"

He lowered his aviators. "I assumed she'd been riding for a few years, and I should know because our older daughter rides collegiate at Cornell. Your girl is *very* good."

"Really?"

"A natural. You can't tell?"

They looked at Q together, guiding her horse through another figure eight. She *did* look more comfortable in the saddle than the other girls out there, more at one with the huge animal beneath her.

"I've never ridden," Rose confessed. "I don't know anything about it."

"Well," he said, conspiratorial now, edging closer to her along the fence. "Look at her lower back. You see how straight that is down there, how you could take a yardstick and put it up against her spine? She's doing it naturally, by instinct. It takes months to get them to do that, because they naturally want to huddle over. Feels more protective. And the way she sits the trot, I mean, look at my poor little Caitlyn."

He pointed out some of the other differences between the girls' competencies, explained certain terms and phrases, and soon Rose started to see it too. There was Emma Z, her face set in frustration, eyes tearing as she tried and failed to put her horse through the basic maneuvers. There was Caitlyn, sweet and open, laughing at her mistakes and trying again. And then there was Q, straight and confident in the saddle, the animal responding to her slight tugs on the reins and the imperceptible movements of her knees and thighs.

Rose rode bikes, not horses; wouldn't have known a canter from a trot. But the man's observations sparked a parental glee that all but erased Q's atrocious behavior in the car. Because Q might be a voracious reader, but Emma Z was *always* the best: at school, at ballet, at violin.

But not, it seemed, at this.

TWENTY-TWO

EMMA Z

There was something extremely *irritating* about Rose. She thought she was the chill kind of mom but really she was tense all the time and watched everything Q did.

For example: the way she got about food when they went to restaurants. Z always decided right away what she was going to order. Today, for instance, Z was really in the mood for Japanese pan noodles, and when Rose had told them on the way out to the barn where they'd be going for lunch she'd known *exactly* what she was going to have. Now, on the way home, she could already taste the crunchy sprouts and the carrot slices and the shiitake mushrooms, the thick soy-saucy strands of the noodles and the gooey way they would feel when she sucked them through her lips.

"What are you going to order, Z?" Emma Q asked her. For probably the third time.

"Japanese pan noodles," said Emma Z.

"Oh." Q looked worried.

Z cocked her head. "What about you? What are *you* going to order?"

Q's eyes widened. "I don't know yet. Do you think I'd like that, the Japanese thing?"

"You never know until you try it," Z said brightly. Something her dad always said.

"Maybe I should just get the buttered noodles."

Z sighed. "You could, I guess. But isn't that what you *always* get?"

Rose frowned in the mirror, then shifted her eyes to Q. "How about the *penne rosa*, Q? Remember how much you liked that last time? The spaghetti and meatballs are good, but we had your dad's brisket last night, so that might be a lot of beef."

"Yeah," Q said doubtfully.

"And if you want more variety, you could get the kids' mac and cheese," said Rose. The car turned into the parking lot and steered toward the wavy awnings. "Remember, it comes with two sides, so you could order apple-sauce and a crispy. Or broccoli and pineapple."

"I guess so," Q said doubtfully.

Z smiled.

In line Emma Z stood in front and listened while Rose kept talking through the options.

"Well, I know you like salad, sweetie. They have the chicken Veracruz, and I personally always like the Med, or there's a Caesar you can get with or without chicken. You like Caesar because of the romaine, that really crunchy kind of lettuce? So how about a salad, Q?"

"*May*be."

"Or there's chicken noodle soup. You like their chicken noodle, don't you?"

"It's too salty," said Q.

At the table Emma Z, chewing on a noodle, observed, "They're not really Japanese, though. I just like them."

"Why aren't they Japanese?" Rose asked.

"Um," said Z, and took a sip of lemonade. "I guess they're *sort* of Japanese? When we were in Yokohama over New Year's my dad took us to the *best* restaurant, which wasn't even fancy and it didn't even have tables. It was in the train station, and there were mostly just businessmen in there. It was really smoky, and you had to stand at the counter and eat noodles and broth from these bowls. They're called soba noodles, and they're made out of buckwheat. They put them in this spicy soup and crack an egg on top and you eat it almost raw. The cook really liked me, because my dad taught me how to order in Japanese. He gave me an extra egg. And it was only three-fifty yen." She looked up from her bowl at Rose. "That's about three dollars."

"Wow," said Rose, blinking fast.

"I don't like this, Mommy," said Q, pushing aside her bowl after probably two bites. Thai green curry with shrimp. Rose had ordered it for her after Q couldn't make up her mind. Definitely the *wrong* dish for Q, who was an incredibly picky eater even though her parents liked to pretend she wasn't.

"My mom makes really good curry," said Z. She picked out a cluster of sprouts and cilantro from her bowl and swallowed it after three chews. "We went to this spice market in Bangkok, I think? Or Chiang Mai? Anyway, she got these special spices there and uses them to make curry and pad Thai. But they're almost gone now."

"Well I guess you'll just have to go back to Thailand and get some more, won't you?" said Rose, with one of her creepy smiles.

Z shook her head. "This summer we have to go to Machu Picchu."

"Oh! Your mom didn't tell me that. Did you tell Silea?"

"Who?"

"Silea. She's from Peru."

Emma Z said nothing.

"The woman who cleans your house three times a week," said Rose.

"Oh, you mean *SilEEa*," said Z, getting bored. "I've only seen her one time, I think." She thought of the paper animals that kept appearing in her room after Silea's cleanings. There had been another one yesterday, a pink elephant on her dresser. Z had unfolded it like the others but still couldn't figure out how it went back together.

"She cleans our house too," said Q.

"Only once every two weeks, though," said Rose hastily.

Z looked up at Emma Q's mom as she finished her lemonade. Rose was staring at her in a way that wasn't nice at all, a way that actually looked kind of mean.

Z just raised her eyebrows and concentrated on her last delicious noodle. Yes indeedy centipedee. Q's mom was *really* irritating sometimes.

Scary, even.

TWENTY-THREE

ROSE

Notification day: mere hours and they would know.

As the light rose in the bedroom she stared at their water-stained ceiling and heard again the Emmas' voices in the car. A small part of her now wanted Q to be rejected, needed this whole thing to be done with, so her daughter could go back to being her sweet self and they could concentrate on raising an ethical child rather than an entitled little brat.

But only a small part. Most of her craved good news from the committee, the kind of news that would allow her to continue parsing the ins and outs of admissions criteria over the coming weeks with Lauren and Samantha, and perhaps Azra too; the kind of news that would give her and everyone else a sense that her daughter, even if ultimately not admitted to Crystal Academy, had passed through an objective assessment of her abilities and intelligence with flying colors.

In the kitchen that morning everyone was brittle and tense. Emma Q whined about the lunch her father was packing ("No egg salad, Daddy, you KNOW I hate egg salad!"), Rose snapped at Gareth when he dropped a table knife on the floor with a teeth-rattling clatter, and Gareth slapped his hand on a cupboard when Rose reminded him to schedule appointments with the dentist and orthodontist for Q. By the time she left for work she and Gareth were speaking to each other through clenched teeth and tightened lips and poor Q was nearly in tears over a piece of homework she'd forgotten at Twenty Birch.

Throughout the day at the lab Rose squirmed and shifted in her chair. As the hours at her desk unspooled—instrumentation costing, hiring proposals, a hastily eaten lunch over spreadsheets—she found herself constantly refreshing her email, just as agitated at work as she'd been at home and no kinder to those around her. She spoke sharply to two of her postdocs and grew impatient with a doctoral student for misunderstanding an equipment protocol. She felt like an ogre, hideous and impossible to be around.

Anything yet? Gareth texted just after three, trying to reach out, share her nervous anticipation of the results.

No, she replied, without further comment.

At four o'clock she logged out of her email and logged back on just to make sure the system was working correctly. Nothing. She walked down to the vending machines on the first floor, bought herself a Snickers bar, and gobbled the whole thing on her way back upstairs. Still nothing.

Finally, three minutes before five, an email dinged in.

Sender: Bitsy Leighton, City of Crystal School District

Subject: Crystal Academy Admissions Results, Round One

Rose took a deep breath and held it in like a cigarette drag. Blew out. Clicked.

A salutation, then three paragraphs.

Dear Dr. Holland:

We are writing to share the results of our initial round of admissions screening for Crystal Academy. We have been working with an excellent team of consultants to ensure that our review process is carried out with the utmost integrity and transparency. Nearly one hundred thousand students in grades five through eleven from throughout the Four Counties and the City of Crystal were given the opportunity to test, and nearly half of these students showed up for one of our testing sessions in March. The tabulated results have allowed us to emerge with a pool of roughly three thousand students from which the initial cohorts in the upper and lower schools will be selected.

Your child's scores on the Cognitive Proficiency test (CogPro) appear on the next page, along with a key to interpreting the results in each category. We wish to stress the importance of multiple assessment measures in determining each child's suitability for Crystal Academy. The results reported here are merely one such measure and do not necessarily reflect your child's abilities as a student or his/her/their promise for future matriculation in the academy itself or in one of the existing school-based programs for exceptional learners. However, this process requires us to make hard choices and clear distinctions so that the end result will be a truly distinguished cohort of young learners in the upper and lower schools.

Your child has scored sufficiently high on the CogPro to be advanced to the next round in the admissions process. Details of the subsequent steps will be provided at an upcoming orientation session for parents, to be held in the main auditorium at East Crystal High School on April 22 at 7:00 p.m. We look forward to seeing you there, and we will of course be happy to answer any additional questions that might arise during or following the information session.

Regards,
Bitsy

Elizabeth Leighton, Head of School
Crystal Academy

As a lapping sea of warm pride spread in Rose's chest a text popped up on her phone. Samantha, edging in.

Hey.

Hey, Rose replied.

Did you just hear?

Yes.

Want to rip off the Band-Aid?

Sure.

I'll go first. Just heard from Kev: Z made the cut.

Bravo!

What about Q?

Rose read the email a second time, just to be sure. Happily she tapped in her reply.

Yup.

Then, from Samantha: ☺☺☺☺☺☺☺☺☺

Rose smiled fondly at her phone. Crazy how a single email could be such a mood lifter. For weeks—months, really, since Thanksgiving at Twenty Birch—a growing part of her conscience had been thinking of the admissions process as a threat to the web of relationships between her family and Samantha's. Emma Z would get in, Emma Q wouldn't, and Rose's constant and low-burning envy of the Zellars would erupt into an open flame.

But perhaps the gifted school would prove less a threat to their complicated friendship than an opportunity for its growth in new and different directions. If the girls were both lucky enough to get a spot, there was no telling how their friendship might develop in the years ahead. The Emmas could continue sharing their interests, Rose and Samantha could continue carpooling and swapping weekends and evenings, their intertwined lives could continue to unfold as they always had.

Maybe nothing had to change.

TWENTY-FOUR

BECK

Leila, an upspeaking millennial and the only full-time designer on staff, was trying to talk Beck into adopting a fancy new software package for their shrinking client base, hoping a new look and new approach might scrape up new business. But Beck was old school. He liked the familiarity and ease of their current package, which happened to be free, unlike the one Leila was pushing, which would set the firm back two grand they obviously didn't have. Plus, the lazy side of him, which was most of him, didn't want to learn all the bells and whistles attached to this new stuff when Adobe worked just fine.

He'd been patiently explaining this to Leila for probably forty-five minutes, demonstrating on her own desktop all the things the current platform could do. She nodded along, reminding him of a shortcut or alternative methodology now and then—*Oh right, yeah, of course I knew about that*, Beck would sputter in reply. He had to admit, she was making a convincing case for this new package, ideal for navigating what looked increasingly like "a post-Adobe world," she'd claimed. Unfortunately, though, they just couldn't afford it—or much of anything else these days.

"Well," Beck said when he decided they were done, leaning back in his chair with his fingers interlaced behind his head. "You raise some good points, Leila. I'll make my decision by early next week, then we'll circle back on this. How's that sound?"

"Fine." She pushed her glasses up her nose. "Though—"

"Look, you made a strong argument here, Leila, don't get me wrong. But as CEO I need to see the big picture, you know? I have to think about overhead, accounts management, payroll."

"Right," Leila said, drawing it out. "Though . . . about that?"

"About . . ."

"Payroll?"

"Uh-huh?" He swallowed.

"My—sorry, but my paycheck hasn't been deposited the last two cycles?"

"Wait, what?"

"I'm on biweekly? And my salary hasn't shown up in my account, which I only noticed because I bounced a check."

"Join the club," Beck muttered.

"Huh?"

"I just meant—that can't be right. Are you sure?"

"Yeah, I'm sure."

"Well damn, Leila, I'm really sorry about that. I'm sure it's just an accounting glitch. In fact there have been some other funky things going on with the financial software. Let me check into it tomorrow and I'll—"

"Circle back?" she said. Her jaw was set and she was coming close to glaring at him. She pushed her glasses up again.

"Yes, I'll circle back," Beck said. "Tomorrow. I promise, okay?"

"Okay," she said, and pushed herself up from her chair, grabbed her purse, and left the studio without another word.

After she was gone Beck settled his frame back in his swivel chair and surfed porn, letting his nerves calm, delaying the drive home. He liked the vintage seventies stuff, straight-haired hippie girls in Woodstock scenarios, less hardcore than today's nastiness, though these days nothing really did it for him, and the sex drought was the least of his problems. Sonja's silent housekeeping strike was well into its second week by now. Stacks of unwashed dishes, Beck's laundry starting to sour, his wife doing the bare minimum to keep herself and Roy healthy and fed. As a result Beck had been spending more and more time at the design studio and in coffee shops, places where his creative juices could flow. There were also some emails from a few credit card companies that he'd have to handle creatively, with some wheedling on the phone. Nothing too worrisome, but things would go more smoothly if Sonja wasn't around for that.

Just after six he was transferring a balance from his corporate Platinum Visa to a somewhat dodgy high-annual-fee Discover card, his plan to deposit just enough of a cash advance to cover Leila's missing pay (or at least half of it), when his phone buzzed. Not a number he recognized.

"Hello?"

"Mr. Chaudhury?"

"Unsworth."

"Right, right. Andy Millward, from Rocky Mountain Fútbol, calling about your lads. Got a few minutes?"

"Absolutely," he said, heart rate notching up.

"Fine, then. We've reviewed Aidan and Charlie's applications, and we'd like to take a look. So let me tell you about our identification process." The coach detailed ROMO's procedures, the levels of evaluation that went into putting together the elite team, the cost for the season. Basically he wanted Beck to know what they might be getting into if the twins got spots on the squad. "A lot of our process will depend on position and fit. What it is, right, we can put twenty kids in the pool, and even with that, only eighteen will be rostered for any given game. The current side's spectacular. Deep. Honestly we could put together two squads in this age group without kicking a lamb."

"Wow." Beck had a lightning flash of the ski slope, Aidan's injured ankle. The sprain was mostly healed, but who knew how he'd feel once he was cleared to play.

"Other thing is, we're strong in the midfield but a little weak up top, meaning we're a tad more interested in Charlie than we are in Aidan, though we haven't seen either of them play yet."

"You don't have a sibling policy? You know, where a sibling gets preferential treatment if his brother's on the team."

Millward chuckled. "Not at this level, friend. ROMO's one of the top youth soccer academies in the country. Every lad for himself."

"I see."

"In any case we'd like to invite your boys to our next talent ID session." Millward gave him the details, then said a hasty goodbye.

Beck stood at a window overlooking the Emerald Mall. With his forehead resting against the glass he remembered the twins, not quite two, in the tub. Azra usually gave them their baths, but that night Beck had been in there with them, having a blast, wondering why he didn't do this more often. Aidan was trying out the word *brother*, a new acquisition, pronounced with his adorable lack of *r*'s as he pointed furiously at Charlie.

"*Bwudduh. Bwudduh. Bwudduh.*"

"That's right, Aidan," Beck said. "Charlie's your brother."

"Bwudduh bwudduh bwudduh bwudduh bwudduh."

"That's right."

Then, after a grunt of effort: "*Chah*wee *bwu*dduh. *Chah*wee *bwu*dduh." Aidan's first attempt at a sentence, a full thought. Not *Mommy milk*, not *Daddy carry*, but *Charlie brother*.

Beck clapped for him, thrilled to witness a leap like that. "Babe, you have to come in here!" he called out the bathroom door to Azra.

Then Aidan, getting up on his knees, arched himself forward and tackled Charlie in the bathtub, pushing him against the side and giving him a long, tight hug, their pinkish-amber skins joined in the water like the slick sides of seal pups as he yelled his two-word string over and over and over into his brother's ear. *Chahwee bwudduh Chahwee bwudduh Chahwee bwudduh.* Meanwhile Charlie smiled against his brother's shoulder and laughed and clapped his hands against Aidan's back—but that was all he could give him, because Charlie had only a few words at that point.

When they separated, Aidan got a confused little frown on his face at his brother's failure to respond. "Chahwee bwudduh?" he said in a squeaky voice, sadly this time. "Chahwee bwudduh?" Peering into his brother's eyes as if to say: *Don't you get it?*

Beck was heading out of the studio when his phone rang again. Azra.

"Any news yet?"

"About ROMO?"

"Didn't you get an email? Rose did and so did Samantha."

"What email?"

"About Crystal Academy, Aidan's CogPro score." She sounded frantic and sharp, as if she'd done a few lines of coke.

"Oh, I might have seen that."

"Well, what does it say? Tell me tell me!"

"Just a sec." He held his phone away, putting her on speaker. He tapped open his email and swiped down to the message from Leighton. "Okay, got it."

"Well?"

"Let's see, uh, 'share the results of our initial round of admissions' yadda yadda, 'pool of roughly three thousand students' yadda yadda—"

"Beck, come on."

"Okay, hold up." He scanned down until he found the key sentence. "Well, huh." Tormenting her.

"Beck, goddamnit!"

He turned off the speaker function and propped the phone against his ear, listening to her soft panting, wishing he could see Azra's face right now. Then he told her:

"Aidan made the cut."

TWENTY-FIVE

EMMA Z

"What was my score, Daddy?"

"That's none of your business, sweet pea."

"Of *course* it's my business, silly," she said. "It's my score."

The Zellars were all in the kitchen, where her mother was putting the finishing touches on something with lamb that smelled delicious. Daddy's old music scratched from the speaker, a man with a very low voice singing about a ring of fire. He Spotified this playlist at least once a week, but Z didn't mind.

"Well?" she said.

Her father took a sip of his whiskey drink, clanking the ice cubes around, then gave a long, exaggerated, funny sigh and shook his head at her mom. "What do you think, kitten?"

Her mom spun halfway around with one hand on her hip and a paring knife in the other. "I don't know about that," she said. "It's kind of private, Emma Z."

"Aw, let's just tell her," Kev said.

Her mom shrugged. "Fine by me. But don't let it leave this house, understood?"

"Understood," said Emma Z.

"You too." Her mom pointed the knife at her dad.

"Heart crossed." He reached to swat her on the fanny as she turned back to the stove.

"Kev," she said with a frown, nodding at Z, but then smiled secretly as she basted the lamb. Whenever she frowned at him she never really meant it. Not like Rose, who frowned at Gareth all the time and *always* meant it.

"Okay, then," he said, leaning over the counter with his mouth near Emma Z's hair. "You ready?" he whispered.

She nodded.

He leaned closer. "You sure?"

"Daddy, come *on*."

He put his mouth right up against her ear as if he were about to gobble it up. "You got a one-forty-five," he whispered.

"Really?"

Her mom looked over her shoulder.

"Really," her father said.

"Can I call Grandpa to tell him?" Z asked.

Her father straightened up and clanked his ice some more. "Sure, give the old man a call," he said, and took a big, long gulp of his whiskey drink.

TWENTY-SIX

ROSE

An April rain shower had blown east, sharpening the air and leaving behind low-swirled mists among the foothills. Rose unlocked her bike and was about to head home when she had a burst of inspiration. She made a few arrangements with a text and a call, then phoned Gareth.

She told him the CogPro news; then, "Let me take you to dinner," she said.

He hesitated. "A little premature, isn't it? And what about Emma Q?"

"Tessa can come over if we want her."

"Kind of a splurge," he said; *and spontaneous,* he didn't need to add. An impromptu dinner date wasn't like Rose at all: more the kind of annoying thing Gareth would spring on her when she had loads of work to get through.

She gently parried his objections, then made the proposition more appealing. "Plus I've achieved the impossible. Reservation for two at Xiomara." A new Chilean place on the mall. The Zellars were the only people Rose knew who had managed to dine there so far. It was too popular after a gushing write-up in *The New York Times* the week it launched: one of LA's top chefs relocating to the Rocky Mountain heartland to explore the diverse cuisines of his Chilean homeland infused with the subtle influence of the American Southwest. Or something like that.

"Six-thirty," Rose said, feeling adventurous. "Two spots at the bar, but they serve the full menu."

"See you in fifteen minutes." Her husband sounded pleased.

Unlike most restaurants on the Emerald Mall, Xiomara offered no out-door seating. Its modest entryway was guarded by window boxes and a phalanx of potted ferns that brushed Rose's neck as she passed by, her hands teasing her hair after the tight press of her bike helmet. Inside, the place had an almost bohemian feel, though the clientele was anything but: the first face she recognized belonged to one of Colorado's US senators.

Eight stools stood at the bar, one empty. Gareth smiled at her from the next. When she walked over, he kissed her on the mouth, lightly, without show, which she liked. He handed her the martini she had just tasted on his lips.

"Dry and dirty," he said. "With top-shelf vodka."

She hadn't intended to drink more than a single glass of wine but ended up ordering a pisco sour, which arrived along with a menu backed with tooled leather. "Meanwhile an amuse-bouche," the waiter said, and put two small cut-glass bowls in front of them, one sea green, one cobalt blue, each mounded with a delicate ceviche of sea bass and lime zest. The flavors bloomed on her tongue.

"This was a good idea," Gareth said. Rose put a hand on her husband's, a small concession.

"How was your day?" she asked.

"Believe it or not, I actually sent a short story in."

"Really?" As far as Rose knew Gareth hadn't submitted a piece of fiction in over a year. "What's it about?"

He shook his head. "Once I hear back from the journal."

"Fair enough."

They huddled over the menu, close together with their elbows touching.

———————

Emma Q's test score didn't come up until entrees, when Gareth wanted to know what happened next in the application process. She read him the results letter from her phone, and they bonded over their possibly exceptionally gifted daughter and her chances of admission. For once Rose felt that she had a full partner at an important moment in their parenting.

"What about Aidan?" he asked at one point.

Rose checked her texts. Nothing from Azra, not that Rose would have expected her to write after that tense exchange in her car.

"Xander?" he asked.

"I haven't heard from Lauren, but I mean, come on."

"Right." He gnawed on a chili-spiced short rib. "And Z?"

"Oh, she made the cut."

"Good for her," he said curtly, then signaled for another round.

Rose smiled down at her snapper, liking the salty edge in his voice. No doubt it would have been a small source of evil satisfaction for Gareth if Emma Z had failed to nail the CogPro, given his long history of distaste for Kev. Rose would have enjoyed that little shiver too, if she were being honest with herself. But the fact that the Emmas both did well was as it should be. There were hundreds of spots in the sixth grade, plenty of room for the two of them.

On the mall she wheeled her bike toward the car, too buzzed to ride. The night air tingled with such sweet possibility that Rose wasn't even a little bit grossed out when Gareth stopped in front of Crystal Books and pulled her in. As her bike crashed to the bricks she lifted up a leg, just for fun, and her husband dipped her in a Doisneau and pressed her lips.

"I've missed that." He stood her up.

"Me too," she said.

"What's with you tonight?" he asked, obviously loving it.

"Who knows." Rose smiled and swayed and let her husband lift her bike, an act he performed with a chivalrous ostentation that, if she'd been sober, would have annoyed her and certainly turned her off, but in the moment she found charming. They walked another block, and his hand went out with his keys to *bleep* the car doors unlocked. When he opened the hatch, they worked together to wedge her bike inside. Their fingers touched, their bodies bumped, and before she knew it Rose was wanting her husband's touch in a way she hadn't for months, maybe years.

Thankfully Emma Q was asleep when they got home. Gareth paid Tessa and Rose walked her out to her car and watched her drive off. She was about to head inside to have nondutiful sex with her husband when she was arrested by a voice in the night.

"Rose."

She peered through the low-hanging branches of a crabapple tree and saw Lauren at the fence with her old dog Aquinas, both of them cast in shadow by the streetlamp.

"Lauren, what are you doing here? Tessa just took off."

"I know. I was waiting until she left."

"Oh." *Well, that's weird*, Rose thought.

"Can I come in?"

"Of course, sweetie."

Rose opened the gate for her. They went inside to the living room, and Rose sat her friend in the middle of the sofa while Aquinas slumped at her feet. Lauren's cheeks were bright pink, eye sockets crimson and chafed.

"Do you want some ginger tea?" Rose asked. Gareth appeared in the kitchen, but she waved him away.

"I'm fine," Lauren said. "And I'm sorry to bother you."

"Oh, stop. Tell me what's going on." Rose sat down next to her so their knees touched.

"It's about Xander." She looked at Rose sidelong. "God, this is embarrassing. I can't believe I'm here." She gazed longingly at the front door.

"Lauren, just tell me."

She huffed out a sharp sigh. "He didn't get in."

"I'm sorry?"

"The CogPro." She blinked. "Xander didn't make the first cut."

"No." Rose kept her eyes poised in sympathy as her fear unwound.

Given Lauren's demeanor, she had been expecting disaster, awful news about one of their friends, maybe a cancer relapse. Her mind quickly adjusted against catastrophe—though for Lauren that's just what this was.

"It's ridiculous." Lauren inched her chin up. "It seems impossible."

"I know, insane." Rose shook her head, worked her sternest frown. "I mean, if anyone was going to ace the CogPro, it was Xander, you know?"

"Yes."

"So what happened?"

"He bombed the verbal. No surprise, but I assumed the other components would bring his cumulative up enough to pass the bar."

"That just really sucks."

"I'm so embarrassed."

"Embarrassed? Lauren, why would you be embarrassed about your son's test score?"

"Because everybody thinks of Xander as a genius. He's a very visible kid. The independent studies, the chess, all of it. Everybody's watching him all the time to see how he does on things, especially on something as *public* as this. Then look what happens. Now I have to face people at work, my friends . . ."

Rose nodded some more, trying to think of a useful nugget to share with her blindered, suffering friend.

"Well, I don't know if this is helpful or not," she said patiently. "But when Gareth used to get blue about his writing—you know, being late with his next novel, thinking his agent must be sitting around laughing at him— he'd keep this one quote taped to his monitor. Something like, 'You'll be a lot less obsessed with what people think of you when you understand how infrequently they do.' Some writer he likes said that. Just the idea that most people are usually thinking about themselves, not about others. The point is, no one will care what Xander's score was."

"But *I* care," Lauren said, offended. "Xander cares."

"Of course *you* care, Lauren. That wasn't my point. What I'm trying to say—"

"I just don't know what to do."

Rose steadied her breath. With Lauren always be practical, she reminded herself, not emotional. "Can you appeal? I thought I'd heard something about a process for that."

"Already on it."

"Good."

"What about Q?"

Rose hesitated.

Lauren said, flatly, "She made the cut, didn't she."

Rose nodded.

Lauren looked away. Her blinking sped up. "That's great. I'm happy for you." She spoke like a movie robot. "So that means Z definitely made it?"

Rose wanted to scream. Lauren simply had this *way* sometimes. You tried to be supportive, accommodating of her unfiltered flow, and she found a way to spatter it back in your face, like a wet cough.

"Y—es," Rose said. "Apparently Emma Z hit the mark too."

"Good for her," she said—exactly the way Gareth had said those same three words not one hour ago.

Lauren sprang to her feet. "Anyway. Thanks for listening."

"Hey, anytime." Rose put on a smile and stood with her. "Do you want me to say anything to the others?"

Lauren's face softened for a moment. "Would you? That would really help. I just can't face more conversations like this."

"Of course."

"Thank you, Rose." Without so much as a smile or a hug Lauren bee-lined out of the house, tugging Aquinas along behind her.

When the door shut, Gareth appeared in the kitchen. It was clear he'd been eavesdropping.

They locked eyes. "Christ," he said.

"I know," Rose said, and maybe it was being wound so tightly all day and now loosened by the alcohol and the rush of adrenaline from the awful yet somehow delicious news about Xander that caused a rare course of energy to thrill through her nerves.

Their therapist had long asked them to be more in the moment, to *jump each other's bones* when the feeling moved them, a phrase Rose despised,

THE GIFTED SCHOOL | 167

unable to recover the early lust this impromptu bone-jumping would require. Sex had become something that happened because therapeutically
prescribed. Perhaps once a month, if that.

Things felt different tonight. Wanton.

When Gareth saw the look on her face, he hesitated at the counter. "Do
you still—"

"Is Q asleep?"

He nodded. "But I mean is that something—"

"Yes but no talking."

In their room she pushed the bedspread aside and wrestled off the warm
socks she'd put on when they got home. He came over to help, and pulled
her shirt up over her breasts and from her arms but left it twisted around
her wrists and held it above her head as she fell back on the mattress. He
started to touch her, but she shook her head and pushed up against him and
they moved together like that, his slightly uncomfortable weight on top but
her hands pinned up there above the pillows in the way she used to like, the
rest of her writhing in unfamiliar pleasure beneath him. His breath moved
across her ear and along her neck; he'd brushed his teeth, maybe even
flossed. He never altered their positions but thrust against her pelvic bone
again and again and brought her almost there before moaning and collaps-
ing on her.

He withdrew and rolled off, leaving Rose frustrated, wanting to yank
him back on with her newly freed hands—but now another surprise as he
lowered himself down over the lower reach of her belly. Gentle pressure,
just right; and her breath went short. She bit her lip, she felt herself flush,
bit harder, she clawed her fingers into his scalp, and at the end she squeezed
her husband's head between her thighs and covered her mouth with a hand
to keep from waking Emma Q.

Afterward, unable to sleep while Gareth's gullet sawed away, she thought
about their lovemaking.

No, not lovemaking. What they had just shared, sparked by an email and seared hot by Lauren's misery, didn't deserve such an ennobling name. It had been, Rose thought with a reluctant but oddly delicious shiver, a carnal expression of parental pride.

But even that was too generous.

It was a schadenfreude fuck.

TWENTY-SEVEN

CH'AYÑA

She rose at dawn to put the coffee on, then took a blanket outside to wait. After five minutes of huddling on the top step she heard a rustle. The foxes appeared, a pair of them that denned in the little woods south of there, between the sprawl of the trailer park and the fancy riding stables on the other side. They always came to see about garbage and discarded food. Once they got a cat, which was nice for everyone; it had been a loud cat.

They nosed in a neglected mulch pile beneath the next trailer where the neighbor's dog liked to go when she was staked out. The dog barked from inside the house, and the foxes straightened their skinny necks, looking startled but unafraid.

Back inside Ch'ayña poured two cups of coffee and took one to her daughter, who was just sitting up. After three sips Silea set the mug on the bedside table and reached for her phone with her good hand.

"You don't need that," Ch'ayña chided her. "Too early for that thing."

"Atikcha will ask," said Silea. "He'll want to know how he did."

Ch'ayña shook her head and rose. Back in the kitchen she made an effort to clatter things.

"Mamay," Silea called down the short hall. "He's sleeping. And come here, let me read something to you."

Ch'ayña stood at the bedroom door and listened as Silea read out a letter from the school. Harder and harder for her, as she translated stumblingly for Ch'ayña. Silea was losing her mother's tongue.

Atik was different. He got better at Quechua by the day, Ch'ayña made sure of it, and not just the speaking. She'd found him a Quechua translation of some old Spanish book about a knight and windmills. It took him a while to work out the letters, but now he was reading everything he could, his school librarian ordering the few titles she could find, Atik wondering why there weren't more. *I'll teach you to read Quechua next, Awicha*, he'd promised her once or twice.

When the letter was done, Ch'ayña felt something go soft in her chest, a kind of reluctant loosening. *So you cared after all*, she scolded herself, but the relieved pride was too much not to share.

"I knew the *wawa* got an A," she whispered. "I knew already."

"The email just came," said Silea.

"But I could tell that very night when I picked him up, from the way he hopped in the truck." Ch'ayña sat on the edge of the bed. "The whole sixth grade came crowding out of the school. Our Atikcha was last. He saw the truck and gave me a wave and just plowed on through everybody and got in, like it was nothing. 'How'd the test go?' I said, and he took off his glasses and cleaned them that way he does with his breath and shirt, like he's forty years old behind a desk. Door's still open and he's wiping the glasses and he turns his head to me and says, 'That was *easy*, Awicha.' Quite a bragger, your *wawa*."

Silea was smiling over the phone.

"That's when I knew. That's when I knew already, that we'd get the news. And look there, we did."

"We did," said Silea.

"Read it to me again. Spanish is fine."

Silea read the email from her phone a second time. Ch'ayña shook her head. "'That was *easy*, Awicha,' he says. Little mouse. Little devil."

Atik's door opened. He peered out, looking scared at first. "Did you hear?" he asked.

Silea gestured for him to come, and Ch'ayña pulled him into the room. Atik sat on the bed next to her.

"Some news for you, Atikcha." Silea set down her coffee and handed him her phone. Atik held it in front of his face. His lips formed a half smile as he read the letter, almost a smirk.

"So you're in?" Ch'ayña asked him.

"Not yet," Atik replied. "But I will be."

He handed the phone back to his mamay, and the glow it made on his face showed his pride.

But it made Ch'ayña shiver a little, to see her grandson swell like this, and all through the day as she cleaned she wondered what it would mean, to send Atik to this new school, to surrender him to a place like Crystal with its flashy glass palaces and its spoon-fed whelps and its sidewalks clean as polished teeth. What it would do to their Atikcha to release him into a world like that, where he'd learn to strut like them, think like them, speak like them, live like them—then be forced to come back to Dry River, a new cock in the yard, bursting to escape.

A Touch of Tessa:
one GiRL's Survival GuiDe to Junior year
A Video Blog

Episode #159: A Big Surprise!!!!
. . . 19 views . . .

TESSA: Yo, guys, check it out!

[*Close-up of laptop opened to email: "Dear Ms. Frye: We are writing to share the results of our initial round of admissions screening for Crystal Academy. We have been working with an excellent team of consultants to ensure that our review process is carried out with the utmost integrity and transparency." Zoom in, scroll down.*]

TESSA: I mean, I didn't even vlog it before because I didn't think I had a chance, but Azra said I should just go for it and I did. Here's the important part.

[*Wobble, then focus on underlined text: "Your child has scored sufficiently high on the CogPro to be advanced to the next round in the admissions process. Details of the subsequent steps will be provided . . ." Reverse to Tessa, rolling eyes and beaming.*]

TESSA: This is *so* hype and my mom will flip. But here's the thing, because this isn't even the crazy part. The abso bizarre thing about all this is that Xander didn't pass. Seriously, you guys, my genius little brother didn't make the cut. And I don't want to throw shade or whatever but—what is *that* about, you know? Anyway. [*Shrugs.*] Low-key now, I am seriously proud of myself. I did this on my own, without her help, without anybody's help. This is *my* thing, not theirs, and it doesn't have anything to do with Xander. So I'm gonna keep going. Whatever it takes I'm doing it. You heard it here first, bitches. I'm getting into that fucking school.

TWENTY-EIGHT

XANDER

His mother was acting strangely tonight. Earlier she'd been stomping around the house cleaning things. Pots and pans slamming into the sink. The vacuum running over the same rugs three times. Finally she put Aquinas on his leash and took him for a walk, without a word.

Xander knocked on Tessa's door.

"What?"

"Fraternal unit."

"Begone."

He opened the door and walked in. Tessa looked up from her phone and gave him a funny smile. "Hey, little brother."

Xander said, "Mom's mad."

"Yeah, no shit."

"What's up her ass?" He used the word just to get his sister's attention. She kept smiling.

Xander sat on the edge of her bed. She stared at his neck, then his forehead. Her eyes went to the left, to the right. She couldn't hold them steady. Her eyes couldn't look at his eyes.

Xander said, "You're nervous. Palpably nervous."

"No, I'm not."

"There's something you're scared shitlessly to say."

"Stop trying to read my mind." She kicked at his leg. "It's creepy. Anyway I have long shifts at BloomAgain this weekend and have to do homework."

"You never do homework."

"Well, people can change," she said, kicking again.

Xander went up to his mother's study and played a game of online chess with a remarkably untalented Canadian man. When he got tired of that, he watched several of Tessa's latest vlogs. Episode 129 was called "Pandora's Box—or Pandora's Bust?" He watched it, then watched it again, slowing it down this time. He took a screen shot and zoomed in.

Ew.

Later Xander wandered into the kitchen, starving, because dinner had tasted like dog anus. He poured himself a bowl of granola and added yogurt. Seven bites in he stopped mid-chew when he heard his mother out on the deck, through the screen door. She was back from her walk. He went around to the darkened living room and crept forward until he could hear.

"His stanine was seven," she was saying. "They took nines and some eights."

The person on the other end said something.

"His nonverbal was astronomical. It was the verbal that killed him. . . . Fortieth percentile, something like that. . . . No, that's freaking *remedial.* . . . Well, it brought down the cumulative enough to sink him."

She listened again, for longer this time. Her head was shaking in the moonlight, and there was a sadness on her face that Xander knew.

"It's a public school, Mom. . . . No, they have to put a set standard in place and treat all scores the same way."

Xander's nana lived in Massachusetts. Apparently his Cognitive Proficiency test had not gone terrifically well.

"Of course we'll appeal it. . . . I've got an appointment with the admissions folks next week. If we can demonstrate some remarkable capacity on Xander's part . . . . No idea, Mom, maybe some kind of original, life-changing discovery? . . . Right, right. . . . I know, I know. But there might be a chance."

Original, life-changing discovery. Xander looked above his mother's head, up at the vast patterns in the stars.

"I know it is. . . . Believe me, Mom. . . . Absurd. I know." She leaned over and her forehead dropped into an open hand. "Well, we tell ourselves that, don't we? We always have. . . . But that's the thing, his last real IQ test was in second grade. . . . I don't know, Mom. Maybe he's just a weird kid with a nut allergy and a big head."

Xander walked back to his room and got into bed and put his hands around his skull. His head wasn't *that* big. He'd even measured it with a measuring tape before and checked it against the percentile charts. Besides, BABIES BORN WITH BIG HEADS ARE LIKELY MORE INTELLIGENT, according to a convincing article he'd seen in *Popular Science* last year at the orthodontist. Plus, his dad's head had been larger than average, or at least it looked that way in pictures.

Aquinas sniffed at his door. Xander helped the dog get his fat butt into bed and crawled in beside him. He squeezed a pillow with one arm and Aquinas with the other and looked out through the branches again, finding patterns he liked, lines and planes and surprising spirals among the stars—

His body shot up from the bed like a jack-in-the-box. He could see them now, the patterns, but also the surprises. What he didn't know was what they meant, or whether they meant anything at all. But he could find out, couldn't he? That was the whole point. So, how?

An experiment, a *real* experiment involving samples, and tests, and actual science, and—best of all—chess. Results he would easily be able to plot on a trifold so any idiot judge could understand them, even one who didn't know what a zugzwang was.

A cloud covered the moon, and as his eyes traced the silver glints along its edges Xander ran through all the things he'd need to do to make it work.

There was a risk, of course. But good science always carries risk, Mr. Aker said.

Rolling away from the window, he faced the darkness of his room. His nerves thrummed so loudly he could almost hear them playing inside him like a banjo. Because, yeah, maybe he wasn't a "voracious reader" like Emma Holland-Quinn. And maybe he couldn't juggle a soccer ball a thousand times like Aidan Unsworth-Chaudhury.

But if there was one thing Xander knew about it was patterns. Like in Maróczy-Bogoljubow (London, 1922), one of his favorite matches of all time, especially that amazing moment when Bogoljubow begins his counterdefense and Maróczy goes for his throat, those moves that tell you everything you need to know about the two players.

P–R3	Q–K2
Q–Q3	R–KKt1
Kt–B5	B x Kt

Set rules and endless variation.

Sequences and strings.

Predictability and uncertainty.

How certain pieces behave. How shapes fit together.

The code, Xander thought. *It's all in the code.*

Plus, it was *simple*. Almost too simple. But Mr. Aker would love it.

Original, life-changing discovery.

He went to sleep full of excitement about his plan. About these amazing things you can learn about people if you're willing to experiment a little.

Who they are.

Maybe especially who they aren't.

PART III

THE WHOLE CHILD

Profoundly gifted children are ones for whom intellectual stimulation and/or creative expression often are clearly emotional needs that may appear to be as intense as the physiological needs of hunger or thirst.

—JAMES T. WEBB,
Misdiagnosis and Dual Diagnoses of Gifted Children and Adults

April 16, 2018

Opinions

WITH STARS UPON THARS

This week, based on the arbitrary results of a single standardized test, the local school districts of the City of Crystal and the Four Counties have divided thousands of local schoolchildren into two camps.

On one side are those few whose performance on the Cognitive Proficiency test (CogPro) yielded a high enough score to pass them into the second round of admissions evaluation for Crystal Academy, the Front Range's newest magnet school for "exceptional learners," slated to open this coming August.

On the other side are those tens of thousands of students already denied any chance of admission to the school on the basis of a single ninety-minute IQ test.

Since the combined school boards announced the founding of Crystal Academy last fall, this paper's editorial staff has been divided on the whole concept of a magnet school for gifted children funded by public dollars.

Some feel strongly that gifted students represent a population with special needs—much the same as our neurodiverse students or those with physical disabilities—and that such needs are best met with additional resources designed to accommodate these unique abilities.

Others believe these same resources would be better spent on underserved student populations in need of remedial or compensatory education, or else spread out more evenly among those already being served by existing gifted-and-talented programs in our public schools.

What we can all agree on, however, is the need to safeguard against the inherent biases exhibited by standardized tests, such as the Cog-Pro, as well as the us-versus-them mentality promoted by some of the school's more avid supporters on the local school boards and City Council. So far we have heard nothing from the school boards about these difficult issues.

Worse yet, we have recently learned that the admissions process for the new gifted school will be overseen by an outside consulting firm, Dorne & Gardener, an outfit located in Washington, DC. Their work—funded at taxpayer expense—has so far been shrouded in secrecy, with little transparency regarding how the admissions process will account for differences of race, ethnicity, economic privilege, national origin, linguistic proficiency, and ability within and among the vast school-age population being evaluated.

How are parents supposed to have confidence in this labyrinthine admissions process overseen by corporate interests with little or no investment in our community and its schools?

We can only hope that the elected officials on the school boards of Crystal and the Four Counties will honor the democratic and egalitarian values of public education as this new venture moves forward—and that their work will promote the best interests of all the students they were elected to serve.

Our children deserve better.

TWENTY-NINE

ROSE

When she got a glimpse of her husband's legs out on the screened porch, Rose smiled and rolled her eyes, last night's mischief still fresh on her skin. Her head throbbed with a mild hangover but her body felt oddly awakened, twingey and alive. She veered into the kitchen and poured herself a cup of coffee and took it to the porch door. Gareth was stretched out on the sun-faded chaise longue with a student's journal opened on his lap.

He looked up at her, crinkling his eyes. "Hey you."

"Hey yourself."

He moved his legs to give her space at the end of the lounger. She stepped outside and breathed deeply to get the cool morning air oxygenating her blood. When she sat, he traced a finger up her spine. She shivered, liking his touch.

"You need to read something," he said.

"Sounds ominous." She sipped her coffee.

"Here." He picked up a quartered copy of *The Crystal Camera* from the side table and handed it to her with the lead editorial facing up. WITH STARS UPON THARS, the title read. It took her half a minute to get through the unsigned piece, the consensus view of the paper's editorial board. Predictable criticism of Crystal Academy for its elitism and bias, the us-versus-them mentality promoted by the school's supporters. Nothing new there.

Then the editorial went after the school's admissions process. Apparently—this was news to Rose—the second phase would be overseen by an outside consulting firm. The paper didn't like it, and the editorial concluded with a full-throated rant against the academy as an assault on the democratic and egalitarian values of public education.

"Well." She let the folded paper fall to her lap.

"What do you think?"

"For one thing, the results of the test aren't arbitrary," she said. "Every kid doesn't have an equal chance of testing well. The results are systematic, not random. That's Stats One-oh-one."

He peered at her over his mug. "You're thinking like a scientist. But to your average parent whose kid didn't make the cut, they're kind of a crock. And this stuff about corporate money? I had no idea."

Neither had Rose, though she said nothing in reply.

"So do we really want to be putting Emma through another gauntlet like this?" he went on. "There's a lot of bad blood out there."

"Of course there is. Parents don't like to have their kids judged against others. If Q hadn't made the cut, we'd probably feel the same way."

"I already do."

"Oh really," Rose said, bristling.

"Kind of. You saw how nervous Emma was the morning of the test. She barely ate her breakfast."

"Well, she's not exactly starving."

"Wait, what?" His stare made her flinch.

"Just—nothing," she said, ashamed. She started to rise, but Gareth reached out and tugged at the hem of her nightgown, keeping her on the chaise.

"Look, Rose." Going into lecture mode. "I want us to be on the same page here. This school—I'm just not liking the vibe. I mean look at Lauren last night. She was a wreck, and for what? Because Xander might have to stay at one school for gifted kids rather than go to *another* school for gifted kids?"

"Yeah, but that's just Lauren," Rose protested. "Plus Odyssey costs her an arm and a leg, and Crystal Academy would be free."

"So are all the other public schools. Besides, it's not as if Q will suffer if she goes to Red Rocks as planned. The schools out here are already some of the best in the country, and then you hear high school kids like Tessa talking about all the stress, multiple APs a year, the massive amount of testing. So why add to that with something like Crystal Academy? It's a pressure cooker inside a pressure cooker. Plus, Q loves the time she gets with Mr. Wilkins every week."

"Who?"

"Um, Mr. Wilkins? The gifted-and-talented instructor she's had at Donnelly for the last two years?"

"Oh, right."

Gareth pursed his lips, a pious look. Rose felt her twelve-hour flush of lust cool back into the familiar mild repulsion she always felt toward her husband. *Well that was quick.*

She leaned away from him, trying to recover her composure. "Why don't we ask Q what she wants?"

"You mean—"

"About Crystal Academy, the whole admissions process. If she wants to pull out, then fine. And if she wants to keep going, we let her."

"Okay." Gareth sounded suspicious. "But what if—"

"Speak of our little devil," Rose said as their daughter appeared at the bottom of the stairs, dragging her favorite fleece blanket behind her. "Hey, sweetie, come on out," she called through the door. Emma Q traipsed out onto the porch, rubbing her sleepy eyes with the back of a hand. Her button nose lifted into the air, she climbed up into Gareth's lap and put her feet on Rose's legs.

Rose stared at their daughter in a new way. One of her colleagues in neuropsychology who researched animal cognition claimed that the minds of dogs could distinguish among an almost infinite array of scents. Three hundred million olfactory receptors in their noses, while humans have only six million. As Q lay there bundled in her pajamas and blanket, Rose imagined her daughter's neuronal receptors sifting the world, the thousand mingled scents of the outdoors.

"Rose. *Rose.*"

She looked up at Gareth.

"What are you thinking?"

Profoundly gifted. She was thinking that Emma Q got a 135. Their daughter had knocked the CogPro out of the goddamn park.

"About oatmeal. Do you want some, Q?" Rose touched her daughter's nose with a fingertip.

Q said, "I'll have cheese eggs, please, plus white toast," and beautifully sniffed again. She turned to watch a squirrel hopping through the weeds in their postage-stamp backyard.

"So, before you eat," Rose said, "we have something we wanted to talk to you about."

"Is this the right time?" Gareth asked.

"Right time for what?" Q said.

"We can wait," Rose answered lightly, but she knew her daughter.

"I don't *like* waiting." Q wriggled on Gareth's lap. He looked over at Rose and shrugged.

"Well, okay then," Rose said. "So listen, Emma. We got some news last night, about that test you took."

"The CogPro?"

"That's right. You did very well."

"Really?"

"Really," Gareth said behind her.

She bent her head back against his ribs and looked up at his chin. "*How well, Daddy?*"

"That's not important."

"You got a one-thirty-five," Rose said.

"*Jesus,*" Gareth snapped. "Rose—"

"*Really?* A one-thirty-*five?*" Q said. "But that's—that's *way* higher than I got on any of the practice tests!"

"I know it is," Rose said, patting her daughter's blanketed knee. "You did just great. But Daddy wants—*we* want to make sure this is all okay with you. The testing, the admissions stuff with Crystal Academy. We want this to be your choice, Emma."

"What your mother's saying is that you don't have to keep going with all this if you don't want to," Gareth assured her. "You've been looking forward to regular middle school all year, haven't you?"

"I—guess so," Q said.

"You know a ton of kids who will be at Red Rocks, plus you could walk there just like you do to Donnelly now."

"Right." Q sat there for a moment, thinking it over. "But are you saying you don't think I can get in? Because Z told me that's what Xander said to Mom."

"Of *course* not, Q, of *course* not," Gareth said soothingly. He squeezed her arms. "We just want this to be your decision, not ours."

Emma Q's brow knotted into a little frown. Then suddenly her eyes widened. "Wait. Did Z make the cut?"

"She did," Rose said.

Q's shoulders slumped. "What was her score?"

"I didn't ask," Rose said. "And you shouldn't either, sweetie, okay? No score-swapping this time."

"But is she still applying?"

"As far as I know," Rose said.

Q pushed herself off Gareth's lap and let her blanket fall to the deck, where it puddled around her ankles. "Well, if Z's still doing it, then I still am. Obvs."

"You sure about that?" Gareth asked, though Rose could tell from the look on her husband's face that he knew Emma Q wouldn't budge—just as Rose had suspected.

"I'm sure," Q said.

Rose stood and took Q's hand. "Let's go see about those cheese eggs." She turned her back on Gareth to lead their daughter inside.

THIRTY

BECK

Azra handed him a glass of wine, and they settled together on her shady front stoop to wait for the twins, who'd left for a walk around the block with Roy. Beck knew he should be getting home, but it was nice up here, sitting with his ex-wife in front of the art-filled, mortgage-free house where she grew up, inherited when her folks died, and where he got to live for what he still regarded—secretly, guiltily—as the best ten years of his life. There was a cool, dry breeze coming in off the foothills and he'd rather have been drinking a hoppy pale ale but the wine was good, crisp and tart.

"I'm really worried about Charlie," said Azra. "Have you talked to him about the school?"

"Should I have?" Beck asked. They hadn't spoken since the test results came in, and Beck had hardly given the matter another thought.

"He keeps bringing it up in these weird ways."

"How did he take it when you first told him that Aid made the cut?"

"At first he just laughed it off and called Aidan a gradetard. You know how they do."

"Uh-huh. But I just can't see Charlie getting jealous about a test he didn't even take."

"It's hit him hard, Beck. He's used to being the best at school, the best at sports, but now all of a sudden he's got his twin brother getting out ahead of him, starting on the soccer team when he's on the bench, maybe going to a new magnet school. He's been saying things like, 'Well, I guess it's the *slow* brother's turn to empty the dishwasher tonight.' Or 'Kind of hard to concentrate on my homework when I know the starting midfielder in the living room could do it for me in like five minutes.' You know?"

Beck thought about it. "I did hear him say something like that the other day. 'Wish I was brilliant enough to make my own lunch' kind of thing." He drained his glass.

She reached for the bottle on the top step.

"Well, look," he said as she topped him off. "So maybe we don't keep going with it."

"The academy?"

"If it's creating friction. Why create such high expectations when it's only going to set him up for disappointment?"

"You mean like soccer."

"That's different."

"How so?"

"The twins have a natural gift for soccer," he said. "It also happens to be the thing they care about the most."

Azra coughed in that way.

"What?"

"Beck, come on. It's the thing *you* care about the most. I see you on the sidelines, pretending not to give a damn while you're boiling inside. It's always been like this. You're the one who took them out to shoot penalty kicks when they were four, the one who pushed them into trying out for travel when they were happy in select. And you were the one who convinced them to go for this ROMO thing."

"Hey, that's bullshit. They've been dreaming about this for almost a year."

"Please. The boys wouldn't have known that league even *existed* if you hadn't put the idea in their heads."

Beck looked down at her hands, at those long fingers crossed over one knee.

"I've told you before how I feel about this stuff," he said. "I say we pull the plug. That's my vote."

"All I'm asking is that you keep an open mind, okay?" she pressed him. "This could be really good for Aidan. Maybe it will bring him out of his shell, introduce him to a new set of kids who won't make him feel embarrassed about being bright."

"What if he doesn't get in?"

"Well, he probably won't," said Azra matter-of-factly. "The important thing is that he try, because I think he actually wants to see if he can. So please be encouraging about it." She rocked forward and looked up the street. "They're coming."

Aidan was out front, dancing backward and singing wildly, swaying his hips back and forth, making Roy scream with laughter. The baby strained against his straps to reach for his big brother. Charlie, unamused, pushed the stroller. Beck smiled and waved, but Charlie's mouth stayed flatlined.

Azra stood and took his wineglass. "There's another thing."

"Uh-oh," said Beck, rising with her.

"A meeting about the final admissions cut. We have to put together a portfolio."

"When is it?"

"Thursday at seven-thirty. We should both go. I'll text you the details."

She stood on her tiptoes to give him an awkward hug, holding the wineglasses wide and away. He felt a familiar surge and squeezed her around the waist, maybe a little too low. Her body stiffened.

"Beck, stop."

"Sorry, sorry." He took a half step back, hands spread in the air.

She looked at him oddly. "Is everything okay? With you, I mean?"

He felt unbalanced, suddenly ill. A zapping sensation shot across the crest of his head and his vision filled with the scrolling flicker of his fuck-ups, like movie credits: maxed-out bank cards and floating balances, the night screams of a baby and the new coldness of his wife, a flabbifying midsection, old food moldering in the pit of a garbage disposal broken for months, Charlie slumped on the soccer bench with the other scrubs.

"Beck?"

"Yeah, I'm good," he said, blinking. She knew him too well, but maybe not well enough.

She bonked a wineglass on his elbow. "Don't forget the meeting."

THIRTY-ONE

ROSE

M om."

A shaky voice from down the hall, drawn out. Rose went to Emma Q's bedroom and found her stretched out on top of her comforter, forlorn, with smeared cheeks and a moist nose and her phone clasped tightly in her hands.

"Oh, honey, what's wrong?" She grabbed a tissue from Q's nightstand and stooped to swipe it across her daughter's upper lip.

"Z got a—a—" Then something indistinguishable. Rose pulled out another tissue and tried again, peeved. Just what they needed: another tiff with Emma Z. They happened every month or so; though no matter how trivial the provocation, Q's face was a wonder when she cried, a splotchy mess of florid pinks and shocking reds.

"Q, what is it? What did Z do this time?"

Emma Q shook her wet head. "Nothing. She got—she texted me. She got a one-forty-five."

"You mean—"

"On the CogPro. That's ten points higher than *me*. She said the cutoff was one-*thirty*, which is almost what *I* got."

"Oh," Rose said, dying inside. So the girls were swapping scores, this time the real thing.

"So I'm already eliminated, right?"

"We don't know that, Q." Though Rose was having the same thought. "That score is just the first step. Now that you and Z are both in the final pool together you'll be treated exactly the same."

"Really?"

"Of course really," Rose said—though was this true?

"But why is Z so *mean* all the time? Why does she want to *beat* me at everything?"

"Oh, honey." Rose pulled Q into her arms and let her sob it out for a little while. But beneath the surge of protective love for her daughter she felt a hard knob of fury at Emma Zellar for inciting this constant, nasty rivalry between the girls, at Samantha for encouraging it—and at herself for marinating in its juices so often.

Q stopped sniffling and backed away, looking at her with eyes wide and sober. Aware of what was at stake; wanting it. "So then how will they make the final cut? I really want to know."

Rose smiled proudly at her daughter and wiped her cheek with the end of a sleeve. "So do I, Emma," she said slowly. "So. Do. I."

She couldn't blame Q for what happened the next morning, the chain of competitive idiocy that started to unspool, link by link. Rose was the one who would pick up her phone at the lab, touch in the number, start a conversation and then a second conversation it would have been so much smarter to avoid. But her daughter's anxious question had planted the idea.

She waited until ten before calling. The phone was picked up on the first ring.

"Bitsy Leighton."

"Oh. I wasn't expecting to reach you directly." Rose swallowed, speaking low because her office door was open to the lab. "My daughter tested recently for Crystal Academy?"

"Our procedures for appeal are laid out on the school's website."

"No, Emma made the cut."

"Wonderful. And you'll be at the second-stage admissions meeting?" Her tone of voice had instantly changed, from dismissive to inviting.

"Of course."

"So how can I help you, Ms.—?"

"Doctor, actually. Dr. Rose Holland." She winced at herself. "Rose."

"How can I help you, Rose?"

"I know you'll be very busy once the next round begins," she said, speaking quickly, "so I was wondering if you might have time to discuss a few matters about the school."

"What sorts of matters?"

The thought came in a startling flash, though later she would recall that she sounded even to herself as if she'd rehearsed every word. "My curiosity isn't just parental. I'm a pediatric neurologist in the med school. Our lab has done some work on childhood brain development."

True, sort of.

"Right now we're thinking of proposing a longitudinal study on gifted children and brain development."

An unambiguous lie. It just shot out, like an unanticipated sneeze.

"Tell me more," Bitsy said, sounding intrigued.

Rose thought for a moment. "Well, given the size of the first intake and the wide range of aptitudes, backgrounds, and demographics, your assessment work during the admissions process might make for an ideal sample."

Rose could almost hear Leighton's mental calculations as she improvised: the braggable prestige such a cooperative venture with the local university would bring to a new school. Bitsy asked a few additional questions, then suggested coffee later that same morning at Higher Grounds, a café on the Emerald Mall.

Rose disconnected and her face quavered on the phone's darkened screen.

She had seen Bitsy Leighton only from a distance, during an informational session about Crystal Academy. Bitsy had appeared the coolest of customers then, a tall and confident woman perhaps five years Rose's senior who had retained her stolid boarding school demeanor while being hammered with anxious, probing questions from all sides. Now Rose would have the woman to herself.

When Bitsy came in, the bell tinkled and banged on the glass. She waved off Rose's offer to treat her, instead standing in line until she got her cappuccino. Rose studied the woman's shoulder-length silver bob, pushed back in a brown band that left the full width of a pale forehead exposed. A simply cut burgundy suit worn over flat loafers gave the impression of a woman entirely unconcerned with style.

Bitsy licked a slug of foam off the side of the cup on her way to the table. After pleasantries Rose said, "So tell me about your background."

"I grew up outside of Boston and graduated from Princeton," Bitsy said. "Then I did my doctorate in elementary education at Columbia."

"Teachers College?"

"That's right."

Rose asked her about the testing regimen for the academy. The choice of the CogPro, the deliberations over next steps.

"I won't pretend the tests aren't important," Bitsy said. "For one thing they've eliminated seventy to eighty percent of the prospective students."

"Wow, that many."

"Yes, and believe me, we're hearing about it from the parents." Her brow went up. Rose thought of Lauren, the desolation on her friend's face.

Bitsy continued. "We want the second-stage evaluations to be as effective as possible. The fewer students we're assessing, the better."

"Tell me about this next stage." Rose poised her pen above her notepad, waiting for the details. "How specifically will applicants be evaluated?"

"For Crystal Academy we're assessing the whole child. Aptitudes and special talents. Perseverance and stick-to-it-iveness. Does she play a musical instrument with particular distinction? Does he have a unique approach to problem solving? Do they express themselves in complex sentences that suggest a level of abstraction that separates them from their peers? We're also on the lookout for the two-E kids."

"'Two E'?"

"The twice exceptionals. Kids with high intelligence and coexisting disabilities that might prevent them from performing to their potential on a test like the CogPro."

"So you're using both quantitative and qualitative data to assess each child."

"That's right." Bitsy nodded with vigor. "The CogPro for an anchor score, and then the individual assessments for a more rounded sense of the child. Also important is fit with the academy's program and curriculum."

"Fit?"

"We want to recruit an active, curious bunch of kids for the first cohort. A diverse community of exceptional learners united by a fierce desire to push the boundaries of learning to transform themselves and the world around them."

"Sounds like a mission statement."

"We're working on one."

"And what will distinguish those selected?"

"We'll be looking for a range of exceptionalities. Stand-aparts in knowledge or abilities or particular talents. Math whizzes. History buffs. Incredible athletes. Kids who've been playing with their chemistry sets since kindergarten and want to tell you everything they know about—oh, I don't know, benzine."

Or Plains leopard frogs.

"An obsession, then," Rose suggested.

Bitsy waggled a hand. "Too negative. More of a spike. Some of these kids, they'll knock you flat. We have an eighth grader in the pool who's already doing second-year calculus at the university. A sixth grader from out in Beulah who's a master origamicist."

"A what?"

"He makes beautiful paper animals and things; his teachers say they're just dazzling. Oh, and he's trilingual to boot. And we have a fifth grader from here in Crystal who performs hip-hop lyrics with a Shakespearean twist. The kid has two million followers on Songbird."

"That sounds familiar," Rose said. An old teammate of Charlie's, she thought; maybe Azra had mentioned him.

The door opened, bringing a breeze. "It's a challenge, I won't varnish the truth for you," Bitsy said. "We're trying to identify a thousand kids out of a pool of, what, a hundred thousand? These kids will be Rhodes scholars and Supreme Court clerks. They'll be international thought leaders; I mean, you can see them giving TED Talks in ten years."

Rose hummed in approval.

"What excites me most of all, though," Bitsy went on, leaning forward, lowering her voice as if sharing a great secret, "is the fact that Crystal Academy will be a *public* institution, with a *public* mission. We're not opening an elite boarding school here, or a private day school removed from the community, with helicopter parents checking in every day with the guidance counselors. We want the academy's culture to be the diametric opposite of all that."

"How so?"

"Well, I don't know where you grew up, Rose. But if you emerge from a certain East Coast background, you'll know what I'm talking about. All the wealth and entitlement disguised as ability and smarts. Because if your grandfather went to Exeter or Andover, *you* can go to Exeter or Andover. If you have a horse to board and a senator in the family, your girl can get into Madeira. If your mom's Speaker of the House, you can bet your bippy you'll get a spot at Episcopal. All it takes is money and the right connections and you can get your child into the most elite private schools in America." She sniffed. "But Crystal Academy? No. I'm sorry, but no. Those old families and elite networks don't mean a darn thing out here on the Front Range. Because I remember those privileged kids, believe me. I was *one* of them." She paused to gauge Rose's reaction. "You can tell I'm rather passionate about all this."

"That comes across," Rose said, though she had to bite her lip, because Bitsy Leighton had no idea how many of her buttons she was pushing. Always that intangible sense of injustice, when she was young, a suspicion that the more polished and affable kids were getting things they didn't deserve: blue ribbons for best essays, the teacherly nods. Rose's chest would split with envy when she saw their easy ways with grown-ups in positions of authority, their new clothes in the right labels. Money, though, had been only part of it. The greater injustices derived from family culture. Rose's parents had possessed neither the time nor the cynicism to shield her from two poisonously cliquish schools, a run of bad teachers, a lazy guidance counselor who, she now saw, might easily have pointed her to the sky like a rocket, fueled and ready to soar.

Meanwhile it had been these same entitled kids who got the invitations to apply for the special summer programs, whose parents enrolled them in prep courses for the PSAT and SAT—tests that Rose had murdered all on her own, which was what had finally gotten her out, though not to Penn or to Bryn Mawr or to Yale. Instead she'd won a full academic scholarship to Lehigh, set aside for first-generation local kids from the surrounding valley, and the least true thing anyone could say about her was that she never looked back. She looked back all the time, most recently through the refracting lens of her daughter, who enjoyed the benefits of a mother's hands-on investment in her schooling that Rose had never received. Unfair to Q, perhaps, all this building pressure; but then its absence had been unfair to Rose.

"So you can see why we're not taking this initial admission cycle lightly," Bitsy continued. "This will be the first intake. Our canaries in the coal mine. We're putting all of our resources and energy into identifying *la crème la plus pure de la crème.*"

She wiped her napkin fiercely over her lips, balled it up, and stuffed it in her empty cup.

"Now." She looked at Rose and tilted her head. "Tell me about this study of yours."

Bitsy Leighton clip-clopped east over the bricks while her thumbs worked furiously at her phone. Rose tried to read Q's admission chances in the woman's profile and gait. When Leighton turned the corner on Lapis Lane, Rose pressed a hand to her temple, and a rare panic rattled through her chest. *A longitudinal study of gifted children and brain development?* She'd done a decent job of faking it in there, but a few questions to anyone who knew her research and Leighton would learn that she worked on tissues from dead people, not the minds of living ones. Rose was no more qualified to design and execute such a study than Gareth was to play second base for the Colorado Rockies. What the hell had she been thinking?

Rose had always been a controlled and guarded person, cautious in what she divulged about herself, protective of her work, her family, her reputation. But somehow this business with Crystal Academy was unmooring. Easy lies spilled from her mouth like water from a broken faucet.

And suppose there were interviews in the second round, and Emma Q showed up for the appointment with her mother and father. Would Bitsy Leighton ask Rose about the study in front of Gareth, forcing her to tell further lies on the spot—or cough out a humiliating confession? Once Leighton discovered that Rose had lied to her, would she hold this against Q?

Before Rose had taken ten steps up the mall her phone buzzed.

So what did you learn? Anything useful?

She stared at Samantha's message for a moment before replying.

???

From your appointment.

Rose stopped walking and texted back a question: **What appointment?**

With BITSY, you sneaky bitch.

She almost dropped her phone. No one else knew she was meeting with Leighton this afternoon. Not Samantha, not Lauren, not Azra, not even Gareth. Leighton must have slipped the news to Sam, or someone who knew her.

Her thumb hesitated, suspended above the screen when the next message arrived.

Look to your right!

She lifted her head and saw a flapping hand through the plate glass window of the Aspen Room, a spa across from Higher Grounds. There, less than twenty feet away, Samantha sat with one foot soaking in a pedicure basin, the other in mid-buffing at the hands of an aesthetician.

Sam held up her phone and blew her a kiss—followed by a knowing smirk, her smooth face twisted and cynical. Rose smiled weakly before turning away.

When she checked her email in the car, a message from Bitsy Leighton already waited in her in-box: *R, Thx for meeting today. I'll be in touch soon about follow-up. Can't wait to hear more. BL*

Rose looked up into the cold half-light of the parking garage, feeling exposed. She wanted to erase, redo, rewind. Fly against the earth's rotation, pull against time. She bent her forehead to the steering wheel and already sensed her stupid bit of deceit festering somewhere, surging and angry, like a boil under the skin.

THIRTY-TWO

XANDER

Charlie Unsworth-Chaudhury was hitting baseballs into a new net in his backyard. Every time he hit a ball at the net the ball bounced back to his feet, and then he picked it up and hit it against the net again. And again. And again.

Xander tried to think of something that would be more boring to do. He couldn't. It just wasn't an interesting pattern. You would never practice the same chess move thirty-one times in a row like

Qc2xh7

Qh7–c2

Qc2xh7

Qh7–c2

Qc2xh7

Qh7–c2

Qc2xh7

Qh7–c2

and so on.

But baseball wasn't chess. It had different structures, different reasons for repeating things. He watched Charlie hit the ball into the net thirty-one more times then went inside and found Aidan playing *SoccerPro19* in the den.

"Yo," said Aidan.

"Yo," said Xander.

"Wanna play *SwordQuest*?"

"Okay."

Aidan switched out the console, and they started slicing and dicing other beings. The twins owned the adult version of the game. Lots of blood and body parts and half-naked ladies. Something Xander's mother would never let him have.

Xander died on purpose. "Gotta poop," he said.

"TMI," said Aidan. He kept slaughtering things as Xander stood and walked upstairs.

Xander went into the twins' bathroom and locked the door. From his pocket he removed the two new toothbrushes he'd bought at CVS. Last time he was over here he'd checked the brand and colors to make sure he got the right ones. Aidan's was a Crest Extra Cleaning with soft bristles and a blue swatch on the handle. Perfect match.

He unwrapped the new one, smeared toothpaste on the bristles, wet them, and brushed his teeth. He rinsed it but not very well, then put it in the holder.

He did the same thing with Charlie's current toothbrush. A Crest Extra Cleaning with soft bristles and a red swatch on the handle. Another perfect match.

Once the new toothbrushes were back in place, he sealed the old toothbrushes inside sandwich bags. He peed, flushed the toilet, washed his hands, and headed back downstairs.

Two down, three to go.

Sonja didn't wear much when she was lounging around the house. That day the silky thing she had on barely covered her buttocks area. When she fed Roy, she pushed her top down and just sat there in the living room without covering anything up. Xander had once asked his mother why the twins' stepmom showed herself like that. "She's Austrian," his mother had said.

Usually Xander looked away, but right now he had to pay attention, watching her from the darkened staircase.

After she burped Roy, Sonja took out a machine and hooked it up to one of her shabangas. Roy scuttled around on the floor for a few minutes until Sonja had half filled a bottle and turned off the pump. She wrote something on the lid with a Sharpie and put the bottle in the refrigerator. Then she took Roy up for his nap, leaving the door to his room open a few inches.

Once she was singing to him, Xander crept up the stairs and down the hall and into the master bedroom. He looked around for a few seconds, then went to one of the nightstands at the side of the king-size bed. He opened a drawer.

A red box of condoms. LifeStyles brand. The box was open and half-empty.

Xander thought about it. The Unsworths didn't empty their trash that often, not like his mother. The house was pretty dirty, actually kind of disgusting. So he might get lucky.

He walked into the bathroom and squatted down in front of the trash can and pushed aside wads of tissue until he found it all the way near the bottom; or rather them. Two used condoms, clumped together. They must have been in there for weeks.

Xander took out a sandwich bag. Using a piece of tissue paper, he pincered the condoms between two fingers. He shook them gently until one of them unclumped and fell back into the trash can.

He held the other one up in front of his face. The condom was interesting. It was dry on the outside, but inside he could see Beck's semen. It looked like spit, like the kind of big loogie Charlie hocked when he wanted to gross someone out.

Xander sniffed the condom. Rubber and something else. He sealed it in a bag and shoved the bag in his pocket as he stood. On the way out of the bathroom he swiped a pair of tweezers from the medicine cabinet.

Three down, two to go.

———

Sonja was still putting Roy to bed. Singing one of her German songs, quite badly out of tune. He could also still hear the thwack of Charlie's bat outside. And the sound of Aidan scoring kills in the basement.

He went down to the kitchen and opened the refrigerator. Sonja kept her milk in the door, on the bottom shelf. He squatted down and felt each bottle until he found the warm one, with that day's date written on the lid. He took out a sandwich bag and put the small bottle inside and slipped it into his pocket. Which was getting kind of full.

Four down, one to go.

The twins were playing *SoccerPro19* in the den. In the living room Sonja was asleep on the sofa, sprawled across the cushions with an arm over her eyes and her knees spread open. Xander tried not to look as he walked past her, but he couldn't help it. He felt really glad his mother didn't lie around like that, almost naked. Glad his house was clean and orderly.

Upstairs Roy's door was cracked open an inch. The hinges squeaked, but just a little.

Inside it was dark and cool—and clean. A ceiling fan made it windy, and there was soft baby music playing. Roy was dressed in a one-piece footie jumper and sleeping on his tummy. He had a blanket clutched in his right hand. His left hand was open and down by his side.

Thick hair for a baby. Wavy, like Beck's, but yellow, like Sonja's. Which made sense.

Xander slipped out the tweezers he'd swiped from the master bathroom. He reached down into the crib, pincered a few of Roy's hairs near the scalp, and pulled.

THIRTY-THREE

CH'AYÑA

When she went to close the back of the truck, Ch'ayña saw them. Two brown paper bags, bulging with clothes. She pulled the near one to her chest and tugged on the hem of a silk skirt, fingered the linen sleeve of a dress.

"What's this?" she called out, but Atik was already in the cab. She walked around to the passenger side. "What's all this?" she demanded, shoving the bag at him.

"Ms. Zellar gave them to us," he said. "We're supposed to take them for Mamay."

She shifted the bag to her hip and dug through. Scarves, a leather jacket, shirts of thin silk, a nightgown. "Your mamay won't wear these ugly things. They're useless. Take them back to her."

"We can't."

"What, they were a gift?"

Atik shook his head. "They're a sorry-for-you because of her elbow. Like the coins you give to a man on the street."

"I never give to those men, and you shouldn't either, Atikcha. Keep your money!"

"We have to take the clothes," he said, looking tired.

As they drove off she let him know what she thought of the gift that wasn't a gift. "And now we'll have to stop at the dumpster."

"Turn right, Awicha," said Atik.

"That's the wrong way."

"Turn right. I'll show you."

So she turned right.

That night she told Silea what had happened next.

"Your son had an idea," said Ch'ayña. "'We'll sell them,' he said. 'We'll keep two or three things so Mamay can wear them and show Ms. Zellar she's wearing them when she goes to clean again. The others, we sell.' So we brought the bags to a store there by the middle city park. You know the place."

"BloomAgain," Silea said.

"They sell used clothes but only those that still look new. I told Atik I'd wait in the truck, but he made me come in the store with him because he's too young to sell them himself. He took the bags to the front and talked to the girl behind the counter. She was wearing a tight short shirt, and you could see her navel with a ring in it there on her bare stomach when she spread out the clothes. And there was one sweater she looked at for a long time, a wool thing the color of turquoise, no sleeves, collar cut like a lizard's neck. I thought she might want it for herself and I warned Atik, but then the girl asked him about the sweater. They both started laughing, and I poked him and asked him to explain. Because she knows the Zellars, he said. One time she borrowed the sweater from the missus and wore it herself. How about that?"

Silea's eyes widened in horror.

"No no no!" Ch'ayña clasped her daughter's good arm. "Don't worry, the Zellars won't fire us. I promise. Atik explained it all. The girl wants us to bring in *more* bags, as many as she'll give us. The people who shop there pay almost full price for clothes like these. The girl makes money too, when she sells the clothes. She's looking out for herself and our Atikcha is looking out for us. It was his idea. And look."

She reached into her bag and held out the bills. "Five hundred, Silea. A week's worth of pay for a few bags of ugly Zellar clothes."

Silea pinched the bills between the thumb and finger at the stubby end of her cast and handed them back with a twenty separated out. "Give him this," she said. "Let him get the origami papers he likes."

Ch'ayña nodded. "Nice idea."

Silea's phone rang. Ch'ayña went to the toilet, and when she came back, Silea was still talking. When she put the phone down, she had an odd look on her face.

"What is it?" Ch'ayña asked.

"It was a lady in Crystal. They want Atik to come to a meeting. They want us both there with him."

"What meeting?"

"It's a big one, about the new school."

"Why him?"

Silea's face, bathed in the dim light of a floor lamp, shimmered with pride. "They want us, Mamay. All three of us."

"But why?"

"Because of who we are."

As Silea explained she nodded along, but the ugliness of the request took root in her thoughts. She could feel the whole thing begin to further entwine them. The school, the town and its little Crystals. She wanted to say to her daughter, *Don't you get it? Don't you see what they're doing here?* Because they were using their Atikcha, she could already feel it. Folding him up and changing him, turning him into something he wasn't, just like he did with his papers. An elm tree with a single delicate limb reaching up to the sky.

And soon that limb will break, Silea, like your elbow, Ch'ayña thought grimly. Then you'll see.

A Touch of Tessa:
one GIRL'S SURVIVAL GUIDE to JUNIOR YEAR
A Video Blog

Episode #172: TESSARACKS!!!
. . . 48 views . . .

[*Tessa on stool at sales counter in BloomAgain.*]

TESSA: So we're in the shop today, and I have to say, you guys, this place rocks. It's like flyover Goodwill meets New York haute couture. I mean, look at this stuff. [*Camera reverses to show overflowing bags and boxes of clothes on counter.*] Sometimes we get these big bags of random donations from the wife of some rich guy who died, and it'll be like a thousand dollars' worth of just silk ties, or five dollars' worth of underwear, which we can't resell anyway. Other times you'll get these women coming in thinking they can actually consign these suits with 1990-era lapels, like it's Old Lady Road Show. [*Shop door chimes.*] Hold up, you guys.

[*Sets phone camera-side down on counter; murmurs with a customer; camera reverses on Tessa.*]

Okay, back, and kind of excited today, and it's all because of Azra, the owner. So for a while now, since maybe the second week I started working here, I've been lifting stuff from the donations pile. Not too much, maybe one piece per shift, say a shirt or a dress or a pair of pants I like the look of. But don't worry, I'm not a klepto, because I don't wear the ones I take or try to sell them somewhere else. What I do is, I take them to the sewing machine in the back room and sort of—cut them up, do these alterations, like put an appliqué on some pants, or maybe I'll dart a waistline of a dress so it's more formfitting. Or maybe I combine three things to make an outfit, like I'll put together stuff from different designers to make a new dress, or a sick pair of pants. Usually I'll sketch out my ideas ahead of time, in here. [*Displays sketchbook.*] Sometimes I take what I make for myself. But usually I hide my stuff on the racks to see if anyone will buy it, and know what? They always do. Just because it's different, you know?

[*Door chimes.*] Hold up. [*Raises voice; camera wobbles.*] No, that's okay, we're all set. Thanks. [*Back to Tessa.*] Just UPS. So anyway, today, right before my shift started, Azra said she needed to talk to me and I was like, I'm toast, she's definitely firing me. But guys, that's not what happened at all. Turns out she's known what I've been doing all along. Not only that, but she's been watching to see what would happen with my rags, keeping track of what sells and for how much. She said she's looked at my drawings, and she thinks—she actually said she thinks I have a "gift." So anyway, this is the amazing part: she wants me to put together my own actual fashion line that I can sell in the store. Nothing major, just nine or ten things to start out with, but I'm supposed to come up with my own logo, and get the clothes ready, and then she's going to set a whole rack aside for my line. "My line," like, can you believe that? For my brand name I've come up with TessaRacks, like the tesseracts from *A Wrinkle in Time*, just—something out of this world. You like it? Azra *loves* it. And you know what, guys? It feels like the first time in forever that anybody's believed I'm capable of something besides abusing their kids or swiping Jäger bottles from their liquor cabinets.

[*Wipes tears, blows nose.*] So that's the good news. The bad news is, when I show everything to my mom and tell her, she's all like,

"Fashion, Tessa? *Really?* You can't get into something more *practical?*" and she gives me one of her chewy-chipmunk looks. So predictable, even just the way she said "Really?" made me want to rip her lungs out, and of course the bitch is wearing khakis and a tucked-in polo shirt, so I'm like, "Yes, really, Lauren. Fashion, Lauren. It's called *style*, Lauren. You should try it sometime, maybe stop dressing like some IT guy on a Best Buy commercial." Which she, um, didn't particularly like. Fighting ensued, as my brother would say. [*Door chimes.*] Gotta go, you guys. Love you!

THIRTY-FOUR

BECK

I n the kitchen he found a semi-clean pan and fried up two hot dogs while the twins went at it in the den, throwing f-bombs that matched the content on the screen. He almost couldn't look at the TV these days. When they first got an Xbox for Christmas a few years ago, Beck bought them sanitized versions of a couple of games, PG-rated at worst. Car chases, minimal gore. But somehow the guys had acquired (hacked?) the R-rated versions, complete with stacked women and avatars with the weaponry of a psychopath shooting up a shopping mall. Way too old for his eleven-year-olds, but what's a laid-back dad supposed to do?

He turned up the heat until the hot dogs sizzled. He'd love to have made them a better dinner, but it wasn't his fault. This standoff with Sonja was really wearing thin. With Azra he could get in a big shouting fight and they'd both end up knowing where they stood. Sonja was different. Things were always set on this low Austrian simmer that made him feel like an unwitting crustacean in a stewpot, being slowly boiled alive by her resentment.

A little while ago they'd had one of their typical low-key tiffs before she left the house with Roy.

Have we thought about dinner at all, babe? Beck began.

We?

Just, yeah. I have this meeting I have to go to, about the school, so.

So?

So what are we supposed to eat?

Well, I know what I am eating.

What do you mean?

I am taking Roy over to Cynthia's for dinner with my mothers' group. It has been on the calendar for two weeks.

The calendar.

On your phone. On my phone. The family calendar.

Well, could you take the boys along?

No, I could not take the boys along. They are not invited. Take them to your meeting.

I can't do that.

Then they will be fine here on their own. They are eleven.

With that she was gone, Beck abandoned on the savannah to spear something for supper. It had been happening more and more lately. Their dynamic reminded him of that year before the divorce, when Azra started taking the twins out of the house, over to Samantha's or Rose's or Lauren's. That year when she'd started deserting him in his own goddamn house (technically *her* own goddamn house, which had made things somehow worse). Leaving him alone with the au pair . . .

"Two minutes, guys," he called into the den. Leaning back from the stove, he saw, on the split screen in front of them, a fat black guy in a bala-clava step out from behind a Jersey barrier on a bombed-out boulevard and heave a grenade toward the viewer. Aidan flinched, thumbed his remote, and the grenade exploded in the air, showering his avatar with shrapnel. "Shit," he said.

"Mouth," Beck said loudly, getting a snicker from Charlie, whose avatar was leaping over some kind of hot-pink futuristic Humvee full of Wonder Woman–looking white chicks wielding machetes. Charlie blew them all away with one sweep of his machine gun.

"Ready, boys," Beck said cheerily.

They paused their game and trooped into the dining room, where Beck was busy clearing small appliances and stacks of Tupperware off one end of the table to give them room to eat. He'd started the project a few weeks ago to get a handle on the food storage and processing situation, which had long been dire. There was a juicer Sonja had used maybe once, a fondue set untouched for a decade, a George Foreman Grill Beck had drunk-ordered off the screen during a martial arts bout a while back, plus dozens of mismatched containers and lids.

"I'm starving," said Charlie sullenly.

"Whadda we got, pops?" said Aidan.

Beck proudly set down their plates, but his bubble popped when he saw their reactions to his offering. Black-striped overcooked franks wrapped in freezer-burned hot dog buns, unwrapped granola bars, and two wimpy carrot sticks each, which he'd managed to sculpt out of the skinned core of the one somewhat firm vegetable he'd found in the fridge.

"Is there ketchup at least?" Charlie asked.

"Nope, you'll have to make do, and don't make me start in about starving kids in Bangladesh. Now I have to run." He patted his pants for his keys.

"Dad," Aidan said.

"What?"

"We can't eat this."

"It's disgusting," Charlie chimed in.

"It's fine," said Beck.

"It's *not* fine," said Aidan. "It's like Bertie Bott's Every Flavor Beans from Harry Potter, but every bean is—"

"Snot flavor," Charlie finished for him.

"Or shoe flavor."

"Or poop flavor."

"Okay okay, I get the idea." Beck sighed heavily and looked at the clock. "I gotta motor though. Can you guys just order pizza?"

"Again?" they said at the same time.

"Or whatever. Walk down to Chipotle, maybe."

"Yes!" Aidan exclaimed.

"Do we have to use our allowance?" Charlie whined.

"What allowance?" Aidan glared at his dad, as if Beck needed a reminder. He'd had to cut the twins off the dole a few months back. Every penny . . .

"They'll take this." Beck pulled a credit card from his wallet without looking at it and slapped it on the counter. On the way out the door he called: "Homework after dinner, guys, okay? No more gaming tonight."

"Gotcha, Dad," said Charlie.

By the time he hustled into the crowded auditorium at East Crystal High, it was already 7:16. Beck took a seat near the back. Some kind of dispute was unfolding onstage, a lot of muttering from parents and uncomfortable looks traded among the administrators up there, including Joe Jelinek, superintendent of the Crystal city schools. There was also a slick-looking bunch of overdressed consultants on one side of the stage who seemed to be garnering a fair degree of parental contempt.

Beck sat back to enjoy the spectacle. A mom standing near the front was almost shouting up at Jelinek: "Look, we are under assault out there just for having our kids get through the first cut. Did you read the *Camera*?"

"I did," Jelinek replied, spreading his hands to placate her. "And nobody's under assault here, ma'am. It's not as if our admissions meetings are being picketed."

"Not yet!" someone called out.

"That's right!" someone else shouted.

"Look," Jelinek said. "Come September, when the Academy is up and running, this controversy will be yesterday's news. The important thing for right now is that we give you the tools you need to feel good about entrusting your children to us starting next fall. So we really need to move on now, okay?" More grumbles but everyone soon calmed down.

Jelinek continued: "Now tonight we're going to fill you in thoroughly on the next stage of the admissions process."

Beck, already bored, slipped his phone from his pocket and scrolled through his Twitter feed. There was this one journalist he followed who really knew how to put the pieces together. She shaded a bit centrist, and occasionally Beck had to give her some pointers about finding less corporatist sources. But she was always entertaining, certainly preferable to the admins onstage.

The next time he looked up Jelinek was introducing Bitsy Leighton, the new principal. Beck hunched forward in his seat as Leighton rose and moved to the center of the stage. She began by giving them a bit of her background, then explained why she'd made the move to the Front Range.

"Now, as you can imagine, I've had a lot of questions since arriving in the Denver-Crystal corridor. What would motivate an educator to leave Los Angeles, one of the most demographically diverse cities in North America, to come to a town like Crystal? Because I look around Crystal and I look around this meeting and I see exactly what you'll see if you turn your heads. Go ahead, let's get it out there. Do it. Look around at yourselves."

Beck turned to his left, to his right. He stretched his neck and saw Azra down near the front, one of the few Asian American parents in the crowd. There was a Turkish couple Beck knew two rows in front of him, plus a scattering of maybe-Latino folks sitting over to the left. But mostly just white people.

"Okay," said Leighton, drawing their attention back to the stage. "Now what did you see?"

A long, awkward silence. "Segregation," Beck called out, looking around for reactions. He heard some clucks, though there were also a fair number of nods in the crowd, reluctant sighs. Someone near the front raised a hand.

"Yes?" Leighton said.

The hand raiser didn't stand. "I'm sorry, but the lack of racial diversity in Crystal is a function of economics, not bias. This is one of the most progressive cities in America by any measure. It's about class, not race."

"Oh, please," Beck huffed.

"Class, not race." Leighton smiled. "Well, let me give you a hypothetical, so I can illustrate this point another way. Are you ready?"

Eager liberal nods.

"Let's say Crystal Academy, for some reason, doesn't open in the fall. Lack of funding, politics, whatever. What would your community say instead to a new magnet school for foreign-language acquisition? You like that idea?"

More heads bobbing.

"Now imagine if I could promise you that by the time your child enters high school she will be fluent in a second language. How would you react to that?"

Several hands flew up.

"Yes, you." Leighton pointed to someone in the second row. Samantha Zellar. She stood and Beck listened carefully, sensing a trap and willing Samantha to walk right into it.

"Speaking personally, I can tell you a school like that would be fantastic." Sam swayed attractively, gesturing with both hands in her speaking-for-all-of-us-oh-and-guess-what-bitches-my-husband-is-on-City-Council way. "We have International Baccalaureate programs in some of the schools, and that's great. But IB only goes so far. Without truly rigorous training in a second language, I don't see how we'll get these kids ready for the most competitive colleges."

"Excellent, thank you," Leighton said. Samantha looked around, smiling broadly as she sat. "Other reactions?" She called on a man in the front right. "Yes, sir?"

A man in a tweed sport coat stood and shot his cuffs. "I do have thoughts on the issue, which is quite close to my heart," said the guy, obviously some douchebag academic from Darlton. "We have a bilingual household. We speak English and Mandarin in the home." Beck could hear the quiet groans as the guy gave a capsule version of his earlier career. Two years of fieldwork in China, a Fulbright there after leaving New Haven with his equally white wife, their devotion in the years since to instilling in their two children *the ethical imperative of multilingualism.*

Leighton called on a few other parents, all of them making predictable points about the importance of foreign languages in an interconnected world. She looked around for more hands. Beck saw one go up, on the right side of the auditorium, in a middle row. Leighton lifted her chin. "Yes, ma'am?"

"My son," the woman called out. She was sitting between a boy and an old woman. "He speaks Spanish and he speaks English too, and—"

"Both of them fluently?"

"*Sí.*"

"What grade is he in?"

"Sixth grade."

"And where is it you live, ma'am?"

"We live in Dry River," she said. A migrant community in Beulah County, one of the poorest towns in Colorado. Beck had detoured through it once on the way to a soccer tournament in Nebraska.

Leighton said something in Spanish, then the woman's son stood, edged out of his aisle, and bounded up to the stage. He was a short kid, pole skinny with round wire glasses and a narrow face. Leighton held the microphone down by her waist and spoke to him softly, then turned to the audience.

"Everyone, this is Atik Yupanqui. He'll be translating for the Spanish-speaking folks. I hope that's okay?" She turned and looked at the senior admins lined up along the middle of the stage.

"Of course." Jelinek nodded vigorously. *Should have thought of getting a translator ourselves*, his embarrassed look implied. Beck started to see where Leighton was going.

"Well, how about that?" she said. "A bilingual kid way out in Dry River."

Parents moved in their seats; the few claps quickly died down.

"So let's think about what this means." Leighton paced the stage. "You want a magnet school for languages so the kids in beautiful Crystal, Colorado, can learn some Chinese or Arabic. Who would argue with that?" She paused so Atik could translate. He had a high-pitched voice, but Leighton's idiom and vocabulary gave him no trouble. "Now I'm not here to burst your bubble. But we need to think about the wider context of language acquisition, the broader contours of the problem. Because you know where most of the bilingual kids on this part of the Front Range live? You just heard it from this bilingual mom right here. They live out in Beulah County, where their parents farm the crops and slaughter the animals that provide the farm-to-table cuisine served at the restaurants down on the Emerald Mall."

Nods, murmurs, hums. They were lapping it up.

"In fact we've got a small but vibrant Peruvian community out in Beulah that— Say, Atik, who is that, sitting next to your mother there?"

The kid said some word Beck didn't catch.

"Your grandmother?"

"Yes, ma'am."

"Does she speak English?"

"A little."

"Does she speak Spanish?"

He held up a thumb and finger spaced an inch apart. "Some. Better than her English."

Everybody laughed.

"Why don't you tell her what I've been talking about here. Just the high points."

Atik started speaking loudly across a dozen aisles to his grandmother. Not Spanish, not English. A Native tongue, Beck guessed, glottal but quick. When the kid finished he looked up at Leighton.

"Wow. What language was that, Atik?"

"That was Quechua, ma'am."

She looked out at the audience. "Quechua. Spanish. English."

More shifting, some muted notes of appreciation. *Wow. Incredible. Holy shit.* Plus a few gentle laughs as people started to catch on.

Leighton rested a hand on the boy's shoulder. "Atik here is one of seven or eight kids in the Beulah County public schools who speak English, Spanish, and Quechua. Those kids are not monolingual, not bilingual, but *tri*lingual. They practice an indigenous trilingualism, with equal facility in a Germanic language, a Romance language, and a Native language of South America. Their brains know how to process multiple languages, how to code-switch, how to move from one tongue to another. Their *lives* have been multilingual. So you start those kids in fifth grade in Arabic? Persian? Mandarin? Pashto? No telling how far they'll go."

She leaned down and stage-whispered to Atik, "You can go back to your seat now, son."

The kid smiled, waved at the audience, and this time received sustained applause from the grown-ups. Beck clapped too but couldn't help feeling a flash of indignant annoyance that the school system would put a student of color on display like that just to make a point to a bunch of white liberals—though the sudden surge of righteousness did little to quell his envy of the Peruvian kid's multicultural fluency. At least Aidan had his bi-racialism going for him, though the twins didn't speak a word of Urdu or Punjabi, as Azra's folks had; and as his ex would be the first to point out, being Pakistani or any kind of South Asian was hardly an edge, given today's pretzel-twisted notions of affirmative action. If anything, his guys would be *disadvantaged* by their race, the same way "demographically over-represented" Asian kids got royally screwed by the Ivies, at least according to an article this one guy had posted on a subreddit Beck frequented. The whole thing was complicated, that was for sure.

"Now just to wrap up," Leighton said when the claps died down. "Will these Beulah kids score a one-thirty on the CogPro? Maybe not. But you get them in a Farsi classroom and I promise you they will run rings around the monolingual kids you have in this city. What I'm talking about, let's call it radical inclusion. How do we bring *these* children into the conversation around gifted education? How do we include *them* in our selection process for this school, and how do we ensure that *they* have every bit as strong a chance of admission as a monolingual and monocultural child from Maple Hill whose family can afford intensive test prep and one-on-one tutoring?"

"Oh snap." Beck said it quietly, though the dad in front of him heard. He swiveled his head around and shot Beck a frown; and there was a lot in that frown, Beck thought as the guy turned away. Anxiety, insecurity, fragility, liberal guilt. Maybe a touch of fear.

THIRTY-FIVE

BECK

Out in the courtyard Beck saw Azra's quad of friends huddled up by a dry fountain. His ex-wife was wearing a clingy black dress, scant for the evening chill in the foothills. The high cut showed off the smooth arcs of her calves, like maybe she'd come here tonight from an early dinner date. The four women stood with their backs to the crowd as Samantha Zellar snitted about something, probably her nontrilingual daughter's admissions chances.

Gareth paced on the far side of the fountain, looking down at his phone, waiting for his wife. Beck sidled around to him. "Hey, man."

Gareth slapped him on the arm. "It's been a while."

"I was just thinking that."

"We should—"

"I know. No time like the present?" Sonja should be home, and the boys would have already grabbed dinner, thanks to Mastercard.

Gareth agreed. "Let me just check with Rose," he said, then approached his wife from the rear as the quad broke up. He took a slow stutter step, like a left back afraid to miss a penalty kick. Rose whirled on him with a *What?* and Beck watched as Gareth made his request. Rose gave Beck a cute frown but fluttered her fingers in a reluctant half wave.

On the way to Beck's car Gareth said, "Rose is freaking out."

"Why?"

"That kid in there, the one who went up onstage?"

"Trilingual dude in glasses?"

"Right. So apparently he's the son of the lady who cleans our house. That was his mom calling out from the audience."

"No shit." Beck smiled. "So why did that flip her out?"

"You know Rose. She gets so self-conscious about stuff like that."

Beck's smile dimmed. They'd had a housekeeper until mid-February, this woman Beck had been forced to let go without notice. He'd felt terrible about it, and Sonja had not been thrilled—but the cash flow just wasn't happening, and for some reason the lady didn't take checks.

Beck drove them to Fourteeners, a microbrewery up in North Crystal, housed in a former car repair shop retrofitted with floor-to-ceiling windows facing the foothills. Even for a Tuesday the place was quiet. The TVs inside showed basketball and hockey, and a string band twanged from the speakers. They sat at an outdoor table and ordered a few pints. Across Broad Street the mass of Mount Caritas blocked the stars. Cars traced their routes up and down Caritas Road like Christmas lights slowly unspooling.

"So what'd you think of that Bitsy chick?" Beck said when their beers came.

"I don't know," Gareth said. "This whole school thing—"

"Yeah."

"Rose is obsessed with whether Q gets a spot. But I'm not feeling great about how all this is affecting Emma Q."

"Same with my guys."

"Oh yeah?"

"They're fighting some, got those competitive juices flowing. Leave it on the soccer pitch, is my feeling."

"Mm." Gareth wiped his lip with a bar napkin. "Well, my feeling is, eleven-year-olds shouldn't be thinking about test scores and spikes."

"Yeah," Beck said, sort of agreeing in spirit but wondering where all this self-righteousness was coming from. Gareth could sometimes sound like a goddamn parenting magazine you'd read at the pediatrician's office.

"So, you and Rose," he said, switching topics to something juicier. "Last time we talked she was icing you. It's better these days?"

Gareth gently swirled his pint glass. "Hot and cold. Who knows."

"You're lucky, man. Azra would never take me back."

"You'd want that?"

"I have no clue what I want. Me and some folks from work were at the bar last month shootin' the shit. I look across the restaurant and see this table of four hot women having mojitos, and guess what? It was the quad, celebrating Samantha's birthday."

"What's that have to do with you and Sonja?"

Beck shrugged. "I just feel like I'm never in the right place, in my head. Because they looked great, and I don't mean for a bunch of middle-aged moms. Azra looks better now than she did at twenty-five, swear to God."

Then they talked about their wives for a while, and then Gareth brought him up to date on Emma Q and all she'd been up to, including the usual drama with Emma Z; after that Beck told Gareth about the twins and the politics of the travel leagues, but the whole thing was kind of dull, Beck admitted to himself by his second pint. Sure, it could be good to catch up like this, to kick around familiar things with someone you'd known for such a long time. But Gareth Quinn was never going to be the kind of friend Beck had had in Julian, they just didn't have enough in common, and Beck had always sensed just the teensiest bit of condescension from the guy. Gareth was a published writer, after all, even if, as Sonja liked to point out, he'd only ever produced one novel, which Beck had never read and even Azra said was dull and pretentious—though it wasn't as if Beck had a host of graphic design awards lining his shelves. And anyway a bud's a bud, and if he'll buy you a hoppy ale and ask you stuff about your life, maybe that's what's important in the end.

"They almost don't need a sitter anymore," Gareth had just observed of the Emmas. "We're having Tessa come one night a week but more as a favor to Lauren than anything else."

"Yeah, I hear you. We've been using her too," Beck said with a fond smile, then had an unsettling thought. "Careful with that one, though. She's still a little messed up."

"What are you talking about?"

Beck leaned forward over the table, his fingers destroying a soggy coaster. "We were up at Breckenridge a couple weeks ago and brought her along to watch Roy."

"Yeah?"

"So I'm sitting in the Jacuzzi after everyone's asleep and Tessa comes out there with a bag of weed and drops her towel and just climbs on in."

"She was naked?"

"Topless."

Gareth looked at him with a new expression. "Were you wearing a suit?"

"Hell no. Sonja had just gone upstairs, and we were—"

"And she brought weed out there, right in front of you?"

"Well, she didn't exactly *hide* it."

"Did you take it away?"

"What? No, man, I—"

"Let me guess," Gareth said. "You smoked with her."

"A little, sure. Then I got the hell out of there. It was uncomfortable. That's why I'm telling you this, bro."

Gareth cocked his head, looking at him like a freaking traffic judge. "Did you tell Lauren what happened? That Tessa was acting like that?"

Beck took a swig of his beer, not sure how this conversation had gone so far off the rails. "I figure it's not my business if she's got a wild thing for a daughter."

"Not your business?" He lowered his voice. "Beck, Tessa's a teenage girl. She was in your care for the weekend even if she was babysitting. You were alone and naked in a hot tub with her, and you guys smoked pot."

"Hey, I didn't *give* her any, and in Colorado the shit's legal."

"Did you tell Sonja?"

Beck's mouth hung open, and for the first time he felt genuine alarm. "Why would I do that?"

"So only you and Tessa know about this Jacuzzi incident?"

"It wasn't an 'incident.' Come on." He thought of Charlie, his dark eyes looking out through the kitchen window at bare-skinned Tessa. "But yeah, that's right," he lied. "Only me and Tessa, and now you."

"Well, keep it that way." Gareth tilted his head back and slugged the rest of his beer. "And be more careful. Seriously."

Though he didn't sound protective when he said it. Didn't sound like a friend. More like an uptight prick.

"I hear you," said Beck, trying to be chill, but the bile rose in his throat.

He dropped his keys on the front table and got a glimpse of Sonja in the kitchen labeling milk bottles. "Hey, cutie. Where are the twins?"

"Asleep," she called.

"Already?"

"It is a school night. I made them turn off the TV at nine o'clock."

"Awesome," he said, loving her spine. "Thanks, babe."

He strolled to the fridge for a beer. Sonja stayed frozen in place, backed up against the countertop, her arms folded, giving him the old Austrian stink-eye.

"You okay?"

She didn't move. "Aidan called me from Chipotle, Beck. Would you like to know why?"

"Um, sure?"

"The credit card you gave them was declined." A pause. "I had to read the clerk my own credit card number." A longer pause. "Over the phone."

Oh fuck. He must have given Aidan the wrong card in his haste to get out the door.

"But why didn't the guys call me?"

She dropped her head forward and looked at him.

He swallowed. "Listen, babe—"

"And I had to do this in front of my friends. My new friends. Friends I would like to keep. Do you think I enjoyed this?"

"Hey now."

"Beck, is there something going on with our money that I need to know about? I have this baby. I have not been paying attention to bills and to other things because I trust you with all that . . ." Her voice trailed off, just like her faith in him.

He took two steps toward his wife and cupped her elbows in his palms and kissed the fragrant part in her golden hair. "Everything's under control," he murmured. She stiffened for a moment before leaning against him.

"It's all good," he said, staring at the blank wall behind her. "I promise, babe."

THIRTY-SIX

EMMA Z

Emma Zellar loved her Darlton days.

Every Wednesday her father picked her up at 11:40 and signed her out of school early so she didn't have to go to gym, which she hated, or stay around for recess, which she didn't mind but also didn't mind missing. Then he took her out to lunch wherever she wanted to go, except for a really fancy place, because that would take too long. Then after lunch he drove her to the Varner School of Leadership at Darlton University for her entrepreneurship class, and then after that he took her back to school by two o'clock for last period.

That day her father took her to Guisados, her favorite taco place, next door to the North Crystal Rec Center. Emma Z ordered the fish tacos, and Daddy ordered tacos *al pastor*, like the ones they'd had in Mexico City. As always they split their orders between them, and as always he tried to cheat by taking two of her tacos instead of one but she didn't let him. The fish was crunchy and the pork was spicy and the guacamole was chunky and fresh, made in front of you right at the counter.

When they finished eating, her father leaned back in his chair with his hands over his stomach. "So, sweet pea, how you feeling about everything?"

"Great," she said, licking *al pastor* sauce off her fingers.

"How are things going at school these days? You happy with your teachers, fifth grade, all of that? Do I need to go in there and raise some hell?"

Emma Z laughed. "No, Daddy. Some of it's kind of boring, but mostly it's okay."

"And how about your leadership class? Because you know I give a lot of money to those folks at Darlton. You liking it?" He put his hands behind his head. "It's pretty special, you know. Other kids your age don't get to do that kind of thing."

"It was your idea."

"Oh, I know that, sweet pea. But do you think it's worth the hassle?"

"I *like* the class. Professor Young is really funny, and the college students in there are so nice. They bring me chocolates and stuff. Plus I'm learning a lot."

And, she didn't say, *I really like to be able to tell my friends and teachers at school that I'm taking a class at a college.*

"Is that right? Like what?"

"Like," said Emma Z, wiping her nose with her wrist, "like that great leaders are also great entrepreneurs. And vice versa. If you're a really smart entrepreneur and you invent something and take it out in the world and show everyone how to use it and even build a company so you can sell it, that makes you a leader, not just an entrepreneur, right? So the two go hand in hand, like . . . like hands." She giggled.

Her father got a huge, handsome smile on his face, brought his hands back around, and clapped slowly. "Wow. Just . . . wow. I am truly blown away, Emma Zellar, and proud as heck of you, you know that? So you really want to keep going with this?"

"I love my Darlton days," she said.

"Well, okay then."

But suddenly his smile disappeared, he got a scared look, and he started twirling his hands around, trying to balance on his tilting chair. "Oh, dang," he said. "I'm—oh geez I'm—I'm—"

"Daddy!" she screeched.

"You gotta help me, sweet pea. I'm going over! *Heeeeeeelllllllp!*"

He reached out his hands and she caught them and pulled him back down just in time, even though he had *obviously* been faking it, then she collapsed on his lap, giggling like crazy as everyone around them laughed and smiled, even though they were probably really jealous.

THIRTY-SEVEN

ROSE

Rose wasted an hour on Saturday morning flicking through the hangers in her shallow closet, looking for just the right outfit. Carl Wingate, dean of the medical school, was hosting a kick-off party for the new capital campaign that night with faculty, local donors, and board members, and Rose needed a dress. Not a formal evening gown but something slightly sexy yet sophisticated that paired well with a cardigan. The dean lived high up in Sunrise Canyon, and his events tended to sprawl outside.

She held a few things up in the full-length mirror on the closet door: a sapphire sheath, a casual maxi in a steel gray, a black number with a flared skirt she liked to wear with flats. But nothing felt quite right. Finally she broke down and texted Samantha. The Zellars, major donors to the Medical Center, were also going tonight. Sam promptly ordered her over to Twenty Birch to find a loaner.

First Rose made a call to Wild Horse, part of the plan to augment Q's portfolio. The schools were giving applicants a few weeks to put everything together. Lauren and Azra had already come up with clear, well-thought-out portfolios to bring out the best in their kids. Xander was toiling away on a science project, and Lauren was optimistic about his CogPro appeal. Azra, tight-lipped about the academy since that melancholy curbside conversation, was suddenly all lit up about Aidan's mad soccer skills; apparently Beck had hours of video he was editing into a highlight reel.

Rose had settled on equestrianism as a sellable extracurricular. Ever since Q's fourth-grade final project on *Black Beauty* and riding styles, her daughter had been obsessed with horses, an interest that had produced last year's science fair exhibit on the horse's gait, as well as the History Day project the Emmas had recently completed on horses in the American West. A perfect spike. The only thing missing from Q's portfolio was a letter from her instructor.

Janelle picked up on the second ring, and Rose asked for a sense of Emma's progress. What she got in return was a gift: *excellent in the saddle . . . a natural comfort level with the horses . . . already posts to the trot, the only girl in the Saturday group who can do that so far . . . intuitive . . . don't see that kind of innate ability very often.* Everything Rose could have hoped for, and Janelle readily agreed to send a letter the next week.

I think we have a winner," said Samantha from atop her duvet an hour later, reclining on her elbows with her bare feet dangling over the foot of the Zellars' super king. They were in Samantha's spacious bedroom, with its high ceilings, walk-in closet, just the right vintage paint colors on the walls. Twenty dresses draped the divan and chaise longue. Open curtains invited late-morning light through the French doors and allowed the shadows of swaying trees in the spacious backyard to play dappled patterns over the scattered outfits.

The dress they had chosen for Rose was a bell-sleeved Milly in navy stretch silk that revealed her wrists and ended mid-thigh. The Emmas came in while she was modeling it, and when Z said, "You look pretty in that, Rose," she was sold. Emma Z already had her mother's taste.

As Rose slipped back into her jeans Samantha returned a text. "Well, that's interesting."

"What?"

"This is Tazeem texting me." Tazeem Harb, the mayor's wife and a friend of Sam's, with a daughter at the Emmas' school. "There's a little rumor going around about the guest list," she said mysteriously.

"Oh yeah?"

"Sounds like your friend Bitsy Leighton will be there."

"Really." Rose ignored the implication.

"Apparently she's your dean's cousin or something."

"Interesting," said Rose, nettled by the coincidence—and wondering whether she should just skip the event tonight. The last thing she wanted to do was talk about the bogus study again. She hadn't yet heard from Bitsy about following up, and worried that her presence at the party might remind the woman about it when she'd probably conveniently forgotten by now.

She waited for an opening to slip in a related question that had been nagging her. "So, what's Emma Z's spike, for her portfolio?"

"What isn't?" Samantha replied. They started rearranging dresses on her silk-padded hangers. "And that's the problem, you know? There isn't just *one thing*. The girl has no Pike's Peak. She's more of a high-altitude steppe, though Kev has some ideas."

"Like what?" Rose lifted two hangers and walked them to the closet.

"Something about leadership, that kind of thing," Samantha said, vaguely again.

Standing in the master closet, Rose thought: Emma Z, good in everything, best in none.

In the kitchen the teakettle whistled and piped. Samantha dropped round bags of anise tea into two mugs. Down the hall somewhere a vacuum cleaner switched off, then one of the house cleaners pushed a blue Dyson from the dining room into the library, pulling at the chord as he went.

When he passed through the hall, Rose got a glimpse of a boy's face. She looked again. "Wait, is that Atik?"

"Yeah, he and Shayna have been coming on Saturdays lately, given the situation," Samantha said casually. "They're an amazing team, don't you think? Almost as good as Silea."

"Who's Shayna?"

Samantha gave her a look.

"What?"

"Shayna is Silea's mother, Rose."

"Oh," said Rose, suddenly uneasy. "Wait, so where *is* Silea?"

"Seriously?" Sam leaned forward and lowered her voice. "Rose, Silea's been out of it. For a while now."

"*What?*"

"You didn't know that? She broke her elbow in three or four places. She had to have surgery, pins, one of those fixed braces. It was a bad one."

Rose felt her stomach drop, the blood drain from her face. "I had no idea. I saw her at the assembly but only from a distance, and I didn't even notice the brace. Plus, she only comes to our house once every—"

"Two weeks. So you've pointed out."

"And I try to stay out of her way, so I just didn't . . . I had no idea. God, I feel *terrible*." It occurred to Rose that she hadn't been physically present at the house for one of Silea's three-hour cleaning jags since before the holidays; if Gareth knew about her injury, he hadn't said anything.

"I've been bagging old clothes for her," Samantha said. "And Kev sent them home with a couple of Whole Foods lasagnas last week to put in their freezer."

Rose looked down the hall again where Atik glossed the wood floor with a Swiffer mop, his grandmother standing behind him to murmur quiet instructions. "What is *he* doing here, though?" she said in a low voice. "He's the Emmas' age, or close to it. Aren't there child labor laws?"

Samantha shrugged. "Kev checked into it with our attorney."

"He did?"

"You know how cautious he is. Apparently as long as their work doesn't interfere too much with school hours and they stay below a weekly minimum, it's fine. Besides, the family lives pretty near the edge. What are they supposed to do?"

As Rose was leaving Twenty Birch she tried to act anonymous while slipping past her housekeeper's son, on his knees wiping down a bookcase in the front hall, but he caught her eye and nodded up at her.

"Hello, Ms. Holland."

"Hi there," she said, with a nervous smile. "You—know who I am?"

"Your family photos, ma'am. I dust them sometimes."

Rose swallowed, at a loss for words. "This all looks great," she said lamely.

"Thank you, ma'am."

"Atik, I'm so sorry to hear about your mother."

He looked at her, puzzled. "What about her?"

"Oh, just—about her elbow."

His lips curled into a confident smile, and his chin tilted up. "She'll be okay. She has a really good orthopedist, and they were able to do the procedure without a bone graft. Now it's just a waiting game for the brace to come off, then she'll be in PT."

Rose narrowed her eyes, taken aback. The kid sounded for all the world like one of her residents. "So who's the ortho?"

"Dr. Bowers."

"Edward Bowers?"

"Yes, ma'am."

"Ted's good. The best elbow guy in Colorado."

"I know. I researched him."

"And your mom's pins? Any problems with infection and so on?"

"Nope, everything looks good." For a long, strange moment they shared a stare. Rose saw him in those same round glasses twenty years from now, scrubbing in for a neck dissection. She searched for some kind of reassurance to give him, but Atik cheerily said, "See you soon," and went back to his work.

On her way to the car Rose tapped out a note on her phone, reminding herself to put a little something extra in Silea's envelope next week.

THIRTY-EIGHT

BECK

ROMO tryouts. Beck had slept in that morning, nothing major but Aidan had to come upstairs to shake his shoulder and rouse him. It had been a late night of financial planning, and when he'd rolled out of bed and called for Sonja, he discovered she was gone somewhere with Roy, again. She hadn't mentioned the Chipotle incident since the other night, and he was trying to straighten a few things out in the credit card department. After a hurried breakfast of frozen waffles and squishy bananas they had all tumbled into the car at ten past nine, already running late.

Now an accident was coming up on the right shoulder, the source of the slowdown for the last ten minutes.

"Did you guys hydrate?" Beck asked the twins.

"Yes."

"And how's the ankle, Aid?"

Aidan didn't respond.

"Ankle feeling okay, bud?"

"Stop *bugging* me about everything."

"Sorry, it's just that the stakes of this tryout—"

"Are high. I know, and you've told us that like twenty times, but you're the one who didn't get up on time and my ankle's *fine*."

Button pusher. Nerve plucker. Thinner of hair. Beck flexed and unflexed his hands on the wheel until the backup finally cleared.

Fifteen minutes later they pulled into the parking lot of the Rocky Mountain Fútbol Academy, thirty flat acres wedged along Peña Boulevard ten miles short of the airport, a fifty-minute drive from downtown Crystal in good traffic. As he tucked the Audi into a space Beck calculated what it would mean to haul the boys down here four evenings a week, then again on game days. Call it two hours a day. Times four is eight, then another two on weekends. Away games might require a four-hour round trip to Cheyenne, an overnight to Santa Fe. Twelve to twenty hours per week on the road, hours that could be occupied playing with their friends, hiking the foothills. Maybe some homework.

But ROMO? It was the pinnacle of youth soccer in this part of the country. If the guys could get spots on the team and keep them for the next few years, who knew where they might land. At the very least full rides to decent colleges, and given the state of Beck's finances, that was nothing to sneeze at. Some things were worth the pressure.

He found a viewing spot up a slight rise from the pitch, along a fence line separating the ROMO complex from a sugar beet field to the east. The digital recorder had a good perspective from that position. The boys finished warm-ups as Beck adjusted a few settings and hit the record button.

"Excuse me there."

He looked up. One of the ROMO coaches was jogging across the pitch, a tall bald guy in a team warm-up jersey. Andy Millward, Beck guessed, the coach he'd spoken to on the phone. When he neared the end line, he stopped and placed his hands on his narrow hips. "With the Rapids, are you?"

A rival club in Denver. Beck smiled. "I have two boys trying out."

"Which boys would those be?"

"Aidan and Charlie Unsworth-Chaudhury, skinny brown dudes over there."

The boys were taking a break between warm-up drills, and they were all staring at him and the coach—all except Charlie, who was standing with his arms crossed, gazing in the opposite direction.

Millward shook his head. "No filming, and camera aside, we can't be bothered with dads watching the tryouts 'cause it rattles the lads, so if you can come back and get them afterward, that'd be fair."

The coach didn't wait for a response, just rotated on a heel and jogged back to the team. Expressionless, Beck packed up his camera, folded his tripod, and skulked toward the gate, careful to avoid looking over at the pitch, risking a glance only once he'd reached the gap in the fence. Charlie met it with a glare, direct and scowling, and when the whistle sounded he turned away.

The next two hours were hard for Beck. He was used to watching every minute of the boys' games, and back in Crystal the CSOC tryouts had always been their own spectator sport. But ROMO's best practice fields were surrounded on all four sides by a high chain-link fence with opaque black liners, making it impossible to see what was going on from outside the perimeter.

Though maybe not. As he trudged back to the car Beck noted a few tears in the liner, on the side facing the parking lot. And if there were some on this side—

With the tripod and camera stowed in the trunk he headed around the fence, a soccer dad on a casual stroll. He followed a gravel path winding through a few stands of evergreens until he spied a decent oval-shaped tear the circumference of a serving platter at eye level. Beck moved his head until he saw Aidan in an orange pinny, standing with his foot on a ball. Charlie was on the next field in a red pinny.

Scrimmages. Aidan's orange team versus yellow, Charlie's red team versus blue, two of three small-sided matches about to kick off. Practice goals with tiny mouths, no keepers.

Before the first game Aidan looked tense and wary, not keeping his studied pregame chill. But from the beginning he played well. Quick passes, good energy, smart movement off the ball. The talent level around him was clearly raised a few notches, but he looked just like he did with his CSOC team, holding the middle of the field with confidence and grit. The game went on for fifteen minutes. Beck couldn't tell what was happening on Charlie's field, but Aidan's team led 3–1 when the first game ended.

The teams changed up. Red went to play green, yellow moved over to battle red, and Aidan's orange stayed put to face black.

This game was different. Black moved the rock with crazy agility, players rarely touching more than once before dishing off, scoring two goals in the opening minute before the game settled down. The kids on black also seemed to know one another's names, spitting them out ahead of passes, instructing teammates on where to send the ball, when to move. These must be the current ROMO players, Beck figured, or eight of them anyway; guys already rostered for this season and probably with secured spots on next year's squad.

He edged a little closer to the gap. The midfielder on black looked familiar.

Oh. Right.

The Egyptian kid from Fort Collins. Baashir, the left-footer Wade had told him about, the kid offered an early spot on ROMO for next year. Strong, fast, nimble as hell, Baashir was every bit as talented as Aidan. Kid looked like a little drill sergeant out there, clapping, encouraging, correcting.

But Aidan held his own, raising his game in the face of the strong competition. He connected every pass, low-headed a great goal, pulled his team together. At one point he even got in a nice tackle on Baashir, who flashed him a nasty scowl. *Amazing.* Beck bounced on his toes.

At the next switch the coaches called all the players in for a water break and ordered them to shed their pinnies, then they reassembled the teams based on what they'd seen so far.

Beck wasn't even aware of what was happening until the damage had been done. First Millward tossed Aidan a black pinny, which he pulled on before joining Baashir and the other ROMO players in a larger cluster of thirteen guys. A second group of kids, a few of them from the original black team, were told to don red. The rest of the kids got either blue or orange, handed out at random, the coaches not bothering to call their names.

The red and black teams began a full-sided game, eleven on eleven, with Aidan and Baashir playing midfield on black, running a four-four-two.

The three ROMO coaches stayed on the sidelines, writing on clipboards, conferring in low voices.

Meanwhile the orange and blue kids had been ordered off to a stubbly secondary field, where they were divided up into a scrimmage supervised by a young assistant coach. The guy blew a whistle for kickoff, then started checking his phone as blue and orange began a sloppy, desultory game.

The striker on the blue squad was Charlie.

"But—" Beck said aloud to the hole in the fence, because this couldn't be right, so he stepped closer, his face just inches from the wire. He saw it all at once, and understood. Aidan looked ecstatic out there, face drenched in sweat, whereas Charlie was just going through the motions, thwacking the ball around with twenty-one other boys. They all knew it was over for them. No second chances, no sibling policy; no ROMO.

As Beck watched helplessly the same strapping coach glanced for a moment along the fence line. Millward fixed him with a stare, a bearded deer in headlights. The fucker actually smirked before turning away with a cool shake of the head.

From the far field Charlie saw the interaction. His head spun and he spied his father, gawking through the tear, and gave him a vicious look. The whistle sounded again. Beck backed away from the ragged hole.

You embarrassed us *so, so* much," Aidan said once they were in the car. "Everybody was looking. Kids were laughing, both times."

"I thought you liked watching yourself play." Beck tried to sound light, as if what had just happened hadn't. "That's why I film every week."

"Not at a tryout. God, Dad, might as well get a stupid *drone* or something so you can spy on us from the car."

"That's not a bad idea, actually."

"Dad!"

"Hey, come on. I'm sorry if I embarrassed you, okay? Won't happen again."

Aidan scoffed, but Beck knew what was going on here, because this wasn't about the humiliation caused by an overinvested father. Aidan was yammering like this to distract them both from the sorry state of his brother, who was staring fixedly out the window as Peña Boulevard blurred by.

The end of the tryout session had been excruciating, the boys called up one by one to shake the coaches' hands and learn their fates: every kid on orange and blue sent home with a better-luck-next-time, half the kids on red invited for callbacks, the players on black, including Aidan, offered roster spots. Lots of tears, stiffened jaws; but also bursts of ecstasy from those boys selected for ROMO.

Not from Aidan. He reacted to the outcome with a taut and glowing unease, not sure what to do with himself. During the whole of the ride home, as Beck observed him in the rearview, Aidan stole furtive glances across the Audi's back seat, and Beck saw no triumph in his son's eyes. Instead Beck saw what he took as loyalty, a will to protect his twin against this new threat to the pack.

*Chah*wee *bwu*dduh.

THIRTY-NINE

ROSE

The dean's sprawling mountain house glowed with a dozen forms of light: ground-level solars lining the driveway, post lamps along the stone path, candles in the front-facing windows, sconces in a patterned brass guarding either side of the door. Inside, gossamer strings of bulbs drooped from terraced beams, pooled luxuriously inside glass vases and bowls.

Rose and Gareth moved around knots of guests through a sunken living room with dark wood floors and colorful area rugs. Catering staff were spreading out a buffet on the dining room table while others circulated among the guests with trays of appetizers.

In the kitchen a bartender smoothed a lime slice along the rims of two hurricane glasses, dipped the rims in a dish of sugar, then filled the glasses with a pink concoction that fizzed as he topped the drinks. Rose, looking around, took a sip. Light grapefruit forward, something deeper beneath.

She didn't see Samantha or Kev inside. She led Gareth out of the kitchen and onto the upper deck. The Continental Divide marched twenty miles to the west. Seven guests sat with their feet in the kidney-shaped pool down below, lit emerald for the coming night.

"Is that Gareth Quinn?" someone said behind them.

It was Tazeem Harb, grand and regal in a long, flowing dress of teal and deep blue silks. The wife of Crystal's mayor, Tazeem was also a partner at a corporate law firm in town and a fixture in Samantha's socialite circles.

"I just finished *Gallows Road*," said Tazeem. Gareth's novel. "It's *wonderful*."

Gareth looked taken aback. "That's really kind," he mumbled as several guests turned their heads.

"Sam Zellar gave me a copy," she explained. Rose blinked.

"Oh." Gareth sounded even more surprised. He gave her a bashful grin. "Glad it's still making the rounds."

Tazeem laughed. "Dawn Jansen is a great character, isn't she?" A smile for Rose. "That scene where she finally understands what's in the trees, and who put it there? I read the whole chapter aloud to my husband."

"I don't know what to say," said Gareth.

"Say you'll write more of them," Tazeem said warmly, with a gentle elbow poke to his arm, and started talking to those guests clustered around them about the need to support Crystal Valley's local writers.

Rose stepped away so Tazeem and the others could draw him out. "Yes, I'm a writer," Gareth said bashfully, in response to someone's question, then told a self-deprecating joke and got a healthy round of laughs.

She watched the exchange from an empty spot on the deck, trying to puzzle it out. Why was Samantha passing around a copy of Gareth's novel? As far as Rose knew Sam had never even read *Gallows Road*; she'd certainly never mentioned it if she had, and now she was recommending it to friends?

Rose sulked by the railing until she saw two familiar faces over by the outside drinks table. Mitch Stephenson, her department chair, stood talking with Carl Wingate, that night's host and dean of the School of Medicine. Rose walked over.

"Why, it's the good doctor herself," Carl boomed. "Hello, Rose."

Mitch raised his eyebrows at her. "Rose," he said, nodding.

"Hi, Mitch. Hi, Carl." She slipped between the administrators' tall frames to lean against the balustrade. "Thank you for having us, Carl. Your home is just beautiful."

"We're glad you're here," said Carl. "Chloe's going to play for everyone a little later, so I hope you'll stay." Chloe was Carl and Vince's eighth-grade daughter; a violinist at St. Bridget's, Rose remembered, or maybe a pianist.

"Wouldn't miss it," she said.

Then Carl looked intently at her. "I understand we'll be bulking up your lab for the NIH scheme."

"Yes, I'm thrilled," said Rose. "And really grateful to the administration for the support."

"It's well deserved, from everything Mitch tells me."

"I appreciate that." Rose beamed, looking fondly at her chair. "He's been incredibly supportive."

Mitch nodded again, and though he participated in their exchange, smiling in the right places, he was acting reserved tonight, not his gregarious self, his eyes slotting away into the crowd whenever she opened her mouth. As the conversation went on Rose started to feel her chair's coolness of manner as a solid thing, like the stainless-steel railing behind her.

Soon Mitch's wife, Sherry, came by. Time to leave, she told him. An event in Denver, at a gallery downtown. Unlike Mitch she seemed fine, breezy and talkative. They bid the dean goodnight, and Mitch pecked Rose's cheek, but again the gesture felt cursory, almost brusque.

Shortly after nine o'clock, and still no Samantha. Carl gave a short speech and a toast to welcome everyone, thanking the doctors for their hard work, donors for supporting the campaign with their time and wealth. As the crowd parted Rose, to her horror, found herself a few feet from Bitsy Leighton. The head of school was helping herself to a napkin of treats from the dessert table, her long fingers pincering a truffle. Rose felt a small explosion in her skull and tried to edge away. Just then Bitsy turned and saw her.

"Well, hello there, Rose."

"Hi, Bitsy," Rose said, with a pained smile. Bitsy bit into her truffle. Desperate to fill the lull, Rose added, "I forgot to ask the other day how you're liking Crystal so far."

"I'm commuting in," said Bitsy. "We have a place out in Elmont."

"Oh," Rose replied, surprised. Elmont was at the eastern edge of Beulah County, not far from Q's riding stable. "I'd have thought you'd want something closer in, near the academy."

Bitsy raised an eyebrow. "I'm on a public school salary. Have you checked out real estate around here lately?"

"Oh yes." *I live in a 1,200-*

square-foot house and my husband is unemployed,
she wanted to shout.

"We also wanted to be in a more diverse community. The air's a little thin in town."

"It is that," Rose replied, eternally self-conscious, like everyone in Crystal, about the city's demographic, the open secret of a town the rest of the state dismissed as a lefty enclave. Pink Quartz, they call it. Mao of the Mountains. Vlad's Valley. One of the most politically progressive towns in America with one of the least diverse populations.

"So you'll drive your kids in with you, to the academy?"

"Why would I do that?"

"Oh, I just thought—since you're head of school—"

"My children aren't profoundly gifted, not like the academy kids will be. Ours will go to the Beulah County schools and do the regular TAG program out there. That's assuming they test in."

"How many do you have?"

"Two."

"And what are their ages?"

"Fourteen and sixteen. So they have a few years on Chloe." Carl Wingate's daughter.

"She's their first cousin?"

"Second, and I'm first cousins with Carl. He and Vince are the ones who talked me into applying and relocating."

"Nice to have family in a new place."

"That's right." She leaned over her plate and bisected another truffle with her long teeth. "You know, Rose," she continued, chewing, "I should apologize. I've been meaning to follow up with you about that study you're proposing on our first intake kids. Now that the first cut is over I'd love to get a drill-down on that."

"Oh—oh yes, of course," Rose stumbled, "though at this point it's really just an undeveloped idea."

"It sounded splendid when you pitched it to me. Can I take you to lunch next week to discuss it, or perhaps you could come in and talk to some of my colleagues?"

"Of course. That would be lovely." Rose pulled out her phone to exchange numbers, though inside she was panicking at the thought of digging this hole any deeper. She promised herself right then to email Bitsy on Monday and tell her the study was off. She could make up some half-true excuse, maybe claim she was too busy preparing an NIH grant, which happened to be the case. But this crazy fabrication had gone far enough.

"Oh, *wonderful*." Bitsy looked toward the house. "My goddaughter is about to play."

They peered into the glassed-in living room, where a crowd had gathered in a wide circle around a grand piano. Bitsy made her way inside, and Rose stayed with her until they were both pushed into the second row of guests. Gareth stood over by the kitchen, leaning on a half wall. They settled in for what Rose assumed would be a few minutes of basic stuff, something suitable for an eighth grader being trotted out for her parents' friends.

The dean's daughter shifted on the piano bench and reached her legs out for the pedals. Bitsy tilted slightly toward Rose and grazed her arm with two cool fingertips. "You've heard Chloe play?"

"I haven't," Rose said.

Bitsy sniffed a chuckle through her nose just as Chloe touched the keys. Chopin, a mazurka. Within the first two measures the room went from mildly charmed to stunned. Chloe's maturing hands splayed and reached for the keys, filling her fathers' house with chromatic ascents, flights of color and contrast. Her left hand kept the mazurka's dancy beat at certain points, at others joining her right hand for a flourish of blended rhythms.

Rose looked around at the faces of her fellow guests. Awe, incredulity, knowing admiration from the few already acquainted with Chloe's skills. Mostly, from fellow parents in the crowd, Rose saw a kind of surprise that was also a subtle sadness like hers, a grim acknowledgment of the lack they all shared.

This girl was a prodigy; this girl was gifted as hell.

Shortly after ten Carl and Vince walked them to the door. Though the party was still humming, Gareth, as always, preferred an early night. They were saying their final goodbyes on the driveway when they heard a group of late guests approaching from the canyon road. A crunch of gravel, a spill of familiar laughter. In a moment the foursome emerged from the darkness, happy and backslapping. Samantha and Kev, and Azra with Glen.

"I hope we're not too late," Samantha called ahead.

"Are you kidding?" Vince stepped forward and wrapped her in a hug. "We're just getting started here."

"The cover band's showing up at midnight," Carl quipped, and Samantha's group shared the kind of loose laughter that comes with long evenings in company you enjoy.

Their unexpected intimacy hit Rose like a brick, this violation of an unspoken rule. Double dates were rare in their group, in part because of Lauren's enduring singlehood, in part because Gareth and Kev just didn't click. Mostly they all went out of their way to avoid making anyone feel excluded, as Rose did right now.

They had enjoyed Thai food, Azra said, and seen a film. "And child-free!" she sang as she spun around, exuberant and annoyingly beautiful, arms in the air, hands splashing at the night. "Tessa is over with Emma Z and the twins."

"At your house?" Gareth asked.

"No, at Twenty Birch," said Samantha, with a self-conscious shrug. "Given how things are going, we thought we'd give her another shot."

"My influence." Azra wrapped her arms around Glen's slim waist. He reached out a hand and grabbed her hip bone. An intimate, casually sexy gesture; Rose couldn't imagine Gareth touching her that way, not that she'd ever want him to.

"That's great," Rose said weakly, coming off tired and sour. "I'm so sorry we have to leave."

Gareth palmed her shoulder, ready to move down the driveway. She shrugged him off as Carl waved goodbye and started heading back in with Samantha at his side. Azra and Glen followed with Vince between them, guiding them along.

But Kev lingered behind, sending a text or an email. "So, Doc, is Bitsy Leighton here?" he asked her without looking up. "Want to buttonhole her if I can."

"She's inside," said Rose.

"I hear she's a Tiger." Kev slipped his phone away and straightened his sport coat with a jerk of the lapels. "Class of Ninety-five."

"A what?"

"Princeton. We overlapped by two years. Wonder if we ever hooked up at Reunions."

"Jesus, Kev," said Rose.

Kev snickered dirtily. "Once a Tiger always a Tiger."

Rose, still feeling bitter and small, imagined clawing out his eyes.

"Well, the barkeep calls. I should get in." Kev rubbed his palms together and strode for the door. "Drive safely, my friends," he called back.

Rose watched him go inside, her blood at a simmer, her temper inflamed by Samantha's confident intimacy with the dean, Azra's ecstatic twirling in the night, and Bitsy Leighton's presence within. The party would now hum along without them.

She turned away from the beautiful house and saw Gareth standing by the car watching her, his gaze darkened, his lips tugged back in what looked like a snarl. As he turned to open the door she heard him say, mockingly and under his breath, "Go, Tigers."

A Touch of Tessa:
One Girl's Survival Guide to Junior Year
A Video Blog

Episode #186: UM, WTF?
. . . 164 views . . .

[Computer screen displaying monthly statement from Front Range Equities in names of Kevin and Samantha Zellar, 20 Birch Street, Crystal, Colorado.]

TESSA: God these people are loaded. Check out this investment account, you guys. [*Zoom in on balance of $10,245,876.90.*] Don't you love the ninety cents at the end? And this is probably just part of it, I mean ten million dollars and here I am logged in. It's amazing, you know? A guy like Kev, so smart about money and computer stuff. "Why go with one of these commission-based index fund managers when you could open an E*TRADE account yourself?" and "I'm telling ya, Tessa, don't go in for that cryptocurrency BS, it's all about to collapse." Um, okay, Kev, I won't, and here's one for you: don't store your passwords on your computer screen. [*Line of yellow stickies across top of monitor: passwords for bank account, Netflix, Amazon, etc.*] He even leaves his email program open and I'm like, whaaaaah? Aww, but look at these sweet messages from Samantha, though, all flirty. And oh wow, he's planning a surprise vacay for her forty-fifth next month. Hawaii! What a guy, what a guy. Let's see, let's see, let's see . . .

[Scrolls down in-box and pauses on email from Bitsy Leighton, City of Crystal School District. Subject: Crystal Academy Admissions Results, Round One.]

Oh snap, this is the same letter I got. *[Clicks email open; camera wobbles, blurs.]* Yadda yadda— *[gasps]* Wait. Wait wait wait wait wait. No. Fucking. *Way.* *[Camera wobbles again.]* Look at this you guys. Just *look* at this.

[Sharpens on last paragraph. Reads:]

"We regret to inform you that your child has not scored sufficiently high on the CogPro to be advanced to the next round in the admissions process. Should you wish to appeal this decision to the admissions committee, details of the appeals procedures can be found on our website at the URL below. We will conduct another round of assessment at the end of the next academic year to fill any additional spots in your child's cohort, though we expect only a very small number of seats to be available at that time."

[Camera reverses to Tessa's face, lit by glow from monitor.]

Okay, officially blown away, but you know what? Also totally unsurprised. Because I've always thought Emma Z was kind of—not slow, but just not that bright. I mean you compare her to my brother and she's an idiot, but that's true of everybody. No, I mean like in comparison to Emma Q, or even the twins, Emma Z just isn't that smart. Not the sharpest tack in the box. Not the brightest bulb in the socket. She doesn't read, she's not—I don't know—sparky when you talk to her, like the others. But these people, the Zellars, they treat her like she's the second coming of everything. And it's all lies, just like her CogPro score. One-forty-five my sweet white ass. I knew that was bullshit when Z told me last week. *So* pathetic. And they give me shit for swiping some pills or whatever? Well . . . screw that. *[Splash of headlights on window.]* Oh shit, they're home. Bye, you guys.

FORTY

XANDER

The clock by his bed read 2:26. He listened for a sound from Tessa's room, because she fidgeted a lot when she was awake, thumped their shared wall with her feet or her butt. But when she was asleep, Tessa was like a car in the driveway.

Nothing.

The next thing Xander listened for was his mother. She was hardly ever awake in the middle of the night, but you never knew if she had to pee.

Nothing.

He swung off the bed. Aquinas lifted his head but Xander wasn't worried. He'd already taken the dog's collar off so he wouldn't make any noise, and Aquinas couldn't get off the bed by himself anymore. He wouldn't even whine.

Xander tiptoed from his room and down the hall to the front door. In the darkness he felt for his mother's purse and took her wallet, then crept up the stairs to her office computer. He opened the browser and went to Amazon, which had a basic version of what he needed.

He had to order eight of the kits, and they weren't cheap. His mother would definitely notice the charge when she did the bills. She'd ask him about it, they'd probably have a "family meeting" in the kitchen, and for once his mother would have something to be as mad at Xander about as she always was at Tessa.

But he had timed the purchase carefully. His mother's credit card bill arrived around the fifteenth of every month, meaning she wouldn't see the charges for three weeks. By then his science fair project would be done, and he'd be admitted, so he was pretty sure his mother wouldn't sweat the money.

Xander logged out, went back down the stairs, and returned the wallet. In the kitchen he poured himself a glass of water. He wasn't thirsty but if anyone heard him walking around the house at 2:47 a.m., he needed an excuse.

Back in his bedroom Aquinas had hardly moved. Xander climbed in next to his fat dog and closed his eyes.

FORTY-ONE

ROSE

His name was Logan. He had lost his fine motor coordination at four, his hearing at five, at six his ability to walk. He had died blind and demented three days before his seventh birthday. The boy's diseased brain survived now in the form of paraffin sections on slides taken from his cerebral cortex.

The sections, though, had buckled. Their appearance was wrinkled and warped, the result of sloppy slide preparation by Franklin Barnes, one of Rose's postdocs—the second time this had happened in a month.

When Rose stepped out of the microscope room, she saw Franklin chatting up one of her graduate students in the far corner of the lab. He had the young woman boxed in by the centrifuge stand, with his right hand on the counter, his left toying with an instrument rack near her head.

Rose, raising her voice, said, "Franklin, could you come into my office, please?"

The lab fell silent. He looked slowly over at her and didn't bother to hide a smirk.

Franklin was a type every female scientist knows, a mildly toxic young man who couldn't stand being supervised by a more capable woman. He behaved himself for the most part, but every now and then Rose would catch him undermining her authority in the lab, always in subtle, deniable ways. A whispered bit of mansplaining to the grad students, a minor proto-col spat with a more senior postdoc.

In her office she spoke to him about the mishap, more sharply than she'd intended. But the stakes could not have been higher—for the lab, for Rose, and, she tried to make Franklin see, for himself. In the end he apol-ogized for the poor slide preparation and promised to be more careful next time.

"Please do," she said, ignoring his tight lips, his stiffened jaw. After she dismissed him she checked her phone. A missed call from Emma Q's school, a voice mail asking her to phone the principal's office.

"We need you to come in," the principal's assistant told her. "Today if possible."

Words no parent ever wanted to hear from a school administrator. Rose leaned back in her desk chair and looked through the slatted blinds into the lab. She'd been hoping the grads and postdocs might all push through until seven or even eight this evening, but she couldn't ask her staff to stay late if she had to cut out in midafternoon.

"And you can't give me any indication over the phone what this is about?"

"All I can say at this point is we're looking at a bullying incident involv-ing your daughter."

"Oh no." She wondered who could be antagonizing Emma. One of the bigger girls, probably, or that awful Keith Duggan.

"So right after the closing bell?" the admin asked.

Rose said, "We'll see you then."

At three-thirty she met Gareth just outside the principal's office, leav-ing no time to prepare themselves before Sue Willis directed them to a circular table in the corner of her office suite. Willis was young to hold a principalship, favoring phrases like "differentiated instruction," "interper-sonal intelligence," and "motivational openings" when talking about her work in the City of Crystal School District. But she was also edgy and smart, with a no-nonsense approach to administration that Rose, not a PTA type, had admired from afar.

Willis steepled her fingers on the table. "So, let me tell you why I've asked you in. It seems that four of the girls in Ms. Avery's class have formed a club of sorts."

"What kind of club?" Rose asked.

"Well, those four girls are the only members so far. They're considering allowing a few boys in, but they're still working out the application protocols."

Gareth snorted. Rose turned and glared at him.

"Who are the other three girls?" Rose said.

"That I can't tell you. Student confidentiality."

"Okay."

"Your daughter is the secretary."

"The *secretary*?" Gareth, still acting amused. "Well, that's kind of insulting."

"Gareth," Rose said under her breath.

"Sorry."

"And what kind of club is this?" Rose asked.

"That's the kicker. Because this isn't about Donnelly Elementary. This is about the new school, Crystal Academy."

"Oh no," said Gareth, his tone changing.

"Oh yes."

Willis, Rose saw, was holding back real anger.

"Four girls and one boy in Ms. Avery's class tested into the next round of admissions. By a strange coincidence these same four girls have taken it upon themselves to form this new club."

The first-cut kids. Samantha's phrase, that blithely superior tone. Smug, exclusive, clubby.

"And what are they calling it?" Gareth said.

But Rose already knew.

"They're calling it the Gifted Club," Willis said with unmasked contempt, her air quotes performed with outstretched arms.

"That's horrible," said Gareth.

"Yes, and a direct violation of our no-bullying policy." Willis pointed a thumb at a poster framed over her right shoulder. Six guidelines screamed in all caps.

WE ARE RESPECTFUL TO ONE ANOTHER
WE ARE KIND TO ONE ANOTHER
WE ARE RESPONSIBLE TO ONE ANOTHER
WE SUPPORT ONE ANOTHER
WE DO NOT EXCLUDE ONE ANOTHER
WE DO NOT ACCEPT CRUELTY TOWARD ONE ANOTHER

"Quite a few of the students are very upset," Willis said. "As you know, we have an existing program that identifies exceptional learners for targeted instruction. But that's an officially sanctioned program, with wide participation. The Gifted Club? That's something else entirely. This club is exclusionary. It's elitist."

"That seems a little harsh," said Rose, feeling defensive for Emma Q.

Willis tilted her head. "I don't think so."

Gareth asked, "Have you seen outright cruelty from any of these girls?"

"Yes. And according to Ms. Avery, it's more than borderline at this point." Willis clasped her hands on top of a folder. "Now this is going to be hard to hear."

Rose folded her legs.

"Three things," Willis said. "First, the spreadsheet. Ms. Avery found it in Emma Q's cubby this morning."

She took out a piece of printer paper and rotated it so they could see. A spreadsheet divided into four columns, each filled with students' names and headed with a word or phrase naming their designated category.

The Ivies | Out-of-State | In-State | Community College

"This is a lovely bit of fortune-telling," Willis said. "The girls have taken it upon themselves to divide the class according to each student's college prospects. What kinds of schools the kids are 'in the ballpark' for, as one of them put it. Over here we have the Ivy League–bound."

Emma Zellar, Emma Holland-Quinn, and two other girls' names Rose recognized, plus a boy named Caleb Sykes.

"Let me guess," Gareth said. "The members of the Gifted Club?"

"No comment." She moved a finger to the top of the next column. "And here we have the one child bound for an 'out-of-state.' A sporty type. The girls feel he's more suited to athletics, kind of a 'dumb jock,' as they've been heard to pronounce."

"Jesus," Gareth muttered.

"As you can see, the chart goes all the way down from the Ivies to that last column: 'Community College.' Only a hair more fortunate than the kids who will be, as Ms. Avery heard one of the girls say, 'stuck in a crappy Colorado state school.' I've had calls from two outraged parents already whose children have been labeled 'in-staters' by the Gifted Club over this last week. That's why Ms. Avery went looking for the spreadsheet."

"Did she confront the girls?" Rose asked.

"She did, and that's the second thing. When she pulled Emma Q aside to ask about the chart, your daughter said to her, 'You're just a teacher. You don't even have a PhD, so how would you know?'"

"She didn't," Rose whispered through her fingers.

"She did. And let me tell you. Tasha Avery? She's a first-generation college graduate and the only black woman on my entire teaching staff. Now she's seriously considering whether to quit and just substitute in Denver for the balance of the school year. Because this town—" She shook her head and didn't finish the thought; didn't need to.

Gareth looked across the table at Rose, one eyebrow raised, a snitty sneer on his lips. *Don't say a word*, she wanted to scream at him.

"Q isn't like this," said Rose, eyes seeping. "She's just not."

"I know that. And her teachers know that, Ms. Avery said it herself when she reported all this today. Q's a good kid." Her voice softened. "And that's precisely why this has us so alarmed."

The wall clock ticked toward the hour.

"What's the third thing?" Gareth said.

Willis took a deep breath. "What your daughter said to me when I called her in. I asked her where she was getting all this, who was putting these awful things into her head. She wouldn't tell me, but what she did say was that she doesn't think quotas are a good idea."

"What?" Gareth sputtered, sitting up.

"As Q put it, 'But they have to let Beulah County kids in because otherwise the school would be too white.'"

You need to address this with Kev and Samantha right away," said Gareth once they were outside.

Rose, incredulous, fixed him with a stare. *You?*

"That crap about in-staters, about the Beulah kids?" he went on. "You can just hear Samantha spouting that shit, poisoning our daughter."

I have heard her spouting it, Rose thought bitterly, *a dozen times*. She looked at her husband: shaken, seething, a rage in his voice that almost frightened her.

"Let me talk to Sam." Rose decided to ignore his implication that this was somehow her sole responsibility. "She and I will address it with the Emmas together."

"I just don't want her bulldozing us. Or blaming the 'club secretary' for all of it."

"I won't let her do that," Rose said, though she knew Samantha's tactics. Once, when the Emmas were three, Z had found some paints Gareth was trying out in the bathroom. She brought the ugly brick red and the hideous burnt umber back to Q's room and smeared the walls, the carpet, the bed. When Rose walked in to check on the girls, Emma Q's room looked like a slaughterhouse. Q herself was perched up on her new big-girl bed just watching, fascinated, clean as a whistle. But when Samantha saw what was going on, she barged into the room, swept her paint-spattered daughter up off the floor, and marched her to the shower, saying, "Did Q want to paint with you, sweetie? Did Q show you some paints?" Couldn't have been Z's idea, of course.

"Another thing to keep in mind." Gareth ran his hands through his hair.

"What's that?"

"This could get a lot worse," he said ominously. "The CogPro was only the first cut. What happens next time, when these kids get the final word on admissions? How will the Emmas handle that?"

And how will I, Rose wondered—*and how will Samantha, and Lauren, and Azra?*

She crossed her arms. "How have we raised these little brats with our friends?"

"They're not *my* friends."

"What's that supposed to mean?"

"Nothing. Just—" Then he said it: "I *told* you this school was a fucking nightmare, Rose. And now look what's happened. I've known all along this was a bad idea."

She examined him closely, with a quiet fury. He was pouting now, despite his anger, like a petulant boy.

"This is not about you, Gareth," she said, with a calm precision. "It's about our daughter."

FORTY-TWO

ROSE

The mistress of Twenty Birch spooned honey out of a pot and smeared it on a wedge of pear and added a small slice of Gorgonzola. She handed Rose the concoction. Sweet and savory dancing on her tongue, a burst of juice. Rose had always loved the kitchen over here, the calming way the light played on the copper countertops, cluttered with bowls of fruit and strainers of freshly washed vegetables, a warming round of cheese on a clay plate, a crusty bread sliced on a rustic cutting board.

She'd been hesitant about coming over after the meeting at Donnelly, wary of Samantha's reaction, but Gareth was right. This couldn't go on, and so she'd texted Sam to ask if she could stop by with Q.

Samantha was still in her gym clothes. She offered a glass of Prosecco but Rose declined, thinking of the missed hours at the lab she would have to make up late into the night. Again.

Samantha took a cherry in her mouth. She pushed out the pit, set it on her napkin, and looked at Rose with a sigh. "So, the Gifted Club."

"Yeah," Rose said.

"Was Sue Willis schoolmarmy with you guys?"

"She was pretty upset."

"Same when we went in."

"And that's not the only thing I wanted to talk to you about."

Rose told her, finally, about the drive out to the stables, the girls' atrocious exchange regarding their classmates. She watched Sam's lips for that defensive twinge they would often make when her perfect parenting was challenged. Instead she nodded along, mouth soft and pooched, and when Rose was finished, she didn't immediately jump in to correct her account.

"It scared me," said Rose. "Made me feel like I don't know my own daughter. Have you had that sense, with all of this?"

Samantha considered the question. "I mean, Z's a Zellar. She felt *entitled* to her test score. Of *course* she's going to top a one-forty, you know? She can be so disdainful sometimes when she doesn't see other kids acting up to snuff. I want to protect her from that side of herself because it's not attractive, but Kev is—well—"

"A Zellar."

"Exactly."

"Hey. Q isn't an innocent here either," Rose said quickly. "That stuff about Xander not really being all that smart, a kid they've known for ten years? And the way Q talked to her teacher? It feels vicious to me."

Samantha smirked. "The vicious part was saying something."

"What do you mean?"

"Come on, Rose. You know it's true. Just be honest: the Emmas are two of the smartest kids in their grade, right?"

"I guess so."

"And what they say about Beulah kids is actually true."

"Sam!"

"Don't be so PC and benevolent. I mean, think how Azra feels. Do you realize that an Asian American kid has to score a hundred points higher on the SAT than a white kid to get into the same elite colleges? It's how they were discriminating against Jews fifty years ago. What, you think a bunch of deserving Crystal and Kendall County students won't lose out to kids from Beulah just so the districts can meet an arbitrary numerical target? Please, girlfriend. The problem isn't that they *think* it. The problem is that they shared it with their classmates."

Rose started to protest, to summon all the arguments Lauren and Azra would make against this regressive view of the school system's diversity strategy. But with Samantha such objections would fall on deaf ears—and besides, there was something darkly alluring about Sam's view of her own privilege, and thus Rose's. If the Emmas weren't admitted to Crystal Academy, this outcome would say nothing about their intelligence or talent or ability; rather it would be an accident of metrics and political compromise, a necessary concession to the demographic realities of the Front Range.

Rose got a weird taste in her mouth: *bad cherry*, she thought, and ate a fresh one.

Samantha toyed with the paper tab of her tea bag. "Obviously this is all Z's fault."

"Why would you say that?"

"You know Emma Z, always the ringleader. Gifted Club president is a natural fit. I'm sure there wasn't a vote."

Rose bristled but calmed herself quickly. Samantha's braggy observation rang true, and this wasn't about Rose's feelings.

"So, shall we call them to the mat?" Samantha asked.

"You mean, right now?"

"Why not?"

"I think I should talk to Gareth before—"

"Men are useless with this kind of thing. Let's just nip it in the bud."

"Should we make some hot chocolate for them, to soften the blow?"

"Oh, for god's sake, Rose. You'd be a horrible general. We need to get these little bitches in line." She pushed herself off the stool and walked to the basement door, then leaned over the head of the stairs and shouted down.

"EMMA Z! EMMA Q! COME UP HERE, PLEASE!"

That felt good," Rose said once the girls were gone. Confessions and tears had been extracted, and Samantha had made the Emmas write letters of apology to the teacher, the principal, and the children they'd most upset.

"Want some of this now?" Samantha held up the Prosecco bottle, dewed, the label sloughing off.

Rose couldn't imagine doing any good work tonight, in the lab or at home. Better to start fresh tomorrow. "Just a sip."

Samantha retrieved two flutes from a cabinet and poured. As she set the bottle down her phone rang. "I should take this," she said. She walked into the next room, far enough from the kitchen that Rose heard only murmurs, then a raised voice followed by a few spits of angry air. Then silence.

When Samantha came back, her face had changed. Rose waited for her to say something, but the silence lengthened.

"Who was that?" she finally asked.

"Just Kev," Sam said tightly. "Some crap at work."

"Are you sure?"

Sam grasped the stem of her flute. "It's fine." Her eyes glazed over and her knuckles went white on the flute; then, with a *crack* that Rose would remember for the rest of her life, the crystal stem snapped in her grip. The narrow, beautiful bowl tipped and fell to the countertop, where it shattered, flinging a wash of Prosecco across the copper.

"Sam!" Rose reached for her friend's hand, but Samantha pulled away. "Are you okay?"

"Ha! Look at that!" A gash of blood rose on her left palm. She shoved it under the sink and turned the faucet on. "And that was Baccarat from Kev's grandma. *Dammit.*"

As Samantha tended to her hand Rose unspooled a length of paper towel and sopped up the mess, gathered the crystal shards. By the time Rose had cleaned up Sam had covered her small wound with antibiotic cream beneath a Band-Aid, the only trace of her injury sterilized and concealed.

FORTY-THREE

EMMA Z

My fingers hurt." Emma Q shook out her right hand. They'd just finished writing their apology letters to teachers, classmates, and the principal, and now they were back in the den figuring out what to Netflix while their mothers talked some more in the kitchen.

"Better than getting grounded," said Emma Z. She really wanted Q and her mom to leave now. It had been a long afternoon already.

"Why did your mom make us *do* all that? It'll be so embarrassing when people get the notes."

Z kept flipping through show choices. Emma Q hated to be punished. This one time when they were both little and everyone was over at Azra's house, she'd loudly repeated something that Emma Z had *whispered* (duh!) about Xander and his big head. Azra had made Q apologize and sit in a chair for fifteen minutes until she promised to be nice. She cried and cried for over an hour and finally had to go home. Q wasn't used to getting consequences, for *anything*.

The main reason was that Rose was so wimpy. She was all squishy about things like discipline. Sometimes Rose told Q she wasn't allowed to do something, and then an hour later if Q whined a little she'd say fine, okay. And Q, surprise surprise, was exactly the same way. She couldn't even pick her own lunch at Noodles.

Which was why Emma Q would never be a strong leader like Emma Z.

She didn't have the qualities a decisive manager or department head needed to succeed in today's dog-eat-dog corporate environment.

Emma Z's mom, on the other hand, *did* have those qualities. That's why her mom's friends always did what she said. They always saw the movie she wanted to see, ate at the restaurant she wanted to eat at, had the kind of party she wanted to have.

Some people would have said this was because Z's mother was bossy. She'd heard people say that before, people like Beck and Charlie and even Rose. But being bossy was really just about having sound leadership skills.

Which reminded her. Emma Z set down the remote on her beanbag chair and went to the table against the wall of the den where the materials were spread out for her portfolio. A stack of glossy papers, a trifold, pamphlets, a copy of a magazine, and the banner, printed in big blocky letters that would make the whole thing look very official once it was all put together.

EMMA ZELLAR:
BORN TO LEAD

Now she just needed to paste it all onto the trifold and arrange her binder, and go with her mom to turn it in.

Q came over and looked at all the stuff on the table. "What's this?"

"My portfolio. It's all about my leadership qualities."

"Really?" Q scratched her nose. "What kinds of things?"

"Well, I was captain of our soccer team last year, remember?"

"Uh-huh."

"And I'm fifth-grade class president."

"Well . . ."

"What?" Emma Z glared at her friend.

"Sorry but I mean—didn't you just *say* you were class president when school started? There wasn't really an election."

"It's in the yearbook that just came out, so." Z picked up the Donnelly Elementary yearbook from the table and showed her the bookmarked page. Emma Zellar with her arms crossed and a stern look on her face. The caption: *I'm only class president now, but when I'm older I'm going to be president of the United States! 2044 is right around the corner!!!!*

"Oh," said Q.

"Plus I have an essay in a magazine and I'm taking a college class at Darlton about leadership and it's *really* interesting."

"You're taking a class at Darlton University?" Q gaped at her and Z felt a flash of superiority. She had saved this bit of information to share with Emma Q at just the right moment. Q read so much that sometimes Z worried there were things she didn't know that Q did. But as her father liked to say, *There's book smart and there's world smart, sweet pea. And I'll take the world over a book any day.*

"It's called Leaders as Entrepreneurs. I'm sitting in on some of the sessions," Emma Z said lightly. "It's at the Varner School of Leadership. My dad gave them a bunch of money for, like, a lobby or something, so the associate dean said I could take the class. Do you want to see the syllabus?"

"The what?"

"That's the class schedule. It lists the readings and assignments the students have to do." Z dug through the papers on the desk until she found it.

Q paged through the packet. "You have to write all these papers?" Her eyes shot wide. "And you have a three-hour *exam* next week?"

Z smiled. "No, because I'm a junior auditor."

"What does that mean?"

"It's a special thing where you get to take the class but you don't have to do any of the work."

"That doesn't sound fair." Q looked up from the syllabus, trying to hide a pout. "Aren't there any rules?"

"A strong leader makes her own rules," Emma Z said, snatching away the syllabus and replacing it on the table, right next to two pink paper roses she'd found in her room yesterday.

With her back to Emma Q she said it again: "A strong leader makes her own rules." Emma Z smiled. I like that, she thought, staring down at the roses. *Her own rules.* She picked one up and brought it to her nose and sniffed, smelling nothing.

FORTY-FOUR

CH'AYÑA

They brought Atik along again, spending the early hours at the Zellars' and the afternoon at some apartments in South Crystal, four of them in a building Silea had been working for five years. Through the day, as Ch'ayña mopped, wiped, sprayed, bent her back and ordered Atik around, she stewed over the thought of him up on that stage. All pageant, all pretense. The Crystals using her Atikcha for his Quechua and his Spanish, taking his gifts so they could feel better about themselves.

"You sang for them, didn't you," she said to him over their lunch, a *sopa de quinoa* they spooned from thermoses on the Zellars' back porch. "Sang like a bird in the mountains."

Atik wrinkled his nose. "That's not how it was. I *wanted* to go up there. I *wanted* to show them."

She snorted. "To show them. So that's what this is about, this school? Showing off?"

He shook his head and looked away. Ch'ayña shot a look at her daughter, but Silea was on her phone, probably texting with Tiago. She vowed to have it out with Silea about the school, but by the end of the day she felt too weary to bring it up again.

---

ilea set out plates for them, some flour-fried pork with stringy greens. Too much salt on everything, and the pork was dry. Silea was a horrible cook, even when she used both hands. She went to doze on the sofa, and Ch'ayña said nothing about the food. After his supper Atik went around the trailer taking pictures on the phone. He was photographing his folded animals and fruits and things but choosing bad positions and poor lighting.

"Not from that spot." Ch'ayña pointed with her fork at the stove. "The light will be better from over there."

He moved to where she told him, took a few shots of the paper cars and trucks on the table, then pointed the phone up to shoot the cluster of birds dangling on strings from the ceiling. Atik had made the mobile a year ago during a blizzard, using a book about South American birds he got from the school library and a whole pack of the fine folding paper you could only find at the art store in Crystal. Many of the birds had fallen since, but at least thirty still hung there, in all their colors and shapes.

"No no no," said Ch'ayña. "You need to get lower."

Atik huffed. "You do it then, Awicha."

She pushed back her chair. "Give it," she ordered.

He handed her the phone, and she pointed the lens at the thicket of his birds to find the best views. Not all the birds at once; that would dull the effect. What you wanted was a nice cluster, some sharp on the screen, others a blur in the background.

"You have the good eye, Mamay," Silea said sleepily from her spot. "You've always had it."

True. You had to get the position right. The angles and lighting. Not difficult but the details mattered.

Ch'ayña went around the trailer with the phone, getting shots of everything. The train and trees on the back of the toilet, the little village and the car park in Atik's bedroom, the forest and orchard in theirs.

In Ch'ayña's opinion her grandson's greatest creation was a small paper replica of Mountain View itself. He pulled it out and she shot it: thirty-seven paper trailers, sixteen cars and trucks, two bicycles leaning against a double-wide, even the dead cat, all taped to a piece of gray cardboard in the precise arrangement of their neighborhood.

Afterward they sat three together on the couch and went through the pictures, choosing the best ones for Atik's portfolio. "Tiago knows a place to print them out," Silea told them.

"We don't need his help," Ch'ayña snapped back. Once again he was butting in where he didn't belong.

Silea tapped her arm brace. "Right now we need all the help we can get."

"Anyways I like him." Atik leaned forward on the couch to look down at his grandmother. "He thinks the school is a good ticket. That's what he said."

"Oh, he did, did he," Ch'ayña said. "Ticket to what?"

Atik just shrugged. "He's smart like you, Awicha."

Ch'ayña scowled at the flattery, though she knew what Atik said was true. Tiago had a clever way about him, and the man was good with his hands. When he came around to fix things, he worked methodically but exactingly, with an eye for detail. Atik was teaching him how to fold animals, and Tiago was pretty decent at it, despite the man's long and thick-knuckled fingers.

Silea sent the pictures through the air to him, and this reminded Ch'ayña of the day Silea got her phone. Three days of pay. How strange it was, to lose half her daughter's mind to that shiny little square.

FORTY-FIVE

BECK

Seen in slow motion, on a giant high-res Mac screen, Aidan's dribbling was a thing of subtle wonder. Sometimes Beck had to watch it up close and slowed down to believe that his son's feet could do what they did. The curve of his left boot caught the ball before flexing it to the outer side, then back again, now to his right foot, *tink tink tink*, then a hard pass across the midfield line. Beck adjusted the framing, cropping in to highlight Aidan's legs and feet. He shaded away the rest and added an artful dissolve.

The highlight reel was eight minutes and thirty-two seconds long so far, with a digital mountain of clips still left to sort through. Beck's goal: twenty minutes, enough to show the admissions folks Aidan's dazzle. With the right production values, good editing, and a few twists here and there, the reel should make a wicked centerpiece for his son's portfolio. Sure, it meant a few extra hours in the basement, but this was probably a good day to stay home. Leila was supposed to drop by the studio downtown to pick up her overdue paycheck, which Beck had vaguely promised her he'd leave in hard copy in an envelope on her desk by lunchtime.

Wasn't happening. Not today anyway.

Thump.

Thump.

Thump.

"Hey, guys, keep it down!" Beck yelled up the stairs.

Thump.

Crack.

"Guys!"

Crack.

"Guys, quiet!"

The basement door squealed open.

"Little *shithead! Liar!*"

Charlie's shout, followed by a clatter of feet down the stairs. Beck turned away from the computer as Aidan hurled himself into Beck's lap, red-faced and sobbing.

"Charlie hit me," he wailed. "He almost hit me with his bat too, but he hit a wall instead."

"*What?*" Beck grasped his son by the shoulders and looked at his tear-drenched face. A red welt rose on his right cheek. "Where's your m— Where's Sonja?"

"Tay—tay—taking a nap," he blubbered.

Beck shouted at the ceiling: "Charlie, come down here!"

No response.

"Stay put," he said to Aidan, jogging up the stairs past three half-eaten cans of cat food sitting on the landing like mines, contents slathered across the sheet vinyl. At the top of the stairs he stopped to gape at a yawning new hole in the drywall.

"Charlie!"

Upstairs, Charlie had locked himself in his room. Music thundered from his speakers and shook the door. Beck grabbed the handle and pounded. "Charlie, open up! Open up right now!" No response.

He stomped toward the master bedroom. "Babe," he said, bursting into one of the few orderly rooms in the house. Sonja was sprawled across the comforter dressed in yoga pants and a running bra with her head propped up on a throw pillow. A big pair of Bose headphones covered her ears. With her eyes closed she looked like a beautiful bug.

"*Babe.*"

Beck went over and tapped her knee. Her eyes opened and she pulled her headphones off and set them down between her legs.

"The boys were fighting downstairs. Charlie almost beat the shit out of Aidan."

"Oh dear."

"You didn't *hear* them?" He planted his hands on his waist.

"No." She indicated her headphones.

"Well, it was bad."

"And did *you* hear them, Beck?"

"I was in the basement."

She raised her eyebrows. "And so? I was upstairs."

"But I was working."

"You were playing with your soccer videos. You have been playing with them all day. You stayed home from work to play with your soccer videos."

"I'm making a highlight reel for Aidan's portfolio. It's *important*."

"More important than what is happening to Charlie?"

"What are you talking about?"

"Azra says he's acting horribly, saying all these things, lashing out at Aidan. She is very worried about him, Beck."

"She hasn't said anything to *me*."

Sonja tightened her lips.

"Okay, maybe she mentioned it. But I didn't think he was going to act on it like this."

She frowned. "What did he do?"

"He swung a bat at Aidan, downstairs when he—"

"A *bat*?" She sat up, focused now, alarmed.

"Yeah, I mean it hit the wall and didn't hit him, and who knows if Charlie was really trying to hurt him, but still. There's a big hole in the Sheetrock."

"Charlie needs help, Beck. What if he hits Roy?"

"There's no way—"

"You need to call Azra, right now, and get him an appointment with that therapist."

Dr. Dan. Beck hated Dr. Dan, the condescending baby voice, the toys, the drawing, the big co-pay. They'd taken the twins to the shrink just after telling them about the divorce. Total waste of time—and money.

He tugged his beard. "I guess I should call her."

"If you don't, I will."

"That would be awesome."

Sonja sneered but started patting the bedspread, looking for her cell. Beck saw it by her ankle and handed it to her.

"Where'd you get those headphones?" he asked.

"What, these?" She stopped scrolling and glanced down at them, as if seeing them for the first time. "They are the noise-canceling kind. Azra gave them to me last week." She looked up at Beck, the flecks in her irises burning an Alpine green, like an alien death ray. "They were a birthday present."

Beck looked at the mirror behind the headboard and saw it happen, a grayness infused across the patches of skin above his unkempt beard. His legs weakened and dropped him onto the bedspread inches from Sonja's smooth knees, which she curled away from him and pushed beneath a pillow like a turtle withdrawing its toes.

When Sonja came to bed in old sweatpants and a T-shirt, Beck took the nightly hint. They hadn't screwed in seventeen days, by his count, even though over the previous months they'd just been hitting their stride again following the inevitable postpartum poontang lull. He was beginning to suspect that this abstinent turn was tactical on his wife's part, another facet of her overall Sun Tzu household strategy. No laundry, no dishes, no sex, which especially sucked because he'd spent the last three hours doing everything he could to make up for his idiocy about her birthday. He'd made reservations at Xiomara for tomorrow, he'd bought her a full spa day at the Aspen Room, he'd even started planning a perfect getaway for them in Denver later in May, with reservations at the Brown Palace for two nights, including old-fashioned high tea in the lobby both days, something he'd heard her mention wistfully more than once. Just another set of charges on another card.

She slipped between the sheets and turned her back to him, nose in some German novel. He pushed up on his elbows. "This is getting ridiculous.

What, so we're in an Adam Sandler flick now, my wife withholding sex until I wash a goddamn dish?"

"Or remember a goddamn birthday," Sonja said. "And the better reference is Aristophanes."

"What?"

"Nothing."

"Babe, I'm really sorry, okay? I just—can I give you a shoulder rub, at least?"

She flipped a page. "I would rather have Roy vomit on my neck."

FORTY-SIX

ROSE

They ran in tandem, Azra and Rose in the lead, Lauren and Sam behind them, street-stepping their way toward the Crystal Canyon path, a wide pedestrian throughway and bike route that started way out east at Eighty-fourth Street and followed the bubbling Crystal Creek several miles along a narrow canyon. Last summer, during a cool-down, they had tried to calculate the total miles traveled on these Friday runs since they'd met. Four miles times fifty-two weeks times eleven years: more than two thousand miles, a vast distance filled with countless conversations and endless opportunities to emote and vent.

But only silence so far that morning, the slap of soles on asphalt and concrete. As they turned onto the creek trail Lauren broke the thin ice with a jackhammer.

"Just so you all know, our appeal was successful," she announced.

Rose almost laughed aloud at her friend's bluntness.

"Good for you," said Samantha. "Xander deserves a spot if anyone does."

"That's for sure," Lauren said.

Rose, looking sidelong, saw Azra shake her head, tight-lipped.

"How exactly did the process work?" Samantha asked. "Did he have to retest?"

"No. We have an old Stanford-Binet score, from back in second grade. He was in the ninety-ninth percentile. So there's that, then the schools got their independent assessor to administer the Wechsler, because his CogPro nonverbal was so high. *Ridiculously* high. Plus some of his teachers at Odyssey wrote in."

"So he's through the first cut?" Sam asked.

"Yep."

"And you didn't have to retest?"

"Not the CogPro."

Samantha asked a few more questions about the process. Her interest in the appeal sounded excessive to Rose's ear. Usually Sam would be the last of them to indulge Lauren's obsession with her son's brilliance.

Azra half-turned her head. "I'm not surprised they have the appeals thing worked out. This school—I mean, I had my doubts but Aidan seems really jazzed about it. Plus I'm blown away by Bitsy Leighton, everything she said about inclusion, the multilingual stuff. Even Beck's starting to fall in line."

"She was great at the meeting," Lauren admitted.

"And one-on-one she's just as passionate. She has this edge I really like."

"Mm-hmm," Rose hummed. *Uh-oh.*

"Wait, you met her?" Lauren's voice was a touch sharp; but Azra, amiable as ever, didn't seem to catch on.

"I talked to her for a while the other night, after you and Gareth left the party," Azra said, to Rose again. "She was pretty chatty by that point. Later I was telling Glen how much I liked her, the thought of Aidan in her hands. She really made me think."

"What party?" Lauren asked.

Azra didn't respond: big mistake. Any one of them could have fixed it right then with two sentences. Instead they met Lauren's question with silence, and the longer it lasted, the more noxious it grew.

"What party?" Lauren said again, this time more deliberately.

Two cyclists passed them, ascending west into the foothills. At the same moment the rising sun flooded the canyon from the east, warming their backs and casting them as long figures on the earth. Rose saw the shapes of

Samantha and Lauren moving ahead of her, mingled with the shadows of her own running legs.

Azra broke their silence with one of her nervous wordfloods. "Glen invited me along, and Sam suggested a double date since we just started seeing each other and I was telling her I really wanted him to start meeting you guys. And anyway it was just a fund-raiser for the medical school."

"Bitsy Leighton is the dean's first cousin," Rose clarified. "That's one of the reasons she moved here."

"So why were *you* there?" Lauren asked Sam.

"Because Kev's on the foundation board. We're major donors to the epilepsy center."

"Let me get this straight," Lauren said. "The three of you were partying with Bitsy Leighton last weekend?"

"It's not like we were doing mezcal shots with the woman," Samantha retorted. "It was a big party. Half of Crystal was there."

Rose cringed as she ran. *Half of half of 1 percent, maybe.*

"Oh, I get it." Lauren sounded bitter now. "So this is the grown-up version of the Emmas' Gifted Club. Do I have that right?"

Rose whipped her head around. "There's no club here, Lauren. There's just not."

"Ridiculous," Samantha muttered loudly, speeding up, putting space between herself and Lauren. They had come to a steeper part of the trail that veered around a corner, narrowing as it hugged a canyon wall. On the other side a waist-high railing separated the trail from the road, requiring them to run in single file. For a full minute no one said a word, and Rose was hoping the stretch might give everyone a chance to cool off.

No such luck. When the trail widened again, Lauren sprang ahead and pushed between Azra and Rose. Her shoes kicked up a puff of dust as she turned on them and stopped. Hands on hips, she glared at Samantha as they slowed to a halt in front of her.

"What's ridiculous, Sam?"

"Oh, I don't know," Samantha panted, bending to put her hands on her knees. "Maybe your paranoia?"

"Sam." Rose reached out for her.

Samantha straightened and shook off the hand. "No, I'm serious. Lauren, I'm sorry that Xander didn't hit the mark on the stupid test, but huge congratulations on your appeal. And I'm sorry this has been hard for you, because no one and I mean *no one* deserves it more than Xander."

Samantha could have stopped there.

She didn't.

"Because I know you're used to thinking of your son as God's gift to the rest of us poor earthlings."

"Sam, stop." Azra sounded scared; Rose felt it too.

Lauren's mouth dropped open. She looked slapped and small.

"But you know what?" Samantha stepped forward until she was almost in Lauren's face. Rose could imagine her two friends back in fifth grade, the ages of their children, the queen bee and the drone facing off.

"Other kids have gifts too," Samantha continued. "Some can play the piano like Rubinstein. Others can play soccer, or ride a horse like a pro, or write beautiful poetry, or—or make friends easily and have a basic curiosity about people other than themselves. Not that you would ever notice what other kids are doing. Do you even know what *our* children have been up to? Have you asked any questions about *them* lately, or shown curiosity about any kid but Xander in the last few years? Because honestly I haven't seen it."

Rose knew where this was going, could feel it coming like a thunderclap. "Samantha—"

Sam thrust out a palm and her voice lowered to a near whisper. "I mean, do you even know what's going on with your own daughter? *Do* you, Lauren?"

Lauren's skin went pale, despite the sweat streaming down her face. Her voice was trembling when she responded, "Don't you *dare* bring Tessa into this, you entitled *bitch*."

"You guys, please." Rose stepped between them, her voice shaky and scared. "She doesn't mean it, Lauren." Desperate to make peace, she looked back at Samantha, just as rattled as Lauren in her own cold way. "Sam? Will you apologize to Lauren? Come on. And Lauren, will you . . . could you . . ."

Rose's voice trailed off and Samantha simply stood there with her lovely chin jutting out, her arms folded, eyes searching the top of the canyon wall.

Rose looked at Azra. *Why aren't you helping here?* she wanted to scream, because normally Azra could dissipate any tension among her friends with her ease and open grace, but right then she was as frozen as the other two.

Finally Lauren hocked and spat on the side of the trail, seething against Samantha's icy demeanor. "I don't *want*. Her *fucking*. A*pology*." Chopping her hands out to the side with every other syllable. She backed away. Azra and Rose surged forward—instinct—but Lauren went rigid and splayed her hands in front of her face, as if to push them away.

"*No*. Do *not*. Fol*low*. Me *home*." More chopping. "Just *don't*. I'm *fine*."

She turned away and sprinted, back through the narrowest part of the trail and toward the sun.

FORTY-SEVEN

BECK

From his window seat at Finnegan's Wake, Beck looked down onto a throng of vapers and smokers crowding the tables out front, all nose rings and ear stretchers and inked skin. Something thrashy and carnal on the speakers. A caramel latte on the counter by his left hand.

Catastrophe on his laptop screen.

The firm had just lost another client, a big account in Broomfield that had covered half his overhead for the last four years. They'd lost major business before, the design trade could be fickle, though usually there was enough of a cushion in the firm's operating account to cover payroll and other expenses.

Not this time. Too much turnover, too much back-and-forth between Beck's personal finances and the firm's bank account. Might have to off-load his full-time admin, he reckoned, maybe even pare Leila down to part-time, if she'd even agree to work for him at all, given the ongoing paycheck fiasco. Might have to fucking fire himself, if it came to that; and hell, maybe bankruptcy wouldn't be so bad. If the president can do it . . .

But then again, anything drastic could be put off for at least a few months. All it would take was another card. He was right in the middle of applying for a new Corporate Platinum Mastercard (*Optimize accounts payable through robust transaction-level reporting!* the promotion encouraged) when a big hand slapped him in the middle of the spine. Beck knew that hand, that slap.

"Hey, partner," said a familiar gravelly voice.

In one motion Beck shut his laptop and twirled around to see Wade Meltzer's wide face beaming down.

"Hey, man," Beck said, surveying him. He was used to seeing Wade on the sidelines in cargo shorts and T-shirts, torturing referees. Today Wade was dressed in a tailored suit, a button-down oxford shirt, and a subtly patterned tie. The getup rendered Meltzer a different person: trimmed and powerful.

"You clean up nice," Beck said. Wade grinned. "But I thought your outfit practiced in Denver."

"Mostly we do." Wade lowered his voice. "Got a little drug thing up here at the courthouse. Kid of one of our major clients peddling ecstasy in the dorms." He rolled his droopy eyes. "I'm at the tail end of my lunchtime constitutional, figured I'd pop in for a cuppa. Anyway." He shot a cuff and looked at a wafer-thin watch.

"You'll be at the tournament next weekend?"

"Oh, hell yeah. I have a feeling we'll take it too. Tough bracket but our boys look solid. Had to give Coach a piece of my mind on our winger situation, though. Joey can't finish these days." Meltzer picked up his coffee from the counter. "Back to the jungle. You take care now."

"You too," said Beck.

Joey can't finish these days. Neither can I, Beck thought, staring glumly at his screen, thinking of his messed-up eldest son, his zeroed-out bank accounts, a sprawling web of debt. And now he wasn't getting laid, or even flirted with by any of the latter-day hippie chicks wandering in and out of the coffee shop.

He minimized the credit card app and opened Facebook, mostly to distract himself with a few political threads. Aside from the occasional porn fix, Beck's only form of therapy these days was to go after neoliberals still wedded to the two-party system, all these lame corporatist Democrats convinced the world would be saved from ruin if the Senate tilted two seats toward the center. He spent ten minutes arguing over voter suppression on one thread, another fifteen enlightening a few fact-challenged DNC die-hards on another.

Meanwhile two new notifications had popped up, both from acquaintances in the area asking him to join a public group and "like" its page. Interesting.

Beck clicked through. The group was calling itself the Alliance of Parents Against Crystal Academy, ALPACA for short. Its mission statement read like standard entitled-activist pablum.

> We are a group of concerned parents strongly opposed to the creation of
> the new public magnet school for allegedly gifted students. We believe
> that gifted education should be democratic, egalitarian, and nonexclusive.

ALPACA. A perfect acronym for a protest group in a city like Crystal. There was an entire store on the Emerald Mall dedicated to clothing and accessories crafted of alpaca wool humanely sourced from South America. You could get a felted alpaca shawl, an alpaca cape, even a onesie for your infant. Alpacas also featured prominently in the city's self-loving iconography, like on those KEEP CRYSTAL STRANGE! bumper stickers you saw on all the Volvos around town. (Beck hated Volvos almost as much as he hated the Clintons.)

ALPACA's page header featured an artist's multiculti rendering of six disembodied forearms and raised hands, each a different hue, from dark brown to pale beige, with the words EQUALITY IN EDUCATION emblazoned in bold red lettering across the top. The page had eighty-six likes so far, but as Beck scanned it for the first time the number clicked up to eighty-seven. Eighty-eight.

With his anxiety mounting Beck started reading the posts. Typical Facebook bullshit, a heady mixture of righteous indignation, scripted bragging, and boozy chattiness.

> **Ann Marlowe** Thank God this group exists! I've been wanting to vent
> for MONTHS and finally it feels like there's a safe space for that. This
> whole thing has been so demoralizing for our family. I guess our

son just isn't "gifted" enough for the Upper School, despite his four AP classes, his perfect grades every quarter (every quarter!) through his sophomore year, etc. etc. Now one stupid test and he's out. INFURIATING!

11 mins

> **Carol Kinsley** With you, **Ann**.
>
> **Midge Wilson** Preach.
>
> **Dave Riggins** Fuck this school.
>
> **Toni Andriesen, Administrator** Let's try to keep the language clean, **Dave**. Our kids could be reading this page!
>
> **Dave Riggins** Noted. Apologies. Just a little worked up!
>
> **Toni Andriesen, Administrator** No worries! ☺   ☺   ☺

Dorothy Ernst shared a link to the *Crystal Camera Opinion Page*
Hope everyone saw the op-ed in the Camera yesterday. Favorite quote: "Crystal Academy, once it opens, will represent one of the biggest blows to equity and equality in public education our local school districts have witnessed in a generation." Follow the link for more. Great stuff!

42 mins.

> **Erin Barnes** Drinking gin while reading it. Feeling better.
>
> **Carol Kinsley** I'm on my second appletini but who's counting?

Tracey Larsen Does anyone on this page know anything about the meeting the other night, the one at East Crystal High where they discussed portfolios? Apparently the superintendents were all there, the new principal from California, etc. Did they explain themselves? Because I'd like to know why the admissions people are considering this "whole child" BS for the second cut but used only the CogPro for the first cut. What am I missing here??????

2 hrs.

> **Toni Andriesen, Administrator** Speaking only for myself (though I think many would agree), this is precisely the reason we started this group in the first place, **Tracey**. They've used the CogPro to weed out, what, 80% of the population, and now they tell us that they won't even be using those scores for the second cut?

Tracey Larsen Thanks for this, **Toni**. I think there needs to be a
community meeting—sort of a town hall type thing. If we can
do it with our state legislators about concealed carry, why can't we
call in the school board and superintendents for our children???

Toni Andriesen, Administrator Great idea, **Tracey**. Let me do
some calling around and we'll nail down a date and venue, then
get some invitations out. Solidarity!

Carol Kinsley Hold my appletini. I'm there!

Olivia Steiner Just catching up on this thread after late-night arrival
from Barcelona—uber jetlagged. But we are shocked! How can this be?
We just moved here over the summer from the Upper West Side of
Manhattan for my husband's new tech job. Our daughter was enrolled
at TAG, a gifted magnet in East Harlem, all the way through elementary
school. And now she doesn't qualify for a magnet out here in Flyover,
Colorado? This is beyond absurd.
4 hrs.

Erin Barnes It's a challenge for all of us, **Olivia**. No need to look
down on our beautiful Front Range!

Carol Kinsley Agreed. No need for any more dividing and
conquering—the schools are already doing that for us!

The posts went on in this vein, fourteen of them altogether since the
page was launched the night before, and each post continued to accrue
likes, dipshit emojis, and replies as Beck read along. By the time he scrolled
back up to the top, dozens of new likes had appeared, approaching two
hundred now. ALPACA was going viral.

Beck wrote up a group email to Azra, Gareth, and Kev.

Hey, all,

You guys see this? Some nasty stuff here about the academy, a lot of
angry folks stirred up about admission, testing, etc. Probably worth
paying attention to, IMHO. Sorry to be bearer of bad news!

Pax,

B

He pasted in the link at the bottom. After he hit Send, he scanned a few more posts, all his ambivalence about the gifted school returning like a bad meal.

an outrageous use of public resources in an age of budget cuts and defunding

just a bunch of lip service to diversity

and the lower school is in the wealthiest neighborhood in Crystal. Coincidence???

Beck chewed his lip. The ALPACA meeting was in two days. A lot of these folks would be attending, some just to vent, some to organize against the school, others to listen, which is what Beck wanted to do. Because maybe his initial instincts had been correct. Maybe this gifted school wasn't such a great idea after all; and besides, it was just a meeting. Azra didn't need to know. He put it on his calendar and packed up and was pushing out the door when he bumped into Tessa Frye on her way in.

"Hey, there," he said, holding the door for her, happy to see a young and optimistic face.

"Oh, hi, Beck." Her eyes widened at the sight of him.

"What's up?"

"Um." Tessa's eyes darted left and right. She showed him her MacBook. "Just some homework, then I have a shift at BloomAgain."

"Cool. It's awesome you're doing that."

"Yeah. Azra's amazing."

"That she is." Beck nodded and lingered, the door still open.

"Well, see ya!" She gave him a nervous little wave, then walked off toward some tables in the far corner.

He watched her for a few seconds then let the door hiss closed behind him. On the sidewalk he stood for a minute, thinking over the encounter. Tessa had looked almost embarrassed to see him, or to be seen with him. What the hell was *that* about?

He sniffed his pits, examined himself in his phone camera to see if he had something gnarly in his nose or his beard. Nope, all good.

Man, he thought as he left the shelter of the awning. Now even Tessa wouldn't give him the time of day. As he trudged off to find his car he opened the ALPACA page again on his phone. More posts, more likes and meanie-face emojis, more hating on the gifted school.

A Touch of Tessa:
One Girl's Survival Guide to Junior Year
A Video Blog

Episode #196: HITS

... 487 views ...

[In BloomAgain, a circular clothes rack with several shirts and jackets hanging from the rod; at the center a colorful stenciled sign: TESSARACKS.]

TESSA: Hey, you guys. So here it is! Can you believe it? Just four things so far, but in a couple weeks I'll have some new rags up. You like this shirt? We sold one just like it yesterday, to this girl from Denver Central who comes in here a lot, and Azra said she wants one for her boyfriend's daughter, so I'm like, sold! And she bought it for forty dollars. I can't even tell you guys what—just what this feels like, to be doing something like this. Designing things, making them, literally selling them, you know? It's like I have an actual life or something.

So, okay, but—awkward!—there is this one thing I wanted to ask you guys about. This is weird but suddenly it seems like more people are looking at our channel. Have you noticed that? Like usually I get maybe six hits on my vlogs and they're all probably from you losers. But yesterday I saw that one of them had twenty-three views, and this other one was on thirty-three, and Maurice, did you see that like a hundred people watched the one about your SATs? So I don't know, you guys. I mean, I'm used to getting lots of eyes on my Instagram, like if I post a fashion sketch, a lot of people will share it and comment and whatnot. That's totally different, though; nobody even knows who I am on there. But some of the stuff I've vlogged, it's just—are you guys worried about it? Jessica, you set this channel up, so maybe you could change the settings, so all of this is private? I don't know if I want to put any new ones up until we figure this out. Anyway. It's probably stupid but I wanted to say something. Love you guys!

FORTY-EIGHT

ROSE

Putting together major grant proposals had always made Rose feel like a coin spiraling around a funnel, moving slowly at first as she surveyed the problem from above, accelerating as she began to tick off action items, spinning madly as she neared her deadline, waiting for the final drop. Her lab staff could feel the vortex of the final sleepless weeks about to suck them in. Data to crunch, controls to design, a whole raft of scientific and budgetary expectations to meet. There had been other major grant applications in her career but never for this amount of money, never with so many eyes focused on her work.

The past week had been filled with one minor disaster after another, from a miscalculated facility costing that affected half the budget to a disagreement with a potential co-investigator at Johns Hopkins. Then, that morning, one of her postdocs, the problematic Franklin Barnes, had transmitted some old erroneous data during a Skype session with the director of a computational neurology center in Berlin. After the Skype call Rose had admonished him in front of the staff. Nothing major, and he'd deserved it, but now she had to deal with his bruised ego along with his sloppy work. She spent the early afternoon checking in on everyone's progress, trying to cheer on her team.

By three her nerves were shot. She retreated into her office to stare out through the blinds into the lab. A mug of fresh coffee steamed on her desk.

Leaning back in her chair, she looked at the mug and read, probably for the ten thousandth time, the words printed in a flowery font on the forest green ceramic.

Friends are the siblings God never gave us.

Azra had had the corny saying printed on four mugs she'd presented one spring evening ten years ago. They'd been gathered around a patio table at a downtown bar when she pulled out four small boxes wrapped in crepe paper and tied with white ribbons. "I know this is kind of hokey, you guys, but I got us all a gift."

"That is so sweet." Samantha leaned over to give her a hug.

"Thank you, Azra," said Lauren, looking solemn.

"What's the occasion?" Rose asked.

Azra smiled shyly. "Well, I don't know if you guys realize this, but today is our one-year anniversary."

"Wait, seriously?" said Sam.

"May twelfth. Our first coffee-and-bagels klatch with the babies."

"Over at Twenty Birch." Sam gave the table a happy slap. "That's right. We were in the sunroom."

"For some reason that date stuck in my head, and I wanted to mark it for us. So I got these." Azra nodded down at the boxes.

They opened them and found their mugs, each a different hue. Burgundy for Samantha, teal blue for Lauren, a forest green for Rose, and Azra gave herself mustard yellow. They cooed appropriately as they read the proverb out loud. *Friends are the siblings God never gave us.*

"Who said that?" Rose asked Azra.

"Found it on ReadyQuotes. Some ancient Chinese proverb."

"Hey, if the shoe fits," said Samantha, and they all laughed, loose and happy and close.

"No, but seriously, you guys." Azra looked around at them. "You know I'm an only child, and you have no idea what this group means to me." They all teared up, even Lauren. Their fingers joined along the circumference of the table. "You're my sisters now. So thank you."

"Let's drink to that," Samantha said as their hands unclasped. She poured half her cosmo into her new burgundy mug and raised it. "To friendship."

The others likewise decanted their cocktails and raised their colorful mugs, a ceramic rainbow over the table.

"To friendship."

Anniversary mugs, like Friday run one of their cherished traditions. Every year, on or about the twelfth of May, someone would order up mugs in the same four colors and emblazoned with a carefully curated quote. The sayings were often saccharine, sometimes funny or irreverent, but they always rang true.

One of the most beautiful qualities of friendship is to understand and to be understood. (Seneca)

One loyal friend is worth ten thousand relatives. (Euripides)

Friends cherish one another's hopes, are kind to one another's dreams. (Thoreau)

Friends are the best to turn to when you're having a rough day. (Justin Bieber)

That year was Rose's turn, and she had already chosen just the right quote, though she didn't know if she'd have the nerve to get it put on four mugs and hand them out. Azra had emailed it to her years before when she was upset with Samantha over some slight long since forgotten, and she had vowed to save it for just the right anniversary. It fit the present occasion like a neoprene glove.

True friends stab you in the front. (Oscar Wilde)

She sipped her coffee, still hot, and finished it in a single gulp that scalded her throat.

At four she allowed herself a glimpse at her phone. Five texts, the most recent one from Gareth.

Read your email!!!!

Rose eye-skipped through several dozen messages until she found her husband's, forwarding something from Beck. The link took her to a Facebook page for a group calling itself ALPACA, for Alliance of Parents Against Crystal Academy. The page had four hundred and twenty-seven likes so far. The most recent post had just gone up.

Elaine Steiner Could someone please repost the info on the organizational meeting for the town hall? Totally disorganized here . . .
2 mins.

> **Toni Andriesen, Administrator** Check the Events tab at the top of the page, **Elaine**—everything you need to know about the meeting is in there.
>
> **Elaine Steiner** Thanks, **Toni**!!

Rose clicked on the Events tab and found a post about the ALPACA meeting at the home of Steve Markley and Toni Andriesen. Rose knew them: Toni was a member of City Council, serving alongside Kev Zellar. Her husband, Steve, was on the med school faculty; pulmonology, maybe. She went back to the main page to read other recent posts.

Tracy Ingham Here's a great piece from Better Parenting magazine about the dangers of "gifted" labels in elementary schools. Really helpful perspective here! Key sentence: "In short, gifted programs may be doing our brightest children more harm than good."
55 mins.

> **Nancy Wooden** Wait, seriously? I'm absolutely appalled at the lack of knowledge displayed in this article, and I say this as a longtime advocate for gifted children and a practicing child psychologist. The author seems to have done no informed reading whatsoever on the subject, despite the extensive peer-reviewed research arguing for the efficacy of TAG programs in the public schools. Would anyone on this list say that a physically disabled student in a wheelchair shouldn't be provided with accommodations that meet his or her specific needs? Should children with learning disabilities be denied specialists trained to deliver instruction to this population? Then why should gifted children not be given adequate resources to

address the unique abilities and attributes that set them apart from their classmates?

Corbin Shaw elitist much?

Tracy Ingham I'm sorry but comparing a kid who scored well on an IQ test with a kid in a wheelchair is offensive as hell.

Nancy Wooden That's not what I'm doing and you know it, **Tracy Ingham**. My problem with Crystal Academy is that it will divert much-needed resources from the EXISTING gifted-and-talented programs in our public schools. THAT'S the real scandal here.

Ron Borton No, the real scandal is the government shelling out more taxpayer money so the snowflakes up in Pink Quartz can have another cream puff to brag about on college applications.

Mark Yopps Let's face it, most "peer-reviewed research" is a crock. Why do we need some social scientist to tell us what we already know?

The ALPACA Facebook page was like a political blog, thick with self-righteous moms, libertarian trolls, mansplainers. Rose scrolled down through six or seven more contributions until she found a particularly worrisome post.

Len Blick I don't want to spread false rumors, but has anyone else been hearing things about Bitsy Leighton, the new head of school? I have it from a reliable source that she's been hanging out with a select group of parents, giving them advice on portfolio preparation, admissions particulars, etc. Something about an exclusive party at some rich parent's house? I find the secretive processes surrounding Crystal Academy quite disturbing, especially given all the lip service to openness, transparency, equity, etc. The hypocrisy on the part of these PUBLIC SCHOOL administrators is stunning. They're supposed to be working for us!!!!!
3 hrs.

    Mary Riggins could not agree more. triple like!

    Tekla Rabinowitz geez is that really true? Is that even legal???

    Carter Dempsey WTAF?

    Mary Nielsen yup

Olivia Kim No words.

Toni Andriesen, Administrator Frankly I'm not sure about this—it's a pretty harsh rumor to be spreading if it's based on secondhand information, especially about a female leader new to our community. Let's stick to the facts, which are bad enough.

Len Blick The fact remains, if she's showing favoritism to certain parents over others during the portfolio review process, we need to know why. Hope we can add this to our list of questions/demands for the organizational meeting.

Toni Andriesen, Administrator Done!

Carter Dempsey I would take Len's suggestion one step further. Any parents who attended an event like that should have their children automatically disqualified from admission to Crystal Academy. Period.

The last comment had already garnered sixty-three likes.

The whole exchange was like a chop to the sternum. Rose stared at the screen, seeing Bitsy Leighton on the stage, at the dean's fund-raiser, imagining how she would react when she saw this vicious piece of public gossip so soon after her move to Crystal Valley. Suddenly the fresh-from-California head of school was hosting parties for the parents she liked, playing favorites, giving some children unfair advantage over others. A mean and ugly distortion of the truth; though it was undeniable that Rose *had* been trying to take advantage of a personal connection to Leighton through her dean.

She looked at the post again, tempted to write a lengthy explanation in response, tell everyone in the ALPACA group how wrong they were. Instead she picked up her office extension. The silly charade had gone on long enough. As Leighton's phone rang Rose imagined standing in front of a dozen school administrators, mocking up a presentation on a nonexistent research project, faking her way through a phony set of questions and objectives. Nipping this thing in the bud was definitely the right decision.

"Bitsy Leighton."

Rose opened her mouth to speak—then froze.

"Hello? . . . Um, hello? . . . Who is this, please?"

Rose slowly set the receiver in the cradle and closed her eyes. Why hadn't she spoken—and confessed? Would caller ID pick up her lab number, identify her as the caller? What must Bitsy Leighton be thinking right now, with some rando making prank calls to her office in the school district?

She looked down at the handset, appalled. Her palm had made sweat prints on the phone.

Only an hour went by before Rose, unable to resist the masochistic lure of all that parental anger and angst, checked the ALPACA page again. More likes, more hand-wringing, more polemics against the admissions process.

Toni Andriesen I wanted to share this very reassuring update on a prior thread. Dr. Leighton has posted a statement on the Crystal Academy home page about the party in question. I take her at her word, and I think the rest of us should as well. Link is below.
27 mins.

Rose clicked on the link to the school's web page and read Leighton's statement.

To Members of the City of Crystal and Four Counties Communities:

In the last twenty-four hours a rumor has spread that I have been "socializing" with a number of parents seeking admission to Crystal Academy for their children. It is true that I attended a social event at which several such parents were also present, including one of the hosts. The event in question was a medical school function at the house of my cousin and my goddaughter, an eighth-grade girl I have known since birth. While I understand how some might have received such an impression, clearly I was not attending the party in an official capacity as head of school. Any parents present at the party who believe otherwise are sorely mistaken.

I also want to assure the community that I personally will play no role in the admissions process, which is being handled exclusively by Dorne & Gardener through a procedure designed to insure the utmost integrity.

Please feel free to contact me directly for further clarification.

Regards,
Dr. Elizabeth Leighton

Founding Head of School
Crystal Academy

"Jesus," Rose muttered. The words *sorely mistaken* flailed at her like a ruler on the knuckles. It was nearly dark when she left the building to grab a sandwich at the student union, a new moon hiding somewhere above. The bats were out as she returned to the lab. Hunting spring bugs, falling through the night.

Many hours later she clicked off her desk lamp and sent a quick safety text to Gareth, letting him know she was on her way home. As she passed the Sub-Zero on her way out of the lab she stopped, seized with an almost childish longing. She set down her bag and pulled a tray from the back of the freezer. The slide she selected was a dated one, a cortex sample from an earlier grant, the tissue probably four years old. The freezing glass edges burned her fingertips as she took the slide to the microscope room.

With the TEM powered up, she slipped the glass slide into the holder and zoomed in and there it was: the invisible zing of countless electrons creating a frozen dance of green and blue. The sight of cells laid out like this was always propulsive, inspiring, slightly terrifying. You thought you knew what you would see, but the cells changed even as they stayed the same. You learned more, you noticed more, you changed along with them. This looking always brought back to Rose her first enchantment with the human brain, long before she knew how much of her life would be devoted to understanding the great intricacies of this majestic organ's life and health, its engines and its pathologies, the mysteries of its work. Rose could go weeks without looking at a cell or euthanizing a mouse, months without touching a patient's hand. Running a lab required a certain detachment from the raw material of her research. She forgot how much she missed it, and sometimes it was good to check in.

A guilty pleasure, this gazing down on a brain sliver without a research agenda or an article to write. To feel like a child again, when all you wanted to do was look.

FORTY-NINE

XANDER

On Thursdays Xander carpooled from Odyssey with Jebanny Ford, a fourth grader. Jebanny's mother was a fast and kind of crazy driver, so Xander almost always got home before Tessa. A bonus, because Tessa could be grumpy after school. But usually he had a good twenty minutes or so to himself.

Sometimes, though, Tessa got home first if she skipped her last class or got a ride or biked extra fast. And today he *had* to get home first, but there was a traffic jam on Range Parkway, a bunch of rescue vehicles up ahead in a sea of colored light. By the time they got past the accident and pulled up in front of the town house, Tessa was just coasting into the garage.

Xander leapt out of the car and pounded up the front steps. Eight small packages were lined up on the porch. He unlocked the front door and gathered them all up awkwardly in his arms.

He heard Tessa coming upstairs through the laundry room. Aquinas lumbered in, shoved his big nose at Xander's balls, and knocked him off balance. The packages fell to the floor. One of them slid off down the hall and hit Tessa in the right foot.

She bent down and picked up the stray package, glancing at the shipping label. She looked at the other packages sprawled on the floor of the front hallway. "What's all this crap?"

"Stuff for my portfolio." He started gathering up the other packages.

When he stood, she was holding out the eighth one, not looking at it, just staring at him.

"Thanks." Xander grabbed the package between his chin and chest.

"There's cookies, little brother," she said, still looking at him strangely. "A no-nut kind."

"Which variety?"

"Mint Milanos."

"That is my all-time favorite kind of cookie."

"I am aware of that, little brother."

"Oh."

"So you'd better hurry."

Xander took the packages back to his room, shut them in his underwear drawer, and went back to the kitchen. Tessa put two cookies on a paper towel and set them in front of him.

"Thanks," said Xander.

"Want some milk?"

"Yes, thanks."

She went to the fridge. "So, little brother."

Little brother again. Tessa only called him that when she was thinking about something Big. It was a pattern. She set a glass of milk in front of him. He dipped a cookie and bit in.

"I have to tell you something," she said. "It's kind of—a secret I've been keeping."

Xander blinked at her and waited. Tessa reached into her school backpack, pulled out a binder, and set it on the table in front of him. It was her portfolio, she told him, for Crystal Academy, and over the next five minutes, as they plowed their way through the bag of Mint Milanos, she showed him her sketches, photographs of her clothing designs, even a special rack for her "new clothing line" that Charlie and Aidan's mom had set up for her at BloomAgain. Tessa had taken the CogPro at the makeup session without telling their mother, she explained, just to see how it would go. She was shocked to make the first cut, but the only people she'd told so far were her friends from Sweet Meadow.

"I'm sorry I didn't tell you, Xander," she said. "Especially because I know you didn't do as well on the test as Mom thought you would. That's probably hard, you know? I'm just glad the appeal worked out."

But was it hard? he wondered, bothered for some reason by what his sister was telling him. He wasn't angry at her, just a little . . . uncomfortable, and for the first time he understood at least part of what had been going on inside his head for the last few weeks.

He bit into another cookie. "I didn't do well on the test," he said as he chewed, "not because I lack the requisitely acute quantitative, abstract, and verbal reasoning abilities but because the test was extremely simplistic and I was bored, and I don't really want to go to Crystal Academy despite our mother's fondest wishes."

He thought the way he said all this might make her laugh, but instead her face froze and her mouth hung open.

"You don't?"

"Well, actually," he said, thinking of Charlie and Aidan and video games, of Emma Quinn and her thick hair, "I think I probably do want to go. I'm just—maybe—confused."

His sister rolled her eyes and smiled at the same time. "It's okay to be confused, Xander. You're not a fucking, like, computer, okay? You're almost a teenager, and believe me, once you're twelve or thirteen things will get a lot more confusing, even for a megadweeb like you." She sighed and dipped the last cookie into his milk. "It just makes me wish Dad were still around, you know? Because he could explain this stuff to you better than I ever could, let alone Mom. Bitch didn't even know when I got my first period."

Tessa closed her binder and started to gather up the other things from her portfolio.

"You're going to get in, you know," he said, aware that the thought made him happy.

"You think?"

He nodded.

"How do you know?

He took a last swallow of milk and looked at her over his glass. "I just know things. Lots of things."

FIFTY

ROSE

In the kitchen Emma Q sliced peppers and Rose peeled eggplants while Bonnie Raitt warbled sadly over the speakers. "Two Lives," a slow track from *Sweet Forgiveness*, one of her early albums, cut the year Rose was born. *If you had a secret, I could take a guess . . . One of us is hiding.* Her lips made the words as strips of dark skin accumulated on the counter.

For Rose the rare comforts of making food with her daughter and ordering Gareth out of the kitchen were usually centering, though today they did nothing. The exchange with Bitsy Leighton at the party was worrying her, and she knew her clumsy lies about the bogus study could yet come back to bite Emma Q. And Samantha's behavior at Twenty Birch the other day had been unnerving. A crystal flute cracking in her hand, a line of blood crawling across her skin. Rose yearned for the quiet of the lab, but tonight would be good for her, for Q, for her marriage and her sanity.

On an impulse she had asked Lauren and the kids over for supper, a small normalizing reparation for what happened on Friday run. Lauren acted surprised to hear from her, to receive a dinner invitation so soon after her outburst, but she accepted. She would have Xander in tow, she told Rose; Tessa had other plans.

"Do I have to play chess with Xander?" Q asked. She held the knife poised above a purple pepper, still whole. Rose examined the sprawling pile her daughter had already produced. Red, orange, yellow, green, a mound of sloppily julienned slivers ready for the sauté pan.

"That's the last one we'll need." She stroked Q's head, the smooth and shiny hair. "Once you're done throw them all in that bowl. And yes, you have to play chess with Xander. At least one game."

The blade cracked through the skin, and Rose smiled because Q didn't really mind. Xander was anything but boring, plus Q loosened up with him when Emma Z wasn't there to boss her around.

There were lots of ways to be with people you knew so well.

X ander came in first when they arrived, wordlessly slipping past. Gareth reached out to shake his hand, but he had already disappeared inside, a boy on a mission.

"That smells so good." Lauren squeezed Rose's hand before getting on her toes and kissing Gareth on the cheek. "Great to see you guys."

"I'm happy you're here," Rose told her, and it was true, because when you got Lauren in a smaller group where she didn't have to show her feathers, she could be disarmingly kind. There was a goodness in her that came out in practical ways too easy to forget.

That time Q came down with the flu, for instance, and they hadn't had their shots. The three of them were laid out with fevers spiking 102, only three hours into their Tamiflu when Lauren showed up with a pot of chicken soup, the stock boiled fresh from the bones. She came right in and got it heating on the stove, then brought the whole family bowls of it in bed. She did the dishes, vacuumed and mopped, took out the garbage, even got down on her knees and cleaned their flu-spattered bathroom. Rose was too weak and delirious to object, and once everyone recovered it felt as if an angel had descended on their home. When Rose tried to thank her for it the following week, Lauren barely remembered they'd been sick.

A blessing, to know the talents and limitations of those closest to you, what they're capable of and what they aren't. One kind of friend who will spend hours sifting through your psyche; another who will sacrifice half a day to scrubbing your toilets.

Gareth set the table and Q ran off somewhere with Xander. Rose was in the kitchen with Lauren drinking chardonnay, and of course what Lauren wanted to talk about once she was loosened up was Crystal Academy. She was cautious at first, nosing around, curious to find out exactly *how* the dean knew the new head of school, *why* the rest of them got invited to the party.

"I don't know what came over me. But when Azra was going on about that wonderful Bitsy Leighton, I started losing it. Then Sam went off about Tessa . . . I had to get away from you guys."

"We all reach breaking points sometimes," Rose said. "Our group can be intense."

"It's not just that." Lauren folded her arms. "I'm jealous, okay? I'll say it. I'm jealous as hell of everyone else's easy kids."

"Seriously? Easy?"

"Admit it, Rose. Emma Q is like an angel."

"She has her darker side," Rose countered, speaking softly, because Q tended to creep up. "That nightmare Gifted Club? Gareth and I were mortified. I wanted to throttle her. And Q is a bright kid, sure, but she's no Xander."

"Oh, please." Lauren looked out the kitchen window. "Xander is off. That's what everyone knows about Xander."

"Lauren! What are you saying?" Rose turned from the counter, showing Lauren her face. "Sure, he's an odd duck. But that comes with the territory. There is *nothing* wrong with your brilliant son." She stepped closer. "I'm a pediatric neurologist, for Christ's sake. If you're going to listen to anyone other than your pediatrician or an actual specialist, it'd better be me."

Rare tears appeared on Lauren's cheeks, running freely now. Her face was wide open in a way Rose hadn't seen it in years.

"Thank you for saying that." She sniffed. "It's just that sometimes other people's kids— It's hard."

Rose nodded along.

"God." Lauren hung her head. "Sure, Emma Z can be a little witch. But do you realize that the Zellars actually go to *plays* together, that they've taken her to chamber music concerts in Denver? Plus they've traveled all over the world with her. And even Azra and Beck's boys are polite and charming, these amazing athletes, so charismatic. And I've got—" She clapped her hand over her mouth. "How can I talk about my kids this way?" she whispered between her fingers. "It's just that ever since Julian died I focus on them, *only* on them, and I know I don't ask about the Emmas and the twins all that much, Sam's right, but I love them all, I hope you guys know that, I would do anything for them, but it's all *focus focus focus* and I've fucked up so badly with Tessa and—and—*god*, I'm such a shit mom."

Rose stepped into Lauren's space. "You're an incredible mother, Lauren, and you've been through hell. But you've got an articulate, beautiful daughter who's coming out of a dark place and doing great." Rose felt her worries recede in the face of this more important truth about a mother she loved, a daughter she loved almost like her own child. "Seriously, Tessa is amazing. Those outfits, her eye for the telling detail. And you've got a brilliant son whose love of science makes me green with envy. It's a cliché, sure, but you've got two kids who could change the world. That's what you've got."

Lauren's shoulders hitched, and Rose rubbed her arm even as her own parenting jealousies clawed for attention, the petty and the profound. How she envied Emma Z's charismatic confidence and her graceful form and wanted both for Q—desperately sometimes. The ways she'd fantasized about Xander's brain and how nicely it might fit her daughter's skull, if you could just lobotomize his weirdness. The relaxed way Azra and Beck had with their boys, who seemed to wear their full emotional lives on their sleeves.

Insidious, these false versions of superiority and ease we project onto other families: how often they blind us to the surer comforts of our own.

After dinner Gareth cleared plates while Lauren and Rose sat in the living room with the kids. Q was on her third round of chess with Xander. He was letting her stay in the games longer than he needed to, stretching them out, taking his dutiful notes. He'd done it with Rose earlier, making just enough weak moves to give her a glimmer of hope before lowering the boom. Testing her somehow, in a way he never had before, though still ruthless at the end; a wily cat toying with a blind mouse. She had never seen him lose, not since he was three.

An undeniable talent, a spike like no other, as Bitsy Leighton might have said. Rose thought anxiously of Emma Q's portfolio, the need for a special finishing touch. But what could it be?

Gareth came in wiping his hands on the seat of his pants. "Xander, how about a game or two?" he said, flashing a grin at Rose. She smiled back, glad he'd volunteered in Q's place. He so rarely interacted with any of the younger kids aside from the Emmas.

Xander looked at him, inscrutable as ever. "Q wants to play again," he said.

"That's okay." Q crab-walked backward. "I've got a book." She lunged for her Kindle and settled in at Rose's feet.

Rose spoke softly with Lauren as Gareth and Xander played. A few minutes into their game a gentle tap sounded from the front door. Q glanced up from her Kindle, recognizing the knock. She bounded up to answer, and when she came back, she had Tessa by the arm.

"Well, hello there," said Lauren from the sofa. "I thought you had plans."

"I did," Tessa said. "They ended early."

Tessa wore a flannel shirt untucked above unpatched jeans, dressed plainly for once. Instead of taking the free chair she slumped down on the floor with her back against the hassock, as far from her mother as possible in the small living room.

Gareth looked up from the chessboard. "Tessa, you hungry? We have plenty."

"I'm okay," she replied softly. "I already ate." She blinked, her pretty eyes fluttering, and a surge of love for this odd broken family swelled in Rose's heart, along with a fierce protectiveness that surprised her.

Tessa stopped blinking and stared at a random spot on the rug, her eyes slitted now, opaque—familiar. Rose shivered and some animal instinct caused her to raise her hands and squeeze the chilled flesh along her upper arms. She remembered the two of them sitting just like this at Julian's wake all those years ago, mother and child huddled on opposite sides of a room, unsure how to go on, bewildered by the sudden absence of a cherished life.

The silence lingered, deepened; then Xander moved a chess piece, and the spell in the room was broken by a capture, the *tink* and roll of another kill.

PART IV

SPIKES

Gifted children often have fears like those of older nongifted children . . . but do not have the emotional control to put these insights aside and go on with their lives.

—NANCY M. ROBINSON,
in *The Social and Emotional Development of Gifted Children*

City of Crystal

SCHOOL DISTRICT

achievement, excellence, equality

TO: Crystal Academy Stage II Applicants

FROM: Dr. Joe Jelinek, Superintendent

SUBJECT: Portfolio submissions

April 2, 2018

Dear Crystal Families:

This is a final reminder about the timeline, format, and procedures for portfolio submission in support of your child's application to Crystal Academy. We will be evaluating upwards of eight thousand students in Stage II for approximately one thousand combined seats in the upper and lower schools. It is of crucial importance that all portfolio submissions conform to the guidelines set out in this memo.

Content

Your child's application portfolio can include virtually anything, from book reports to ribbons won at a gymnastics tournament, and we are eager to recruit a well-rounded student population. However, the admissions committees will pay particular attention to those parts of an applicant's portfolio that demonstrate concentrated ability or proficiency in a specific area, whether scientific, athletic, or artistic. Parents are advised to help their children compile the materials that will best showcase the applicant's one special talent, achievement, or competency.

Format

The contents of portfolios should be submitted in a single container, whether a box, a portfolio case, or an accordion folder. The container should be clearly labeled with the child's name and parent contact information. In the case of web-based or online materials, please provide a cover sheet with full URLs and detailed instructions for accessing the relevant components of the application.

Procedure for Submission

Portfolios must be submitted in person at the Lower School for students applying for grades 6–8 and at the Upper School for students applying for grades 9–12. *No exceptions.*

Deadline

All portfolios must be submitted by 5:00 p.m. on Wednesday, April 18, in advance of the Open House on Sunday, April 22. *Again, no exceptions.*

FIFTY-ONE

ROSE

Am I really doing this?

On Monday morning Rose sat in her lab with the door closed and a cold slug of guilt inching up her throat. Xander's chess, Aidan's soccer, Emma Z's well-rounded perfection—Emma Q's what?

She looked down at her unpainted nails and then at her fingers, poised over the keyboard. *Am I really doing this?*

The trifold lay flat and open at the side of her desk. The Emmas' joint History Day project, returned the week before with an A+++ scrawled on the banner in red ink.

THE HORSE IN THE AMERICAN WEST
BY EMMA ZELLAR AND EMMA HOLLAND-QUINN

The last names weren't in alphabetical order, Rose noted with a frown, but otherwise the girls had done a beautiful job with the project. At least two dozen discrete artifacts were arrayed across the surface, from old post-cards and movie stills to cutouts from magazine articles about modern breeds and siring. Everything was laid out neatly but artfully, creating a real sense of visual wonder while conveying an enormous amount of information about the chosen subject.

The trifold was all ready to be clipped and zipped into the poster-sized portfolio case, along with the other evidence of Q's dedication to equestrianism, beginning with Janelle Lyman's testament, which Rose had placed on top of it all. She was tempted to frame it.

To Whom It May Concern:

I am delighted to provide this assessment of Emma Holland-Quinn's equestrianism. Although Emma has been enrolled in introductory lessons with me for less than three months, she has already developed into a truly gifted rider, with a natural grace in the saddle that comes across in a variety of ways: a mature sense of posture, balance, and form, a quick mastery of rein length and leg alignment, and, most remarkably, an intuitive touch and manner with the animals, who respect her and yield to her commands without the slightest hesitation. Usually I have our young riders wait many months before competing against representatives from other stables. In Emma's case, I have little doubt that she could compete against some of the best riders her age if she wanted to—and would have an excellent chance of coming away with ribbons!

Having taught hundreds of girls her age over the last ten years, from up and down the Front Range, I can say with confidence that Emma Holland-Quinn is among the most promising young riders in Colorado today. Please don't hesitate to contact me if you would like me to elaborate on any of the points above.

Sincerely,
Janelle Lyman
Owner and Principal Instructor
Wild Horse Stables
Edgemont, Colorado

It was perfect. Couldn't be better if Rose had written it herself. But the trifold. The subject had been plucking at her nerves for days, and frankly it didn't seem fair that Emma Q should get only half the credit for a project to which she had contributed 75 percent of the imagination and labor—and who knew how the admissions committee would evaluate joint projects. At least with Rose's neurology papers you could tell who the lead author was, because hers was always the first name in the list on the title page. In this case, though, the consultants would assume the Emmas had played an equal role in producing this gorgeous display of inquiry and knowledge.

She looked back at her screen, at the new banner she'd typed up to replace the original version glued on by the girls a few weeks before. Same rustic typeface, same size, same title. Only one small difference.

THE HORSE IN THE AMERICAN WEST

BY EMMA HOLLAND-QUINN

Rose bit her lower lip. She remembered that first moment she saw Emma Zellar, a sweet baby girl bobbing in the pool, riding Samantha's hip when she came out of the locker room, seeping into her daughter's life with the slow, invisible osmosis of water itself, until the two girls became nearly indistinguishable.

Am I really doing this?

She closed her eyes. She exhaled. She printed.

It was only Monday, portfolios weren't due until Wednesday, but Rose wanted to submit Q's early, just to be on the safe side. The handover would take place in the model classroom at the lower school, now in its final stages of renovation.

Rose's first impression when she entered the building for the first time: clean lines and gleaming planes, everything new, details glistening from surfaces of polished wood, stainless steel, smooth slate. Walls a muted gold, built-in bookcases stained cedar. The ceiling lights pleased the eye, tuned just bright enough to complement the natural Colorado daylight pouring in from the south.

The whole place was being prepared for an event advertised on posters as a big community open house the following Sunday, designed to allow the administration to celebrate the new school and welcome townspeople to its grounds. Two fresh-faced young women sat behind the intake table to process portfolios and greet parents as they flowed through. Laminated Dorne & Gardener name tags shone from their suit jackets: AINSLEY and MIRIAM.

Rose stood in Miriam's line. When her turn came, she set Emma Q's portfolio down on the table, then filled out a brief form identifying Q as the submitting applicant and signing over the contents to the school to do with as they wished. Miriam handed her a receipt and turned to place the portfolio gently in a canvas basket truck behind the table, a huge hotel laundry bin on wheels, already half full. Seeing spots, Rose watched the portfolio disappear into the bin's depths.

This is what cheating on taxes must feel like, she thought—or committing a hit-and-run.

With an effort she turned away and nearly bumped into Bitsy Leighton, whom she hadn't seen since the dean's party—and whose voice she hadn't heard since hanging up on her a few days ago.

Leighton smiled, her face unreadable.

"Rose," she said, and held out her spotted hand. "Everything running smoothly for you, I trust?"

"It is, thanks," Rose said, and immediately erupted in a nervous coughing fit. Bitsy put a hand on her back and signaled to Miriam, who tossed her a bottle of water. She cracked it open and Rose took it from her and swallowed, eyes watering over the plastic, glad to have her mouth stopped up for the moment. When she recovered, she thanked Bitsy and tried to start a conversation, desperate to appear normal and unflustered.

"You all are busy, aren't you? Quite a job ahead of you."

"We'll manage," said Bitsy. "In fact we're quite looking forward to the next stage."

"I'm sure you are."

Bitsy scanned her face, and Rose felt herself wilting under the scrutiny. Any moment the woman would mention the bogus study again and try to nail her down on next steps. Rose braced herself, waiting for it to come up as she knew it inevitably would, about to broach the subject herself when Bitsy said, "Remind me. Your child's name is—?"

"Emma Holland-Quinn. We call her Q."

"And why is that?"

"Her best friend is also named Emma. Emma Zellar. We call her Z."

"Oh yes, I know the Zellars," Bitsy said with a smile Rose took as familiar, insidery.

Rose tried to summon a question about the school's facilities. Bitsy cut her off with a curt and inexplicable "Well." She raised her eyebrows. "Best of luck to you, Rose, and to Emma Q."

Rose waggled the bottle in front of her face. "Thanks for the water," she said.

"You betcha," Bitsy said briskly, and whirled away.

Rose exhaled. Such a relief, to feel free of the woman's scrutiny, let alone the nagging itch of her own idiotic deception. Bitsy must have simply forgotten about the study in the whirlwind of admissions. Next time they talked, Rose promised herself, she would come clean.

That evening after gymnastics Rose drove Emma Z home along with Samantha's borrowed dress, dry-cleaned and paper-wrapped on a hanger. She followed Z up the front walk, hoping to catch Samantha. They hadn't exchanged more than a few texts since the blowup on Friday run. A distance had opened up between them, not yet a chasm but something worrisome and odd.

"Is your mom home?" she asked Emma Z.

"Dunno," said Z as she clattered up the porch steps. She opened the storm door and went inside without looking back. Before the door could shut Rose caught the edge and went inside. Kev, passing through the hall, saw his daughter first.

"Dinner's mac and cheese," he grumbled at Z. "It's on the stove."

Rose stopped just inside the door. Kev was standing at a slouch, clad in running shorts and a T-shirt torn above the waist, showing the lower half of his well-worked abdominals. He hadn't shaved in a few days.

"Q's mom's here." Z disappeared into the kitchen.

Kev looked up, the ice cubes rattling in his nearly empty tumbler. "Doc," he said.

"I'm sorry to intrude like this, Kev, I just thought—"

"Sam's at the gym." He leaned against one of the built-in bookcases lining the front hallway. With his arms crossed Kev wedged his tumbler up against an armpit, and the channel of bared belly widened. Rose looked down, embarrassed, though what surprised her more than his unkempt appearance was the attitude. Kev usually showed the manners of a gregarious southern senator. Right now he was surly, quietly furious.

"You guys get your portfolio turned in?" she asked brightly, just to make conversation.

His face contorted, a twist of his mouth and a narrowing of his eyes. "Sensitive subject at the moment, to be quite honest."

"Oh," she said, still baffled by his manner. She lifted his wife's dress. "Mind if I return this?"

"Be my guest," he said with a shrug, and shuffled into the kitchen.

Rose went upstairs to the master suite, where she slipped the dress between two others in the main closet. Back on the porch she leaned against a column, a hand over her chest as the exchange replayed in her mind. Was it something she'd said? But Kev had already been growling at his daughter before he even knew Rose was there.

She heard Samantha's voice behind her. Rose looked through the shrubbery at her car, parked by the curb. Sam leaned over the opened passenger door to speak with Emma Q.

"Just returning your dress," Rose explained, approaching.

"Yeah, Q said." Samantha reached through the gap and showily fluffed Emma Q's hair, then turned and started strolling with Rose up the block. They walked in a thick and awkward silence until reaching the stop sign.

Rose stopped and turned to face Samantha. "Hey, so is Kev doing okay?"

"What do you mean?"

"He seemed upset just now. I got the feeling I'd ticked him off."

"Oh, Kev's just been pissy lately."

"About Crystal Academy?" Rose said.

A sharp frown. "Why would you say that?"

"I don't know. I just mentioned portfolios and he seemed—put off somehow."

"Well, it's difficult." Her face went rigid. "I've been meaning to say something, Rose. Honestly we're having second thoughts about the whole thing."

"You mean the school?"

"I'm afraid so."

"But why?"

"Well—for a while there we thought everything would simmer down and people would chill out. Admissions would be over, the construction done. The controversy would go away. But that's not what's happened. You've read the editorials, Rose."

"Yeah?"

"And Kev has to think about reelection next year. City Council, maybe even mayor, I mean who knows. But that battle-ax who's spearheading ALPACA—"

"Toni Andriesen."

"Right. We've heard she's about to announce for City Council. Kev's seat. And she's planning to exploit the school as a central campaign issue."

"Is that group really going anywhere?"

"Are you kidding? They're meeting right now in her living room. Apparently dozens of people are there." She waved her phone as if to flag a secret source, a spy on the other end of a text chain. "And it's getting ugly. Have you looked at their Facebook page?"

"Of course I have."

"Kev's worried it could all blow up in our faces. And that's the thing, you know?" Samantha's perfect nose leaked out a disapproving sigh. "It's a real shame. It's just not about the kids anymore."

FIFTY-TWO

BECK

Sign the petition—or pass it on?

Beck read the six sentences that represented ALPACA's argument against Crystal Academy, the same language opposing the school on the group's Facebook page. *We, the undersigned . . .* Addressed to the school boards of the Four Counties and the City of Crystal, the petition demanded an immediate suspension of construction and renovation, a redirection of moneys already budgeted for the school's first two years, a reassignment of faculty and staff back out to their home districts, and, to cap it off, a system-wide review of policies on gifted-and-talented programs in the public schools.

Quite an ask, but the tone was reasonable and the style plainspoken, crafted to make the group's requests seem both logical and inevitable. Because who wouldn't oppose the costly opening of a new academy targeting the most elite group of students on the Front Range?

Beck didn't want to be seen not signing. On the other hand, there was no way he'd put his name to the thing, not with Aidan's acceptance hanging in the balance. If the admissions committee got their hands on the petition, all it would take was a quick name match between signatories and applicants to finger the hypocrites.

Azra would kill him.

He looked around. There were a few folks he recognized in the crowd. Amy Susskin, the boys' soccer team manager, for one. The tense gathering was being held in one of those hideous scrape-and-replace mansions you found more and more around the older Crystal neighborhoods, all glass and steel and molded concrete. Beck was one of about thirty parents sitting cross-legged on the floor as Toni Andriesen, ALPACA's self-designated leader, stood in the curve of a baby grand piano, prattling on about action items.

"You done with that?" said the woman to his left, a cute, fortyish redhead with nothing on her ring finger.

"Just a sec," Beck said.

His delay with the petition was starting to feel uncomfortable. A few nearby parents glanced over at the clipboard the same way you'd stare at restaurant diners lingering at a table.

He decided on compromise. He scrawled his name on the next open line, but illegibly, so it looked more like Tom Valiant than Beck Unsworth, and gave a fake email address. As luck would have it the line he filled was the last one on the current page. He flipped the top sheet, covering his deliberately sloppy handwriting, then passed the clipboard to the left.

"Thank you," the ringless woman said, showing him the bare finger. Or maybe she was just taking the clipboard. Beck pretended to listen.

When the crowd broke up for refreshments he slipped out to the back deck, looking for the redhead. She wasn't around but he found a decent lager in the drinks cooler. He glugged it down and grabbed another, downing it while leaning against the railing, watching the herd mill in and out.

"Hey you." Amy Susskin approached from around the corner of the deck.

"Amy." Beck kept one hand on the railing behind him and the other clutched around his bottle.

"How's Aidan's ankle?"

"All better."

"Our game schedule for the tournament changed. I'll send out an update tonight."

"Great."

"How'd the ROMO tryouts go?"

"Just fine," he said tightly.

"Rough, though, to have one kid make it and the other not. You doing okay with that?"

He smiled. "Word gets out, huh?"

She waved a hand. "Your wife told me."

"Azra?"

"No, the young one."

Azra is still young. Beck's first, defensive thought. "Sonja," he said.

"Right. Wow, I'm bad with names, terrible for a team manager, isn't it?" She flashed him some perfect teeth. "I was calling around to nail down snack sign-ups, and Sonja said you were out with the twins at a tryout. I put two and two together, and so." She shrugged. "Sorry if I stepped in it."

"No worries."

"Anyway." She bent back at her waist and turned her round little head to look inside. "Don't know about you but I'm convinced. This school is a menace."

"You think?"

"Worst thing to happen to public education in this town since I moved here."

"What, did Will not test in?"

This stopped her short. "Excuse me?"

"I'd bet most of the people here are just pissed their kids didn't do well enough on the CogPro."

She crossed her skinny arms. "Well, you'd be wrong, Beck."

"You sure about that, Amy?"

"You think ALPACA is just a club for sour grapes?"

Beck shrugged. "Hey, I didn't say it."

"Well, that's—" She glared at him. "I'm surprised at you, Beck. I didn't think for one minute you were the high-flying gifty type. You've always seemed down to earth. Real liberal."

He arched an eyebrow. "Don't call me a liberal. And actually the academy is one of the most progressive experiments in gifted education in the country right now. It's one of the few chances the schools around here have to desegregate themselves, be inclusive for once."

She threw her head back in a laugh. "You've really gulped the Kool-Aid, haven't you, Beck?" A few other parents sensed the heat. Some heads turned. "Why the heck did you even come tonight?"

"I came to see if I could learn from you freaks. But *fuck* that," he said, way too loudly.

Amy went slack-jawed.

"I'm out of here." Beck drained his second beer and pushed out through the living room, setting his moist bottle on the polished surface of the grand piano and avoiding the stares.

"Douchebag," someone mumbled at his back.

On the way to his car he got light-headed and disembodied, as if looking down on a stranger. His hands shook on the steering wheel. He drove a block, turned the corner, then pulled over to the curb. A blunt and a lighter screamed at him from the glove compartment. With the driver's-side window cracked and the ignition still running he lit up, dragged deeply, leaned his head against the headrest, and let the weed do its work in him before he exhaled.

What is wrong with me?

And Amy Susskin. *Christ.* She'd been saying exactly the sort of stuff about the gifted school that Beck really believed, not even that deep down, and now she'd think he was the worst kind of prick, just a Front Range Bernie Bro telling a woman off on some rich dude's deck.

Plus, now he was stoned. A midlife cliché. Worse than that.

He dragged again and held his breath and thought about how he must have sounded to Amy and the others. Self-righteous, haughty, arrogant. Like he was having a nervous breakdown. Maybe he *was* having a nervous breakdown. Indecisive, liable to sudden bursts of inexplicable anger, signing a fake name to a petition. Schizo soccer dad, obsessed, angry, broke.

Just—off.

He moaned quietly, choking out the smoke.

FIFTY-THREE

EMMA Z

Her parents almost never fought, or even argued about anything except in a playful way that always made Z laugh. Tonight, though, they seemed really angry, and everything in the house felt just—wrong. Her father's unadorned mac and cheese was already cold by the time she sat down to eat. She'd had to heat up the bowl in the microwave *herself*, and her parents had been in really bad moods for the last two hours.

At around eight the arguing stopped. Shortly before eight-thirty the doorbell rang. No one ever came over this late on a school night.

Z went to the top of the stairs and leaned out over the banister. Her father answered the door. The man standing there was Mr. Jelinek, the boss of all the schools in Crystal. He'd been to parties at their house before.

Usually when people came to the door, Daddy invited them inside and offered them a whiskey drink with the big ice cubes. Not this time. Instead he went outside and started talking to Mr. Jelinek on the front porch. Their voices were soft at first, too quiet to hear. Emma Z crept down the stairs into the foyer and pressed her ear to the crack between the door and the frame.

"—don't have the authority to do this, Joe," her father was saying in a low voice.

"You're right about that," Mr. Jelinek responded. "I'm just the goddamn superintendent. I'm not Bitsy Leighton, I'm not with Dorne & Gardener. But I sure as hell will let them know about this."

"You'd yank her app based on a hunch?"

"We'd have to, Kev, if it's true."

"Which you don't know."

"Easy enough to confirm. And until we do we can't keep her in the pool."

"What, so you're seriously going to call this guy?"

"I have to."

Whack.

Emma Z's head went back. Her father's hand, she thought, slapping the side of the house right by the door.

"Joe, don't," her father said. "*Please.* This is my daughter we're talking about here, my only kid. Look. We've known each other for a lot of years—"

"We have. But really, Kev? You're this desperate? First you try to gin up an ADHD exemption for your daughter so she can have more time on a second CogPro. Convenient timing, don't you think?"

Emma Z held her breath. They were talking about *her.*

ADHD? But she got a one-forty-five!

"Soaring all those years through the honor roll and class presidencies only to get a diagnosis just as she's heading for middle school?" Mr. Jelinek said. "Then we get a letter from—let me see here—the associate dean of the Varner School of Leadership at Darlton, extolling Miss Zellar's, quote, exemplary qualities as a young leader full of promise for a shaping role in our nation's future, unquote. Okay, fine. One of these kids has a recommendation from a goddamn US senator in his file. But now I find out you paid this guy under the table to work with you on the whole portfolio? Plus you've given the Varner School, what, five mil over the last few years?"

"Joe, listen, I'm telling you—"

"You paid him a consulting fee, Kev. And that's strictly forbidden here. We went over that at every orientation, it's in all the literature. What the hell were you thinking?"

"Joe. Be reasonable here."

"You're asking *me* to be reasonable? You're the one who turned this into such a goddamn shit show."

A shadow fell across the door.

"Z, what are you doing?"

She spun around. Her mother loomed over her.

"Is Daddy in trouble?" she whispered.

Her mom frowned at her and reached for her arm. "Let's get you up to bed, sweetie pie."

Her mother didn't seem angry as she climbed the stairs with Emma Z and watched her brush her teeth, then tucked her in. Instead she seemed—sad. She sat on the side of Z's bed for a while and then lay down with her head on the pillow and told her one of her favorite stories, the one about a brave blue horse and a brave blue girl and how together they rescued a handsome blue boy who was trapped in a dungeon with blue walls. While her mother told the story she rubbed her fingers along the top and sides of Emma Z's skull, scraping along the skin. She wasn't as good at scraping as Tessa, but she was still pretty good, her fingers long and strong as they combed through Z's hair.

Sleepiness leaked into her brain, but before it got her completely Emma Z said, "Mommy, am I stupid?"

Her mother stiffened next to her, and the hand in her hair went still.

"You, Emma Zellar," her mother whispered across the pillow, "are the smartest, most special girl in the world."

Emma Z smiled automatically and her mouth stayed that way until at last she fell asleep.

FIFTY-FOUR

XANDER

Xander, up early at his mother's computer, was just checkmating a thirty-year-old Class B from Singapore when the first email from GenSecure arrived. The ping sounded at 6:03 a.m., followed by another, all the way up to eight pings, one for each test.

The first email he opened was a cover letter, explaining how the tests had been completed and how to interpret the results. There was an explanation of the basics of the process, an illustration of the principle behind base pairs so that stupid people would understand the probability levels. Guanine, adenine, thymine, cytosine, stranded together like a ladder, a code that you could spool out like

AT
TA
GC
TA
CG
AT
AT
GC
GC

but every bit as complex as chess. Actually even more complex, probabilities and variations in the millions and billions and trillions.

Then there was a whole paragraph about how the results were legally inadmissible, which Xander already knew, because the legally admissible tests would have cost over three hundred dollars each and that would have been *waaaay* too much to put on his mother's credit card.

The messages had links that took you to the actual result. He stared at the fifth email in the GenSecure stack.

Save that one for last, Xander told himself. He opened the first link and scanned the chart and glanced at the probability index. *Yep.* No surprise there.

The next one. Same thing.

Next one. *Yep.*

Next one. *Yep.*

Yep.

Yep.

Yep.

Finally the important one. The big enchilada.

And there it is.

Xander got a calm feeling inside, like after a really good poop. Now he knew for sure. Hypothesis correct. It wasn't a hypothesis anymore, actually. It wasn't even data.

It was a conclusion. A result.

The chances that he was wrong? Almost zero.

The chances that he was right?

For inclusion, 99.999 percent. For exclusion, 100%.

One hundred percent!

It didn't get any better than that. Not even in chess.

He spent the early morning hours before breakfast up in his mother's office getting all his materials together and mounting everything on a trifold. His question, his hypothesis, his algorithm, descriptions of his data and notations. Then he made color printouts of all the charts from the downloadable PDFs linked on the results pages. Next he took screenshots of the GenSecure logo, pasted them into a document, and wrote up a summary of the testing process, including an account of how he'd gathered samples.

Xander had already chosen good photographs of all the grown-ups and kids in the five families, from baby Roy all the way up to Xander's mother. Some of the pictures he had taken himself or screenshot from Tessa's vlog. Others he had "borrowed" during playdates and dinners. Once everything was glued onto the trifolds, he drew lines between certain pictures, just as he'd planned out in his research notes. When the whole thing was done, he set the trifold up on his desk and stood there looking at it.

If this project didn't get Xander into Crystal Academy, nothing would.

It was simple. It was perfect.

And it was most definitely life changing.

He waited at the top of the stairs with the trifold tucked under his arms. His mother, he thought, was still out on a run, and Tessa was in the shower. All quiet on the domestic front. He padded down the stairs and stopped on the bottom one.

His mother sat on the couch, still sweaty and scrolling on her phone.

"Hey there, Xander," she said, looking up.

"Hello."

"All done?"

"I have completed the project." He started walking toward his room.

"Aren't you going to let me see?"

He kept walking.

"Xander?"

He stopped.

"Come on, give your mom a peek. You've been working for weeks on this thing. I can't wait to see what you've done."

Xander saw what was on his trifold, imagined his mom seeing it and learning what he'd discovered.

He had a thought:

A Feint is a trick whereby the enemy is induced to defend a vital point against

a false attack; or compelled to defend such vital point against an attack which read-
ily may be developed into a true attack, should proper defensive precautions be
neglected.

From Franklin K. Young, *Chess Generalship*, volume 2, part 1 (1913).

He turned to his mother. "Is Tessa finished with hers?" he asked.

She frowned at him. "What?"

Xander's feint: lift bus, throw big sister beneath.

"What about Tessa's portfolio? She's been working on it very hard."

His mother gave him a weird grin. "Xander, you're such a joker."

"I'm not joking," he said. "Tessa did exceptionally well on the CogPro. She didn't tell you?"

"Xander, what—" His mother got a peculiar look on her face. Whether angry or happy or both at the same time Xander couldn't tell, and in that moment didn't particularly care.

"And for her portfolio," he said, "she submitted drawings and photographs of her clothing line and a letter of recommendation from Azra."

"Her *clothing line?*"

"It's a really good portfolio. You should check it out."

His mother got another look in her eyes. The look of putting two and two together, as the earthlings said. Down the hall the shower went off with a clank.

"*TESSA!*" her mother yelled. She stomped past Xander and zoomed toward the bathroom, Xander's portfolio forgotten as she rapped on the door with her angry knuckles. "Tessa, we need to talk *right now.*"

"Um, I need to dry my hair?" Tessa's muffled voice said from the bathroom.

"*Right now.*"

"*I NEED TO DRY MY HAIR JESUS FUCKING CHRIST MOM!*"

As the fight predictably escalated Xander turned back toward the kitchen, snagged his lunch from the counter, popped it in his backpack, and left the house with his portfolio tucked under his arm. Jebanny's mom was already waiting at the curb.

Xander smiled as he climbed in the minivan. Feint accompli.

Eat that, Bobby Fischer.

FIFTY-FIVE

CH'AYÑA

Silea's arm brace had come off that afternoon. She would be in a flexi-cast for at least another few weeks, but it was a small thing to celebrate, and Ch'ayña would cook. On the way to Dry River she detoured to the Latin store in Loving to get the spices and other items she needed. Back at home she seasoned two chickens with a rub of salt and tamarind worked into the skin. There would also be roasted potatoes with cheese and boiled eggs, bowls of *cancha* on the side, a sugary pudding for dessert.

Tiago showed up at eight, dangling a pack of beer from a bent knuckle. Ch'ayña didn't look at him when he came in, though she also didn't offer him a glass of cold water this time. Instead she busied herself in the kitchen while Tiago murmured with Silea on the couch. The frying pan sizzled, drowning out their soft words. After the corn popped, she spooned the toasted kernels into two small bowls and set the *cancha* on the table.

Tiago got up from the couch and approached the stove. She could hear a glug of beer when he walked up, offering her a bottle. She ignored him but he persisted, held the bottle there and pointed to the label.

Reluctantly she turned to look. *Cusqueña*. That word. She stared at it, mouthed it. Peruvian beer, words and colors that blared from half the trucks on the Huánuco roads. She hadn't seen a bottle of Cusqueña in thirteen years, not since leaving with her pregnant daughter for the States.

"Tiago got it at that big liquor barn in Crystal," Silea said with a sly smile. "They have everything there."

"I would like for you to having this," said Tiago, haltingly—and in Quechua. Ch'ayña frowned at his grinning face but took the beer.

After supper Atik cleared the dishes, then the four of them sat around the table again to look over Ch'ayña's pictures. Tiago had had the twelve shots of Atik's foldings printed on glossy paper to the size of a full page. The shapes and colors shone out from inside plastic covers keeping them clean. Tiago had also brought along a new binder for everything. The three adults watched as Atik arranged the pictures in the order he wanted and used his markers to write his name on a square paper that he taped to the front.

When the binder was complete, Atik slid it across the table to Ch'ayña. "The folder has to be at the school by the end of the day tomorrow," he said. "You and Mamay can take it in, Awicha, after you clean the houses?"

Ch'ayña shrugged. Maybe she could toss it in a sewer on the way. "Fine," she said gruffly.

"I've got homework," Atik said. He said his good-nights, then went to his room.

Silea looked down at her phone calendar. "Tomorrow we've got that new mountain house in the morning, Mamay, then Hollands in the early afternoon."

"Lot of driving," Ch'ayña grumbled.

Silea raised her bad arm, still wrapped tight in a cloth bandage. "One more week, Mamay, then *you* can start sleeping in the truck again."

They all laughed.

"Mountain house?" Tiago asked.

"It's along Opal Canyon a few miles," Silea explained. "We've been there twice and nothing's good enough for the lady of the palace."

Ch'ayña said, in Spanish for Tiago, "Last time I mopped the floor in the kitchen just before we left. It was wet but she let the dog in."

"It tracked mud and dirt all through the first floor," Silea said.

"Which she made me mop again," Ch'ayña added.

"Why not find a different house?" Tiago asked.

Silea shook her head. "The pay is too good. The lady said, 'I simply cannot *abide* paying a house cleaner less than thirty an hour. What kind of *monster* would that make me?'"

Tiago laughed. "She said that?"

"That and other things."

"Guilt always pays extra around here." Ch'ayña stood and went to the sink.

No one spoke for a little while, then Silea asked quietly, "Do you think it will get him in, this origami stuff? Maybe they'll see it as a silly thing, to spend all that time folding paper. Frivolous."

Ch'ayña said nothing.

"It's not just folding, is it," Tiago said. "Origami is knowing shapes and angles and even weight. I've seen structural engineers on sites who aren't half as brainy as your son."

Ch'ayña lifted her head and stared at Tiago's reflection in the small, darkened window over the sink.

"He'll build things, that boy," Tiago said, and Ch'ayña felt a shiver in her old legs.

FIFTY-SIX

ROSE

She sat at her kitchen counter with her head full of fog and her initial grant deadline looming and her ears ringing with the sporadic scream of the vacuum as Shayna visited each room in turn. The intricacies of the budget, sieved through a hodgepodge of university rules and federal regulations, had assaulted Rose from the moment she opened the first of the spreadsheets. There was, she sensed, a minor error somewhere in the cost-share column. She had almost put her finger on it, but then the vacuum went off and the sound of Shayna's spray bottle distracted her. Normally she went to the lab on house cleaning days, but the schedule had been irregular since Silea broke her arm—for good reason, of course, as every job must take them a little longer now, but that did nothing to mitigate her minor irritation as she scanned through the numbers, looking for the snag.

A new torrent of Quechua broke in from the front hall, Silea and her mother discussing something. Rose thought nothing of the exchange until she sensed the two women in the kitchen doorway. She looked up, mildly annoyed. "Yes, Silea?"

"Ms. Holland." Silea stepped into the kitchen. "Very sorry to interrupt you."

"No problem at all. What can I help you with?"

"We are having a problem today. At another house."

"Oh?"

"Up in Opal Canyon. I just got a call from Ms. Emory, the owner."

"Okay?"

"And she says we forgot two rooms, and that we didn't dust correctly in the others."

"It is a big house," Shayna added, the first time Silea's mother had spoken to her.

"I see," said Rose, puzzled. "But can't you just take care of it next time?"

"She is a new client," Silea said. "She—wants us back now. This afternoon."

"Oh. God. Of course," Rose said, suddenly getting it, and part of her was relieved that her house would soon be silent. "Well, of course you should go, Silea. You're almost done here anyway. Go now. *Ve—ahora.* And don't worry about any of this, okay?" She gestured toward the door, waved away the vacuum.

"Thank you, Ms. Holland," Silea said. "Thank you for understanding." She turned and said something to her mother, trying to rush them out the door. But the mother stood there mutely, holding a Pledge can loosely in her left hand and staring at a spot on Rose's neck.

"Is there something else?" Rose asked curtly, anxious to get back to work.

The mother held up a finger. "One moment." She spoke to Silea softly. They seemed to be arguing about something.

"Yes yes," Silea said, looking annoyed. She turned toward Rose as the mother walked out to the truck. "Ms. Holland, may I ask you an enormous favor?"

"Of course."

"It's about my son. About Atik." She seemed almost embarrassed.

"Is he okay? He's not sick, is he?"

"No, ma'am, nothing like that. But—there is something we have to do today, and I'm afraid we won't have time."

"What is it?"

Silea hesitated.

"Here," said her mother, bursting back inside clasping a navy blue three-ring binder. She rotated it and placed it in Rose's hands as if presenting an award or honorary degree.

Rose read the name on the cover—ATIK YUPANQUI—and immediately understood. The binder was Atik's portfolio, for submission to Crystal Academy. Rose had turned in Emma Q's days ago, knowing this would be a hectic week, but today was the actual deadline. If the two women had to work in Opal Canyon this afternoon, there was no possibility they would have time to bring Atik's portfolio back into town before five o'clock.

With an almost tearful surge of understanding Rose started to nod. "Of course," she said loudly. "I'll do it on the way to the lab." Technically she wasn't planning on going in that afternoon, but they didn't need to know that, and a drive over to the lower school would take her all of ten minutes. "I will take the—um, *Yo llevaré la—una—le—portfolio a la escuela?*"

"*Sí sí.* Thank you so, so much, Ms. Holland." Silea reached out to clasp Rose's forearm. "*Muchas gracias.*"

"It's no problem, Silea. *De nada.*" Rose smiled broadly, oddly grateful to the woman for giving her a chance to help, to do something for their beleaguered family. She set Atik's binder on the counter, and the two women hustled out to their truck.

It took her twenty minutes more to find the cost-share error: a discrepancy in one of the fringe benefit rows. The correction affected this entire portion of the budget, ticking everything up a few thousand dollars that would have to be found elsewhere. She wrote a two-line email to the department's fiscal tech asking him to address the issue. Just as she was clicking Send her cell vibrated at her elbow.

"Hello?"

"Is this Dr. Holland?"

"Yes, and who is this?"

"This is Darla Robbins." Mitch Stephenson's admin. "Dr. Stephenson would like to see you as soon as possible. Does two-fifteen work for you?"

She glanced at the wall clock. Ten minutes. "I'm not in the building this afternoon," she said, suddenly self-conscious about working from home.

"Two-thirty, then," said Darla. Not a question.

The short notice was puzzling, as was Darla's snippy tone. Rose drove in to the med school, and at 2:29 she was jogging up to the fourth-floor administrative suite. Darla waved her into Mitch's office without comment. She found him speaking in a low voice with a woman about her age who looked vaguely familiar.

"Have you two met?" Mitch stood and came around from behind his desk.

"We haven't," Rose said. The woman turned to face her, ID card bouncing from a lanyard on her chest. A grim-faced corporate type with a dead fish handshake and cool skin. An anemone of keys jangled at her waist.

"Jean Byer is the interim associate vice provost for human resource management here at the School of Medicine," Mitch explained. "She'll be sitting in." He gestured at a small conference table in the corner of his office. When they were seated, he cleared his throat. "Rose, two things have come up that we need to discuss with you."

"Sounds ominous," said Rose.

Mitch flashed a glance at Byer. "First item," he said. "Can you tell us how things are going in your lab?"

Rose adjusted herself in her chair. "Well, we've got the budget pretty much nailed down. There was a little hiccup with Berlin that I'm hoping to resolve—"

"With that computational neurology lab," Mitch said.

"That's—right." Rose wondered how her chair could know this. "And I have an equipment share I'm proposing with the Marino lab at Hopkins."

"I'm talking about morale."

"Excuse me?"

"Your postdocs and grads. How are they handling the stress of the grant prep? How are *you* handling it?"

"Just fine. I've had to pull some late nights, and the lead time isn't everything I could have desired. But for the most part everyone's working well together. We're getting there."

He shifted, crossed his legs. "Well, here's the thing. We've received some complaints. It seems you've spoken sharply to a few of your postdocs in recent weeks. Haven't set clear expectations for certain tasks, haven't been organizing workflow among the various studies you have going. Your staff members feel adrift."

"You mean Franklin Barnes."

"Not just Franklin. There are others."

"Oh." Rose felt chastened, unsteady.

"More than that, you've been spending less and less time in the lab. Some days you come in after lunch, some days you're not coming in at all."

"Wait, that's happened maybe three or four days in the last month."

He held up a hand. "The details aren't important. What's important is the message you're sending. There have been meetings missed or left early, reconciliations unapproved."

"Mitch," she protested, "I have five different studies running at the same time while trying to put together this grant that *you* urged me to take on. So, yes, I've had to let some of the postdocs and grads manage themselves more than they're used to. But that's because I need all my focus to be on the NIH scheme. And that in turn involves a lot of working from home, because if I'm in the office, I'll be interrupted every ten minutes. I've explained all this to them, several times over. You need to cut me some slack here."

"Look, Rose, don't make too much of this. I'm sure you'll work this out with your staff. Until now we've never received a single complaint about you or your lab. Isn't that right, Jean?"

"That is correct," said the interim associate vice provost.

Rose sighed. "So what do you suggest I do?"

"Jean?" Mitch said.

"Our office has some strategies we can share with you for supervising personnel," Byer said. "Some management modules you can go through with one of our specialists."

"Fine. I can do that."

"I'll set something up." Byer looked pleased with herself.

Rose turned to Mitch. "You said there was a second thing."

His lips tightened. "There is. What concerns me more than the lab issues—and frankly it's a concern I share with the dean—is this business about Crystal Academy."

Rose felt her cheek twitch, two planets colliding. "Excuse me?"

He lifted his fingers into a sharp-angled steeple and air-quoted as he spoke. "What can you tell us about this 'longitudinal study of intelligence and outcomes' you've proposed to the public school system?"

"There's—no study, Mitch," she said, suddenly light-headed. "That's something that just came out of my mouth a few weeks ago, when I was talking to a school official."

He looked at his notes. "But from what I've been told, you scheduled a meeting with the head of school for this new gifted academy. Told her about some elaborate study you were designing here in the School of Medicine that would draw on testing data from the academy's initial cohort. You had a number of people quite worked up about it."

"That wasn't my intention," Rose assured him, realizing why Bitsy Leighton was acting so strangely at the lower school the other day: distant, cold even. "Again, it was just an idea. That kind of thing is way outside my area of expertise."

"Certainly is."

"It was a slip of the tongue, Mitch," she said, genuinely alarmed now.

He took off his glasses. "This is a small town, Rose. There's a certain— well, there's a certain layer of folks around here who all see each other at the same fund-raisers and openings and so on. Members of the school boards, City Council, the Medical School Foundation Board, our donors. So you've struck a little nerve, and I want you to think about it from our position. From Carl Wingate's position. Carl runs into Shirley Ames, the chairman of the school board, at a cocktail reception. Shirley tells the dean how eager her central admins are to be working with the School of Medicine. And this is the first he's heard of it. You see the problem?"

A certain layer of folks. Folks like Bitsy Leighton, with her East Coast pedigree. Folks like Kev Zellar, a Princeton man on City Council.

Suddenly Rose understood why she'd been hauled in here. The squabbling among her staff was standard fare for a science lab preparing a major grant application—and it was merely an excuse. Mitch never would have called her to the mat like this if not for the tongue-lashing he'd probably received from above about her bogus study.

Mitch said, "The dean wants this whole thing to go away."

"So do I," Rose replied meekly. "It was just an offhand idea, a stupid one, sure. But I've never done anything more than talk about it."

"I'm relieved to hear that. Because this kind of thing is beneath you, Rose. You're one of the pioneers in the field. No one would be surprised if the MacArthur Foundation gave you the nod. A neurologist of your abilities, faking up some social science bullshit just to win the ear of an admissions committee for your daughter?"

She turned away from the administrators, poised between tears and rage. Byer set her notepad on the table. Mitch intertwined his fingers and leaned forward slightly. "You've done meaningful work here, Rose. You are a scientist we like to brag about. None of that has to change, whatever happens in the short term. But truth and integrity are at the core of the science we do here at Darlton, especially in an era of scant resources and diminished federal funding. And frankly, we have to prioritize where we put our investments. A thing like this . . ."

His words pinned her to her chair.

"What are you saying, Mitch? Am I—being pulled from the neuro scheme?"

His right hand lifted a few inches, dropped again to the table.

"Is that what the dean wants?" she asked, incredulous that it had come to this.

He looked meaninglessly at his watch, then at Rose. With a deep sigh he told her, "I'm afraid so."

FIFTY-SEVEN

BECK

Grand Junction this time. An overnight, meaning a Marriott for $127 plus tax, breakfast not included. The twins sprawled on a double-wide sofa in the lobby while Beck attempted to check in. The clerk wore a white cowboy hat above a big smile that Beck barely noticed, because three of his credit cards had been declined so far and he was afraid to hand over the fourth. Instead he gave her his newest corporate AmEx. It went through just fine, but now there was an unambiguously personal expense on one of his business accounts, which the accountant wouldn't like at all, even if he paid her on time this month, which he obviously wouldn't, just as he hadn't paid Leila, who was now threatening to take him to small-claims court.

Thankfully the clerk hadn't said anything out loud, because a line of CSOC parents was growing behind him. The card finally went through. She handed him his room keys, and when he turned from the counter, he saw a small group of teammates gathered around the twins.

"Is it true?" Bucky Meltzer was saying to Aidan. "You're going to ROMO next year?"

"I was going to tell you guys this weekend," said Aidan, looking both pleased and embarrassed by the attention.

"Hey, it's awesome, man. You deserve it." Bucky gave Aidan a high five. The other guys followed suit, then Bucky turned to Charlie. "You too, Char-char?"

Charlie shrugged and looked down at his phone. Bucky okay-thenned with his eyebrows and turned back to the knot of teammates.

"You guys ready?" Beck hoisted Charlie's bag.

"I got it," Charlie snarled, pulling his bag off Beck's shoulders and slumping toward the elevator.

At the hotel bar after team dinner Wade Meltzer bought him a beer and toasted Aidan's good fortune. "But how'll you manage the double driving duty?" he wanted to know. "Aidan down to Denver, Charlie out to CSOC Park? Helluva haul."

"We've got it handled," said Beck. "On my weeks Sonja can take Charlie, then on Azra's weeks I guess I can take Aidan, because there's no way she will. Or we could pay our regular sitter to drive him."

"Damn. Every night?"

Beck spun his empty bottle on the bar. "We'll see."

The next morning's game began with Aidan starting at attacking mid and Charlie again warming the bench. The match should be an easy one, Wade had pronounced, and sure enough the Crystal team looked dominant. But Grand Junction fought back, thanks in large part to a striker named Zeke, tall and lightning fast, the embodiment of hope and gruff adoration for the opposing parents.

"You got it, Zeke!"

"Good one, Zeke!"

"Get 'em, Zeke!"

Zeke was a rangy white kid with sandy-blond hair pulled back in a headband, face washed a ruddy tan. Not the nimblest feet, but he made up for them with size, volume, and a brash attitude with his teammates and coach, demanding the ball, barking orders, arguing spiritedly with the refs—basically having a blast. He reminded Beck of Charlie at his self-confident peak, just a few short months ago.

Twelve minutes in, Zeke drew first blood on a powerful free kick from thirty yards out, putting Grand Junction up 1–0.

"Now I remember that boy, that big foot," Wade observed grimly. "Kid was great in U-10, but he was injured when we played these guys last year. Looks like he's back. *C'mon D!*" he hollered at Bucky and the other backs.

The first CSOC goal came ten minutes later. Taking space, gathering speed, Aidan dribbled up the middle and faked right. He touched the ball with the outside of his left foot, then slowed and dished to Will. Will nutmegged one defender and spun with the ball toward the opposing centerback. The Grand Junction kid defended well, bodying him up and away from the eighteen, but as the defenders closed, Aidan overlapped and got a perfect through ball from Will. The ball bent around the leaping keeper and hit the net in the upper ninety, tying the game.

"All *DAY!*" Wade Meltzer bellowed, leading the cheer, always the loudest for other people's kids. "All damn day, boys!" He turned with a big palm opened wide, and Beck high-fived him. "We got these guys. We got 'em." Wade bent to put his hands on his knees.

The boys jogged back to midfield for the next kickoff. Ten more minutes of play, then the whistle blew for halftime, the game tied at one.

B eck walked off alone, his gaze drawn to a knot of buzzards or vultures circling above a fallow field adjacent to the soccer complex. Six of them, poised above the Rockies, from this distance a long pile of rubble laid out to the east. Must be something big.

He bought a Mountain Dew at a drinks tent, found some shade in a picnic pavilion, and looked at his phone. Three texts from Sonja.

At store cannot buy groceries wtf

Checking account overdrawn. wtf???

CALL ME RT NOW BECK

It had to happen eventually. The fourth credit card he hadn't tried last night was their main family card, the sacrosanct Visa that Beck and Sonja used for their household expenses. For months Beck had been hiding all the mounting balances from his wife, letting the minimum payment keep that one account in good standing. Problem was, their checking account had been set up to pay the minimum on that card automatically, and as the minimum payment had grown—$100 one month, $250 the next, now something like $800—his cash balance hadn't kept up, and with all the other balance-kiting he'd had to manage with his other home and business accounts, he'd forgotten last month to make sure there was enough cash in checking for the payment, then didn't transfer in a cash advance off a credit card to handle *this* month's minimum either, let alone any cash withdrawals Sonja might want to make, so now he was utterly fucked. It was all basically over.

He looked up at the sky where the circle of buzzards had narrowed tornadically, descending on the corpse of whatever beast had been lucky enough to die in the middle of that wide, dry plain.

The second half began with both teams playing defensively, feeling out the opponent, waiting for the right break. Fifteen minutes in, the coach took out Will and Aidan, giving the starting striker and midfielder a quick rest before the final push. The game was still tied at one.

Charlie subbed in for Will. Soon after taking the pitch, Charlie had the ball at midfield, looking for a pass, when Zeke, coming back on defense, sprinted up behind him.

"*Man on! Man on!*" Wade Meltzer yelled.

Too late. Zeke got in a slide tackle, and a teammate recovered the ball. Just a turnover, hardly a disaster.

But things quickly got worse.

A few plays later Zeke, dribbling up the middle, came right at Charlie and juked him badly, throwing him so far off-balance Charlie fell to the turf. Cheers from the opposing parents, even Charlie's teammates oohing and aahing at the sneaky move.

Beck palmed his face. When he looked through his fingers, Charlie was still on the ground. Not hurt but angry, like when Beck whipped him at Ping-Pong or Aidan changed the TV channel without asking.

Charlie stood and brushed off his shorts. He took a hard pass from Bucky but received it with a poor first touch. The ball caromed off his foot into Zeke's stomach. The big kid gutted it to the turf and spun away, dribbling up the field.

This time Charlie didn't even try to defend. Instead he left his position and sprinted up behind Zeke, taking a slight off angle. As Zeke neared the goal Charlie slid into his ankles from behind with both cleats up. Zeke's right knee buckled and he sprawled forward, landing on his stomach in the middle of the pitch, five feet from the goal line.

Someone screamed. The whistle blew. Grand Junction parents and teammates leapt from their chairs, hollered for blood.

"Referee!"

"PK!"

"Sir!"

"Red card!"

"What's wrong with that kid?"

"PK!"

The whistle blew again, three swift shrills as the ref ran over and pulled out a red card, separating Charlie from Zeke's advancing teammates. He held the card stiffly aloft as Charlie marched off the pitch, kicking up turf beads as he went.

Through all of this Beck had watched, stunned, horrified at the sight of his son running so far just to take out an opposing player in such a gratuitous way. It was the dirtiest thing Charlie had ever done on a soccer field.

The trainer and the coach jogged on to help Zeke, but the kid popped right up, uninjured, and took the crowd's raucous applause with casual cool. His teammates pushed him toward the spot. Zeke sank the penalty kick and Grand Junction went up 2–1.

As the CSOC kids trudged up to midfield for kickoff Beck stood bleak and helpless, watching his son getting chewed out by his coach on the opposite sideline. When Charlie collapsed on the bench, a big Grand

Junction mom standing just down from Beck stepped onto the field and let out an approving holler.

"Now keep that little thug off the pitch!"

The world went red. Beck took three giant steps until he was in the woman's face. "What the *fuck* did you just say?"

He pushed her shoulder. She staggered back a step.

"Whoa, now." Her husband stood with his hands apart.

But Beck kept going at her. "You do *not* talk about my son that way, you fucking *sow*, you white trash—"

"*Whoa* now." Another Junction dad came forward. Two other men jumped up, and things were about to get really bad when someone grabbed him from behind.

"*Hey hey hey hey hey.*"

Huge arms pinned Beck's elbows to his ribs, lifting and spinning him away. Wade Meltzer had Beck off his feet in a bear hug and crushed out his breath. The man turned him aside and wrestle-dragged him away from the pitch as the opposing parents taunted him.

"Freak."

"Chubby hippie."

"Snowflake."

Wade spoke gruffly in his ear while backing him off. "Hey now, Beck, hey now hey now, big fella, let's just step over here for a minute and calm down, shall we? Come on now, Beck. Deep breath."

His heart was beating wildly, his breaths coming ragged and short. Finally he managed a deeper inhale. Wade loosened his grip.

"*Christ,*" Beck said. Palming his cheeks, covering his eyes. "I don't know—goddamn, I don't know what that was—what came over me."

Wade was in his face. "Yeah, well, that lady could charge you with assault, you know that?"

"Assault? I just pushed her."

"Which is a class one misdemeanor in Colorado, you dumbass, even if she ain't hurt." Wade squatted down like an angry coach, so he could see Beck's face. "Now listen the fuck up. Words are one thing. But you can't go at somebody like that, you hear? You could be in deep shit."

"I know, I know."

Wade put up a warning finger. "You stay over here. You don't go back to the sideline, you don't come within a fuckin' mile of that game, you hear? You stay right here by the cars."

Beck nodded.

"I'm going to walk over there and talk to that nice lady, see if I can get her in a nonlitigious frame of mind. Capiche?"

Beck nodded again.

Wade barreled back toward the field. A Grand Junction dad tried to block his way, but Wade held his palms open, then shook the guy's hand. Beck heard him speaking with the offended woman and the men who'd stood up for her, calming everyone with his charm and cheer. Soon there were even some relieved chuckles from the opposing parents as the game resumed.

Easy for them to laugh, Beck thought grimly. *They're winning the goddamn game.*

He looked over at the far sideline. Charlie was slouched on the end of the bench. A wide gap separated him from his teammates. Even from the edge of the parking lot Beck could see the misery on his son's reddened face. Humiliated on the pitch, mortified by his father's behavior.

Down along the near sideline some CSOC parents whispered and sneered. Amy Susskin stood at the center of the group, arms folded, penciled eyebrows working the other moms. Beck knew what they were thinking. Wasn't my kid who flattened the other team's star. Wasn't my kid who got a red card and forced the team to play out the rest of the game one man down. Wasn't my psycho husband who went after another parent like that.

Soon the final whistle blew. The opponents and their parents erupted in cheers, hard-edged and righteous. Reveling in the win over CSOC, that dirty striker, and his batshit dad.

After the game Charlie made a beeline for the Audi, but Aidan wouldn't even glance Beck's way. A text dinged in from Wade offering to take Aidan to the team lunch and bring him home later. Beck looked up and gave the man a nod and a weak wave.

Charlie took shotgun, complaining of a stomachache. In the car, creeping along, snaking from the crowded parking lot to the road, Beck reached over to squeeze his son's knee. Charlie flinched at his touch and pulled away, huddling against the door.

"Look," said Beck. "The whole thing was tough. It was really intense and I overreacted. And everybody makes mistakes. I mean, don't get me wrong. That was a *big* one, to take out a kid like that. But you're an amazing player and I'm really proud of you."

The words felt pale and mealy coming from his mouth. Charlie didn't respond, and the truth was, Beck *wasn't* proud of his son, and he was even less proud of himself. He had never felt more ashamed.

Hours later they topped the final rise of highway. Bear Mesa, an elevated butte with a panoramic view down over springtime in the valley, everything in bloom. Easy to feel like you owned a wedge of heaven living in Crystal, they said, but Beck was starting to hate the place. Monochrome suburbs, sprawling trailer parks tucked away on side roads and hidden from the gleam, sad old Birkenstocked potheads and self-publishing poets longing for the days when the town was dodgy and weird. To Beck, now, the place seemed almost bleak, the sun too harsh and close. He wondered sometimes if a wetter city might better suit the next, gloomier phase of his midlife. Tacoma, maybe. Or Portland, Maine. Someplace less intense, less soul sucking. A city closer to the sea.

A boyish grunt to his right. He glanced over at Charlie. His son's eyes were just fluttering open after a long postgame snooze. "Bounced check for your thoughts."

Charlie frowned. "Huh?"

"What are you thinking about?"

His son stayed silent. The kid was growing so fast, but *Christ* he looked young right now, more seven than eleven.

"You can say it, man. You can say anything to your old dad. That was messed up back there, what I did. Let me have it." Beck set a wrist on the wheel, shepherding them down from the butte.

"Okay, I have a question."

"Shoot." Beck sat up in his seat, hoping for a heart-to-heart.

"You won't like it."

"Try me," Beck said, feeling on the verge of something.

Charlie uncrossed his arms. He turned to watch Beck's face. "Are we getting a divorce again?"

FIFTY-EIGHT

ROSE

On Thursday Rose left the lab at six, reluctantly, and stopped off to pick up a pizza on the way home. Emma Q's violin lesson had been rescheduled, Gareth hadn't had time to run to the store, and though Rose would have preferred a healthier alternative, the truth was, she needed comfort food right now. She still hadn't told her lab staff that the dean had pulled support for the grant. Without the infusion of new funding, half of her postdocs were facing the prospect of unemployment in the not-so-distant future.

At the Sarnelli counter she put in her order, and after the clerk rang her up, she stepped aside to wait, glancing idly outside. The windows faced the wide patio beneath a yellow awning curved to match the mounded hills to the west. She looked more closely. Azra and Glen were eating at one of the larger round tables. Rose hadn't noticed them on her way in.

She waved but Azra didn't see her through the rippled glare on the window. Rose tilted her head to look around the back of a sign taped to the glass and saw Xander, sitting next to Aidan and across from his sister. Tessa was talking animatedly with another girl about her age, a young black woman Rose didn't recognize; Glen's daughter, she guessed. There was no sign of Lauren.

When Rose went outside to wait for the pizza Azra's face lit up, and she moved over to make room on her chair. Glen looked up from a deck of cards he'd been using to show magic tricks to the boys. For a few minutes they traded med center news. Rose got to confirm a rumor she'd heard about his elevation to the chairmanship of the department of radiology, a major promotion. He asked about her lab. She complained about some minor personnel issues, saying nothing about her lost opportunity for the NIH grant. Glen and Azra exchanged fond looks as the three of them chatted, the couple's fingers flitting back and forth to touch across the table.

The girl talking to Tessa was Glen's daughter, Kiana, a round-faced beauty with a ring around every finger, including her thumbs.

"You're a junior too?" Rose asked her.

"Senior, at St. Bridget's," said Kiana.

"She's heading to Oberlin in the fall." Azra sounded sweetly proud of her boyfriend's daughter. "I thought those two might hit it off, so I asked these guys to come along. Lauren had a little crisis at work, so."

As Glen and the boys went back to their cards, Rose looked around at the happy intertwinement of kids, young adults, grown-ups out for pizza; members of three families, a fresh combination. As she listened to the babbling around the table an unwelcome possessiveness reminded her of another recent moment of friend envy: Azra's surprise appearance with Glen and the Zellars at the dean's party. Things were already difficult with Samantha; now alternative friendships were sprouting everywhere, none of them including Rose, let alone Gareth.

"Where's Charlie?" Rose asked foolishly. A wounding thing to say, and she instantly regretted it.

"He's at a friend's in Denver for a sleepover," Azra said softly, "this kid from St. Bridget's. It's a three-day weekend and we're shaking things up, trying to separate them some, give them more one-on-one?" Her eyes started to water. "Dr. Dan's suggestion."

"Oh god, right," said Rose, feeling small. "That makes sense."

"Therapy. It's good, actually. Not just for the boys."

"Tell me."

Azra was staring at her wineglass. "I'm having a hard time, Rose. I swear

I've never been this worried about Charlie, and so I haven't even been thinking about myself, just them. And Dr. Dan asked me some questions the other day that really . . ." Her eyes came up and the golden haloes around their middles contracted.

"What were they?" said Rose. "Can you say?"

Azra, rotating away from the kids, told her about Beck. His worsening money troubles, his unkempt appearance and erratic behavior, the chaotic state of his household. Sonja, she said, was on the verge of leaving him just as Azra had, and what would that do to the twins?

Their exchange was hurried and hushed beneath the din, but Rose hadn't talked to Azra like this in weeks, and despite the subject she was almost giddy to feel their familiar closeness. Azra was talking about an unpaid tuition bill she'd received a few days before when the girls laughed loudly about something.

"No, but seriously?" Kiana said. "I could *totally* see you there. I mean yeah, it's, like, Ohio, but you should visit me in the fall."

Tessa glowed with the compliment. "I doubt I could get in," she said.

"Of course you could, sweetie." Azra turned away from Rose and reached out to pat Tessa's arm. "With your crazy designs, those clothes you make?" She looked back at Rose. "Tessa's putting together her own clothing line at BloomAgain. She's the next Coco Chanel. Plus, did you hear what she got on the CogPro?"

"You took the CogPro?" Rose asked Tessa. "I thought your mom—"

"Oh, she had no idea," Tessa said with a light and careless laugh. "She does now, though, thanks to my little brother."

Xander turned and gave Rose one of his weird smiles.

"And you know my mom," Tessa said. "As soon as she found out I kicked ass on an IQ test, she took all the credit. Now we're best buds, at least for now."

"Well, I think you're the bomb, girlfriend," Azra said, trying too hard to sound young and coming across, to Rose's ear, as goofy and insincere. But Kiana laughed and said, "To TessaRacks!"—whatever that meant— raised her bottle of cream soda, and clanked it against Azra's wineglass and her father's Peroni and Tessa's lemonade, and then the boys joined in with their lemonades, and Rose, unbeveraged, had to watch all of them toast while she sat simmering in her dark thoughts.

W hen she walked into the kitchen with the pizza box she could feel it instantly. See it in the set of her husband's weak chin, in the red rims around Q's little eyes. Something off.

"What's the matter, you guys?"

Her husband and daughter exchanged looks.

"Mommy—I saw something," Emma said.

Rose set the pizza down on the kitchen table and sat between them. "What did you see, sweetheart?"

"Z sent it to me. She got it from a group text that I wasn't on. Rich kids from St. Bridget's."

"Okay."

"It's—about Mr. Unsworth."

"About Beck?" She recalled Azra's worry just now. What could the kids at the twins' school possibly be saying about Beck? Had there been an incident, some erratic behavior on his part? An accident?

"Q, why don't you go on up to your room," Gareth said. "I'll show your mom what you saw."

"Okay." Q slid off her chair and scuttled upstairs.

Gareth opened his laptop.

B eck told me all about this when we were having a drink," he said five minutes later. He explained Beck's version of what had happened in the Jacuzzi: hot-tubbing nude and alone, Tessa coming out topless, the two of them sharing a joint.

"Why didn't you tell me this?" Rose demanded. "It's really alarming." By now she was busily panic-scrolling through Tessa's vlogs, dozens of them, watching short fragments as her mind detonated with the implications. Some of the videos had been shot in Tessa's bedroom, but others took place at Azra's store, at Azra's house, at Beck and Sonja's, at Twenty Birch, some of them in this very kitchen. God knew what was in them, what words and moments they exposed. Views were accumulating on Tessa's videos even as Rose scrolled up and down.

"Why didn't you tell me?" she repeated.

He shrugged helplessly. "So what's the right call here? Do we talk to Lauren? Because she hates Beck. The first thing she'd probably do is call the damn police. And from what I can tell Beck didn't really do anything wrong."

"Of *course* he did," Rose snapped. "He smoked pot with a teenage girl and sat in that hot tub naked with her. It's disgusting. Anything could have happened."

"But that was just Beck being Beck, moronic and bro. I mean, come on, there's no major crime on that video."

She wanted to disagree, but Gareth's predictably rational assessment rang true. Rose had known Beck for more than ten years, saw him as much an/ersatz father to Tessa as any of the men in their group. Despite his slobby cluelessness at times, she couldn't see him making an actual move in such a situation.

Still, the contents of the video needed to be thought through. What would Rose want to happen if Gareth ever acted as Beck had? Would she want to hear about it from a third party, with all the sticky suspicion this might provoke? Or—if nothing untoward had happened—would she want it to disappear without her knowledge?

Either way they couldn't keep this to themselves. If a bunch of fifth graders were already sharing Tessa's vlogs in texts and social media, it was only a matter of time before Azra and Beck saw them too—if they hadn't already.

She picked up her cell and called Azra. Her phone went to voice mail. Rose saw again the happy group at Sarnelli's, babbling around the table. For a painful moment after the beep she hesitated, then said, "Sweetie, call me, okay? There's something you need to see."

FIFTY-NINE

BECK

He sprawled on the green sofa, looking out the front window, sipping some instant because nobody'd bothered to clean the coffee machine in weeks. The position afforded him a good view of the spot along the curb where Azra had pulled up five minutes before. Charlie in the passenger seat, gesturing wildly, Aidan in the back with his arms folded across his stomach, Azra turned around with her spine to the steering wheel.

His ex-wife leaned through the gap with her head pushed forward on her swanlike neck. She was pressing the boys about something and waving her phone around. Finally a hand bladed between the seats, a *that's enough* gesture. The twins unbuckled and they all popped out, and Azra walked them up to the door.

The boys hustled inside without looking at their dad. "Hurry up and don't forget your cleats and shin guards," Azra called after them.

Beck frowned at her. "But I have them this weekend."

"No you don't," said Azra. Now she wasn't looking at him either.

"What's going on?"

Azra sniffed.

"What?"

She said nothing.

"What were you guys talking about in the car?" he demanded.

She leaned against the doorjamb, big sunglasses perched on the neat gloss of her hair. Beck hadn't seen those shades before. Probably a present from her new boyfriend.

"Look, Azra, do you want to come in?"

"I'll pass." She waved a hand in front of her nose. "Hurry up, you guys," she hollered inside.

Beck looked over his shoulder at the kitchen. Unwashed dishes lined the counter. A half-empty KFC bucket from last week hulked on the microwave.

Azra put a hand on her chest and forced in a deep breath. When she turned back, she said, "You need to talk to someone, Beck, and soon. It scares me what you did, pushing a woman like that over a soccer play."

"It was a red card."

"Red card, green card, purple card, who gives a fuck. Charlie takes out another kid's legs on purpose, then his dad goes after some poor lady on the sidelines? Amy Susskin thought you were about to strangle her. And she told me you said something racist and mocked the woman's weight. Real nice."

"She was *white*."

"Thank God for Wade."

"Look, Azra—"

"There's more." She stopped him with an open palm. "I'm worried about your judgment right now. Charlie said he saw you with Tessa up at Breckenridge. That you were both naked in the Jacuzzi?"

Beck felt short of air. He breathed in sharply, thinking of Charlie's question in the car, and for a second or so he felt sorry. But then he realized that in this case, at least, for once in his goddamn life, he had nothing to apologize for.

"Yes, I was naked, Azra. She was topless." He said it slowly, as if explaining something to one of the twins. "We were in a Jacuzzi."

"Have you told Sonja?"

"No, and I'm not going to. I mean, Christ, we were in a hot tub, okay? She got in with me and we talked for a while. This is Colorado, for god's sake. Why is everybody making a big deal out of this? Gareth, Charlie, now you."

"Gareth?"

"I told him about it, guy acted like I'd molested somebody. Smug fucker."

She waited before responding. "Beck, you have to know how this looks. If there's nothing to this, then—"

"*If?* Did you seriously just say *if?*"

"Look. You need to tell Sonja. Right away, I'm warning you. Before—"

"It's none of her goddamn business, yours either. We're divorced, remember?"

"And thank God for that."

He turned away seething, the taste of snot on the root of his tongue.

She slowed her breaths. "Beck, you need to be careful. You're off-kilter right now. Your house reeks, honestly *you* reek. Sonja tells me you've been canceling client meetings, bouncing checks. And St. Bridget's says we're late again on tuition?"

He crossed his arms. His heart pumped against his right wrist. "I just need to straighten some shit out. It's fine."

The boys hustled up with their soccer bags. Beck leaned down to give them hugs but they dodged away from him, from their own dad, like cars swerving around roadkill.

"Guys, what the hell?"

Azra looked right at him, finally so he could see her eyes, the gravity in them. There was something she wasn't telling him. That she was afraid to, maybe.

"Azra—"

"Think about it," she said, cutting him off. "Seeing someone."

She looked about to turn for her car when Roy let out a big squawk from upstairs.

"Wait, is Sonja here?" She glanced toward the stairs.

"No."

She narrowed her eyes at him. "So it's Tessa who's with him?"

Beck nodded.

"Get her down here." A spit of words.

"What?"

"*Now.*"

He went to the foot of the stairs and called up. A minute later Tessa came down with the baby on her hip. "Hi, Azra," she said with a glowing smile—then saw Azra's face. "Is everything okay?"

"No, it's not," Azra snapped.

"Well, what—"

"Did you think my sons would enjoy it, Tessa? Seeing their father humiliated like that?"

Tessa frowned, stared at Azra, then her eyes widened and her face fell. "No. No no no, please, Azra, that wasn't supposed to—that was just—for my friends."

"Your *friends*?"

"My rehab group." Roy, sensing Tessa's upset, batted at her face. "We were all supposed to journal with each other this year, and this one girl, Jessica, she set up a vlog. But it's a private thing, I swear it's not—"

"That's not a journal, Tessa, what you did," Azra responded. "It's a goddamn TV channel. Do you realize that all the things about your mom you put up there—and about your brother, about the Emmas, the Zellars, Rose and Gareth, about me and Beck and the twins, about all of us—that all of that is now *out* there, that everybody's been watching it? And I mean *everybody*."

"But it's private."

"Tessa, for god's sake, I saw two of them on my phone just now, in the car. Charlie showed me. Talking about people's children that way? Hacking into Kev's computer?"

"It wasn't hacking, it was—"

"You assumed nobody would see your vlog when it was on YouTube? Surely you're not that naïve. The vlogs tell you how many views they have. Some are in the thousands already."

Tessa's mouth widened. She held the baby between them, like a shield. "I guess—I mean I just didn't think—Are you mad at me, Azra?"

The question hung there, and Beck saw how important his ex-wife's approval was to this once-fucked-up-but-recovering girl. The expectation on her pretty young face. The sad hope.

"I'm disappointed, that's all," Azra said calmly. "Just—very disappointed."

Beck knew that tone and those words, what it was to be the object of this woman's disappointment. He'd endured it so often when they were married, especially near the end of things. And he felt it now, like a weight on his shoulders or a fog around his head that he could never quite swim through.

Tessa's face had gone a shade of beige. She whirled on Beck, handed him his son, and dashed out the open front door with a hand over her mouth.

"Tessa," Azra called, but the teen was already at the curb. The twins gawked at her from Azra's minivan. Tessa got in her car and zipped off down the cul-de-sac toward North Main.

Meanwhile Beck felt like he'd been watching a scene in a German opera Sonja had dragged him to see one time in Denver, a bunch of screeching Teutonic women speaking a language he couldn't understand—except in this case he had a horrible inkling.

Vlog? YouTube? Everybody's been watching it?

"What the hell is this even about?" he demanded, going for tough because he felt so weak right now. "This is insane."

Azra nodded at his flat-screen. "Can you open YouTube on there?"

"Hell yeah, it's a smart system, top of the line," Beck boasted. "It has a browser and all the apps and—wait, why?" he asked suspiciously.

She bent over and grabbed the app remote and started tapping buttons. "How do you—how do you fucking—?"

Beck put his hand over hers and opened the YouTube app. He pressed the enter button, and a search box came up. Azra used the arrow keys to enter the phrase "touch of tessa." A YouTube page appeared with a still image of Tessa smiling from the top and a long line of videos stacked along the right-hand side of the screen. Azra scrolled down until she reached the one she wanted.

Episode 138: Breck with Beck.

Beck swallowed and his skin prickled everywhere. A sense of vertigo came over him, a feeling of abandonment.

"Prepare yourself," Azra said, then hit Play. She handed him the remote and left him there alone.

SIXTY

XANDER

Tessa shook him awake. "Hey, little brother."

His sister almost never came into his room. He sat up and rubbed his eyes.

"I'm quitting school." She handed him his glasses.

"You are?"

"Yeah."

He sat up and looked at the clock: 2:17 a.m. "Why?"

"I'm moving to New York. Like Williamsburg maybe, or the East Village."

"How will you pay for food?"

"I'll find a job."

"When are you leaving?"

"Tomorrow, probably. I just came to say goodbye."

"Aquinas will miss you," said Xander. Saying it felt like a giant hand squeezing the middle of him.

"Well he's like the only one who will."

Xander started crying. Which was actually quite unusual.

"You can come visit me, you know." She patted his head.

"Do you have a house there yet?"

"People in New York don't have houses, dumbass. I'm getting a sixth-floor walk-up. They have them in the East Village."

His face was hot and already sticky. "I want you to stay."

"Sorry, I like *literally* can't stand being here one more day. That's how much I hate it."

"Well, um." He wiped some snot off his lip with a wrist. "Well if you leave, you won't get to see my science project."

"Um, no offense? But why would I want to see your lame-ass science project?"

"It's not lame. It's an original, life-changing discovery that's going to get me into Crystal Academy."

"Fuck that school," she said.

"Mom says maybe I'm just a weird kid with a nut allergy and a big head."

"She did *not* say that."

"Yes, she did."

"That's messed up." Her eyes narrowed. "God, I hate these people. All of them. They hate me too now, which is fine, I mean what else is new. But they're such fakes, you know? So hypocritical. It's just—pathetic."

"Yeah," Xander said, and in the silence that followed he thought about his sister's observation. "Do you know the etymology of *hypocrite*?"

"No, Xander, I don't. Would you like to tell me?"

"It's Greek. *Hupokritēs*, which means 'actor.'"

"So?"

"A hypocrite is a really good actor. Someone who pretends to be one person but who is, in actuality, another person."

"What are you saying?"

"Just that—I think you might really like my project."

"So show it to me."

He shook his head. "It's already turned in."

"Well what's it about?"

"It's a surprise."

"You have to tell me or I'm definitely leaving tonight."

So he told his sister everything.

When he was done, she stared at him. "No," she said.

"Yes," he said.

"*Xander*." Tessa's eyes enormous in the darkness of the room.

"Think about it," Xander said. "Just think about it."

And he could see his sister thinking, with him on his bed.

A Touch of Tessa:
one GIRL's SURVIVAL GUIDE to JUNIoR year
a Video Blog

Episode #201: TOMORROW
. . . 879 views . . .

TESSA [*whispering*]: So, guys, I hope I can get this to work. I'm doing it on my mom's computer, since she took my phone away, and I don't even know if the camera's on, and I'll have to find a way to save it somewhere or else I'll DM it to you guys. Anyway this may be my last vlog for a while, and I just want to say, if I don't post again for a long time, it's because of that, because my mom found it. She found everything. They all did, and right now they're probably looking at my whole life, everything I've said about them for, like, the last nine months, since I left Sweet Meadow. I warned you guys we were getting hits. But you know what? I don't even give a fuck. I *want* them to see it all, hear it all. Because maybe that way they'll finally get a clue about who they are. Who they *really* are. Speaking of.

[*Looks over shoulder, leans closer to camera.*] My brother told me something tonight that blew my fucking top. I don't even know if it's true, I mean I doubt it, but part of me's like—like, did he really figure it out? *Really*, Xander? Maybe so, and anyway it'll all come out tomorrow, supposedly. Yeah, tomorrow. [*Sighs.*]

There's this thing my dad always said to me every night, when he kissed me before I fell asleep. It's basically the main thing I remember about him. He'd say, "See you tomorrow, my little rainbow." Then he'd whisper part of a poem in my ear, and it went something like, "Be the rainbow in the storm of life, the evening beam that smiles the clouds away, and tints tomorrow with prophetic ray." I googled it a few years ago and turns out it's by Lord Byron, this sweet-ass poet who also died way too young, and I've always wondered if my dad knew somehow that he'd get sick like he did. But that poem really used to make me feel like a rainbow. Like I was *his* rainbow, *his* sunbeam. That I could light up anything, you know? And now . . . god. Now I'm just the storm.

PART V

THE FINAL CUT

Life is not easy for any of us. But what of that?
We must have perseverance and above all confidence in ourselves.
We must believe that we are gifted for something and that this
thing, at whatever cost, must be attained.

—MARIE CURIE

YOU'RE INVITED!!

It's An Open House

On behalf of the City of Crystal School District, you are cordially invited to attend a Community Open House to celebrate the "soft opening" of Crystal Academy!

After a nine-

month renovation project, our newest magnet school will soon be opening its doors to teachers, administrators, and staff, who will spend this summer preparing the building and all it contains for our first cohort of students this August. But first we are opening our doors to you, our community members, in hopes that you will join us for a festive afternoon featuring tours of the renovated school, displays of student work, entertainment for younger siblings, and a variety of foods (including vegan and gluten-free options) for all to enjoy free of charge.

Please join us on Sunday, April 22, from 1:00 to 3:00 p.m. in the playground and courtyard of the Crystal Academy Lower School (formerly Maple Hill Elementary School), 243 Fourth Street, Crystal, Colorado.

SIXTY-ONE

ROSE

The shot comes in from above, distant and blurred at first, angled down from a great height before panning right and panning left, then focusing on a single spot below.

The face of a boy, staring out from a dark blue field, wide-eyed with hope and ambition. A familiar face, visible for only a moment before its features flicker, then fade into the background.

Now the navy plane brightens through other shades of blue—azure, royal, sky, turquoise—and slowly starts to throb, then pulse, then flicker, and the oscillations grow in frequency and intensity until their beat drums at the darkness like the siren on a police car. Blaring, flashing, screaming—

Rose woke with a start, seeing it all at once. She sprang up in bed, threw her feet over the side, and leapt, catlike, toward the door.

"You okay?" Gareth grumbled sleepily from his side, but Rose ignored him. She turned the lights on in the kitchen and over the dining room table. She slapped at every surface and her head turned wildly from side to side as she searched half her house for the pulsing object in her dream.

She found it on an end table in the living room, covered with a pile of Gareth's papers. She brought the whole stack to the kitchen and let it all sit there on the counter, the binder still hidden from her full view while she brewed a pot of coffee.

She glanced at the microwave clock: 6:42. The open house at Crystal Academy started in less than seven hours.

The shame settled in like a flu.

The last few days had been one long gut punch as Rose's friends, their husbands, and their children absorbed the impact of Tessa's vlogs, parsed privately and among themselves.

Aside from her withering words for Lauren, there were revealing tours of the Holland-Quinn house (including lovely shots of Rose's underwear drawer and some old sex pictures Gareth had kept since Palo Alto), some choice words about Samantha and her moneyed lifestyle, covertly filmed interactions with several of Azra's customers at BloomAgain (one featured the president of Darlton University grousing over the price of a used blouse), and, worst of all, the humiliating and disturbing footage of Beck smoking a joint with a sixteen-year-old girl, then pushing his naked, bearish body out of a Jacuzzi.

Around midnight Rose had been sitting up in bed watching a vlog shot in her own kitchen when the screen filled with an error message: *Video no longer available*. But just before the notification something in the episode had caught her attention, hooked her eye. A flicker of navy blue, down in the lower corner of the screen, below Tessa's elbow. Rose couldn't put her finger on what it was, and when she tried to restart the video, the whole vlog seemed to be down.

Soon after midnight Lauren sent out a group text informing her friends that Tessa had, at Lauren's insistence, changed the settings to disallow the public viewing of her channel. Promptly enough to avert total disaster, perhaps, though Tessa's violation of all of their newfound trust was a cold reality these families and friends would have to face.

And now, with trust foremost on her mind, Rose sat at the kitchen table nursing herself with a cup of coffee and staring at Atik Yupanqui's navy blue binder—the subject of that morning's dream, the object that had caught her attention in Tessa's vlog before it was closed down. The portfolio due days ago at the lower school.

She opened the cover and flipped numbly through the glossy pages, looking at the boy's extraordinary origami arrays. Cars, trucks, trains, houses, whole villages of animals. Unbelievable, what this kid could do with a piece of paper and his fingers.

Rose would take the binder in on Monday, of course, explain to Bitsy Leighton what she'd done. Silea had a broken elbow, had just gone through surgery, and the family had nothing. Surely the admissions process would allow for such extenuating circumstances. A frank confession would go a small way toward making up for Rose's betrayal of Silea's faith in her: that simple but trusting request to an employer to deliver the portfolio by the deadline.

As she drained the mug her eyes wandered to the stack of papers that Gareth—she assumed it was Gareth—had placed on top of Atik's binder. She tugged at one of the printed papers, recognizing his handwriting in the margin. She looked at the first page.

WHAT MAKES A GREAT LEADER?
BY EMMA ZELLAR

Emma Z's essay, for her portfolio. Four double-spaced pages of the girl's youthful ramblings on "the qualities of a great leader," the combination of "discipline, drive, and determination" required of a successful manager or boss. Rose marveled at the absurdity of a fifth-grade girl spouting off in the language of leadership studies, a jargon she'd learned as a junior auditor in a class at Darlton.

The whole thing was a joke, and Rose wanted to laugh—but couldn't. Because what she immediately recognized was Gareth's careful edits. They covered the page in a tangle of red ink. Correcting Z's grammar, suggesting stronger verbs, retooling her sentences to give them the kind of spark Z's pedestrian prose otherwise lacked. As if Emma Zellar were one of his students, in her early twenties rather than her tweens.

At the bottom of the third page he'd written her a note.

This is really wonderful, Emma Z! I've made a few suggestions for revision, and we can discuss it more if you want. Great work!!!! Gareth

A few suggestions? Gareth had virtually rewritten the paper from top to bottom. If Z followed his editorial insertions and deletions, her revised paper would read like a little gem, the work of a budding corporate prodigy.

Rose set the paper down, full of quiet fury at her husband for giving Z such detailed and expert assistance with her portfolio submission. Didn't he realize that this was a zero-sum game? Didn't he understand that the admissions process was, in fact, an intense and brutal competition? That the Emmas were likely vying for the same spot at Crystal Academy?

As if Z needed any more help with admissions than her privileged situation had already afforded her. A test tutor for the CogPro. A glossy portfolio on her leadership skills. Now Rose's own husband lending her his expertise while *their* daughter sat fingertipping her way through the latest juvenile crap on her Kindle. Wonderful, just wonderful.

Two hours later, as Gareth fixed breakfast for Emma while Rose huddled in bed over her laptop, her phone dinged.

Are we still doing this, guys?

A text from Samantha. Perfect timing, as always.

It was Azra who replied first: **We should cancel.**

Rose went next: **Agreed.**

Then, a moment later, from Lauren: **Absolutely not. I need a Bloody Mary and it's our anniversary! Plus I have Tessa's phone lol**

Rose stared at the text. Lauren could be so tone-deaf, taking her daughter's serial invasions of their privacy lightly enough for an *lol*—and if Tessa's mother felt like she could handle their long-scheduled brunch after yesterday's revelations, who were her friends to refuse? Lauren almost seemed to be enjoying the whole thing. These embarrassments, these exposures. Rose squeezed her phone until her knuckles ached, longing to stay in bed, to surrender her bit part in this ridiculous charade.

SIXTY-TWO

ROSE

The bag of anniversary mugs thunked heavily against her knee. Today marked their eleventh full year in this tangled friendship, and the brunch had been on their calendars for months, though even while trudging the last block of the Emerald Mall, Rose considered blowing it off. The plan was to troop up Maple Hill afterward for the open house at the lower school, which started at one. Kids, spouses, and exes would meet them there. Rose was locked in for at least three hours. Three hours of griping, of jealous suspicions; three hours of a crowded schoolyard and hallways, all under the distorting pall of Tessa's vlog.

Fifty feet short of the restaurant someone leaned against a brick wall, smoking. Rose walked by and did a double take. Azra, holding a cigarette for the first time in years.

"Hey," she said as Rose approached. Her voice was husky, her body framed in a window with smoke curling up from her slim fingers.

Rose stopped a yard short. "When did you start . . . you know." Rose noodled a hand.

Azra shrugged. "Yesterday around eight. Want one?"

Rose declined the offer. They watched a squirrel on the bricks nibbling away at a piece of popcorn, shifting the puffy fragment around in its tiny paws like a steering wheel. Looking at the squirrel, Azra said, "So, I need to ask you."

"Shoot."

"That video of Beck. The boys are so upset. But—do you think something happened between them? That he could have done something with Tessa—*to* Tessa?"

Rose considered it with a squint. "You know Beck better than anyone. What do you think?"

"Don't get therapeutic on me, Rose, please? I need to figure this out. Beck and I have had a great relationship since the divorce, you know that. He's basically a good guy, he loves our boys. But do I need to get a lawyer? Do I need to be worried about protecting my kids if things go further south with him?"

Rose said, "I don't know, sweetie. I don't want to give you false reassurance, but Gareth is positive that nothing happened. Not that the video itself isn't pretty damning, about his judgment at least. But an actual—*physical* thing? I just can't see it."

"Yeah," Azra said, wiping at a tear. "I'm sure Gareth's right." She took a long, final drag and kept her eyes fixed on Rose as the smoke billowed out the side of her mouth. The butt fell from her fingers to the bricks and her right foot squished it dead. She started to say something else but then looked over Rose's shoulder. Rose turned and saw Lauren approaching from Crystal Books across the mall, backpack humped high on her shoulders.

"Well, don't be so happy to see me, you guys," Lauren said, catching their glum looks. Her hands waved away the lingering smoke. Her face was grim, but there was an eerie sparkle in her eyes. "Let's go in, shall we?"

Samantha threw her jacket over a chair and dropped her bag on the floor. Still standing, she loudly ordered an Oyster Bloody Mary from a passing server, then collapsed in her seat, performing a chirpy normalcy, though beneath it, Rose could tell, she was just as agitated as the rest of them. She herded them into ordering shrimp skewers and an eggplant dish, and all of them sat on the edges of their seats.

As the waitress arrived with their drinks Lauren started to text, eyebrows angled into a sharp frown, then set down her phone.

"How is Tessa doing?" Rose leaned in, though the others had heard her say Tessa's name, and now all three of them listened intently for news.

"She's—not doing well," Lauren said. "I took away her phone last night, so she can't do her vlogs, at least, and she swears she's going to write apologies to everyone. To all of you. Again."

Lauren flushed, and impulsively Rose clutched her arm, as did Azra on her other side. They sat in silence for a long moment. Rose remembered Tessa's last series of apologies, which had arrived in the form of handwritten letters from her rehab facility.

"She's going to be okay, Lauren," Azra said. "I was harsh with her yesterday at Beck's, but I didn't fire her, and I don't intend to. There haven't been drugs this time, right?" Lauren shook her head. "And she's been amazing with our customers, Sonja says she's incredible with Roy. She's a teenager and she's made another mistake."

"Several of them," Samantha said, looking angrily away. "She violated our trust again, our sense of privacy. Filming our homes, our kids. Our goddamn investment account."

"That's true, Sam," Azra allowed. "But some embarrassing videos that she thought were private? It's not the end of the world here. And she's a teenager. How many of us didn't make big mistakes when we were sixteen?"

Or forty-six, Rose thought bitterly, thinking of Bitsy Leighton, her chair, her dean.

"Well, maybe she's doing us a favor," Samantha said. "We can use all this as an excuse to take the kids' phones away. Kev's been looking for one."

Rose and Azra laughed, but Lauren stayed stone-faced. She wouldn't look at Samantha. Instead her eyes remained focused on her glass as she said, "Apparently she told Xander she's moving to New York. A sixth-floor walk-up."

Azra said, "God, I remember that time she ran away when she was, what, thirteen?"

"No, she was twelve," Rose corrected her. "Just about the Emmas' age. And she ended up—"

"At my place, hiding out in the doghouse all night," said Azra. "She and our old collie Beecham came to the back door at the same time for breakfast.

His tail was wagging, and Tessa had the biggest smile on her face, like she'd just gotten away with murder."

"Always doing her own thing," said Rose.

"Tell me about it." Lauren perked up. "And Azra helped her put a portfolio together of her designs. I can't thank you enough."

Azra freed her hands and raised her mimosa. "To Tessa," she said. Samantha and Lauren started to lift their glasses.

"Wait." Rose reached down along the wall for the bag hidden there. She set it on the table and handed out the anniversary gifts. The women all dutifully unwrapped the boxes and set their mugs on the table. Rose read the year's friendship quote out loud. *"Being honest may not get you a lot of friends but it'll always get you the right ones.* John Lennon." She decanted the rest of her Bloody Mary into the new mug and raised it for a toast.

But the mood around the table had subtly shifted. Azra held her mug high, but Lauren was staring at Samantha, waiting for something.

Uh-oh, thought Rose. All the feelings from Friday run came flooding back.

"I saw it, Samantha," Lauren said. "Episode—what was it—one-eighty-six? Title: 'Um, WTF?' Is that ringing a bell for you?"

"Missed that one," Rose said lightly.

"What is going on, you guys?" Azra asked.

Samantha sat stiffly in her chair with her hands clasped around the new mug. She stared somewhere over Rose's left shoulder. Her eyes started to flutter, but she controlled the impulse to cry by sucking in her smooth cheeks and filling her lungs with air. Finally she took a quick drink of her Bloody Mary, like a calming shot—from her glass, not the still empty mug.

"Fine." She huffed out a sigh. "Emma Z didn't make the cut."

"What are you talking about?" Azra said dismissively. "They don't even announce until next month. Nobody knows about admissions decisions yet." She looked around the table for affirmation.

Samantha said, "That's not what I'm talking about."

Rose knew before Sam said it, could feel her jaw loosen, her mouth fall open.

"I'm talking about the first cut," Samantha went on. "The CogPro."

"What do you mean?" Azra still wasn't getting it.

Sam sighed. "Emma Z didn't score high enough. She was eliminated weeks ago."

Rose stared at her while adding up a few weeks of lies. How fragile, this family, she thought, and how sad: the pressure of all that Zellar perfection, those Zellar genes. "Exactly how long have you known?" she managed to ask.

Samantha gave her a plaintive look. "Since I cut my hand on that champagne flute, Rose. I've known for—a while."

Though she hadn't been the first to lie about it, Samantha told them. That would be Kev, who'd listed his own email address under first point of contact. When he received the bad news about the CogPro, he texted Samantha right away, telling her that Emma Z had made the cut. Just lied impulsively, Samantha put it, like the president. He even lied to their daughter, telling Emma Z she'd earned a ridiculously high score when in reality her CogPro put her around the eightieth percentile. Samantha only learned about the deception the day Rose came over after the Gifted Club debacle. Then she started lying too, covering for her husband, trying to whack down the moles of his stupidity.

"And it's gotten even worse since I found out," Samantha said. "Kev was so panicked that he started exploring an ADHD accommodation."

"ADHD?" Azra couldn't keep the disgust out of her voice. "Since when has Emma Z been diagnosed with ADHD?"

"Since never, okay? That was part of my husband's brilliant plan, to take her in and get her officially assessed. So she could get time and a half on a retest."

"You have got to be kidding," said Rose. "That is just—"

"Pathetic," Samantha said. "I know, and how do you think I feel? My husband was lying to me for *weeks*. But that didn't stop him from putting a portfolio together, oh no, and now we're getting guff about *that*."

"How so?" Rose asked, selfishly alarmed.

"Because Emma Z got paid help on it from some associate dean in the leadership school at Darlton. Kev gave him a consulting fee. A *consulting* fee!"

"Geez," Azra said.

Samantha rested her cheeks in her hands and glumly shook her head. "Kev won't give it up. This whole thing has made him absolutely insane."

I know the feeling, Rose wanted to say.

"But why would he do all that?" Azra asked.

"Because he thinks—" Samantha winced. "He actually said it's all for me. He somehow thinks that getting Z into Crystal Academy is so important to me that he'll move mountains to make it happen, and I just don't know *where* he's been getting that idea. I think it's some weird Freudian thing with his dad and his siblings. I frankly don't give a damn anymore."

Rose almost spit out her drink.

"Even before this I'd been warning him we should pull out of the admissions process." She looked at Rose. "That's what I was telling you the other day. We could have stepped away gracefully and no one would have known, especially poor Z, who, thanks to my clueless husband, now knows that she didn't score high enough to make the cut *and* that her parents have been lying about it. But now Kev's insisting there's still a chance, I mean, he's even taking Emma Z to the open house as we speak. Kev's been like a man on a mission, and I'm just sitting back and watching this train wreck."

"And it's *not* important to you anymore?" Lauren had been listening to the hiss of the punctured Zellar balloon with a barely disguised glee. "That seems a little disingenuous after all these months of hand-wringing."

"What can I say?" Samantha spread her hands in a you-got-me gesture as their food arrived. "I mean, sure, a kid in that school, who wouldn't want bragging rights. But not at the expense of my dignity, or what's left of it after all this." She forked a sweet potato wedge. "At this point I just want it to be over."

In the bathroom Rose opened a stall. She sat on the closed seat and stared at the metal door. There was no thrill in this news, no smug shiver of superiority about the Emmas' comparative CogPro scores, only a sad and desperate charge. To Rose the revelation about Z was like a mirror reflecting back her own deranged ambitions for her child, her own hypocrisy in judging the Zellars for their misdirected aspirations.

Because what had Kev Zellar done that Rose hadn't—and worse? Conniving, lying, stealing half a project from an eleven-year-old girl; and now, if Q did get in, the Emmas would be at different schools for the first time ever.

What was really twisting her insides, though, was Samantha's newly blasé attitude toward admission, the process, the academy. *Cut our losses*, she'd said, and Rose suspected her friend was being sincere. For months the pressure had been like a yoke over their shoulders; and how unfair it seemed that Samantha suddenly got to set hers aside without real consequence. Rose almost envied Sam her indifference to the whole thing.

At the sink she splashed water on her face, dried off, checked her phone. Gareth was leaving with Emma Q for the open house. *Be there soon*, she texted back, then pushed out the bathroom door. The four women joined the Sunday rush on the Emerald Mall, the buzzing and milling hundreds, churning with youth and beauty. They turned left toward the mountains and moved hearselike through the crowd.

SIXTY-THREE

XANDER

After his sister dropped him at the curb, Xander went through the gate and into the schoolyard of Crystal Academy. He stood there for a while, getting the lay of the land, fingering his lower lip and trying to decide between the bouncy house and the sundae station.

While he considered his options, two familiar legs appeared at the entrance and then a head that belonged to Charlie Unsworth-Chaudhury. Charlie slid off the bouncy house platform, sweaty and grinning. Some little kids followed him out.

If the house wasn't too lame for Charlie, then it definitely wasn't too lame for Xander. He went up to the bulging front of the platform and hoisted himself through the entrance flaps and onto the rubber surface, rocking along to the leaps and rolls of the four other kids inside. He jumped too, tentatively at first, then with more purpose.

He landed on his butt. He bounced to his feet.

Tried it again. And again.

Butt.

Feet.

Butt.

Feet.

"Yo, Xander."

Aidan, climbing in. He scrambled up to standing and took a test jump. Soon he was bouncing even higher than Xander, landing on his knees, back, legs, and every time coming up to his feet again. The other kids were loving it, how good he was, especially two girls with long ponytails that thrashed back and forth as they jumped. The two littler kids left and now it was just the four of them.

Aidan started throwing his head around. "You gotta *shake* it!" He nodded in an almost violent way that made his hair flop down over his face, back up over the top.

Xander thought: *Doesn't that hurt?*

But the girls started imitating his movements, thrashing their heads like Aidan. They were giggling a lot, throwing their ponytails back and forth, thwacking their backs and chests with thick ropes of hair.

"Come on, Xander, *do* it!" Aidan yelled in his face, looking at him weirdly as they both bounced. "Your head. Just like this."

Xander tried it. Just a little bit the first time, because it didn't look comfortable. His head went forward, backward. Forward, backward. It was kind of fun. And kind of scary.

"Harder!" Aidan yelled. "You gotta let loose!"

More screeches from the girls, smears of wild whipping hair in the blue half-light of the bouncy house. Xander did it harder. Back, forth. Back, forth.

Then his glasses flew off and suddenly everything was smeared like fingerpaints.

"Wait!" he yelled. "My glasses!"

But no one responded. Just more bouncing, giggling, bouncing.

He went down to his knees, hands and forearms searching for them. "Guys, can you help?" he whimpered.

No one listened. But Xander could hear them bouncing, feel the easy power of their bodies going up and down above and around him, and all he could do was smack the roiling rubber.

Then he heard his glasses as they bounced on the smelly, quivering surface somewhere to his left. A *tip-tip-tip* above the heavier thuds of all the feet, like someone fingertipping on a drum.

He reached that way, fingers spread. The glasses grazed his hand as they leapt up. He grabbed for them, but they bounced away.

A few seconds later there was a bad crunching sound; a laugh.

"What was *that*?" Aidan said in a fake exaggerated voice. Because Xander was pretty sure Aidan knew exactly what *that* was. He'd seen the glasses and stomped them on purpose. But *why*?

The rubber churned and seethed around him, then Aidan was right next to Xander with his mouth to his ear. "Tell your sister she's a *slut*," he said, sounding like a high schooler, then he pushed Xander over.

"I'm outtie," Aidan said loudly, jumping away. With a brittle laugh he took two very hard, blurry hops toward the flaps. The two girls followed him out.

Xander was alone in the bouncy house.

He continued his search, starting in the middle of the platform, spreading out in a panicky spiral, slapping at the rubber until at last, along the hemmed edge of the bouncy house floor, his fingers found a lens, and then a portion of broken-off rim, then the rest of his glasses. He wrapped all the pieces in the bottom of his shirt and pressed them to his stomach while scooting toward the exit. Out in the daylight the whole loud everything was a blur that smelled of cotton candy and grilling meat and tofu and the coconut sunscreen on someone passing by. Squinting didn't help at all.

Xander closed his eyes, trying to remember the pattern of the schoolyard, how everything was laid out. The bouncy house, the sundae stand, the cotton candy cart, the stairs to the school. He opened his eyes, took three steps in what he thought was the right direction, and bumped into his sister.

"What happened to your glasses?" she demanded.

"Aidan broke them, on purpose." Xander, squinting up, showed her the pieces. Tessa had her phone pointed at him. Filming again.

"Didn't Mom take that away from you?"

"A girl has ways." Tessa lowered the phone. "So where's your project?"

"Inside."

"Don't you want to go find it?"

"I have to fix my glasses."

She glanced at her phone again. "Shit," she said under her breath.

"What?"

"It's Beck. Come on, let's go." She pushed ahead of him through the crowd.

"Fine," Xander mumbled, and wandered the blurry path.

SIXTY-FOUR

ROSE

They passed through the gate into the crowded schoolyard. "Where's the bar?" Samantha quipped. No one laughed.

Rose looked around at the spectacle, her spirits sagging lower at the sheer number of potential students in attendance, surely only a small fraction of those still vying for a spot in the lower school. The parents milled around, showing their tight smiles, assessing, comparing.

"Oh! There's Xander!" Lauren's hand rocketed up just as Xander reached the top step and disappeared inside the building. "Why isn't he wearing his glasses?" Lauren wondered aloud, then slipped away in pursuit.

They passed a sundae station, a long table already glopped and smeared with ice cream and spilled toppings, gooey jars of caramel, fudge, strawberry sauce. Two lines of parents and kids passed down either side.

"You want sprinkles, Brie? Can you put your own sprinkles on? Just one spoon. Good job!"

"Flu season's over, so yeah, I'm doing this."

"What, they couldn't spring for organic maraschinos?"

"Sorry, Caden, the caramel sauce has high fructose corn syrup, so no, you can't."

They reached the bouncy house. Rose lifted the flap and peered inside. No Emmas, no twins, just a half-dozen littler kids. They pushed on past a line of gas grills laden with burgers and hot dogs, another labeled VEG

ONLY!!!!!!! Portobello discs, veggie burgers, and squares of seared tofu sizzled over the flame.

A rank of benches shaded by an enormous sycamore defined the edge of the crowd. Azra stepped up on a bench. "The boys are probably on the basketball court," she said, standing on tiptoe, peering through smoke billowing from the grills. She hopped down and her knuckles brushed Rose's arm. "I'll catch up with you guys inside."

Rose watched glumly as Azra moved away. She had no wish to be alone with Samantha right now, but the Emmas were almost certainly together somewhere.

"I know what you're thinking," Sam said as she sat.

"What?"

"Just, you know." A hand thrown up, gesturing at the melee. Rose took the place next to her. "The craziness of all this. How crappy it's made everything. How crappy it's made me and Kev."

"Don't be too hard on yourself," said Rose, not meaning it.

"I'm just so embarrassed." Her voice dropped. "What we've done to get her in? You don't know the half of it. The way Kev conned them into a retest, the time and money we've invested in her portfolio. I mean, *Born to Lead*? I know I was blaming it all on Kev back there, but I've bought in too. And you know what, in the end? Z's about as profoundly gifted as my big toe."

"Samantha, that's ridiculous. Emma Z is—"

"A smart, capable kid who's comfortable in her own skin. But come on. Why are we trying so hard?"

Self-awareness, so rare from a Zellar.

Rose's tongue felt suddenly heavy in her mouth, but when she spoke, her words were clear, strong, honest. "You know, Sam, I have a confession too." *It's not too late.* "Two confessions, actually."

"Do tell," Sam said with a pretty smirk, and Rose got a flash of their old closeness, the rush of intimacy she had once felt all the time around Samantha. It was muted now, with time and age, but could still give her a buzz.

"You remember that day you saw me on the Emerald Mall with Bitsy Leighton? You were getting a manicure."

"You were all mysterious and befuddled. I figured it had to be something."

"You have no idea." Rose told her about the bogus study she had proposed, the cold treatment from Bitsy Leighton, the angry bafflement of her chair. "And now I've lost the chance to put in for a major grant from the NIH. I've set my lab back a few years in the administration's eyes. All because of a desperate lie I told on the spur of the moment to give Q an edge. So." She leaned back. "All you guys did was futz with Z's application."

Samantha looked at her fondly.

"What?" Rose said, actually enjoying the moment. Telling her friend about the debacle felt cleansing, almost restorative.

"It's just so unlike you, Rose, to spin yourself into a web like this. You're such a rational person it can be scary sometimes. The fact that you'd do something that batshit makes you seem, I don't know." She shrugged and smiled. "Human."

They laughed together, the first deep, genuine laughter Rose had enjoyed with Samantha in a long time, and as they watched the anxious crowd a cool relief settled around her heart. The gifted school can be a blip in our lives, she told herself, if we let ourselves see it that way. Something to laugh about next Thanksgiving while the Emmas set the table and their mothers stand watching them, sharing a glass of sparkling wine.

Rose turned to her friend. "Speaking of honesty." Her face was warm. Something deep in her wanted to break, or break out.

"The theme of the day," Samantha said. "Mugs and all."

"Right." Rose cleared her throat. "There's something else, and it's kind of worse. So for Emma Q's portfolio I—"

SQUEEEEEEEEEEE!

They clapped their palms to their ears as a blaring whine erupted from the sound system in front of the school, amplified by remote speakers set up around the yard. The horrible sound persisted until a technician adjusted something, fixing the problem. As the feedback faded into a chorus of relieved laughs from the crowd, the two friends looked at each other. Rose remembered a certain moment long past, and saw the same recollection in the smile lines around Samantha's eyes.

The squeal of feedback over water, two Emmas bobbing, a chorus of babies screaming in the pool. A friendship built over eleven long years that seemed, in that moment, a single blur.

Almost nothing. Almost everything.

Rose started to speak, determined to push through, when the amplified voice of Bitsy Leighton broke in. She stood at a microphone stand on the school's main staircase. "On behalf of the City of Crystal school board, our host today, I'd like to welcome you all to the Crystal Academy's lower school for our inaugural open house." She beamed over the hearty applause, owning her moment.

Rose tilted herself against the slatted back of the bench, and Samantha reclined with her. Settling in, they listened together, bare skin touching along their arms.

"Though not every deserving student in the Four Counties will attend Crystal Academy, we want our school to serve as a beacon for gifted education on the Front Range and throughout Colorado. And it's in this spirit that we've invited our community here today to celebrate our children's many gifts—and believe me, they are many. But first, our gifts to you! Great food going on the grills, a sundae bar just over there, a bouncy house for the little ones, and I'm told a taco truck from BeulahRitos will be pulling up in a few minutes."

More clapping.

"But once you're full and happy, please do come inside and look under the hood with us. Because we want to show you our wonderful school. How we've imagined it, how the spaces are laid out, what it will offer the students. The lower school incorporates the best practices in instructional design, the latest learning technologies aimed at enhancing the classroom experience for children from throughout the Four Counties."

Bitsy clasped her hands. "And speaking of the children, we're especially excited about the portfolio display."

The what? Rose felt her breath hitch.

"We've spent hours over the last several days setting up, and now the building is full of your children's work. Every student who passed into the second round has submitted a portfolio of excellence for the committee's review. We've got budding mathematicians, scientists, dancers, equestrians, origamicists, artists, and engineers—a whole rainbow of talents displayed in our new facility."

But instead of a rainbow Rose saw streaks of jagged red, and a dull ringing began in her skull. Not feedback this time: a steady droning between her ears, as if a rock had struck her head. A shudder rose from the base of her spine, from her sacrum, an almost sexual throbbing that shivered up her back and along her shoulder blades as Bitsy wrapped up her welcome speech.

Rose didn't hear another word, the image of the trifold's new header engraved on her conscience like an epitaph:

THE HORSE IN THE AMERICAN WEST
BY EMMA HOLLAND-QUINN

In one movement she rose from the bench and plunged into the crowd.
"Rose, where are you going?" Samantha called behind her.
But Rose was already gone.

SIXTY-FIVE

BECK

He pushed and nudged his way along the clogged hallway, looking inside each classroom in a desperate search for Tessa. He'd texted her probably five times that morning and again just now, but she still wasn't answering his increasingly panicked messages.

Tessa, we need 2 talk

Call me pls

URGENT!! CALL ME!!!

But nothing.

He leaned into another classroom, scanned the dozen-odd kids and parents, pushed out. Next classroom, same thing.

Why would Tessa have posted a video like that, especially one so humiliating and messed up? And why would Azra—or, like, what was it about Beck that would make anyone believe—for instance his sons, and especially his ex-wife—that he could ever, *ever* be capable of something so, just— messed up and—*fuck*. What was *wrong* with everybody?

Because the credulity of the people he cared most about in the world, the lack of faith they'd have to have in Beck to make them think he'd messed with Tessa Frye? That was somehow worse than the bizarre accusation itself. To imagine them all out there just *thinking* this shit—not acceptable. And now, what, he was going to be called out for some pervy shit he didn't even *do*?

He reached the foot of the staircase to the third floor. As he jogged up, each step seemed to clang with one syllable in a long, pained question thudding up through his head.

Why
me
what
the
hell
why
the
fuck
did
you
smoke
weed
and
drink
beer
with
a
top
less
six
teen
year
old
girl
in
a
Ja
cuz

zi
what
the
fuck
is
wrong
with
you?

"What is *wrong* with you?" he said aloud when he reached the top and had to take a lean to catch his breath.

But then with a shiver of self-disgust he saw it. The certainty lodged in his throat.

Not what was wrong with *them*—with Charlie and Azra and Gareth and anybody else who'd wondered about him and Tessa—but what was wrong with *him*. With *Beck*.

A lot of things. Money work marriage gut school parenting soccer anger anger anger. Sex drought. Money again. Gut again. Anger again.

His life had basically spun out of control. All of it. *And if I can be so out of control about everything else, why should it be so hard for people to believe I lost control with Tessa?*

That's it. *That's fucking it right there, dumbass.*

He twisted around with the top of his head against the wall until he was facing the third-floor hallway. He slapped his hot open palms on the surface, willing the cool stone to calm his raging thoughts.

So this was all about control, then. That's what all of this had in common.

Control.

Losing it—

Getting it back?

He squeezed his eyes shut and pinched the bridge of his nose, fingers pressed into his eyelids. To get control again. What would that even look like? What would that *feel* like?

He thought of Sonja, the calm beauty, the competence, the *control*. He could almost taste her right now, her lips and her thighs and the line of sweat she sometimes got along the vale of her lower back, and a feverish, sad longing swelled inside him as he stood twisted against the school wall. He couldn't lose her, not like he'd lost Azra. This couldn't be happening. Not again.

When he opened his eyes, Tessa was there, not five feet away.

SIXTY-SIX

BECK

"Tessa! Hey Tessa!" He waved through the crowd and bumped right into her as she emerged from a classroom.

"Hey," he said breathlessly.

"Oh god." She shielded her face with a hand and tried to push past.

He matched her steps as she strode up the hall. "Why haven't you answered any of my texts?"

"My mom took my phone last night," she muttered. "I stole it back this morning, okay?"

"Well, listen—"

"Just a sec." She dodged into the next classroom. Her pirouettes took her around tables and desks and parents and kids and a school staff member or two, looking at all the student projects displayed on the tables and walls. When she came back out to the hallway, she looked tense.

"What's going on?" he said.

"I need to find Xander." She jerked her hair back over an ear. "He's putting on a little show today. I think you might really enjoy it."

"A show? What—look, Tessa, I don't have time for that. We have to talk."

"Not right now, Beck. This is important."

"Well, so is this, goddamnit."

She stopped and took in his out-of-control beard, wrinkled her nose at his BO, which Beck kept forgetting about because he couldn't even smell himself.

"Fine," she said, then dodged into the small tiled vestibule of a custodial closet. She leaned against the door frame tapping her foot, impatient with him in that way only teenagers can be impatient, as if nothing in your lame fortysomething, kid-having life could possibly be as important as the most minor detail of their own.

"So, what?" she asked.

"You know exactly what, Tessa. That fucking video."

"What about it? I took it down, just like all the others. My mom made me, and I'm in deep shit. And I'm sorry I ever put it up, okay?"

"Okay," he said, somewhat mollified. Beck had downloaded the video to his phone and watched it probably fifty times since yesterday. Huge relief to know it no longer lived online—though this took care of only half of his current worry. "But listen. Have you said anything to the twins, or your mom or Azra or whatever, about—about us?"

"*Us?* What does that even *mean?*"

"Like, that we—I don't know. That I tried to make a move on you, up in Breck?"

Her eyes widened. "No. God. *Yuck.* That is so cringey, I can't even. Who would say that?"

Beck could have done without the *yuck* and the *cringey*, but he also got a relieving crackle in his chest. "You have to tell Azra that nothing's going on," he demanded softly, glancing at the crowds shuffling past. The skin beneath his beard started to prickle. "Seriously, you have to tell her that I never even hinted at making a move like that, okay? Because you *know* I didn't, you *know* I'd never do that. And you have to tell Sonja if she says anything. I can't have my wives thinking—"

"Your *wives?*" she snorted.

"Whatever," he said. "The point is, my life's fucked up enough already as it is. I can't have Azra and Sonja believing that I'm—that we're—"

Her face changed, going all lit and righteous. "*Your* life, Beck? You think this is about *you* and your lame problems? You're seriously clueless enough to believe that?"

Beck gaped at her.

"The twins are messed up, Beck," she spat at him. "You have no idea. Especially Aidan. He just broke my brother's glasses on purpose. Like, *stomped* on them in the bouncy house."

"Aidan wouldn't do anything like that," he protested. "It must have been Charlie."

"Wrong. And besides, that vlog you saw? Okay, it's gross, but it's also basically proof that nothing happened. So chill out, okay? And seriously, bro, take a shower. I'm going." She whirled off and left him there in a fug of mute, gelatinous helplessness, a stinking waste of skin huddled against the door of a custodial closet.

Just then Lauren passed by, saw him, and stopped, her face lit with fury. "Why were you texting my daughter last night?"

"Oh shit, Lauren, just don't—" He glanced over her shoulder, half expecting the cops to be right behind her. "Look, you gotta ask her, because we just talked and it's all straightened out."

She shook her head and hedgehogged off to wherever.

Control.

Beck had lost all semblance of it—but then so had his sons' lives. Routine, predictability, stability. Maybe Tessa was right. Maybe this wasn't about Beck at all.

Because when your parents split up and then your dad marries your au pair and then your au pair has a baby who's your new brother but not the same kind of brother as your twin because he has a different mom and then you see your totally baked dad get out of a Jacuzzi and finger Nutella out of a jar while a half-naked teenager who's your current babysitter gets out of the same Jacuzzi a few minutes later, all of this while your dad's freaking out about money and you don't even know where you're going to school next year and your brother's kicking your ass in soccer when you've been the star for years and now he's also getting higher test scores, not to mention your mom getting closer with this *Glen* motherfucker who apparently has a whole family of his own—

—well, then, yeah, you might start thinking and saying some weird-ass shit too, no matter how outrageous it might sound. Because what you're asking for is some sense of *order* in your life. Some sense of predictability. Security. Balance.

But then what about Aidan and what Tessa had just told him about Xander's glasses? Why would Aidan pick on a sweet kid like Xander?

Well, Christ. Maybe they both needed help; but so did he, Beck admitted to himself for really the first time. *Bigly.*

He fumbled his phone out of his pocket and looked down at the screen and called up "Breck with Beck." He hit Play, and as he watched once more he understood that Tessa was right, that this was evidence of a sort in his favor, showing him not as some skeezy middle-aged perv but as a bumbling idiot, as harmless as he was clueless; yet somehow these same moving images of himself, this vision of his big hairy ass and his shaking gut and the pathetic false bravado on his thickly bro-bearded face as he posed in a towel and tried to suck in his stomach and straighten his shoulders—because he still thought of himself as a man with shoulders that could straighten, a man with an abdomen that could flatten—somehow this, more than anything he had experienced in his adult life, throbbed through him like the low, intense pulse of an electric bass with Beck as its single string, a long, thrumming nerve stretched and tensed to a breaking point he could feel coming but had no power to hold off.

But shit, man. Maybe he did.

He lifted his eyes from the phone screen and looked down the hall, where his ex-wife stood staring at him from an open doorway. He saw her in that photo from Burning Man, on that perfect day in the desert, Beck poised at the top of the wheel beneath an impossible flood of sunlight with his whole life—

He blinked. Azra was gesturing toward the classroom. *They're in here*, she mouthed, and when Beck staggered into the room, he saw the twins at the front of a crowd watching a video on a wide-screen monitor affixed to the wall.

Beck's video, sleekly produced over hours in his basement and showing off Aidan's mad soccer skills to their best advantage. His son's deft dribbling through the legs of his opponents. His son's virtuosic juggling with the ball bouncing on his ankles and shoulders and head, the traps and feints and turns, tricky assists, goals rocketed into the net or slammed in with a buck of the head. Every move introduced with a flashy text graphic naming the opponent and listing Aidan's stats for the match in question, then a starburst identifying him on the field in freeze-frame, so viewers wouldn't confuse him with his teammates when play resumed.

His teammates. And there they were, in the background of each play, working just as hard as Aidan—though Beck's camera followed only his son. Only one of his sons, actually, despite the fact that Charlie appeared in every third or fourth clip playing with his brother, doing his best, but treated by his father as so much background noise.

Beck looked down from the monitor and watched his incredible boys watching themselves, being watched by the parents and other kids crowded into the room to see Aidan Unsworth-Chaudhury burn it up on the soccer pitch. Aidan's face glowed with unabashed pride but also, and he noticed it for the first time in that moment, something cold and arrogant that chilled Beck while he stood there inside the doorway.

Charlie's gaze was more opaque, brooding and confused as he experienced his brother's talent through the rapt and admiring looks of so many others. Including, it occurred to Beck, a father who seemed to have eyes only for his twin.

Azra turned to Beck and flashed him a proud-mama smile that faded when she saw the look on his face, the tears he could feel streaming from his eyes.

"Impressive," said some dad in the crowd. "So is this film of both of you playing?"

"Nope," Charlie said, voice tight and edgy. "Just him."

"My brother's playing left bench this season," said Aidan, prompting a few mean chuckles from some other kids. The dad raised his eyebrows and whispered something to his wife. Something about Aidan.

For a moment Beck saw flashes of crimson, just as he had on the sideline in Grand Junction last weekend. For a second there he wanted to deck the guy for the smug, superior look.

But then the red mist of his anger cleared, and what he saw instead was Charlie's humiliated little face, he saw the hidden gritting of his son's teeth, he saw how hard the kid was working to hold all that fury in. But Beck could see the anger and shame just under the surface. He recognized it; knew it.

He looked at Azra, who was staring now at Aidan, visibly stricken by their son's cruelty. In one long movement Beck pushed through to the monitor, switched it off, and squatted down in front of his boys.

"You know what, guys?" he said quietly. "Let's get out of here."

"But the best part's coming up," Aidan protested.

"We need to go. Right now." He held out both his hands, and maybe it was some new calm in his voice that made his sons step forward and grasp them without a fuss.

Control.

They trooped out of the room together and into the milling crowd. When they reached the top of the stairs, Beck turned back to Azra.

"Please let me take them," he said, keeping his voice steady and cool. "I'll bring them to my place, get them cleaned up and fed, sort through how we're going to deal with St. Bridget's. Then we'll talk about all this. That okay with you?"

He liked the surprised look on Azra's face. "Yes, okay," she said nodding. "That sounds good."

He let go of his sons' hands and stepped closer to her. "And that Tessa thing is total bullshit," he said with a deeper kind of calm, looking into those kind eyes he'd always loved. "You know that, right?"

His ex-wife nodded, then reached out and touched his hand. Just for a moment, but it was enough. With his sons at his side Beck walked down a flight of stairs, out the front entrance, and down to the sidewalk, heading for home.

SIXTY-SEVEN

CH'AYÑA

The new school was on the hill, tucked up against the mountains. From the truck Ch'ayña saw for the first time the height and size of the place. Without knowing it she had driven past the school thirty times on the way to the Zellar house but had never once looked at it. Today all the people swarmed like flies, up and down the stairs and on the play equipment in the yard.

Maple Hill Lane was full of cars, so they had to park around the corner on a side street. The three of them climbed out of the truck. Atik, sweating through his buttoned shirt. Silea, the skin of her healed forearm grayish and loose. Ch'ayña, heart thumping madly against her ribs. She dreaded the event, had always been bad with crowds, though today there was something else eating her from the inside out.

In the packed yard the first thing they did was join a line.

"For ice cream," Silea explained, up on her toes, looking about.

Ch'ayña stood behind her daughter, peering through the thick crowd of Crystals. The women in their short dresses and the men standing on their bare, hairy legs, all their spoiled children demanding more of everything, in English but Ch'ayña could still understand them.

More ice cream. Another burger. A blue cloud of spun sugar.

Atik didn't belong here among these spoon-fed whelps glued to their phones. Ch'ayña felt the conviction start to harden, a contempt for the place, a clawing certainty that it could never be right for her *wawa*.

On the far side of a sliding board a familiar face appeared. Tiago, sauntering toward the cooking meats, looking for Silea. Ch'ayña watched as their eyes kissed across the schoolyard.

He hurried up and spoke to Ch'ayña first. *"Alli-lla'n'chu, doña?"* he said, mangling the hello. She stared at him, took in the way Silea stapled herself to his arm.

Ch'ayña waited in the playground until the others finished their ice cream, then they made their way up the stairs and into the building. The air was soured with the hot bodies mingling, and there was a nervous current in the crowd. Along the hall and in every classroom the talents of the children were displayed. On tables, on walls, on television screens. The gifts shone out from every corner of the school, a spot for every child who had given them something. Atik was skipping ahead of them now, looking for his pictures, the proof of his gifts.

They climbed up to the second floor. As they went down the hallway Ch'ayña saw Ms. Holland—their employer saw her too. Ms. Holland's eyes went wide with surprise, and with something else. She sidestepped to the middle of the hall and put up her hands, stopping them, her face a ruddy blushing mess as she spoke with Silea.

Ch'ayña listened as Ms. Holland huddled with her daughter. Silea stared at the woman, giving her nothing. She caught some of Ms. Holland's feeble excuses. . . . *my fault, Silea, my fault entirely . . . a meeting with my boss . . . feel just TERRIBLE . . . some trouble at work . . . just forgot . . . next week, first thing Monday I'll bring it in and explain everything, I promise . . .*

I promise, I promise. But it wasn't enough, of course; could never be enough.

Ch'ayña clung for a few moments more to her denial, but she understood what she had done, how it was all her fault.

Because Silea had wanted to drop by the school first, turn in the portfolio themselves, on their way up Opal Canyon. It was Ch'ayña who'd suggested asking Ms. Holland, Ch'ayña who'd rushed out to the truck and grabbed the portfolio from beneath the seat, placed it in Ms. Holland's ir-responsible hands. Ch'ayña didn't even know the lady, didn't know a thing about her soul, and yet she'd trusted her with all of Atik's hopes that day, just to save them fifteen minutes.

Atik's binder in her mind became a stiff bird with blue vinyl wings, smashing out the windows of Ms. Holland's house and flying through town and into the schoolyard and up the outer stairs with its panels flapping wildly to disgorge the glossy pictures, to show these people Atik's gifts, to show them what the boy could do with his hands and his intricate mind.

She felt her knees wanting to give out. Moisture beaded up in the pits of her knees and arms and the blood rushed to her face and her limbs went cold.

Sweet Atikcha had heard none of this, she saw, hadn't even noticed Ms. Holland stopping them in the crowded hallway. There he was, walking ahead, chatting with Tiago, happy as you like.

Atik peered through the doorway at the end of the corridor, then looked back at Ch'ayña with a smile and a little nod and a come-on gesture with his right hand. Ch'ayña had to look away. Ms. Holland was finishing up her wet-cheeked apology and Silea was being nice to her, of course, fawning and flattering, because what choice did she have, the lady was one of her bosses. Ch'ayña glared at the woman until she turned and walked away. Silea glanced again at her mother, but Ch'ayña couldn't meet her gaze. To-gether they walked unspeaking down the hall after Atik, who had just dis-appeared into the classroom.

They went in together, Ch'ayña first and Silea right behind her. Once in the classroom she didn't see it at first. Then Silea made a happy little moan, and then—

Ch'ayña stared past Atik and Tiago at the far wall, transfixed.

"*Chekaqchu!*" she blurted, clapping a hand to her lips.

Because there, on the wall, were Ch'ayña's photographs, arranged around a window in a display of Atik's skills—and something more.

Beneath the window on a table sat Atik's paper model of Mountain View Mobile Park alongside a small gathering of his animals and flowers

and trees. An elephant, a cat, a moose, a gorilla, a giraffe. A daisy, a sun-
flower; roses in pink, purple, orange. An oak and a pine tree and an aspen
shedding golden leaves.

Her grandson's origami foldings: perfect in this rich light, like cut
gems. But how had they gotten here? Who had brought them?

Atik walked over to the display, and the boss of the school started
talking to him. Ch'ayña couldn't speak, she could only shake her head and
look on mutely as Atik moved his magical hands and explained the work of
his fingers.

Tiago was talking to Silea. Ch'ayña couldn't hear what they said, but
once they were finished, Silea came over and took her mother's hand.

"It's my fault," said Ch'ayña, her eyes flooding.

"It's not your fault, Mamay." Silea patted her hand. "You've had so much
on your shoulders these last months with all the houses, the driving. Taking care of us."

Ch'ayña shook her head. "But how—"

"Tiago made another folder for him and drove it here, that same day,"
Silea said, gesturing for the man to join them, "along with the model and
some of his other designs. He got everything in on time."

"I thought they should see the origami itself, not just the pictures,"
Tiago explained. "I made a second binder and brought it in with the mobile
park and those animals. I told Atik, but I should have said something
to you."

Tiago raised his eyebrows and gave her a meek look, a shrug of his
bulky shoulders.

Ch'ayña made a decision right then, as she stood with her arms folded
stoutly and watched her grandson boast to the school boss. No more cold
water for Tiago. From now on she would offer the man a cup of tea when
he came over. Coca, mint, lemongrass, any kind he asked for. A whole damn
pot if he wanted it.

SIXTY-EIGHT

EMMA Z

The Emmas strolled along the third-floor hallway sharing a rasp-
berry-lemon scone from the pastry cart. You weren't supposed to
bring food inside the school, but Z didn't care. She ate first, breaking off a little piece from the first flaky corner before handing it over to Q.
She watched as Q snapped off the next corner.

Emma Q always had to be a copycat, even with a scone. Z sighed
loudly.

"What?" Q looked alarmed.

"Oh, nothing," said Z in a singsongy way. "Just—nothing."

"But tell me."

"It's not important." Z led them through a door into a classroom full of
light and color.

It was an art studio. There were easels, there were shelves full of clay
bricks wrapped in plastic, there were famous paintings on the wall ("Look,
Mommy, that one's Klimt!" an annoying girl said in a very shrill voice). A
big wall of windows faced outside. The classroom was high up, on the top
floor of the school. You could see the Redirons way off, shoving their
pointy blades at the sky.

A big television monitor at the front of the room showed a girl who
looked the same age as the Emmas sitting at a potter's wheel making a bowl
out of clay. The girl shown in the video was standing there with both her

parents watching, like she hadn't seen her own video a million times already. The real bowl, mustard yellow and spiraled from top to bottom with an aqua stripe, sat on the shelf just below the monitor.

Z took another pinch of scone. "This is boring." She chewed loudly, dropping crumbs.

"*So* boring," Q agreed, taking the scone.

The girl's father turned and glared at them.

Z said, "Let's try a different room."

She made them skip the next two doors, because those classrooms didn't look that interesting and there were no kids in them, and so far she hadn't seen *Born to Lead* displayed anywhere. And maybe it *wouldn't* be displayed anywhere, because if her CogPro score wasn't high enough and what that man said to her father was true . . .

In the third classroom there was a family who looked maybe Hispanic, staring at some photographs on the wall. A boy, a mother, a father, and an old lady who was probably the boy's grandmother. The mother looked familiar. Emma Z stared at her, trying to figure out where she'd seen the woman before.

The boy was talking to Dr. Leighton, the lady who had been speaking into the microphone outside. He had brown skin like Azra's but a little darker. He wore round glasses with silver rims. The lenses weren't thick like Xander's, but the shape of the glasses made him look like an owl.

"This is really ingenious, Atik," Dr. Leighton was saying to the boy.

"Thank you, ma'am." The boy's chin went up a little, which was annoying.

"Where did you learn to do this kind of work?" Her head moved in a slow, exaggerated circle, as if she were taking in some museum exhibit and wanted everyone to see her seeing.

"From myself, ma'am."

"Your parents must be so proud."

"Yes, ma'am," he said, then spoke to the old woman in Italian or Spanish or something. The grandmother beamed at the teacher and the boy. They talked a little more to Dr. Leighton before heading toward the door.

When they were gone, Emma Z went up to look at the pictures. There were seven of them, the first two showing views of a mobile suspended from a ceiling in someone's house. From the mobile dangled about twenty paper birds of every shape and color. Flamingoes, pelicans, hummingbirds and cardinals and bluejays. The next picture showed a bunch of house trailers in rows, and seeing the model gave Emma Z a strange rush of familiarity, because it looked just like the trailer park they would pass every Saturday before turning into Wild Horse Stables way out in Beulah County. Other photos showed paper cars, paper trucks, paper people. On a narrow table just below all the pictures stood ten actual paper animals. Including a giraffe exactly like the one that somebody left in her room all those weeks ago.

Emma Z's eyes fixed on one of the four thumbtacks attaching the lowest picture to the wall. She wanted to pull the tack out and keep it. She was just reaching for it when she realized the boy had come back into the classroom without the others and was standing nearby, watching her look at the pictures.

"You're Emma," he said.

She put her hands on her hips like her mother did and frowned at him. "How do *you* know my name?"

He mumbled something.

"What did you say?"

"From pictures," he said.

"What pictures?"

"In your house."

"What were you doing in my house?"

He smiled. "Cleaning," he said, and Emma Z thought of her yellow sweater pushed under her bed; of all her books, neatened and organized on the bookcase. Of the paper animals left on her shelf.

"Is your mother Silea?" she asked him. Now she knew who the familiar woman was. She remembered her own mother saying something about

Silea's other family members, how they had to do the cleaning while Silea's arm was healing.

"Yes," he said.

"Oh." She blinked, not knowing what to say.

The boy stepped closer to her and nodded at the pictures and the folded animals.

"Those are from my portfolio. It's called origami. Do you like it?"

Emma Z turned toward the animals on the small table. All the shapes, the folds, the impossible intricacies of the boy's creations.

For some reason she thought of the CogPro. She thought of Question 15.

A square, a circle, a parallelogram, a cone, a rhombus.

Blue, red, green, yellow, purple.

The boy was staring at her, but in a way she sort of didn't mind.

She shrugged. "Paper isn't really my thing. My project is on leadership."

"What does that mean?"

Emma Z rolled her eyes at the boy like she rolled her eyes at all boys. "It means I'm a leader. It means leadership is my spike. I'm a junior auditor at Darlton University."

"What's a junior auditor?"

"Someone who takes classes there, same as the college students."

"Wow. That's amazing."

"I guess."

He stood there until finally she raised her eyebrows and gave her head a little shake, like she saw Tessa do sometimes when she was impatient.

"Well . . . good luck," he said, and his face looked kind of disappointed.

Emma Z decided to smile at him. "You too," she said.

Without saying goodbye he turned away and said something to his grandma, who'd just come back in the room to find him. She frowned at Emma Z and patted the boy on the head, then pushed him toward the door. As they left the classroom she kept her head turned back, her old eyes fixed on Emma Z's.

———

Once they were gone, Z's gaze swept across the small crowd. There were ten or twelve people in the room, but no one was paying attention to her. With a fingernail she plucked one of the thumbtacks out of the poster, slipped it into her pocket, and pressed the pad of her thumb against the point. It didn't hurt that badly. She removed her hand from her pocket and sucked a bead of blood off her thumb.

When she turned from the photograph display, she noticed that Emma Q wasn't moving. Her friend looked frozen in place, and her eyes were wide, and she was standing in front of a trifold.

There must be something *verrrrry* interesting on that trifold, Z thought, because Q was staring as if the flaps might close on their own and bite off one of her chubby cheeks.

"What is it, Q?" Emma Z called across the room.

Q broke her stare. "Huh?" she said dumbly. She looked scared.

"What's on that poster?" Z started toward her.

"Nothing." Emma Q moved away from the trifold and stood there, blocking Z's way.

"Move," Z said.

"Let's go down the hall," Q replied. "This stuff is all stupid."

"No, it's not. That origami's not stupid. Could *you* make paper animals like that?"

"No, sorry, I mean *some* of it is, like, all that stuff over there."

"What stuff?"

"Let's just go." Q grabbed Z's arm and tried to face her toward the door. Z pushed her hand off.

"What is your *problem*?" Emma Z kept her voice down so the parents wandering the room wouldn't hear.

But it was too late. Dr. Leighton frowned at them. "Is there an issue, girls?"

"No, ma'am," Z said sweetly.

Q got an I-give-up look on her face, then Z spun away and walked to the table where the trifold was displayed. When she saw the front of it, she laughed. "Q, you're so *weird*. This is just our History Day thing."

But then she saw the new header unfurled across the top.

THE HORSE IN THE AMERICAN WEST

BY EMMA HOLLAND-QUINN

Z stared at their project. "That's funny. How did—"

Then she understood.

"*Ohhhh*," she said, turning to look at her friend. Q had her mouth open and her head was shaking and she was about to start crying, and obviously Q knew this was going to make Z very angry, and Q also knew how much Z would enjoy telling her mom that her very best friend's daughter basically *stole* Z's work for her portfolio. And right now Dr. Leighton was walking over to them.

So this was *big*.

It was weird, though, but the new caption didn't really make Emma Z all that mad. In fact she felt almost proud of Emma Q for stealing so openly from her and thinking she could get away with it. The theft showed a side of Q she'd never seen before. It was sneaky, it was dishonest, and it was almost, like, kind of *brave*.

But Z was going to have to punish her for it anyway. Maybe a week without talking at all, or even two weeks or a month. Or maybe having a big party at her house or at JumpGym to which Q wouldn't be invited.

Oh yes, this was *definitely* big.

SIXTY-NINE

ROSE

S he leaned against the tiled wall, humiliation burning her cheeks, as Silea and her mother continued down the hallway. Would she ever forget the disappointment in Silea's eyes just now, or that look of pure hatred from her mother, that gut-punching contempt? All her privilege, all her benevolence, all her smug self-satisfaction that she had a house cleaner come just once every two weeks when the Zellars had theirs come three times a week—and now an abject failure to fulfill this simple yet infinitely meaningful request: a ten-minute detour to do an easy favor for a woman who'd scrubbed her toilets for the last five years.

And now Rose had to find Emma Q, her portfolio, and Samantha— hopefully all three of them, and in the right order—before yet another catastrophe struck.

The crowd moved slowly and with deliberation, pooling and congealing at doorways and in the narrow spaces between tables, but despite the throngs Rose made quick work of the east side of the third floor. She crossed into the first classroom on the west side, then the second, and had made it all way down to the last room when she saw her daughter across the hall.

Two tables in, the Emmas stood together in front of a trifold with Bitsy Leighton squatting between them, her head wedged between their pretty faces, their attention clearly riveted by the enormity of what Rose had done.

For the second time in five minutes she found herself rooted to the floor, unable to move.

She looked past them, the misery gathering in her head like a sneeze—and saw a table full of Atik's origami animals standing beneath a window. Above them a dozen photographs from his portfolio, arranged attractively to show off his talents. She stared at the array, baffled.

"Why, this is lovely, Emma," Bitsy Leighton said to her right. Rose looked away from Atik's creations. Bitsy's arm had settled on the shoulders of Emma Q.

The classroom was pitched at a low murmur that Emma Z's voice snicked through like a blade when she said, "It was a *lot* of work."

Bitsy turned her head. "What's that?"

Rose held her breath. Emma Q's eyes went wide as pancakes. Emma Z grinned up at Bitsy, then turned to look at Rose. Samantha's daughter gave her a bitchy little smile.

"I'm going to go look for my mom and dad now. I can't find *my* trifold *anywhere*," Z said, then skipped from the room.

Rose let out air. Q's milky face was flushed a fierce and blotchy red. She dashed out of the classroom with her fists pumping, darting for the stairs. Rose wanted to go after her but couldn't leave the project here like this, bared and exposed, almost pornographic in its raw disclosure of her dishonesty; and Samantha could be anywhere. Bitsy Leighton frowned as Rose meekly approached the table, folded up the trifold, and tucked it under her arm.

Before leaving the room, she took one look back at the woman's face. Rose saw confusion there, then a glimmer of understanding. Worst of all: a hint of pity in the woman's eyes.

SEVENTY

XANDER

After taping his glasses back together in the main office, Xander went upstairs to a chemistry and biology lab, stocked with two empty terrariums, microscopes, beakers, and test tubes for show; posters of the periodic table and instructions on laboratory safety. Dozens of science fair trifolds stood like skyscrapers on the high lab tables.

Water pollution, jet propulsion, rocketry, lake biology, ocean biology, creek biology, aerodynamics, asteroids: exactly forty-four science fair projects were displayed in the lab.

But not Xander's. There must be another lab, on a different floor.

When he left the classroom, he saw Emma Q coming down the hall, tears and snot smearing her face. Xander crossed the hall and followed her into another classroom. This room was different from all the others, quieter somehow. There was music on, a cello, and a girl was performing gymnastics on a television screen. There was no pattern, though. It looked as if the teachers had stacked the room with a bunch of projects they hadn't known where else to put. Everything was very—miscellaneous.

A few adults stepped away, and Xander saw Mr. Quinn staring down at a trifold, his face unmoving and his right arm crossed over his chest. It looked like he was holding his heart. His left arm dangled at his side.

One of Xander's favorite things to watch was this old clip of Mikhail

Botvinnik winning the Soviet championship against Salo Flohr (Leningrad, 1933). You couldn't find a video of the whole match, but the part Xander liked best came near the beginning, when you saw Botvinnik staring down at the table with his lips pooched and a dark pit in his sucked-in cheek and his spectacles tight against his eye sockets, so they looked more like goggles than glasses. The champ's face was one big, brainy ball of unmoving focus. You got the feeling that his whole life had come down to this one moment. That everything he did afterward began right here.

That was exactly the way Mr. Quinn's face looked, minus the glasses. He had the same kind of head as Botvinnik's, and his right arm was crossing the top of his chest, squeezing his ribs. He looked like a tense hunting dog about to spring forward and go for a squirrel. Quivering, even. Trembling, like Aquinas.

Emma Q walked over to her father, breaking the spell. He took her hand. His eyes were blinking crazily.

"What does it mean, Daddy?" she asked, taking in the trifold. Her puzzled frown deepened. Xander's stomach burbled as he watched Q begin to understand the truly life-changing significance of his discovery. Her forehead smoothed, her face went blank with surprise.

"*There* you are," said a low voice behind him.

"Hello," Xander said to his sister, hearing his own voice tremble on the two syllables, like Mr. Quinn's hands. His lenses wobbled as a piece of tape gave way.

They stood there together, looking at Gareth and Emma Q. Father and daughter, their lives changing by the moment.

"I am indubitably grounded," said Xander.

Tessa held up her phone.

SEVENTY-ONE

ROSE

s Q with you? Rose texted Gareth as she speedwalked with Q's trifold pressed to her side. Descending to the second floor, she ran into Azra.

"Have you seen Emma Q?" Rose asked, breathless.

"No, I was just coming to look for you. Beck took off with the boys, so—"

"What about Samantha? It's important." Rose could hear the desperate clawing in her own voice.

"I saw her just now, with Kev. Coming up from the main floor."

"Will you show me?"

"Of course." Azra led her along the hallway. By silent agreement they took the classrooms on opposite sides, keeping pace as they went along.

First room: no Q, no Sam.

Second room: no Q, no Sam.

Third room—

"Rose!" Azra called, waving her over. "They're all in here."

Rose dodged around a few parents and kids on her way to the door. Through the glass panel she first saw Xander, standing with his back to a wall, Lauren in front of him with her hands on his shoulders. Farther in were Kev and Samantha, walking slowly toward Gareth, who stood at the far side of the room with Emma Q pressed to his side, her face buried in her father's ribs.

Rose felt her stomach lurch. She knew Q was upset, but the scene was wrong somehow; she sensed this on her skin and wanted to turn and slink away.

"What the hell?" Azra pushed unceremoniously on the door.

Rose had her eyes drawn first to a large monitor showing a gymnast doing an impressive routine on the uneven bars. The familiar arpeggios of a Bach cello suite lilted from a speaker somewhere. Across the room her husband and daughter stood in front of a trifold. The look on Gareth's face was sober, almost funereal.

The door opened again to a wave of hallway noise, and Emma Zellar burst into the room, her pretty face lit with a smile that remained fixed despite the presence of the disgraced Rose. She started skipping over to her parents.

"Where's my trifold, Mommy? I can't find it anywh—" Z stopped in mid-skip. One look at her father's glowering scowl and the joy dropped from her face.

Around the far table Rose could see them all: a tableau of pale familiar faces running a gamut of strange emotion. Xander pressed against the wall as Lauren gripped his shoulders; Gareth, an arm clutched around his middle, almost cowering now and casting up a furtive, ratlike glance at Rose; Samantha with her palms pressed against Kev's heaving chest, holding him back. Tessa, ignoring everyone as she stared at her phone. (*Filming again?* Rose wondered.)

And the Emmas, looking never more alike.

"What's going on?" Rose said, and the eight heads turned as one.

Gareth was the first to break the silence. "Rose?"

"What is this?" she said, cutting him off.

"Rose?" he said again.

Samantha detached herself from Kev's chest and held up her palms at Rose. "Wait—Rose—please—"

Gareth reached for the trifold. At the same moment Kev lunged forward and knocked her husband's arms away. Gareth brought his hands to his mouth, cupping his panic-heavy breaths.

"Don't you touch it," Kev seethed. His eyes darted back and forth between his wife and Gareth. "Let her fucking see it. Let *everybody* see it."

"See what?" Rose asked.

Kev's mouth contorted into a broad smile, the familiar shape of his public face, yet not the same at all: furious, threatening. "Why, it's Xander's goddamn science project. Brilliant piece of work." He beckoned her with an old-fashioned gentleman's flourish, then, as she stepped forward, stormed past her toward the exit. "It's all yours, Doc. All yours." His voice cracking as he threw open the door. "Enjoy!"

The others made room for her, as if honoring a mourner approaching a casket. Her grip on Emma Q's trifold loosened, and it fell from her hands to smack on the floor.

Once in front of Xander's presentation—its pictures, graphs, charts, lines—Rose felt her scientist's brain kick in instantly, a familiar detachment that allowed her to focus on what was before her.

Hypothesis, data collection, experimentation, results, conclusion. Allowance for error.

Evaluate, she told herself. Across the top of the trifold's middle panel stretched a banner title:

CHESS PERSONALITY: HEREDITARY OR LEARNED?
By Xander Frye

Rose scanned the left panel, a statement of the project's guiding question and hypothesis, printed on separate squares of paper and glued to the trifold.

QUESTION: Is a player's chess personality determined by genetics or environment? Is chess personality hereditary or is it learned?

HYPOTHESIS: Chess personality is determined in part by heredity. Players who are closely related genetically will display similar personality traits in their tactical and strategic approaches to the game, even if they live in separate households.

A bizarre proposition, and as she scanned down through the predictions, research plan, and project description, she summoned her initial objections. Parents and siblings will play each other more often, absorb one another's tendencies through repeated encounters at the chess table. There was also no way to determine whether any given behavioral tendency was genetic or learned: the notion was absurd. Plus—

Yet Xander had controlled for these problems, or at least attempted to. As he argued in his longer description of the project, which Rose read and absorbed in mere seconds, his data analysis would consist of a combination of algebraic chess notations and genetic testing. The notations would be put through an algorithm Xander had designed himself to map a set of behavioral tendencies through the data: aggression, deference, defensiveness, fear, indifference, carelessness, and so on. The genetic analysis would be used to confirm whether the familial relations suggested in his data analysis correlated with the evidence garnered from DNA testing.

The amount and quality of raw data from the chess side of the project was evident from the large middle panel and the stacks of paper piled in front of it. Xander had played every child and adult in every family multiple times—in some cases many dozens of times; had remembered and recorded every move of every game he'd ever played.

One hundred seventy-nine games with Aidan Unsworth-Chaudhury. Two hundred twelve games with Charlie Unsworth-Chaudhury. Sixty-seven games with Emma Zellar. Ninety-four games with Rose Holland. And the list went on. He had also recorded the many matches between others that he had observed over those same years: Charlie and Emma Z, July 5, 2012; Beck and Kev, Best of Seven, Thanksgiving Day 2014 (a pitched battle, Rose remembered, fueled by testosterone and single-malt Scotch).

In all Xander had more than three thousand chess matches transcribed in algebraic notation, every one of them churned through his algorithm to yield a written "assessment of chess personality type" for each member of the families.

Rose, deaf to the rising mumbles around her, scanned quickly through them, catching the odd phrase here and there, lingering on her own assessment.

Azra Chaudhury: very smart player . . . overly accommodating . . . avoids sequential exchanges . . . steers clear of conflict . . .

Aidan Unsworth-Chaudhury: crafty but aggressive . . . avoids sequential exchanges . . . retreats when necessary . . . discourages concession . . . cruel to inferior opponents . . .

Rose Holland: deceptive and sneaky . . . ruthless but insecure . . . squanders pawns, hoards opportunity . . . unwilling to sacrifice for tactical advantage . . . tendency to risk everything in pursuit of a weak endgame . . .

For the lower part of the middle panel Xander had created a chart of familial relationships based on what he'd gleaned from these personality types: the unwritten code binding brother to brother, father to son, daughter to mother, patterns that altered somewhat yet remained largely stable as children grew and parents aged.

Rose's eyes blurred and focused and blurred again as she scanned the chart, absorbed its meaning, saw the obvious error at its center. Because—

"Oh," she said, and blood rushed and throbbed in her ears as she awoke to the room and the people around her. Behind her someone coughed.

Without moving her head, she forced her eyes to look at the right-hand panel, an organized presentation of the genetic data Xander had compiled to test his chess algorithm. Thumbnail photographs of the samples he'd collected, from strands of hair taken from Rose's hairbrush to semen collected from a used condom in Beck's master bathroom. A series of DNA-matching results, all from a national lab called GenSecure. Xander had included his "lab notes" as well as several explanatory bubbles of prose.

Finally, a series of abbreviated family trees. Paired photos of six discrete sets of parents linked with poorly drawn branches to images of their children. Gareth and Rose in a black-and-white wedding photo, matched with

Emma Q in her fourth-grade school picture, their nuclear family unthreatened and secure.

An old beach photo of Julian and Lauren, linked to a picture of Tessa in a bikini and Xander at a chess tournament.

A glorious color photo of Beck and Azra years ago at Burning Man, a shot Rose had never seen before but that Xander's caption revealed had been found in Beck's basement study. They were linked to Charlie and Aidan with photos snipped from a shot of their soccer team.

Then a more heavyset Beck, linked to Sonja in cobra pose and a newborn Roy, connected with a dotted line to the twins, his half brothers.

And at the bottom of the middle panel was the final tree. On the left, the same wedding shot of Gareth but with Rose cut out of the photo—and in her place a beaming Samantha Zellar, holding up a glass of champagne and blowing a kiss over the crystal flute. Their tree revealed them as the biological parents of Emma Zellar—linked to Emma Holland-Quinn, her half sister, with a dotted line that ran from the bottom of the panel all the way to the first family tree at the top.

Rose could sense the millions of nerve cells that coated the tissue of her retina absorbing the images and sending their electrical pulses to her optic nerve and through it to her frontal lobe, which started a cool assessment of the visual information in front of her, as if one of her postdocs were presenting lab results to her skeptical eye. She leaned slightly forward and looked at the side panels again, assessing the probabilities, costing out the damage to her marriage, her friendships.

Her daughter. Samantha's daughter.

Everything.

Finally she straightened. "Is this—Gareth—is this true?"

But she already knew it was, and even as the question left her mouth she felt the gulf that was their marriage widen, its cliff walls finally begin to crumble and plunge.

Around her a dozen strangers murmured and softly questioned. The confrontation was harvesting attention now.

"Oh, Rose," she heard Samantha say as the ringing faded in her ears. "It happened before I knew you, over a year before we even met. I never thought—"

"Stop," Rose said.

Gareth again: "Honey, I don't—"

"Just *stop*. And tell me if it's true."

There was a thick and short silence, broken by Xander's squeaky rasp: "The results are accurate to within 99.99998 percent."

Rose's head spun toward the boy, who was staring wide-eyed through the broken and taped-up mess of his glasses. Lauren had already clapped her hand over his mouth.

"But how did *you* know?" Rose said, still somehow a scientist tangled in the mystery of hypothesis: the spark of thought that made knowledge possible. "What made you do this in the first place?"

Xander simply shook his head, saying nothing between his mother's fingers.

Rose felt like a spectator at the scene of a violent crime, except she didn't know whether she was a victim or a witness—or both at once. Ten feet away Samantha, hands over her face, wept openly, shoulders humping with emotion.

Azra was the first to risk touch; sweet Azra. She put a hand on Rose's arm. "Oh honey," she said tentatively, "maybe we should go. Do you want to go?"

"Listen, Rose," Lauren began. She pushed Xander behind her protectively. "I feel horrible about this." A practical tone that infuriated Rose more with each syllable. "I just wasn't keeping track of Xander's portfolio. You know how he's so independent with his schoolwork, he always has been, really, and I tend to let him do his own thing, which obviously in the case of this science project—"

"Wait." Rose's open hand snapped up with a will of its own, silencing Lauren. "You're . . . you're actually trying to tell me this is—you think *this*—"

For two seconds no one moved. Then Rose grabbed Xander's trifold, clutching it by its side panels and thrusting it toward Lauren's face.

"That this *shit* is *science*?"

She shook the trifold at Lauren.

"This isn't *science*," she seethed, "this is a few drugstore DNA kits and a malicious little sociopath who decided to ruin a bunch of lives."

"Rose—" Gareth started to say. With a burning stare she shut his soft mouth.

She went on: "As if—as if we're *chess* pieces he can just knock over however he wants. Are you proud of your profoundly gifted son, Lauren, for what he's done?" She threw the trifold on the tiled floor and stomped on it with her flats, shoots of pain up creeping up her rubbery legs.

"Rose, stop," Samantha said.

Rose whirled on her. Samantha backed off a step, but Rose moved forward and put a finger in her heart-shaped face. "Oh, don't you start, you evil *bitch*, you lying, cheating—with your perfect precious little brat of a dau—oh, wait, I'm sorry, your perfect precious little brat of *my husband's* daughter. I mean, you and *Gareth*? *Seriously*? And what's her gift? *What*? What's her 'spike'? Leadership? How many millions did you have to give to Darlton University to get them to give you what you wanted? Or did you have to fuck a dean or a provost like you fucked *him*?"

She pointed at Gareth, ignoring the gasps.

"Because guess what, you two? Guess what, everybody?" She pointed with both hands at Gareth and Samantha. "*Their* daughter didn't even score high enough to make the first cut. How about *that*? Your fake family shouldn't even *be* here today."

More gasps, murmurs, a harsh laugh somewhere.

Then Emma Zellar's quiet voice:

"Well, you stole my whole History Day project."

Rose was about to scream a response down into the little brat's face when Z stooped to the floor and picked up Q's trifold, which Rose had dropped minutes before.

"She did, Mommy." Z held the horse project up and open so Samantha and everyone else could see. "Her and Q. Rose only put Emma Q's name on it when I did half the work. At *least* half. Q doesn't even know how to type. See?"

Rose stared at the trifold.

"She's right," Rose keened, throwing up her arms. "She's absolutely right. Oh god oh god oh god." Her face sank into her open hands. A long, wretched moan escaped her chest. "It's this school," she said into her palms; then, looking up through her tears, "It's this goddamn school, it's—it's made us all—just—I mean, look at this, just *look* at all this."

She lunged toward a nearby table and picked up a random trifold. "Chrissy Baker," she said, "on the geochemistry of volcanoes." She showed it to the many gawking witnesses to her unraveling. "But I know Dave Baker. He's a geochemist at Darlton. He chairs the goddamn department! You don't think he gave her the idea, did ninety percent of the work?"

She dropped the trifold and cast her eyes around the room. "And how about this one, our little cello prodigy right here." She stomped over to the speaker playing Bach and lifted up the framed photo of the cellist, showing his downcast eyes and the elegant bend of his bow arm.

"I happen to know that Carter Stanhope *hates* the cello, okay? The poor kid's been complaining for the last two years about his lessons, but it doesn't matter, because his mommies *insist* he's a prodigy when actually he's just a diligent kid who can't say no when they tell him he needs to *get his goddamn ten thousand hours.*"

With one movement she smashed the frame on the edge of the table. The glass exploded in a hundred pieces that scattered across the table, tinkled to the floor. The noise and the sensation of breaking stirred something deep within, and for the first time since seeing Xander's results she felt a faint ping of self-consciousness, a sense of how she must look to everyone else in that room.

But she couldn't stop. Not yet.

"And look at me!" she cried, jamming her knuckles into her ribs. "*Look at me!* I'm the worst of all! This is the worst person I have *EVER BEEN!* I forgot to turn in a portfolio for the son of my housekeeper. I made up a bogus research project and risked my career. I literally deleted the name of my little girl's best friend from a trifold, just *erased* her, and now she's—"

"*JUST SHUT UP, ROSE!*" Emma Zellar screeched, stamping her foot on the floor. "*NOBODY CARES!*"

Rose's head snapped back, and during the horrible gasp of silence that followed she saw the reddened face of Emma Z, the tight little fists held clutched at the top of the girl's chest. In the same awful moment Xander's assessment of her own personality spangled through her skull.

. . . deceptive and sneaky . . . ruthless but insecure . . . squanders pawns, hoards opportunity . . .

Emma Z, her daughter's best friend practically since birth. This girl whose life was changing beneath her little feet, altered so much more profoundly than Rose's could ever be by such a revelation.

Because Rose had just learned that her husband cheated on her over twelve years ago. A revelation that was almost a confirmation, and came as a kind of relief.

Emma Zellar, on the other hand, had just learned that Kev wasn't her biological father—a fact that even Kev hadn't known until minutes ago.

"Oh, Z," she said, wanting to pull the girl in, to comfort her somehow.

But then her own daughter stepped up, with an angry, ashamed look on her round face. "Yeah, Mommy. Please please *please* stop talking."

"But I—I can't—"

Then:

"That's *quite* enough."

A woman's voice, loud and authoritative, sounded from the doorway. Bitsy Leighton marched into the classroom. Rose followed the woman's administrative gaze as it took in the scatter of glass shards across the table, the shredded hunks of cardboard on the floor. For the first time Rose noticed the disturbing number of phones held up and pointed in her direction.

Bitsy clapped her hands. "I'd like everyone to clear the room, please," she said. "*Now.*"

After a brief reluctant pause the rubbernecking crowd shuffled forward around the tables and chairs, making for the door. The parents wouldn't meet Rose's eyes, but their children gaped at her, still thrilled by the fading spectacle.

Lauren, pushing Tessa and Xander out the door, glanced back at her with teary eyes. Azra was right behind them, lips pursed and brow furrowed in a sympathy that Rose found deflating rather than comforting.

Then she felt clammy hands on the bared skin of her upper forearms. She turned her head and saw Gareth's watery eyes and the grotesque shape of his face, smelled the stale, hideous breath of him.

"Let's go now, Rose," he said calmly, as if she were a mental patient, or a child. "Let's get our daughter out of here."

Our daughter.

Over his shoulder Rose saw Samantha and Emma Z slinking an arced path around the tables to avoid further contact. Samantha's face was slick with tears, and there was an unfamiliar stoop to her frame. She was texting madly, probably trying to reach Kev.

"We can talk about all this when we get you home," Gareth said.

Home. A word suddenly and irrevocably ruined.

Rose bent her neck sideways so her lips were nearly touching his ungroomed ear.

"Get your hands off me," she whispered to her husband, "you *miserable* worm."

SEVENTY-TWO

BECK

When Beck pulled up to the house, he told the twins to run in ahead of him. "But don't get too comfortable," he warned them. They looked at him strangely as they climbed out of the Audi, maybe with a little fear. *Good.* Once they were inside he pulled out his phone and saw a text from Sonja.

In Denver w Roy. Beck, I need to think.

He started to thumb out a panicked reply but stopped himself. He held in a breath.

His wife needed to think. Of course she did. Who wouldn't, in her situation, living with fucking Beck Unsworth every day? So let her think.

Next, email.

He scanned through urgent messages from various creditors. His unpaid accountant, three credit card companies, the head of school at St. Bridget's warning of the immediate expulsion of his sons, Leila threatening a lawsuit over missing paychecks.

Debt, hills and hills of it. But at the moment he didn't give a rat's ass.

His phone and keys landed on the table by the door, raising a puff of dust. The table was littered with junk mail old and new, a dirty mug and a crusted plate latticed by two pairs of soccer socks like the shell of a mince pie.

He stomped up to his room and ripped off his clothes and threw on a T-shirt and a pair of cargo shorts, then returned to the kitchen, passing on his way through a gauntlet of disorder. His hands twitched for a rag, his nostrils flared for the astringent tang of bleach.

Charlie was sprawled on the couch playing a game on his phone. Beck clapped his hands three times. "That's enough lying around, kiddo. Right now we're going to work."

"What does that mean?"

"Is that a serious question?"

"Um, yes?"

"Where's your brother?"

"In the den."

"Call him in."

When Aidan walked into the living room, Beck looked his sons over, like a drill sergeant inspecting a platoon. "You guys need a snack before we get started? Granola bar maybe?"

The boys just stared at him.

Aidan said, "I'll have a fresh mouse. There's two of them in the mudroom."

For the next three hours, while his wife and youngest son were gone, they cleaned. Beck tackled the dishes first. Then pots and pans, countertops, tiles, rugs, wood floors, toilets, furniture, the fridge. He did three loads of laundry, he wiped baseboards, he dusted bookshelves and dressers, he threw away old food and recycled mounds of containers. He made the boys take turns with the vacuum, covering every room of the house.

There was an organic chicken in the freezer. He YouTubed a recipe to roast it with some potatoes that looked okay once they were peeled. After thawing the chicken in hot water, then the microwave for a few minutes, he got it all in the oven after the kitchen was done.

Meanwhile the twins cleaned their rooms and their shared bathroom, top to bottom. There was a fair bit of grumbling, but they got into it. Tub, toilet, under the sink, everything. They straightened the den and put away all their crap piled on the ping-pong table. By the time Beck was mopping up the mudroom floor they were outside cleaning the car with music on and having an actual blast.

With the chicken cooling on the stovetop, he went into the clean master bathroom and looked at himself in the mirror. *Let's do this.* He grabbed scissors from the medicine cabinet and hacked off most of his beard and shaved the rest, down to his smooth skin. He had butt-ugly tan lines, but other than that he looked pretty decent. Younger, the shape of the old Beck somewhere in there. After a quick but thorough shower he got dressed in newly clean clothes and started scrubbing again, this time under the kitchen sink, where he discovered that the garbage disposal had been unplugged from the safety outlet this whole time—not broken after all. He turned it on and ran water while it hummed itself clean. He even organized the god-damn silverware drawer and was just closing it when Sonja got home.

"What is going on, Beck?"

He turned from the counter to see his wife at the front door, their son bouncing on her hip.

"I'm home," he said stupidly. "I'm home."

She scanned his smooth face, then he followed her gaze around the kitchen and dining room. Garbage emptied, counters wiped, dishwasher humming and sloshing in mid-cycle, ceramic tiles gleaming underfoot. On the cleared-off front table the mail sat stacked and sorted, and on the pegboard by the garage door the boys' school backpacks hung neatly side by side.

Who knew where it had come from, this deep and vital urge to clean, to scrub, to purge, to feather the nest. All Beck knew was that this whirling dervish of three hours and change had nourished him like nothing had in years.

He went up to Sonja and pulled her in with Roy. "You do too much." He kissed her forehead, smoothed his hand over Roy's bald pate.

She looked at him suspiciously. "You are on drugs."

"I'm not on drugs."

"Drunk, then."

"No." He sniffed. "Does he need a change?"

Sonja, staring, handed him their son. Beck went back to the nursery, took care of Roy's diaper, and let him crawl around behind the safety gate while he emptied the diaper pail, his first time doing this task since the kid was maybe three weeks old. When he came back in from the garage, Sonja was collapsed on the sofa, feet on a freshly defilthed hassock, still eyeing him suspiciously as he washed his hands. He checked on Roy, messing with little plastic things in the playroom, then went back to the kitchen and poured a glass of chardonnay for his wife, a glass of water for himself.

The money, the cards, he showed her all of it: bank statements, fund statements, credit statements, threatening letters from creditors. With everything spread out on the kitchen table Sonja whipped out her phone and coldly totaled it all up on the calculator app. Beck felt like a whipped puppy when she showed him the final figure; but within half an hour she'd come up with a plan. Consolidate the debt onto two cards, burn the others, put both kids in the publics next year, sell the Breckenridge condo, stop leasing a new luxury SUV and buy a used station wagon, get flip phones, refinance the mortgage again, use the overage to pay off what he'd loaned himself from the company—and pay his employees right away, beginning with Leila. Beck texted her right there from the table, truthfully this time, to let her know the deposit was already in her account. He'd have to work out a separate plan to keep the firm afloat, but given the way Sonja had with numbers, he thought maybe she could help out there too.

They'd also have to make some lifestyle changes at home. No more takeout every other night, no more twice-daily lattes, a lot more mac and cheese. After a calm chicken dinner Beck filled the boys in on the situation, the belt-tightening to come. They were sitting on the sofa in the living room, Sonja starting dishes in the kitchen. She was only allowed to scrape and rinse, though, Beck had warned her. The rest of the mess belonged to him.

"You guys like mac and cheese, right?" he said.

Sliding off the sofa, Charlie said, "Long as you put some hot dogs in." He pushed off and ran up to his room. Beck watched him go, wistful, reluctant to initiate the talk they needed to have.

That's when his second son surprised him. Aidan stayed behind, sitting still. The look on his face reminded Beck of that morning in Colorado Springs all those months ago. The first day Charlie didn't start.

"What's up, Aid?" he said. "Is it about Xander, breaking his glasses today? Because we need to talk about that."

Without warning Aidan started to cry. Not a little hiccupy kind of cry but a full-bore snotfest, full-chested and prolonged. Beck pulled him to his side. They waited it out together, the boy's skinny body warming him.

"Whenever you're ready, okay?"

Aidan nodded. Beck waited some more.

"Charlie," Aidan finally said, voice hitching on his brother's name, "Charlie didn't try to wipe me out at Breckenridge. I made that up."

Beck stared at his son. "Why would you do that, Aidan?"

"I was mad at him, for making us go again."

"So what, you wiped out on purpose?"

He shook his head. "I thought I could stay up, make it look like he tried to hurt me."

"God, Aidan." Beck smoothed a hand along his back, and as his boy calmed down Beck asked him other questions and soon learned of additional transgressions for which Aidan had been letting his brother take the blame—including the broken drywall, which Aidan, not Charlie, had smashed in with a bat. Even telling Azra about Tessa and Beck, spinning his brother's quick glimpse of a topless babysitter into something more sinister.

"But why has Charlie been admitting to stuff he didn't do?" Beck pressed him.

Aidan shrugged. "He says if you believe he'd ever try to hurt me when we're skiing, then you might as well blame him for everything."

Beck closed his eyes. Charlie's bleak assessment of his father was a shiv between the ribs, as was Aidan's considerable skill in the lying department. "And that was okay with you?" Beck asked. "To let him take the hits for all that stuff?"

"He's my brother," Aidan said, and the sweet repentance started shading into his new tweeny cool. Beck sat back and considered what he'd heard over the last few minutes, all he hadn't bothered to learn about his sons while swimming in his own narcissistic pond.

God he loved these boys. But what kinds of things had he let slip by over the last year or two? What else had he missed, and what might it be too late to fix?

But the twins weren't even twelve yet. There was still time. There had to be.

Aidan pulled away. "So what are my consequences, Dad?"

Beck didn't answer for a while, letting the question linger. What was heartbreaking was that Aidan clearly *wanted* some consequences, *wanted* to be reined in. The kid needed some control in his life, beginning with his own recent behavior.

"I'm going to work that out with your mom and Sonja," said Beck, liking how it sounded. *Command and control.*

"I don't want to go to that gifted school, Dad," Aidan blurted out.

Beck hesitated. "You're sure about that?"

"I hate it."

"Oh-kay," Beck said slowly. "I'll need to discuss things with your mom, but I can understand that, and obviously we won't force you to go if you get in. And anyway you'll be busy with all those ROMO practices, am I right?"

Aidan shook his head. "I don't want to do that either."

Beck stared at him. "You're kidding."

"I hate all that riding in the car, plus none of my friends are there.

Maybe in high school, but for now I want to stay at CSOC, with Charlie. And isn't it a lot cheaper?"

"I mean, sure," Beck said. In the sense that any youth sport costing almost three grand for a seven-month season could be considered *a lot cheaper*. "But you've had your heart set on this for so long. Think about the competition, the travel, those wicked uniforms. Also the college opps—"

Sonja's face appeared, Germanic and stern. His wife was leaning in from the kitchen and wagging a finger. Aidan didn't see her, but Beck had a clear and beautiful view.

"You know what?" he said. "CSOC is awesome. I'm proud of you for staying with your team. That's loyalty, son." This last said gruffly, a little like Wade Meltzer might say it.

"So you're okay with that?" Aidan asked his dad, incredulous.

Beck stretched an arm over his son's skinny shoulders, alive to the impossible yawning privilege of it all. "Honestly what I am right now is just—relieved."

SEVENTY-THREE

ROSE

Rose braked to a stop on the driveway and turned off the ignition. The porch light was off, but the door stood open, letting a pale wash of interior light spill out to gild the dogwood buds, the effect like tinsel on a curbed Christmas tree. The keys dangled over her knee, and the cooling of the engine made a steady *tick-tick* that took its time to fade.

She stayed in the car, finding her breath. There was a flash of movement to her left. Emma Q dashed out of the house and across the yard. Rose heard a car door open and close, but two lilac bushes blocked her view of the street.

The doorway darkened and Gareth came outside—no, not her husband. It was Azra, her long black hair glowing as the porch light flicked on. She propped one foot up in the doorway and the other on the porch, a muscled arm holding herself against the jamb as she spoke. Gareth stood lit from behind, his face darkened in shadow. They hadn't noticed Rose yet, nor marked the arrival of her car.

She looked out the front windshield at the dim white door of the garage, six windows lined up like voids. Her fingers, slick and weak, pulled at the handle, and with her elbow she pushed open the car door. Azra looked over first, then Gareth. Something flat and distant in his pocketed eyes; only warmth in hers.

Azra walked over and pulled Rose into a hug. "Q can sleep over at my place if you need that, and so can you," she whispered. "Or I can bring her back when you guys are done. Just let me know."

Rose nodded against her hair. She stayed where she was until Azra drove off with Q. Fatigue settled on her shoulders like a shawl, though the feeling of warmth was a false thing. She shivered. The chinooks were blowing up, air crisped with pine, cut grass, a hint of smoke.

Her eyes watered. She watched Gareth, his face a smear in the night. He turned away and she followed him inside.

Rose found the worn spot along the Formica where she had leaned so many times as they fought through their fading marriage. Atik's portfolio was still propped sadly against the wall adjoining the counter, and Gareth sat slumped in the chair opposite, looking small.

"Rose," he began, "you have to understand."

"I think I do understand, actually," she interrupted him. "I understand everything." And had rehearsed her opening response to it. "I understand the smug, superior way you've always regarded my parenting in relation to yours. I understand how you disapprove of my 'workaholism,' my 'ambition,' the value I place on hard work and earned success. I understand why you've enjoyed scolding me for being so obsessed with Crystal Academy, the way my overinvestment in the whole thing might be—how did you put it?—oh, right, 'ruining our daughter.' I understand all of that, Gareth. And yet here we are. You've spent years living in this self-righteous bubble of yours, convinced you're the greatest father and most long-suffering husband in the world, and now . . ."

She shrugged, let her voice trail off.

"Are you done?" he said, and she sneered at him.

What he said next was so out of context, it bewildered her. "I never wanted to move here, you know. You had five offers, we could have gone anywhere, a city where my writing could really thrive."

"What does that have to do with anything?"

"Just reminding you what it was like for me. You were a rock star in your field, Rose. You turned down jobs at Harvard, Duke, UCLA, Chicago. All to come to Darlton so you could be the big fish in this perfect little pond."

"You know that's not true," she protested. "This was the most attractive offer, the most beautiful place—"

"And that was a bad time for me. My novel flopped, I couldn't get another contract, my agent stopped returning my calls. We were going in opposite directions, and I felt like such a dismal failure."

Rose bit her cheek. She had heard all of this before, a hundred times.

"You were building out your lab," he went on. "A million-dollar start-up package from Darlton, or was it two milllion? I barely saw you for months. Then you won that huge grant your first semester on the faculty. Meanwhile I'm cowering at home, trying to keep my writing career going."

"Just a dry spell, you called it."

"It was more than that. Not that you were paying attention."

She sighed, almost bored.

"I joined the gym, North Crystal Rec," he continued. "I went every day that first fall, sometimes twice a day. It was good for me, kept me balanced. When you join, they comp you four sessions with a personal trainer."

Rose saw Samantha in one of her training outfits, the violet one. Lycra, running bra, stomach a circumference of muscle and effort.

"I don't even know how it happened," he said. "Maybe she thought it was glamorous somehow, to have a novelist as a client."

"Oh yeah, like George Clooney," Rose knifed him.

"She asked me all these questions about my writing, my process."

"Your *process*?"

"She'd even bought and read my novel before our third session."

Rose made the disconcerting connection. Samantha loaning her copy of *Gallows Road* to Tazeem Harb, her surprising interest in a novel published over twelve years ago: a book written by her daughter's biological father.

"When did it end?" she asked him. "Did you keep going after she had Emma Z—after I met Sam?"

He shook his head. "Never. I tried to steer you away from that mothers' group, but it was already too late. Once—I guess—I mean one time you were at a conference and they had one of their midwinter parties and for some reason I went. She was helping me look for my coat on their bed. I made some suggestive remark, not even serious, I was drunk, and I remember exactly what she said. 'Back off, Gareth. Rose is my best friend.'"

Rose felt a sob rising but edged it back, refusing to show him anything. She reached to the top of the fridge for a bottle of Herradura—a gift from Samantha. A double shot sloshed in a chipped anniversary mug—one of Samantha's selections: *Some people go to priests; others to poetry; I to my friends* (Virginia Woolf). Rose didn't know which was worse, the knowledge that Samantha could keep such a massive secret for so many years—or that she'd found Gareth compelling enough to cheat with in the first place.

She took a burning gulp. A second pour. A second gulp. She wiped her mouth on the back of a hand. The tequila's sting sparked nettles across her chapped lips.

"So Emma Z," she said finally. "She's yours."

"Looks like it," he said glibly, and for a while no one spoke. Small house noises filled the room. Shift of clock hands, the hiss of a refrigerator hose.

"I stopped going to the Rec Center after things ended," he said. "I assumed I'd see Samantha around town, but we never even bumped into each other again, not once, until that first dinner at Julian and Lauren's over a year later. And there she was, with a baby the same age as Q. With the same goddamn name."

"Lovely coincidence."

"I actually looked it up. Emma was the third most popular girl's name that year."

"So did you two chew over the fact that you'd been together?"

He was looking at his hands. "She never wanted to. Neither did I, I mean I assumed she was on the pill, we never even talked about the possibility that Emma Z might be—honestly we both acted as if it'd never happened. The girl has always seemed like pure Zellar, and I've always thought of Q as my only child."

The kind of lie you can see anyone telling himself, Rose thought. And as for Samantha, why tell your husband that a child might be another man's if you don't have to—and ruin your marriage, your friendships, the life you've made?

Yet what was missing from all this, in a way that Rose found vaguely disappointing, was the shock of recognition. Where were the clues, the dark adumbrations of false paternity over the years? She could see them now, of course, lined up like dominoes: Gareth's instinctive dislike of Kev, his antisocial attitude toward Rose's friends. Yet Rose had never once questioned whether Emma Z was Kev's daughter. She was a beautiful girl— beautiful like Samantha, and like Kev. Outgoing and confident—

like

Samantha, like Kev. A strong jaw and hooded eyes—like Kev's. Perfect— like a Zellar.

But gifted? Well . . . maybe not.

The thought stopped her cold. She pushed herself off the counter and went to the sliding door and stared southwest, where the full moon splashed pearl on the Redirons. *God that's gorgeous*, she thought, and with this incongruous perception of beauty came a jarring epiphany, so unexpected it almost knocked her forward against the glass.

Gareth had sculpted his own well-wrought story to tell about his unacknowledged child; so had Samantha. He had decided that Emma Z could not be his, just as Samantha had decided Emma Z was Kev's, just as both of them had gone through the last twelve years of their lives within the palatable narrative enabled by these self-deceptions, the stories they had chosen to tell about themselves and the daughter they shared.

Yet weren't they all cheaters, of a sort? And were these deceptions so different from the carefully cultivated fictions Rose had built up around her own daughter over the years? Were they any worse than the parenting habits Rose and her friends indulged, telling themselves what they wanted to believe about their children—their gifts, their talents, their milestones— and doing what they could to sustain these impressions and project them out into the world, then acting as if this same world owed them something in return?

She thought of Xander's project, the personality traits he had been tracking for years through those countless games of chess, catching them all out on their feints and fakery, their striving, their little cheats. Gareth and Samantha's affair was but one example of a collective crime against childhood they had been committing together, its outcome no more controllable than the amount of snowfall on a mountain. No wonder the admissions process had resulted in such a pile of catastrophes, and it wasn't even over yet.

Now the consequences.

The glass door shimmered as Gareth came up behind her. The thought of those moist hands touching her shoulders ever again—

"Look, Rose," he said. "Maybe this whole thing can be for the good, help us be honest with each other in new ways. All the therapy we've already done this last year could get us through this, if we want it to. If we try."

When she turned around, his lower lip started a puerile tremble. Has Gareth's chin always been this weak, she wondered, his view of our marriage this delusional? He opened his mouth, but she held up a hand.

"You need to leave," she said. "Now."

He flinched, and she was expecting him to cower out. Instead he straightened his spine, backed away three steps, and fixed her with a withering glare.

"Let me tell you something, Rose," he said. "I fucked up a long time ago. Obviously. *Hugely.* But you want to know one of the reasons I liked being with Samantha so much, even for just a few weeks? Because she let me be who I was, even if who I was back then was just a failing writer who couldn't finish another book. She never treated me as an extension of herself, as if my flaws were hers, or would somehow make her look bad. For you, though, it's all about self-reflection, isn't it? How smart your daughter is, how talented your husband is, how successful your lab is, what value we all add to your stock and the way you look at the world. And you like to go after everybody else for how 'inauthentic' they are. Hate that 'fraudulence,' don't you. But really? Look at all you've done over the last few months, the shit you've tried to pull. You're a worse cheater than I am, Rose. You're just about the most dishonest person I've ever known."

He looked down at his hands, as if he had struck her physically with his frankness. Rose experienced a rush of what felt like longing. Where had this candor been all these years? Why now, when it was far too late?

"So yeah, I'll get out of here," he went on, looking up but not at her. "Happy to."

With that he grabbed his keys and his wallet from the coffee table and left her alone, flattened against the glass.

SEVENTY-FOUR

EMMA Z

Her parents might *think* she couldn't hear them from her bedroom but she could, and the longer she lay in her bed, the longer they cried. Her mother whimpered like a dog left outside, and her father cried almost like Emma Q, cried in these hiccupy little chokes that made his voice sound high and girlish. It was *disgusting*.

She wished they would stop, but they probably wouldn't for a while. They'd brought her upstairs together and put her to bed almost two hours ago (*much* too early), sitting on either side and stroking her hair and using those fakey voices they used when they pretended nothing was wrong. They'd spent a few minutes explaining things, and at least they hadn't tried to lie to her.

Mommy made a bad choice a long time ago. And Emma Q's daddy made a bad choice too. But all of it happened waaaaayyyyy before you were born, okay? It doesn't have anything to do with our family now.

"You know we love you just the same, right? This doesn't change anything," her mother had told her.

"I've always been your daddy, I'm your daddy now, and I'll always *be* your daddy," her father had said before kissing her on the forehead. "I know you know that, Emma."

And Z had nodded in all the right places, returned their hugs.

But she could tell her parents were pretending, for her. And more than that, she could feel, in her own muscles, how scared they were, and beneath the fright she could sense their anger in the tense way they moved around the house, in how they wouldn't look at each other like they always did. No one reached out to squeeze an arm or pat a bottom. Her mom was crying, a lot.

Emma Z was scared too.

She got out of bed, went downstairs and down the hall to the library and listened outside the door. She heard only sniffles now, no talking.

She took a step around the corner and looked at her parents. The low lamp on the coffee table made creepy oval shadows of their heads, and even in the dim light she could see how red her mom's eye sockets were. Her father's face was pale and swollen and sick-looking.

"Hey, baby." Her mom dabbed her eyes with the corner of one of her fleece blankets, the blue one. The rest of it was spread over her legs and her feet. She looked too tired to get up. "You want to come up here with us?"

Emma Z hesitated, then climbed on the sofa. Her parents kind of smelled bad. Her father looked at her in a way she didn't particularly like, with his lips all pressed together and ugly, but she didn't blame him for it. This whole thing was just *too weird*.

She leaned back and nestled between them. Her mother lifted the bottom flap of the blanket and covered her knees and feet. Part of the blanket settled on her father's leg. He reached over and patted Emma's knee. She put her hand on his and felt him start to cry again, but not as loudly this time; less like Q.

No one was saying anything, so maybe it was up to Emma Z to say something.

She took a deep, deep breath, held it for a five-count, and when she let it out, she said, "Xander's a loser and his science project wasn't even smart."

She looked up at her mother, then her father.

"Plus all he did was buy a bunch of test kits," she went on, remembering what Rose had said, because even though Rose was really annoying, she'd been right about stupid Xander Frye. "It was the dumbest project ever."

Her parents stared at her some more, then they started to stare at each other the way they sometimes did just before they started to kiss.

"Besides, it doesn't matter, that stuff he found out." She folded her arms across her chest. "Everybody *knows* we're all Zellars. I don't care. It doesn't even matter."

She heard her father clear his throat and swallow. Then both her parents leaned in across the middle of the couch, toward each other. They hugged, with Emma Z in the warm roasty center of it. The family stayed like that for a while, faces down in the near dark.

"How about some hot cocoa?" her mother said, sitting back up again. "We have some Ghirardelli, I think. Kev, are there marshmallows?"

"There are indeed," said her father, looking surprised to hear her nice voice. "Hoof-free to boot. Shot of Frangelico in yours, hon?"

"Make it two," said her mother.

After midnight. Emma Z stared out at the moon. It had been a *really stressful day*, and now for some reason she kept thinking about that thumbtack, the delicious sensation of the point going into her finger. The tack had fallen out of her pocket sometime after the open house, but her thoughts kept circling back to it.

She slid to the floor and padded her way silently out of her bedroom and down the hall to her mother's sewing room. The door stood halfway open, and the space was filled with silvery light and the lemony smell of the Pledge that rose up from the shining wooden floor.

Her mother's sewing machine, covered in a dustcloth, sat against the left-hand wall. Z pushed the cloth aside, then felt around on top of the machine until her hands discovered the pincushion. Her fingers quickly located a thick needle buried right in the middle. She pincered it out carefully between her right thumb and forefinger.

Back in her bedroom she shut the door and locked it, then went into her bathroom and shut the door and locked that. She turned on the light and sat on the closed lid of the toilet.

She looked down at her legs. With the needle in her right hand she pushed up her nightgown enough to expose her thighs. There was a spot just above her left knee that she'd been thinking about since the open house.

With her left hand Emma Z lowered the needle and was about to push the point into her skin when she saw them.

The built-in cupboard against the opposite wall was normally closed, but tonight the white wooden door stood ajar. The bottom three shelves were stocked with bathroom supplies. Neat ranks of toilet paper to replace on the roller, extra washcloths and hand towels, a pretty basket of soaps, and two containers of Emma Z's favorite kind of bubble bath, in lavender and lemon scents.

And on the top shelf, the animals. A tawny lion, an emerald dragon, a creamy dog, a yellow giraffe; at least twenty altogether. All the origami creatures the boy had made over the last few months and that Emma Z had taken apart, one by one, to leave as flattened, curling sheets of thin paper on her dresser. The used papers would disappear every time; to the trash, Z had assumed, thinking nothing of their absence.

But no. The boy had folded all the same animals back together again, one by one, and left them here, together, hidden in the bathroom cabinet for Emma Z to find. A loose company of paper beasts, all repaired.

She lifted the nearest one delicately between her right thumb and pointer finger. It was a rhinoceros. Red, not brown, with a triangular horn jutting out the front.

She wanted to take the animal apart again, but for once Emma Z stopped herself. The point of the sewing needle relaxed against her skin. She looked down at her thigh. No blood, just a small indentation above her knee. She set the needle on the edge of the sink and nested the rhinoceros in the bowl of her palms. For a long time Emma Z stared at it, then she started to turn the creature about in her hands, to squint at the angles and the joints, to see the wonder in its many folds.

SEVENTY-FIVE

XANDER

On the morning after the open house Xander helped Aquinas get out of bed at 7:10 and walked into the living room. His mother and sister lay sprawled across the sectional sofa, asleep with their heads almost touching in the middle. Tessa's arm hung off at an awkward angle. When Aquinas went over to sniff at it, she pulled her hand up with an angry grunt, turned over, and went back to sleep. The dog wandered into the kitchen and glopped down a bunch of water. Despite the noise his mom and sister didn't move an inch.

Upstairs in his mother's study he whipped an Italian guy at chess, and when he came back down, they were still asleep. He fixed himself a bowl of nut-free oat flakes, and even after he finished that, they were still asleep.

Last night they'd talked for a long time and kept talking after Xander went to bed. His father's name had come up, along with a bunch of stuff he didn't understand, but at least they weren't screaming at each other. The last word he remembered hearing from the living room was *college*.

No one had mentioned consequences yet. Maybe his mother would forget about his science project. Maybe Aquinas would learn to fly.

But was it really so bad, what Xander had discovered? It was just science. The truth. Data. It wasn't even the interesting part of the experiment, and now Emma Z got to have two fathers when Xander and his sister didn't even have one.

I mean, geez, he thought. That's like having two queens, and who couldn't kick ass if you had that? Why was everyone so flipped out?

Xander took a pillow from a nearby chair and stretched out on the floor against the couch. Aquinas came over and flopped his fat self down next to him. Xander snuggled back against the corner of the sofa, as close as he could get to his mother and sister while still levered against the dog.

Xander Frye: . . . patient, deliberate, but swift to capture when advantageous . . . quickly adapts to opponents' strategic shifts . . . main weakness: overconfidence in temporary tactical advantages . . . willing to risk defeat for an artistic endgame against inferior opponents.

Nothing about the warmth of bodies, or their smells, or nonhuman factors like dogs. The algorithm might need some adjustment. Though even so it would never capture the profile Xander most wished he could recover.

Julian Frye: . . . ???

It was his father who had played Xander in his first match, and his second, and his third, and all the way up to his two hundredth, probably; and yet the only game Xander could recall move-for-move was their last, the game that changed everything. Xander won on his own, for the first time. He remembered his father's widening eyes, the stunned look on his face during Xander's endgame as he stared down at the bishop pair and those passed pawns, the way he reached proudly across the board to concede to his three-year-old son. His hand was big and warm and it was shaking a little, and sometimes Xander could still feel his father's touch if he brushed his own hand just the right way.

After a while Tessa turned over on the couch and her arm dropped down again. Her knuckles grazed the dog's back, right next to Xander's face. He looked through the slats of his sister's fingers and out the back window at the lightening sky.

SEVENTY-SIX

CH'AYÑA

She stood unmoving in the doorway, watching her grandson's fingers skitter over the keys and move on the square pad. On the screen a thin-lined triangle bent and folded. He used a finger to move it on top of a rectangle, where it sat as he adjusted it to fit, then used some other way to color and shade the combined shapes. Next he made a circle, then a tube. He floated it across the surface and brought it down to rest against the other shapes. Another triangle but this one turned into a cone that he moved to the top of the cylinder. All of this took him no more than two minutes. Now other shapes, smaller ones he used to fill in the plain surfaces.

She squinted over his shoulder, seeing it now. Windows, door, tower, porch: Atik was making a house. Not just any house but the Zellars' house in Crystal, with its wide front porch and its three-story tower, the dormer window in Emma's room. He had even copied the siding and the trim, colored in soft peach and white. Capturing all the details as in his paper model of Mountain View.

Her lips tightened and she shook her head, disappointed. Fancy new computer, not a used one like Tiago tried to give him—and the first thing he makes on it is *this*?

But then his fingers moved again. He took the cone from the top of the tower and flipped the tower on its side, turning it into a tubular passageway from the square house to another building he started assembling with lines and angles and curves. Next the roof came off the Zellar house. He used it to make a second story over the tube, stretching out the corners until the two pieces fit. Then he added round windows and an outer staircase connecting the bottom to the top. He clicked something and made the staircase move, and soon the structure on his screen began to resemble some building from an imagined future where rooms floated in the air and escalators led only to the sky.

She left him to it. In the kitchen, standing at the sink, she asked Silea, "Where did he get that thing?"

Her daughter half turned from the burner where she was overcooking something. "They're allowed to bring them home, Mamay. The school loans them out so the students will have them for the whole summer. Like books."

Ch'ayña sniffed. "Well, he hasn't been outside all day."

"It's a good thing. With what's on the computer he'll learn how to make buildings and bridges. Ships, planes, tunnels. Solar engines, that kind of thing."

"Like Pachakuti but without all the mess."

Silea smiled at her. "He's just a boy, not a god."

"We'll see," said Ch'ayña, making her daughter laugh. "That's why they let him in. He knows how things go together and how they come apart."

"I suppose," Silea mused. "That's what Tiago says."

"How will he get to the school?" Ch'ayña reached over to turn down the burner.

"There's a bus. It will pick up every kid in Beulah County who goes."

Ch'ayña grimaced. "An extra hour every day. Better to take him ourselves."

"Not with our schedule," Silea said with a shrug. "He'll manage."

Ch'ayña thought about it. The Crystal kids all had their own drivers. Maybe that was important. Maybe you needed that, to thrive up here. Well, if she couldn't give him rides, she'd give him something else.

"He'll need more, for those long days," she said. "He'll need a bigger lunch, more snacks."

"He will," Silea agreed.

"So let me make all the food." Ch'ayña bumped hips with her daughter. "You just stay out of that. The *wawa*'s brain won't stay gifted for long if he has to eat your chicken every day."

A Touch of Tessa:

ONE GIRL'S SURVIVAL GUIDE tO JUNIOR YEAR

A Video Blog

Episode #202: THE ENVELOPE, PLEASE . . .

. . . 5 views . . .

TESSA: Aaaaaaaand she's back, this time with privacy settings. Guys, I can't even tell you what these last few weeks have been like. Read my DMs if you aren't caught up, but god, everybody I know hearing all the shit I've dished about them and their kids this year, watching all of that? The worst part was feeling their old scorn coming back, that snotty condescension I used to talk about in group. So it's been hard, and okay, I got fucked up a couple times with this one girl I hang with, and I even swiped a bottle of smarties from her mom. But you guys'll be proud of me, because I put it back in the medicine cupboard right after without popping a single pill. You believe that?

And I have to say, my mom's friends have really surprised me, like Rose came and picked me up and took me out for lunch the other day, just to see how I was doing, she said. It was awkward and all, but it was nice. And then Samantha and Kev came into the store and Kev got a vintage sports coat that's not him at all and Samantha bought one of my TessaRacks, this sweet jacket I designed, I mean she'll probably just forget about it in a few weeks and toss it in a Hefty bag for her maid and it'll end up back at the store, but still, it's the thought, you know? Oh, that's right, I got to keep my job! Azra's been amazing.

So, they're kind of here for me, these crazy women, and it's a weird surprise. I'll never forget how they pulled my family out of a really dark well after my dad died. They can be so bitchy and sneaky and competitive sometimes, like about who's going to more parties, or whose kid is busier or whatnot, especially my mom. But even when they're stabbing each other in the back, they know how to help you through things, you know? It makes me think of this story Beck told me, that hairy guy in the Jacuzzi. Him and my dad were on this cliff, and one of them started to fall and the other caught him and saved his life, like these two climbing bros clinging to each other hundreds of feet above the ground, laughing over something that almost killed them. Maybe that's what we all need, you know? Someone to grab you and swing you to safety when you're losing your grip. Someone to keep you up and hold you there, pinned against the stone. For me that was you guys, seriously, and I hope I'm there for you too, helping you stay up. But maybe we also have to learn to let go, which is a lot harder. Anyway.

[*Leans off screen, comes back waving an envelope from City of Crystal School District addressed "To the Parents of Tessa Frye."*]

And now, the moment of truth. Will Tessa's sizzlingly high Cog-Pro scores and her immense talents in fashion design earn her a highly coveted seat? Or will she be one of the also-rans, the hoi polloi, the plebes? The suspense is killing you, am I right? Okay, here goes, you guys.

[*Works envelope open with finger, pulls out letter, reads. Looks up with enigmatic smile.*]

ENDGAME

On the eighth of May, two weeks and three days after the open house, the letters arrived.

No email this time but hard copy, a thin envelope from the school district that Rose found in the mailbox that afternoon. When she opened it and read the form rejection, she felt next to nothing: a small prickle of regret, a shiver of new embarrassment sparked by visceral memories of her fifteen minutes of fame as the hysterical mom who lost it at the gifted school. The act of staring blankly down at those meaningless words stirred a different longing that surprised her with its keenness and depth.

She hadn't spoken to Samantha since that day. Azra was doing her best, running peace missions back and forth with texts and stop-bys, acting like a NATO treaty negotiator as Zellars and Hollands and Quinns and Holland-Quinns started adjusting to the all-too-public revelation about their families and what it all might mean. Yet these potential new configurations seemed less important at the moment than taking care of the two little people all of this change risked hurting the most.

She was tossing the letter and envelope in the recycling bin when a text from Samantha flashed up on her screen.

Rose, I love you. Can we try to get past it, for the Emmas?

She smiled sadly at her phone.

They met at the corner of Azure and Main. Neither spoke as they walked west toward the foothills. Rose paced slightly behind Samantha and cast furtive glances at her friend's face, as if scrutinizing one of her neurology patients for a visible symptom.

Finally she plunged in. "Just got the official rejection. For some reason we were still in their database, even after that scene."

"We were too," Samantha replied. "Which, I have to say, does not speak well of our friend Bitsy Leighton and the all-star admissions team over there. I mean if they can't get something like this straight, how can they expect to hire the best teachers or come up with a cutting-edge curriculum?"

"Or design a strong slate of extracurriculars for the brilliant little Crystals?"

Samantha said, "Aside from the sour grapes, Mrs. Lincoln, how was the play?"

They laughed, though tentatively, testing the waters. Samantha was about to speak again when their phones buzzed together. A group text from Azra.

Rejected.

Same, Rose replied.

Ditto, Sam wrote.

Five seconds later Lauren chimed in: **Been meaning to tell you guys. We heard yesterday. Both of mine were accepted! Go figure.**

They looked at each other and burst into laughter, happy for the one parent among them who needed this most.

Finally Samantha took a deep breath and reached for Rose's hand. The story she told began with what she once regarded as her own failure: her inability to conceive in the five years following her marriage to Kev. The eldest Zellar child but the last to reproduce, constantly harangued about it by Kev's progeny-obsessed parents and siblings. Kev, of course, had acted the typical caveman: the problem couldn't possibly be his sperm count, as a test soon confirmed. They'd been headed for more serious testing and possible IVF, fighting all the time, when she met Gareth.

He could have been anybody, Samantha claimed now. "It was such a bonehead, ugly thing to do, but I was *so* angry at Kev, *so* ready to walk out. Screwing a client was just an escape valve, and I wasn't even thinking about pregnancy, I thought that was all over for us so we didn't even use birth control, I just told Gareth I was on the pill. But then right after it ended, Kev and I finally decide to go for it, and we're literally at the initial appointment with a fertility specialist when I find out I'm pregnant."

"Kev was thrilled, I'm sure."

"And I was terrified. I even considered an abortion, but after six years of trying to get pregnant I just couldn't. Then, when Emma Z came along, everybody said she was pure Zellar. They saw Kev in her eyes, Edgar in her chin, freaking Blakey in the shape of her hairline. And I let myself believe it too, I mean with the timing it could have gone either way. Genes be damned, we see what we want to see."

"What did you see?"

She considered it. "After a certain point I didn't care anymore. Emma Z is Kev's daughter in every way that matters. Though . . ."

"What?"

Her face sagged. "Honestly it was this admissions process that made me wonder for the first time whether that was really true. Whether there might be—something of Gareth in my daughter that I'd never recognized before. Whether I should be doing things to nurture it, help it grow. So a few weeks before the CogPro, I was reorganizing the library and came across Gareth's novel."

"*Gallows Road*," Rose said. "You loaned your copy to Tazeem."

"I reread it," Samantha said, "and it wasn't as if the story itself moved me or anything, but the experience made me question things in a way I never had. About Z, about Gareth. My Emma's never been a reader, not like Q. But then neither have I, and neither has Kev, even though we have a library at Twenty Birch, for god's sake, and buy ourselves books all the time and spread them around the house like wallpaper."

Rose smiled.

"But what if Z was *supposed* to be a reader, or even a writer?" Samantha went on. "What if that was supposed to be her gift? Is it fair to keep it from her, the knowledge that this might be a hidden talent, like some atrophied muscle that hasn't been exercised? So one day at drop-off I suggested casually to Gareth that maybe he could work with Emma Z on her essay, give her some writing tips. He didn't even register why I was asking. But it just shows you how messed up these last months have been. The way they've twisted us with these crazy fantasies about our kids' unrecognized genius."

They stopped at the corner of Zircon Lane to wait out the loud beeps of a truck backing up. When the vehicle moved, they passed out from beneath a long row of shade trees and Samantha lifted her face to the sun. "I'm sorry, Rose. I'm so sorry, and someday I hope you can forgive me."

Rose swallowed against a hardness in her throat. "Forgiveness is overrated."

"You should put that on a mug."

"No more mugs," Rose snapped.

"Deal."

"Maybe the school was just an excuse," Rose said a few moments later, startled by the thought.

"For what?"

Rose Holland: deceptive and sneaky . . . ruthless but insecure . . . squanders pawns, hoards opportunity . . . unwilling to sacrifice for tactical advantage . . . tendency to risk everything in pursuit of a weak endgame . . .

"For doing openly what we've been doing since before our kids were even born."

"For lying, you mean," Samantha said, almost under her breath.

"Well, there's that. We tell our kids these innocent lies about Santa Claus, about how, no, of course not, there won't be a war, or a school shooting in our town—"

"Comforting lies."

Rose thought of Gareth's parting shot; the hard truth in it. "Maybe what you did with Gareth was just a version of all this. Thinking you could control what would ultimately happen with Emma Z, that she'd never find out. And even if she did, that she'd somehow believe you were acting in her best interests. Parents always want to manage the narrative instead of letting kids write their own." She clapped a hand over her mouth.

"What?"

"I think Gareth said that. I think he wrote it, in some godawful freelance parenting piece."

Samantha snorted. "Well, I guess it's mostly true. But then you leave them alone for a second and look what happens. Tessa's vlog, Xander's experiment. Total catastrophe."

They had reached the peak of Azure Hill, a gentle rise before the first foothills, their beautiful town spread out below them like a brain scan, the colors, the forms, the unknown dangers lurking among the wobbly shapes and blurry lines. Somewhere down there a mother was ripping open an envelope and chirping with delight, like the thrush Rose heard warbling and trilling from a nearby tree. Up past the reservoir and over the shimmering mirage of the plains, an endless space stretched east a thousand miles and more.

Who could ever leave this perfect valley? she asked herself for perhaps the hundredth time, though the question felt tainted now, hollow.

Samantha's hand brushed her shoulder. Rose felt the sharp tip of a diamond ring as she turned away from Crystal Valley. Together they looked west.

High against the serrated crest of the Continental Divide two eagles danced in an updraft. The majestic birds climbed the thermal until they hovered in tandem above the horizon, almost motionless in a deep and cloudless blue. They spiraled lazily until one of them glimpsed movement below. The eagle separated from its companion and took a line downward, straight and sure, dropping for the kill. When it reappeared above the tree line, a young rabbit was dangling from its talons.

Samantha gasped. Rose pressed a hand to her throat. The eagle's wings beat the air, the bird rising with its struggling prey.

Then, as they watched in astonishment, the second eagle swooped in and knocked the rabbit loose. It plummeted back to earth like a dropped stone. The first eagle dove again—but this time, when it emerged, its talons clutched only air.

"Poor thing must have gotten away on its own," Samantha said, her voice full of hope as the majestic birds lifted away.

Rose wasn't so sure, and the scene would stay in her mind for weeks, years even, and she would always wonder whether the rabbit had learned enough to save itself when the eagles came again.

ACKNOWLEDGMENTS

The Gifted School was conceived and its earliest sections drafted some fifteen years ago while I was living in Boulder, Colorado, the inspiration for Crystal and its surroundings, including the (fictionalized) Four Counties, the Emerald Mall, the Redirons, and other features of the landscape and built environment. I have taken some necessary license with the details of IQ testing (for example, there is no "CogPro" test, my answer to the ubiquitous CogAT), though depictions of the admissions process, selection bias, and evaluation are based on research and interviews with experts. For their input and thoughts on these subjects, I am especially grateful to Jeff Danielian of the National Association for Gifted Children as well as to Ruth Lyons, former director of the Renzulli Gifted and Talented Academy in Hartford, Connecticut. Many thanks as well to Dr. Laura Jansen at the University of Virginia's School of Medicine for inviting me into her pediatric neurology lab and answering my uninformed questions about brain scans and hospital rotations; to Officer Eric Ketchum of the City of Charlottesville Police Department for his informed views on assault and battery (and aggressive sports parents); to Campbell and Malcolm Brickhouse for their soccer pointers and play-by-play suggestions; and to Yuliana Kenfield, who lent the manuscript her expertise and experience in Quechua language and Andean culture. I have benefited greatly from the reading and critique of early drafts by a number of friends, colleagues, and fellow writers, including Jabeen Akhtar, Steve Arata, Carol Holsinger, Christian

McMillen, John Parker, Jim Seitz, Andy Stauffer, and Rachel Thielmann. Thanks to my students at WriterHouse and the University of Virginia for their energy and enthusiasm, and to my friends in the Fiction Writers Co-op for their discretion and support. I owe an enormous debt to my agent, Helen Heller, for championing my work at every turn, and to the remarkable team at Riverhead and Penguin Random House, including Alison Fairbrother, Delia Taylor, Candice Gianetti, Jaya Miceli, and especially Sarah McGrath, a brilliant, tireless, and truly collaborative editor whose vision for this novel far surpassed my own. Anna Brickhouse gave the manuscript the inestimable gifts of her attention and insight. My mother, Sheila (née Moore), is responsible for the opening epigraph, and the dedication speaks for itself.